Molloy
Malone Dies
The Unnamable

Other Works by Samuel Beckett

Novels:
MURPHY
WATT
FIRST LOVE
MOLLOY
MALONE DIES
THE UNNAMABLE
HOW IT IS

Short Prose:
MORE PRICKS THAN KICKS
FROM AN ABANDONED WORK (with Faber)
TEXTS FOR NOTHING
IMAGINATION DEAD IMAGINE
NO'S KNIFE
LESSNESS
THE LOST ONES

Poems:
POEMS IN ENGLISH
AN ANTHOLOGY OF MEXICAN POETRY (translations)

Criticism:
PROUST AND THREE DIALOGUES WITH GEORGES DUTHUIT

Plays:
(with Faber and Faber)
WAITING FOR GODOT
END GAME
ACT WITHOUT WORDS I
ACT WITHOUT WORDS II
ALL THAT FALL
KRAPP'S LAST TAPE
EMBERS
HAPPY DAYS
CASCANDO
WORDS AND MUSIC
PLAY
EH JOE
COME AND GO (with Calder and Boyars)
THE OLD TUNE (translation in PINGET, PLAYS VOL. I,
with Calder and Boyars)
BREATH
NOT I!

Film Scenario:
FILM (with Faber and Faber)

SAMUEL BECKETT

Molloy
Malone Dies
The Unnamable

LONDON
CALDER AND BOYARS

Published in Great Britain by John Calder (Publishers) Ltd. 1959
Reprinted by Calder and Boyars Ltd. 1966, 1973
First published in French by Editions de Minuit as follows:
Molloy: 1950; *Malone Meurt:* 1951; *L'Innommable:* 1952
Molloy translated by the Author in collaboration with Patrick Bowles
first published 1955 by the Olympia Press.
Malone Dies in the Author's translation first published by John Calder
(Publishers) Ltd. 1956, and the whole Trilogy including *The Unnamable*
first published by John Calder (Publishers) Ltd. 1959

ISBN 0 7145 0112 3 Case Bound Edition
ISBN 0 7145 1053 X Paperback Edition

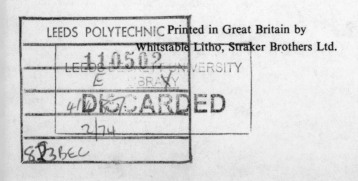

Printed in Great Britain by
Whitstable Litho, Straker Brothers Ltd.

CONTENTS

PART I

★

MOLLOY

I

I am in my mother's room. It's I who live there now. I don't know how I got there. Perhaps in an ambulance, certainly a vehicle of some kind. I was helped. I'd never have got there alone. There's this man who comes every week. Perhaps I got here thanks to him. He says not. He gives me money and takes away the pages. So many pages, so much money. Yes, I work now, a little like I used to, except that I don't know how to work any more. That doesn't matter apparently. What I'd like now is to speak of the things that are left, say my good-byes, finish dying. They don't want that. Yes, there is more than one, apparently. But it's always the same one that comes. You'll do that later, he says. Good. The truth is I haven't much will left. When he comes for the fresh pages he brings back the previous week's. They are marked with signs I don't understand. Anyway I don't read them. When I've done nothing he gives me nothing, he scolds me. Yet I don't work for money. For what then? I don't know. The truth is I don't know much. For example my mother's death. Was she already dead when I came? Or did she only die later? I mean enough to bury. I don't know. Perhaps

they haven't buried her yet. In any case I have her room. I sleep
in her bed. I piss and shit in her pot. I have taken her place. I must
resemble her more and more. All I need now is a son. Perhaps I
have one somewhere. But I think not. He would be old now, nearly
as old as myself. It was a little chambermaid. It wasn't true love.
The true love was in another. We'll come to that. Her name? I've
forgotten it again. It seems to me sometimes that I even knew my
son, that I helped him. Then I tell myself it's impossible. It's impossible I could ever have helped anyone. I've forgotten how to spell
too, and half the words. That doesn't matter apparently. Good. He's
a queer one the one who comes to see me. He comes every Sunday
apparently. The other days he isn't free. He's always thirsty. It was
he told me I'd begun all wrong, that I should have begun differently.
He must be right. I began at the beginning, like an old ballocks,
can you imagine that? Here's my beginning. Because they're keeping it apparently. I took a lot of trouble with it. Here it is. It gave
me a lot of trouble. It was the beginning, do you understand?
Whereas now it's nearly the end. Is what I do now any better? I
don't know. That's beside the point. Here's my beginning. It must
mean something, or they wouldn't keep it. Here it is.

    This time, then once more I think, then perhaps a last time,
then I think it'll be over, with that world too. Premonition of the
last but one but one. All grows dim. A little more and you'll go
blind. It's in the head. It doesn't work any more, it says, I don't
work any more. You go dumb as well and sounds fade. The
threshold scarcely crossed that's how it is. It's the head. It must
have had enough. So that you say, I'll manage this time, then perhaps once more, then perhaps a last time, then nothing more. You
are hard set to formulate this thought, for it is one, in a sense. Then
you try to pay attention, to consider with attention all those dim
things, saying to yourself, laboriously, It's my fault. Fault? That
was the word. But what fault? It's not goodbye, and what magic
in those dim things to which it will be time enough, when next
they pass, to say goodbye. For you must say goodbye, it would be
madness not to say goodbye, when the time comes. If you think of
the forms and light of other days it is without regret. But you
seldom think of them, with what would you think of them? I don't

know. People pass too, hard to distinguish from yourself. That is
discouraging. So I saw A and C going slowly towards each other,
unconscious of what they were doing. It was on a road remarkably
bare, I mean without hedges or ditches or any kind of edge, in the
country, for cows were chewing in enormous fields, lying and standing, in the evening silence. Perhaps I'm inventing a little, perhaps
embellishing, but on the whole that's the way it was. They chew,
swallow, then after a short pause effortlessly bring up the next
mouthful. A neck muscle stirs and the jaws begin to grind again.
But perhaps I'm remembering things. The road, hard and white,
seared the tender pastures, rose and fell at the whim of hills and
hollows. The town was not far. It was two men, unmistakably, one
small and one tall. They had left the town, first one, then the other,
and then the first, weary or remembering a duty, had retraced his
steps. The air was sharp, for they wore greatcoats. They looked alike,
but no more than others do. At first a wide space lay between them.
They couldn't have seen each other, even had they raised their
heads and looked about, because of this wide space, and then
because of the undulating land, which caused the road to be in
waves, not high, but high enough, high enough. But the moment
came when together they went down into the same trough and in
this trough finally met. To say they knew each other, no, nothing
warrants it. But perhaps at the sound of their steps, or warned by
some obscure instinct, they raised their heads and observed each
other, for a good fifteen paces, before they stopped, breast to breast.
Yes, they did not pass each other by, but halted, face to face, as
in the country, of an evening, on a deserted road, two wayfaring
strangers will, without there being anything extraordinary about it.
But they knew each other perhaps. Now in any case they do, now I
think they will know each other, greet each other, even in the depths
of the town. They turned towards the sea which, far in the east,
loomed high in the waning sky, and exchanged
a few words. Then each went on his way. Each went on his way,
A back towards the town, C on by ways he seemed hardly to know,
or not at all, for he went with uncertain step and often stopped to
look about him, like someone trying to fix landmarks in his mind,
for one day perhaps he may have to retrace his steps, you never

know. The treacherous hills where fearfully he ventured were no
doubt only known to him from afar, seen perhaps from his bedroom
window or from the summit of a monument which, one black day,
having nothing in particular to do and turning to height for solace,
he had paid his few coppers to climb, slower and slower, up the
winding stones. From there he must have seen it all, the plain, the
sea, and then these selfsame hills that some call mountains, indigo
in places in the evening light, their serried ranges crowding to the
skyline, cloven with hidden valleys that the eye divines from sudden
shifts of colour and then from other signs for which there are no
words, nor even thoughts. But all are not divined, even from that
height, and often where only one escarpment is discerned, and one
crest, in reality there are two, two escarpments, two crests, riven
by a valley. But now he knows these hills, that is to say he knows
them better, and if ever again he sees them from afar it will be I
think with other eyes, and not only that but the within, all that
inner space one never sees, the brain and heart and other caverns
where thought and feeling dance their sabbath, all that too quite
differently disposed. He looks old and it is a sorry sight to see him
solitary after so many years, so many days and nights unthinkingly
given to that rumour rising at birth and even earlier, What shall
I do? What shall I do? now low, a murmur, now precise as the
headwaiter's And to follow? and often rising to a scream. And in
the end, or almost, to be abroad alone, by unknown ways, in the
gathering night, with a stick. It was a stout stick, he used it to thrust
himself onward, or as a defence, when the time came, against dogs
and marauders. Yes, night was gathering, but the man was innocent,
greatly innocent, he had nothing to fear, though he went in fear,
he had nothing to fear, there was nothing they could do to him, or
very little. But he can't have known it. I wouldn't know it myself,
if I thought about it. Yes, he saw himself threatened, his body
threatened, his reason threatened, and perhaps he was, perhaps they
were, in spite of his innocence. What business has innocence here?
What relation to the innumerable spirits of darkness? It's not clear.
It seemed to me he wore a cocked hat. I remember being struck
by it, as I wouldn't have been for example by a cap or by a bowler.
I watched him recede, overtaken (myself) by his anxiety, at least

by an anxiety which was not necessarily his, but of which as it
were he partook. Who knows if it wasn't my own anxiety over-
taking him. He hadn't seen me. I was perched higher than the road's
highest point and flattened what is more against a rock the same
colour as myself, that is grey. The rock he probably saw. He gazed
around as if to engrave the landmarks on his memory and must
have seen the rock in the shadow of which I crouched like Belacqua,
or Sordello, I forget. But a man, a fortiori myself, isn't exactly a
landmark, because. I mean if by some strange chance he were to
pass that way again, after a long lapse of time, vanquished, or to
look for some lost thing, or to destroy something, his eyes would
search out the rock, not the haphazard in its shadow of that un-
stable fugitive thing, still living flesh. No, he certainly didn't see
me, for the reasons I've given and then because he was in no
humour for that, that evening, no humour for the living, but rather
for all that doesn't stir, or stirs so slowly that a child would scorn
it, let alone an old man. However that may be, I mean whether he
saw me or whether he didn't, I repeat I watched him recede, at
grips (myself) with the temptation to get up and follow him, perhaps
even to catch up with him one day, so as to know him better, be
myself less lonely. But in spite of my soul's leap out to him, at the
end of its elastic, I saw him only darkly, because of the dark and
then because of the terrain, in the folds of which he disappeared
from time to time, to re-emerge further on, but most of all I think
because of other things calling me and towards which too one after
the other my soul was straining, wildly. I mean of course the
fields, whitening under the dew, and the animals, ceasing from
wandering and settling for the night, and the sea, of which nothing,
and the sharpening line of crests, and the sky where without seeing
them I felt the first stars tremble, and my hand on my knee and
above all the other wayfarer, A or C, I don't remember, going
resignedly home. Yes, towards my hand also, which my knee felt
tremble and of which my eyes saw the wrist only, the heavily veined
back, the pallid rows of knuckles. But that is not, I mean my hand,
what I wish to speak of now, everything in due course, but A or C
returning to the town he had just left. But after all what was there
particularly urban in his aspect? He was bare-headed, wore sand-

shoes, smoked a cigar. He moved with a kind of loitering indolence which rightly or wrongly seemed to me expressive. But all that proved nothing, refuted nothing. Perhaps he had come from afar, from the other end of the island even, and was approaching the town for the first time or returning to it after a long absence. A little dog followed him, a pomeranian I think, but I don't think so. I wasn't sure at the time and I'm still not sure, though I've hardly thought about it. The little dog followed wretchedly, after the fashion of pomeranians, stopping, turning in slow circles, giving up and then, a little further on, beginning all over again. Constipation is a sign of good health in pomeranians. At a given moment, pre-established if you like, I don't much mind, the gentleman turned back, took the little creature in his arms, drew the cigar from his lips and buried his face in the orange fleece, for it was a gentleman, that was obvious. Yes, it was an orange pomeranian, the less I think of it the more certain I am. And yet. But would he have come from afar, bare-headed, in sand-shoes, smoking a cigar, followed by a pomeranian? Did he not seem rather to have issued from the ramparts, after a good dinner, to take his dog and himself for a walk, like so many citizens, dreaming and farting, when the weather is fine? But was not perhaps in reality the cigar a cutty, and were not the sand-shoes boots, hobnailed, dust-whitened, and what prevented the dog from being one of those stray dogs that you pick up and take in your arms, from compassion or because you have long been straying with no other company than the endless roads, sands, shingle, bogs and heather, than this nature answerable to another court, than at long intervals the fellow-convict you long to stop, embrace, suck, suckle and whom you pass by, with hostile eyes, for fear of his familiarities? Until the day when, your endurance gone, in this world for you without arms, you catch up in yours the first mangy cur you meet, carry it the time needed for it to love you and you it, then throw it away. Perhaps he had come to that, in spite of appearances. He disappeared, his head on his chest, the smoking object in his hand. Let me try and explain. From things about to disappear I turn away in time. To watch them out of sight, no, I can't do it. It was in this sense he disappeared. Looking away I thought of him, saying, He is dwindling, dwindling. I knew what

I meant. I knew I could catch him, lame as I was. I had only to
want to. And yet no, for I did want to. To get up, to get down on
the road, to set off hobbling in pursuit of him, to hail him, what
could be easier? He hears my cries, turns, waits for me. I am up
against him, up against the dog, gasping, between my crutches. He
is a little frightened of me, a little sorry for me, I disgust him not
a little. I am not a pretty sight, I don't smell good. What is it I
want? Ah that tone I know, compounded of pity, of fear, of disgust.
I want to see the dog, see the man, at close quarters, know what
smokes, inspect the shoes, find out other things. He is kind,
tells me of this and that and other things, whence he comes,
whither he goes. I believe him, I know it's my only chance to—my
only chance, I believe all I'm told, I've disbelieved only too much
in my long life, now I swallow everything, greedily. What I need
now is stories, it took me a long time to know that, and I'm not
sure of it. There I am then, informed as to certain things, knowing
certain things about him, things I didn't know, things I had craved
to know, things I had never thought of. What rigmarole. I am even
capable of having learnt what his profession is, I who am so interested in professions. And to think I try my best not to talk about
myself. In a moment I shall talk about the cows, about the sky, if
I can. There I am then, he leaves me, he's in a hurry. He didn't
seem to be in a hurry, he was loitering, I've already said so, but
after three minutes of me he is in a hurry, he has to hurry. I believe
him. And once again I am, I will not say alone, no, that's not like
me, but, how shall I say, I don't know, restored to myself, no, I
never left myself, free, yes, I don't know what that means, but it's
the word I mean to use, free to do what, to do nothing, to know,
but what, the laws of the mind perhaps, of my mind, that for
example water rises in proportion as it drowns you and that you
would do better, at least no worse, to obliterate texts than to
blacken margins, to fill in the holes of words till all is blank and
flat and the whole ghastly business looks like what it is, senseless,
speechless, issueless misery. So I doubtless did better, at least no
worse, not to stir from my observation post. But instead of observing I had the weakness to return in spirit to the other, the man with
the stick. Then the murmurs began again. To restore silence is the

role of objects. I said, Who knows if he hasn't simply come out
to take the air, relax, stretch his legs, cool his brain by stamping
the blood down to his feet, so as to make sure of a good night,
a joyous awakening, an enchanted morrow. Was he carrying so
much as a scrip? But the way of walking, the anxious looks, the
club, could these be reconciled with one's conception of what is
called a little turn? But the hat, a town hat, an old-fashioned town
hat, which the least gust would carry far away. Unless it was
attached under the chin, by means of a string or an elastic. I took
off my hat and looked at it. It is fastened, it has always been
fastened, to my buttonhole, always the same buttonhole, at all
seasons, by a long lace. I am still alive then. That may come in
useful. The hand that held the hat I thrust as far as possible from
me and moved in an arc, to and fro. As I did so, I watched the
lapel of my greatcoat and saw it open and close. I understand
now why I never wore a flower in my buttonhole, though it was
large enough to hold a whole nosegay. My buttonhole was set aside
for my hat. It was my hat that I beflowered. But it is neither of
my hat nor of my greatcoat that I hope to speak at present, it would
be premature. Doubtless I shall speak of them later, when the time
comes to draw up the inventory of my goods and possessions.
Unless I lose them between now and then. But even lost they will
have their place, in the inventory of my possessions. But I am easy
in my mind, I shall not lose them. Nor my crutches, I shall not lose
my crutches either. But I shall perhaps one day throw them away.
I must have been on the top, or on the slopes, of some considerable
eminence, for otherwise how could I have seen, so far away, so
near at hand, so far beneath, so many things, fixed and moving.
But what was an eminence doing in this land with hardly a ripple?
And I, what was I doing there, and why come? These are things
that we shall try and discover. But these are things we must not
take seriously. There is a little of everything, apparently, in nature,
and freaks are common. And I am perhaps confusing several different occasions, and different times, deep down, and deep down
is my dwelling, oh not deepest down, somewhere between the mud
and the scum. And perhaps it was A one day at one place, then C
another at another, then a third the rock and I, and so on for the

other components, the cows, the sky, the sea, the mountains. I can't believe it. No, I will not lie, I can easily conceive it. No matter, no matter, let us go on, as if all arose from one and the same weariness, on and on heaping up and up, until there is no room, no light, for any more. What is certain is that the man with the stick did not pass by again that night, because I would have heard him, if he had. I don't say I would have seen him, I say I would have heard him. I sleep little and that little by day. Oh not systematically, in my life without end I have dabbled with every kind of sleep, but at the time now coming back to me I took my doze in the daytime and, what is more, in the morning. Let me hear nothing of the moon, in my night there is no moon, and if it happens that I speak of the stars it is by mistake. Now of all the noises that night not one was of those heavy uncertain steps, or of that club with which he sometimes smote the earth until it quaked. How agreeable it is to be confirmed, after a more or less long period of vacillation, in one's first impressions. Perhaps that is what tempers the pangs of death. Not that I was so conclusively, I mean confirmed, in my first impressions with regard to—wait—C. For the wagons and carts which a little before dawn went thundering by, on their way to market with fruit, eggs, butter and perhaps cheese, in one of these perhaps he would have been found, overcome by fatigue or discouragement, perhaps even dead. Or he might have gone back to the town by another way too far away for me to hear its sounds, or by little paths through the fields, crushing the silent grass, pounding the silent ground. And so at last I came out of that distant night, divided between the murmurs of my little world, its dutiful confusions, and those so different (so different?) of all that between two suns abides and passes away. Never once a human voice. But the cows, when the peasants passed, crying in vain to be milked. A and C I never saw again. But perhaps I shall see them again. But shall I be able to recognise them? And am I sure I never saw them again? And what do I mean by seeing and seeing again? An instant of silence, as when the conductor taps on his stand, raises his arms, before the unanswerable clamour. Smoke, sticks, flesh, hair, at evening, afar, flung about the craving for a fellow. I know how to summon these rags to cover my shame. I wonder what that means. But I shall not

always be in need. But talking of the craving for a fellow let me
observe that having waked between eleven o'clock and midday (I
heard the angelus, recalling the incarnation, shortly after) I resolved
to go and see my mother. I needed, before I could resolve to go and
see that woman, reasons of an urgent nature, and with such reasons,
since I did not know what to do, or where to go, it was child's play
for me, the play of an only child, to fill my mind until it was rid
of all other preoccupation and I seized with a trembling at the mere
idea of being hindered from going there, I mean to my mother, there
and then. So I got up, adjusted my crutches and went down to the
road, where I found my bicycle (I didn't know I had one) in the
same place I must have left it. Which enables me to remark that,
crippled though I was, I was no mean cyclist, at that period. This
is how I went about it. I fastened my crutches to the cross-bar, one
on either side, I propped the foot of my stiff leg (I forget which,
now they're both stiff) on the projecting front axle, and I pedalled
with the other. It was a chainless bicycle, with a free-wheel, if such
a bicycle exists. Dear bicycle, I shall not call you bike, you were
green, like so many of your generation. I don't know why. It is a
pleasure to meet it again. To describe it at length would be a
pleasure. It had a little red horn instead of the bell fashionable in
your days. To blow this horn was for me a real pleasure, almost a
vice. I will go further and declare that if I were obliged to record,
in a roll of honour, those activities which in the course of my interminable existence have given me only a mild pain in the balls, the
blowing of a rubber horn—toot!—would figure among the first.
And when I had to part from my bicycle I took off the horn and
kept it about me. I believe I have it still, somewhere, and if I blow
it no more it is because it has gone dumb. Even motor-cars have
no horns nowadays, as I understand the thing, or rarely. When I
see one, through the lowered window of a stationary car, I often
stop and blow it. This should all be re-written in the pluperfect.
What a rest to speak of bicycles and horns. Unfortunately it is not
of them I have to speak, but of her who brought me into the world,
through the hole in her arse if my memory is correct. First taste
of the shit. So I shall only add that every hundred yards or so I
stopped to rest my legs, the good one as well as the bad, and not

only my legs, not only my legs. I didn't properly speaking get down
off the machine, I remained astride it, my feet on the ground, my
arms on the handle-bars, my head on my arms, and I waited until
I felt better. But before I leave this earthly paradise, suspended
between the mountains and the sea, sheltered from certain winds
and exposed to all that Auster vents, in the way of scents and
langours, on this accursed country, it would ill become me not to
mention the awful cries of the corncrakes that run in the corn, in
the meadows, all the short summer night long, dinning their rattles.
And this enables me, what is more, to know when that unreal
journey began, the second last but one of a form fading among
fading forms, and which I here declare without further ado to have
begun in the second or third week of June, at the moment that is
to say most painful of all when over what is called our hemisphere
the sun is at its pitilessmost and the arctic radiance comes pissing
on our midnights. It is then the corncrakes are heard. My mother
never refused to see me, that is she never refused to receive me,
for it was many a long day since she had seen anything at all. I
shall try and speak calmly. We were so old, she and I, she had had
me so young, that we were like a couple of old cronies, sexless,
unrelated, with the same memories, the same rancours, the same
expectations. She never called me son, fortunately, I couldn't have
borne it, but Dan, I don't know why, my name is not Dan. Dan
was my father's name perhaps, yes, perhaps she took me for my
father. I took her for my mother and she took me for my father.
Dan, you remember the day I saved the swallow. Dan, you
remember the day you buried the ring. I remembered, I remembered, I mean I knew more or less what she was talking about, and
if I hadn't always taken part personally in the scenes she evoked,
it was just as if I had. I called her Mag, when I had to call her
something. And I called her Mag because for me, without my
knowing why, the letter g abolished the syllable Ma, and as it were
spat on it, better than any other letter would have done. And at
the same time I satisfied a deep and doubtless unacknowledged need,
the need to have a Ma, that is a mother, and to proclaim it, audibly.
For before you say mag, you say ma, inevitably. And da, in my
part of the world, means father. Besides, for me the question did

not arise, at the period I'm worming into now, I mean the question
of whether to call her Ma, Mag or the Countess Caca, she having
for countless years been as deaf as a post. I think she was quite
incontinent, both of faeces and water, but a kind of prudishness
made us avoid the subject when we met, and I could never be
certain of it. In any case it can't have amounted to much, a few
niggardly wetted goat-droppings, every two or three days. The room
smelt of ammonia, oh not merely of ammonia, but of ammonia,
ammonia. She knew it was me, by my smell. Her shrunken, hairy
old face lit up, she was happy to smell me. She jabbered away with
a rattle of dentures and most of the time didn't realize what she
was saying. Anyone but myself would have been lost in this clat-
tering gabble, which can only have stopped during her brief instants
of unconsciousness. In any case I didn't come to listen to her. I got
into communication with her by knocking on her skull. One knock
meant yes, two no, three I don't know, four money, five goodbye.
I was hard put to ram this code into her ruined and frantic understanding, but I did it, in the end. That she should confuse yes, no,
I don't know and goodbye, was all the same to me, I confused them
myself. But that she should associate the four knocks with anything
but money was something to be avoided at all costs. During the
period of training therefore, at the same time as I administered the
four knocks on her skull, I stuck a bank-note under her nose or in
her mouth. In the innocence of my heart! For she seemed to have
lost, if not absolutely all notion of mensuration, at least the faculty
of counting beyond two. It was too far for her, yes, the distance
was too great, from one to four. By the time she came to the fourth
knock she imagined she was only at the second, the first two having
been erased from her memory as completely as if they had never
been felt, though I don't quite see how something never felt can
be erased from the memory, and yet it is a common occurrence.
She must have thought I was saying no to her all the time, whereas
nothing was further from my purpose. Enlightened by these considerations I looked for and finally found a more effective means
of putting the idea of money into her head. This consisted in replac-
ing the four knocks of my index knuckle by one or more (according
to my needs) thumps of the fist, on her skull. That she understood.

In any case I didn't come for money. I took her money, but I didn't
come for that. My mother. I don't think too harshly of her. I know
she did all she could not to have me, except of course the one thing,
and if she never succeeded in getting me unstuck, it was that fate
had earmarked me for less compassionate sewers. But it was well-
meant and that's enough for me. No it is not enough for me, but I
give her credit, though she is my mother, for what she tried to do
for me. And I forgive her for having jostled me a little in the first
months and spoiled the only endurable, just endurable, period of
my enormous history. And I also give her credit for not having
done it again, thanks to me, or for having stopped in time, when she
did. And if ever I'm reduced to looking for a meaning to my life,
you never can tell, it's in that old mess I'll stick my nose to begin
with, the mess of that poor old uniparous whore and myself the
last of my foul brood, neither man nor beast. I should add, before
I get down to the facts, you'd swear they were facts, of that distant
summer afternoon, that with this deaf, blind, impotent, mad old
woman, who called me Dan and whom I called Mag, and with her
alone, I—no, I can't say it. That is to say, I could say it, but I
won't say it, yes, I could say it easily, because it wouldn't be true.
What did I see of her? A head always, the hands sometimes, the
arms rarely. A head always. Veiled with hair, wrinkles, filth,
slobber. A head that darkened the air. Not that seeing matters, but
it's something to go on with. It was I who took the key from under
the pillow, who took the money out of the drawer, who put the
key back under the pillow. But I didn't come for money. I think
there was a woman who came each week. Once I touched with my
lips, vaguely, hastily, that little grey wizened pear. Pah. Did that
please her? I don't know. Her babble stopped for a second, then
began again. Perhaps she said to herself, Pah. I smelt a terrible
smell. It must have come from the bowels. Odour of antiquity. Oh
I'm not criticizing her, I don't diffuse the perfumes of Araby myself.
Shall I describe the room? No. I shall have occasion to do so later
perhaps. When I seek refuge there, beat to the world, all shame
drunk, my prick in my rectum, who knows. Good. Now that we
know where we're going, let's go there. It's so nice to know where
you're going, in the early stages. It almost rids you of the wish to

go there. I was distraught, who am so seldom distraught, from what
should I be distraught, and as to my motions even more uncertain
than usual. The night must have tired me, at least weakened me,
and the sun, hoisting itself higher and higher in the east, had
poisoned me, while I slept. I ought to have put the bulk of the rock
between it and me before closing my eyes. I confuse east and west,
the poles too, I invert them readily. I was out of sorts. They are
deep, my sorts, a deep ditch, and I am not often out of them. That's
why I mention it. Nevertheless I covered several miles and found
myself under the ramparts. There I dismounted in compliance with
the regulations. Yes, cyclists entering and leaving town are required
by the police to dismount, cars to go into bottom gear and horse-
drawn vehicles to slow down to a walk. The reason for this regula-
tion is I think this, that the ways into and, of course, out of this
town are narrow and darkened by enormous vaults, without exception. It is a good rule and I observe it religiously, in spite of the
difficulty I have in advancing on my crutches pushing my bicycle
at the same time. I managed somehow. Being ingenious. Thus we
cleared these difficult straits, my bicycle and I, together. But a little
further on I heard myself hailed. I raised my head and saw a policeman. Elliptically speaking, for it was only later, by way of induc-
tion, or deduction, I forget which, that I knew what it was. What are
you doing there? he said. I'm used to that question, I understood
it immediately. Resting, I said. Resting, he said. Resting, I said.
Will you answer my question? he cried. So it always is when I'm
reduced to confabulation, I honestly believe I have answered the
question I am asked and in reality I do nothing of the kind. I won't
reconstruct the conversation in all its meanderings. It ended in my
understanding that my way of resting, my attitude when at rest
astride my bicycle, my arms on the handlebars, my head on my
arms, was a violation of I don't know what, public order, public
decency. Modestly, I pointed to my crutches and ventured one or two
noises regarding my infirmity, which obliged me to rest as I could,
rather than as I should. But there are not two laws, that was the next
thing I thought I understood, not two laws, one for the healthy,
another for the sick, but one only to which all must bow, rich and
poor, young and old, happy and sad. He was eloquent. I pointed

out that I was not sad. That was a mistake. Your papers, he said,
I knew it a moment later. Not at all, I said, not at all. Your papers!
he cried. Ah my papers. Now the only papers I carry with me are
bits of newspaper, to wipe myself, you understand, when I have a
stool. Oh I don't say I wipe myself every time I have a stool, no,
but I like to be in a position to do so, if I have to. Nothing strange
about that, it seems to me. In a panic I took this paper from my
pocket and thrust it under his nose. The weather was fine. We took
the little side streets, quiet, sunlit, I springing along between my
crutches, he pushing my bicycle, with the tips of his white-gloved
fingers. I wasn't—I didn't feel unhappy. I stopped a moment, I
made so bold, to lift my hand and touch the crown of my hat. It
was scorching. I felt the faces turning to look after us, calm faces
and joyful faces, faces of men, of women and of children. I seemed
to hear, at a certain moment, a distant music. I stopped, the better
to listen. Go on, he said. Listen, I said. Get on, he said. I wasn't
allowed to listen to the music. It might have drawn a crowd. He
gave me a shove. I had been touched, oh not my skin, but none
the less my skin had felt it, it had felt a man's hard fist, through
its coverings. While still putting my best foot foremost I gave
myself up to that golden moment, as if I had been someone else.
It was the hour of rest, the forenoon's toil ended, the afternoon's
to come. The wisest perhaps, lying in the squares or sitting on their
doorsteps, were savouring its languid ending, forgetful of recent
cares, indifferent to those at hand. Others on the contrary were
using it to hatch their plans, their heads in their hands. Was there
one among them to put himself in my place, to feel how removed
I was then from him I seemed to be, and in that remove what strain,
as of hawsers about to snap? It's possible. Yes, I was straining
towards those spurious deeps, their lying promise of gravity and
peace, from all my old poisons I struggled towards them, safely
bound. Under the blue sky, under the watchful gaze. Forgetful of
my mother, set free from the act, merged in this alien hour, saying,
Respite, respite. At the police station I was haled before a very
strange official. Dressed in plain-clothes, in his shirt-sleeves, he was
sprawling in an arm-chair, his feet on his desk, a straw hat on his
head and protruding from his mouth a thin flexible object I could

not identify. I had time to become aware of these details before
he dismissed me. He listened to his subordinate's report and then
began to interrogate me in a tone which, from the point of view
of civility, left increasingly to be desired, in my opinion. Between
his questions and my answers, I mean those deserving of consideration, the intervals were more or less long and turbulent. I am so
little used to being asked anything that when I am asked something
I take some time to know what. And the mistake I make then is
this, that instead of quietly reflecting on what I have just heard,
and heard distinctly, not being hard of hearing, in spite of all I
have heard, I hasten to answer blindly, fearing perhaps lest my
silence fan their anger to fury. I am full of fear, I have gone in
fear all my life, in fear of blows. Insults, abuse, these I can easily
bear, but I could never get used to blows. It's strange. Even spits
still pain me. But they have only to be a little gentle, I mean refrain
from hitting me, and I seldom fail to give satisfaction, in the long
run. Now the sergeant, content to threaten me with a cylindrical
ruler, was little by little rewarded for his pains by the discovery
that I had no papers in the sense this word had a sense for him,
nor any occupation, nor any domicile, that my surname escaped
me for the moment and that I was on my way to my mother, whose
charity kept me dying. As to her address, I was in the dark, but
knew how to get there, even in the dark. The district? By the
shambles your honour, for from my mother's room, through the
closed windows, I had heard, stilling her chatter, the bellowing of
the cattle, that violent raucous tremulous bellowing not of the
pastures, but of the towns, their shambles and cattle-markets. Yes,
after all, I had perhaps gone too far in saying that my mother
lived near the shambles, it could equally well have been the cattle-
market, near which she lived. Never mind, said the sergeant, it's
the same district. I took advantage of the silence which followed
these kind words to turn towards the window, blindly or nearly,
for I had closed my eyes, proffering to that blandness of blue and
gold my face and neck alone, and my mind empty too, or nearly,
for I must have been wondering if I did not feel like sitting down,
after such a long time standing, and remembering what I had learnt
in that connection, namely that the sitting posture was not for me

any more, because of my short stiff leg, and that there were only
two postures for me any more, the vertical, drooping between my
crutches, sleeping on my feet, and the horizontal, down on the
ground. And yet the desire to sit down came upon me from time
to time, back upon me from a vanished world. And I did not
always resist it, forewarned though I was. Yes, my mind felt it
surely, this tiny sediment, incomprehensibly stirring like grit at the
bottom of a puddle, while on my face and great big Adam's apple
the air of summer weighed and the splendid summer sky. And
suddenly I remembered my name, Molloy. My name is Molloy,
I cried, all of a sudden, now I remember. Nothing compelled me
to give this information, but I gave it, hoping to please I suppose.
They let me keep my hat on, I don't know why. Is it your mother's
name? said the sergeant, it must have been a sergeant. Molloy, I
cried, my name is Molloy. Is that your mother's name? said the
sergeant. What? I said. Your name is Molloy, said the sergeant.
Yes, I said, now I remember. And your mother? said the sergeant.
I didn't follow. Is your mother's name Molloy too? said the sergeant.
I thought it over. Your mother, said the sergeant, is your mother's
—Let me think! I cried. At least I imagine that's how it was. Take
your time, said the sergeant. Was mother's name Molloy? Very
likely. Her name must be Molloy too, I said. They took me away,
to the guardroom I suppose, and there I was told to sit down. I
must have tried to explain. I won't go into it. I obtained permission,
if not to lie down on a bench, at least to remain standing, propped
against the wall. The room was dark and full of people hastening
to and fro, malefactors, policemen, lawyers, priests and journalists
I suppose. All that made a dark, dark forms crowding in a dark
place. They paid no attention to me and I repaid the compliment.
Then how could I know they were paying no attention to me,
and how could I repay the compliment, since they were paying no
attention to me? I don't know. I knew it and I did it, that's all I
know. But suddenly a woman rose up before me, a big fat woman
dressed in black, or rather in mauve. I still wonder today if it
wasn't the social worker. She was holding out to me, on an odd
saucer, a mug full of a greyish concoction which must have been
green tea with saccharine and powdered milk. Nor was that all, for

between mug and saucer a thick slab of dry bread was precariously
lodged, so that I began to say, in a kind of anguish, It's going to
fall, it's going to fall, as if it mattered whether it fell or not. A
moment later I myself was holding, in my trembling hands, this
little pile of tottering disparates, in which the hard, the liquid and
the soft were joined, without understanding how the transfer had
been effected. Let me tell you this, when social workers offer you,
free, gratis and for nothing, something to hinder you from swoon-
ing, which with them is an obsession, it is useless to recoil, they will
pursue you to the ends of the earth, the vomitory in their hands.
The Salvation Army is no better. Against the charitable gesture
there is no defence, that I know of. You sink your head, you put
out your hands all trembling and twined together and you say,
Thank you, thank you lady, thank you kind lady. To him who has
nothing it is forbidden not to relish filth. The liquid overflowed,
the mug rocked with a noise of chattering teeth, not mine, I had
none, and the sodden bread sagged more and more. Until, panic-
stricken, I flung it all far from me. I did not let it fall, no, but with
a convulsive thrust of both my hands I threw it to the ground,
where it smashed to smithereens, or against the wall, far from me,
with all my strength. I will not tell what followed, for I am weary
of this place, I want to go. It was late afternoon when they told
me I could go. I was advised to behave better in future. Conscious
of my wrongs, knowing now the reasons for my arrest, alive to my
irregular situation as revealed by the enquiry, I was surprised to
find myself so soon at freedom once again, if that is what it was,
unpenalised. Had I, without my knowledge, a friend at court? Had
I, without knowing it, favourably impressed the sergeant? Had they
succeeded in finding my mother and obtaining from her, or from
the neighbours, partial confirmation of my statements? Were they
of the opinion that it was useless to prosecute me? To apply the
letter of the law to a creature like me is not an easy matter. It can
be done, but reason is against it. It is better to leave things to the
police. I don't know. If it is unlawful to be without papers, why
did they not insist on my getting them? Because that costs money
and I had none? But in that case could they not have appropriated
my bicycle? Probably not, without a court order. All that is in-

comprehensible. What is certain is this, that I never rested in that way again, my feet obscenely resting on the earth, my arms on the handlebars and on my arms my head, rocking and abandoned. It is indeed a deplorable sight, a deplorable example, for the people, who so need to be encouraged, in their bitter toil, and to have before their eyes manifestations of strength only, of courage and of joy, without which they might collapse, at the end of the day, and roll on the ground. I have only to be told what good behaviour is and I am well-behaved, within the limits of my physical possibilities. And so I have never ceased to improve, from this point of view, for I—I used to be intelligent and quick. And as far as good-will is concerned, I had it to overflowing, the exasperated good-will of the over-anxious. So that my repertory of permitted attitudes has never ceased to grow, from my first steps until my last, executed last year. And if I have always behaved like a pig, the fault lies not with me but with my superiors, who corrected me only on points of detail instead of showing me the essence of the system, after the manner of the great English schools, and the guiding principles of good manners, and how to proceed, without going wrong, from the former to the latter, and how to trace back to its ultimate source a given comportment. For that would have allowed me, before parading in public certain habits such as the finger in the nose, the scratching of the balls, digital emunction and the peripatetic piss, to refer them to the first rules of a reasoned theory. On this subject I had only negative and empirical notions, which means that I was in the dark, most of the time, and all the more completely as a lifetime of observations had left me doubting the possibility of systematic decorum, even within a limited area. But it is only since I have ceased to live that I think of these things and the other things. It is in the tranquillity of decomposition that I remember the long confused emotion which was my life, and that I judge it, as it is said that God will judge me, and with no less impertinence. To decompose is to live too, I know, I know, don't torment me, but one sometimes forgets. And of that life too I shall tell you perhaps one day, the day I know that when I thought I knew I was merely existing and that passion without form or stations will have devoured me down to the rotting flesh itself and that when I know that I know nothing, am only crying out as I have always cried out, more or less piercingly, more or less openly. Let me cry out then, it's said to be good for you. Yes, let me cry out, this time, then another time perhaps, then perhaps a last time. Cry out that the declining sun fell full on the white wall of the barracks. It was like being in China. A confused shadow was cast. It was I and my bicycle. I began to play, gesticulating, waving my hat, moving my bicycle to and fro before me, blowing the horn, watching the wall. They were watching me through the bars, I felt their eyes upon me. The policeman on guard at the door told me to go away. He needn't have, I was calm again. The shadow in the end is no better than the substance. I asked the man to help me, to have pity on me. He didn't understand. I thought of the food I had refused. I took a pebble from my pocket and sucked it. It was smooth, from having been sucked so long, by me, and beaten by the storm. A little pebble in your mouth, round and smooth, appeases, soothes, makes you forget your hunger, forget your thirst. The man came towards me, angered by my slowness. Him too they were watching, through the windows. Somewhere someone laughed. Inside me too someone was laughing. I took my sick leg in my hands and passed it over the frame. I went. I had forgotten where I was going. I stopped to think. It is difficult to think riding, for me. When I try and think riding I lose my balance and fall. I speak in the present tense, it is so easy to speak in the present tense, when speaking of the past. It is the mythological present, don't mind it. I was already settling in my raglimp stasis when I remembered it wasn't done. I went on my way, that way of which I knew nothing, qua way, which was nothing more than a surface, bright or dark, smooth or rough, and always dear to me, in spite of all, and the dear sound of that which goes and is gone, with a brief dust, when the weather is dry. There I am then, before I knew I had left the town, on the canal-bank. The canal goes through the town, I know I know, there are even two. But then these hedges, these fields? Don't torment yourself, Molloy. Suddenly I see, it was my right leg the stiff one, then. Toiling towards me along the tow-path I saw a team of little grey donkeys, on the far bank, and I heard angry cries and dull blows. I got down, I put my foot to the ground the better to see the

approaching barge, so gently approaching that the water was un-
ruffled. It was a cargo of nails and timber, on its way to some car-
penter I suppose. My eyes caught a donkey's eyes, they fell to his
little feet, their brave fastidious tread. The boatman rested his elbow
on his knee, his head on his hand. He had a long white beard.
Every three or four puffs, without taking his pipe from his mouth,
he spat into the water. I could not see his eyes. The horizon was
burning with sulphur and phosphorus, it was there I was bound.
At last I got right down, hobbled down to the ditch and lay down,
beside my bicycle. I lay at full stretch, with outspread arms. The
white hawthorn stooped towards me, unfortunately I don't like the
smell of hawthorn. In the ditch the grass was thick and high, I took
off my hat and pressed about my face the long leafy stalks. Then
I could smell the earth, the smell of the earth was in the grass that
my hands wove round my face till I was blinded. I ate a little too,
a little grass. It came back to my mind, from nowhere, as a moment
before my name, that I had set out to see my mother, at the beginning of this ending day. My reasons? I had forgotten them. But
I knew them, I must have known them, I had only to find them again
and I would sweep, with the clipped wings of necessity, to my
mother. Yes, it's all easy when you know why, a mere matter of
magic. Yes, the whole thing is to know what saint to implore, any
fool can implore him. For the particulars, if you are interested in
particulars, there is no need to despair, you may scrabble on the
right door, in the right way, in the end. It's for the whole there
seems to be no spell. Perhaps there is no whole, before you're dead.
An opiate for the life of the dead, that should be easy. What am I
waiting for then, to exorcize mine? It's coming, it's coming. I hear
from here the howl resolving all, even if it is not mine. Meanwhile
there's no use knowing you are gone, you are not, you are writhing
yet, the hair is growing, the nails are growing, the entrails emptying,
all the morticians are dead. Someone has drawn the blinds, you
perhaps. Not the faintest sound. Where are the famous flies? Yes,
there is no denying it, any longer, it is not you who are dead,
but all the others. So you get up and go to your mother, who thinks
she is alive. That's my impression. But now I shall have to get
myself out of this ditch. How joyfully I would vanish there, sinking

deeper and deeper under the rains. No doubt I'll come back some day, here, or to a similar slough, I can trust my feet for that, as no doubt some day I'll meet again the sergeant and his merry men. And if, too changed to know it is they, I do not say it is they, make no mistake, it will be they, though changed. For to contrive a being, a place, I nearly said an hour, but I would not hurt anyone's feelings, and then to use them no more, that would be, how shall I say, I don't know. Not to want to say, not to know what you want to say, not to be able to say what you think you want to say, and never to stop saying, or hardly ever, that is the thing to keep in mind, even in the heat of composition. That night was not like the other night, if it had been I would have known. For when I try and think of that night, on the canal-bank, I find nothing, no night properly speaking, nothing but Molloy in the ditch, and perfect silence, and behind my closed lids the little night and its little lights, faint at first, then flaming and extinguished, now ravening, now fed, as fire by filth and martyrs. I say that night, but there was more than one perhaps. The lie, the lie, to lying thought. But I find the morning, a morning, and the sun already high, and the little sleep I had then, according to my custom, and space with its sounds again, and the shepherd watching me sleep and under whose eyes I opened my eyes. Beside him a panting dog, watching me too, but less closely than his master, for from time to time he stopped watching me to gnaw at his flesh, furiously, where the ticks were in him I suppose. Did he take me for a black sheep entangled in the brambles and was he waiting for an order from his master to drag me out? I don't think so. I don't smell like a sheep, I wish I smelt like a sheep, or a buck-goat. When I wake I see the first things quite clearly, the first things that offer, and I understand them, when they are not too difficult. Then in my eyes and in my head a fine rain begins to fall, as from a rose, highly important. So I knew at once it was a shepherd and his dog I had before me, above me rather, for they had not left the path. And I identified the bleating too, without any trouble, the anxious bleating of the sheep, missing the dog at their heels. It is then too that the meaning of words is least obscure to me, so that I said, with tranquil assurance, Where are you taking them, to the fields or to the shambles?

I must have completely lost my sense of direction, as if direction
had anything to do with the matter. For even if he was going towards the town, what prevented him from skirting it, or from leaving it again by another gate, on his way to new pastures, and if he
was going away from it that meant nothing either, for slaughter-
houses are not confined to towns, no, they are everywhere, the
country is full of them, every butcher has his slaughter-house and
the right to slaughter, according to his lights. But whether it was he
didn't understand, or didn't want to reply, he didn't reply, but went
on his way without a word, without a word for me I mean, for he
spoke to his dog who listened attentively, cocking his ears. I got
to my knees, no, that doesn't work, I got up and watched the little
procession recede. I heard the shepherd whistle, and I saw him
flourishing his crook, and the dog bustling about the flock, which
but for him would no doubt have fallen into the canal. All that
through a glittering dust, and soon through that mist too which rises
in me every day and veils the world from me and veils me from
myself. The bleating grew faint, because the sheep were less
anxious, or because they were further away, or because my hearing
was worse than a moment before, which would surprise me, for my
hearing is still very good, scarcely blunted coming up to dawn, and
if I sometimes hear nothing for hours on end it is for reasons of
which I know nothing, or because about me all goes really silent,
from time to time, whereas for the righteous the tumult of the
world never stops. That then is how that second day began, unless
it was the third, or the fourth, and it was a bad beginning, because
it left me with persisting doubts, as to the destination of those sheep,
among which there were lambs, and often wondering if they had
safely reached some commonage or fallen, their skulls shattered,
their thin legs crumpling, first to their knees, then over on their
fleecy sides, under the pole-axe, though that is not the way they
slaughter sheep, but with a knife, so that they bleed to death. But
there is much to be said too for these little doubts. Good God,
what a land of breeders, you see quadrupeds everywhere. And it's
not over yet, there are still horses and goats, to mention only them,
I feel them watching out for me, to get in my path. I have no need
of that. But I did not lose sight of my immediate goal, which was

to get to my mother as quickly as possible, and standing in the
ditch I summoned to my aid the good reasons I had for going
there, without a moment's delay. And though there were many
things I could do without thinking, not knowing what I was going
to do until it was done, and not even then, going to my mother
was not one of them. My feet, you see, never took me to my mother
unless they received a definite order to do so. The glorious, the
truly glorious weather would have gladdened any other heart than
mine. But I have no reason to be gladdened by the sun and I take
good care not to be. The Aegean, thirsting for heat and light, him
I killed, he killed himself, early on, in me. The pale gloom of rainy
days was better fitted to my taste, no, that's not it, to my humour,
no, that's not it either, I had neither taste nor humour, I lost them
early on. Perhaps what I mean is that the pale gloom, etc., hid me
better, without its being on that account particularly pleasing to
me. Chameleon in spite of himself, there you have Molloy, viewed
from a certain angle. And in winter, under my greatcoat, I wrapped
myself in swathes of newspaper, and did not shed them until the
earth awoke, for good, in April. The Times Literary Supplement
was admirably adapted to this purpose, of a never failing toughness
and impermeability. Even farts made no impression on it. I can't
help it, gas escapes from my fundament on the least pretext, it's
hard not to mention it now and then, however great my distaste.
One day I counted them. Three hundred and fifteen farts in nine-
teen hours, or an average of over sixteen farts an hour. After all
it's not excessive. Four farts every fifteen minutes. It's nothing.
Not even one fart every four minutes. It's unbelievable. Damn it,
I hardly fart at all, I should never have mentioned it. Extraordinary
how mathematics help you to know yourself. In any case this whole
question of climate left me cold, I could stomach any mess. So I
will only add that the mornings were often sunny, in that part of
the world, until ten o'clock or coming up to eleven, and that then
the sky darkened and the rain fell, fell till evening. Then the sun
came out and went down, the drenched earth sparkled an instant,
then went out, bereft of light. There I am then back in the saddle,
in my numbed heart a prick of misgiving, like one dying of cancer
obliged to consult his dentist. For I did not know if it was the right

road. All roads were right for me, a wrong road was an event, for
me. But when I was on my way to my mother only one road was
right, the one that led to her, or one of those that led to her, for
all did not lead to her. I did not know if I was on one of those right
roads and that disturbed me, like all recall to life. Judge then of
my relief when I saw, ahead of me, the familiar ramparts loom. I
passed beyond them, into a district I did not know. And yet I knew
the town well, for I was born there and had never succeeded in
putting between it and me more than ten or fifteen miles, such was
its grasp on me, I don't know why. So that I came near to wondering if I was in the right town, where I first saw the murk of day
and which still harboured my mother, somewhere or other, or if I
had not stumbled, as a result of a wrong turn, on a town whose very
name I did not know. For my native town was the only one I knew,
having never set foot in any other. But I had read with care, while
I still could read, accounts of travellers more fortunate than myself,
telling of other towns as beautiful as mine, and even more beautiful,
though with a different beauty. And now it was a name I sought,
in my memory, the name of the only town it had been given me to
know, with the intention, as soon as I had found it, of stopping, and
saying to a passer-by, doffing my hat, I beg your pardon, Sir, this *is*
X, is it not? X being the name of my town. And this name that I
sought, I felt sure that it began with a B or with a P, but in spite of
this clue, or perhaps because of its falsity, the other letters continued
to escape me. I had been living so far from words so long, you
understand, that it was enough for me to see my town, since we're
talking of my town, to be unable, you understand. It's too difficult
to say, for me. And even my sense of identity was wrapped in a
namelessness often hard to penetrate, as we have just seen I think.
And so on for all the other things which made merry with my senses.
Yes, even then, when already all was fading, waves and particles,
there could be no things but nameless things, no names but thing-
less names. I say that now, but after all what do I know now about
then, now when the icy words hail down upon me, the icy meanings,
and the world dies too, foully named. All I know is what the words
know, and the dead things, and that makes a handsome little sum,
with a beginning, a middle and an end as in the well-built phrase

and the long sonata of the dead. And truly it little matters what I
say, this or that or any other thing. Saying is inventing. Wrong,
very rightly wrong. You invent nothing, you think you are inventing, you think you are escaping, and all you do is stammer out your
lesson, the remnants of a pensum one day got by heart and long
forgotten, life without tears, as it is wept. To hell with it anyway.
Where was I. Unable to remember the name of my town I resolved
to stop by the kerb, to wait for a passer-by with a friendly and
intelligent air and then to whip off my hat and say, with my smile,
I beg your pardon Sir, excuse me Sir, what is the name of this town,
if you please? For the word once let fall I would know if it was
the right word, the one I was seeking, in my memory, or another,
and so where I stood. This resolution, actually formed as I rode
along, was never to be carried out, an absurd mishap prevented it.
Yes, my resolutions were remarkable in this, that they were no
sooner formed than something always happened to prevent their
execution. That must be why I am even less resolute now than then,
just as then I was even less so than I once had been. But to tell
the truth (to tell the truth!) I have never been particularly resolute,
I mean given to resolutions, but rather inclined to plunge headlong
into the shit, without knowing who was shitting against whom or
on which side I had the better chance of skulking with success.
But from this leaning too I derived scant satisfaction and if I have
never quite got rid of it it is not for want of trying. The fact is, it
seems, that the most you can hope is to be a little less, in the end,
the creature you were in the beginning, and the middle. For I had
hardly perfected my plan, in my head, when my bicycle ran over
a dog, as subsequently appeared, and fell to the ground, an inept-
ness all the more unpardonable as the dog, duly leashed, was not
out on the road, but in on the pavement, docile at its mistress's
heels. Precautions are like resolutions, to be taken with precaution.
The lady must have thought she had left nothing to chance, so far
as the safety of her dog was concerned, whereas in reality she was
setting the whole system of nature at naught, no less surely than I
myself with my insane demands for more light. But instead of
grovelling in my turn, invoking my great age and infirmities, I
made things worse by trying to run away. I was soon overtaken,

by a bloodthirsty mob of both sexes and all ages, for I caught a
glimpse of white beards and little, almost angel faces, and they
were preparing to tear me to pieces when the lady intervened. She
said in effect, she told me so later on and I believed her, Leave
this poor old man alone. He has killed Teddy, I grant you that,
Teddy whom I loved like my own child, but it is not so serious as
it seems, for as it happens I was taking him to the veterinary surgeon, to have him put out of his misery. For Teddy was old, blind,
deaf, crippled with rheumatism and perpetually incontinent, night
and day, indoors and out of doors. Thanks then to this poor old
man I have been spared a painful task, not to mention the expense
which I am ill able to afford, having no other means of support
than the pension of my dear departed, fallen in defence of a country
that called itself his and from which in his lifetime he never derived
the smallest benefit, but only insults and vexations. The crowd was
beginning to disperse, the danger was past, but the lady was in her
stride. You may say, she said, that he did wrong to run away, that
he should have explained, asked to be forgiven. Granted. But it is
clear he has not all his wits about him, that he is beside himself,
for reasons of which we know nothing and which might put us all
to shame, if we did know them. I even wonder if he knows what he
has done. There emanated such tedium from this droning voice
that I was making ready to move on when the unavoidable police
constable rose up before me. He brought down heavily on my
handle-bars his big red hairy paw, I noticed it myself, and had it
appears with the lady the following conversation. Is this the man
who ran over your dog, Madam? He is, sergeant, and what of it?
No, I can't record this fatuous colloquy. So I will merely observe
that finally in his turn the constable too dispersed, the word is not
too strong, grumbling and growling, followed by the last idlers who
had given up all hope of my coming to a bad end. But he turned back
and said, Remove that dog. Free at last to go I began to do so. But
the lady, a Mrs. Loy, I might as well say it now and be done with it,
or Lousse, I forget, Christian name something like Sophie, held me
back, by the tail of my coat, and said, assuming the words were
the same when I heard them as when first spoken, Sir, I need you.
And seeing I suppose from my expression, which frequently betrays

me, that she had made herself understood, she must have said, If
he understands that he can understand anything. And she was not
mistaken, for after some time I found myself in possession of certain
ideas or points of view which could only have come to me from
her, namely that having killed her dog I was morally obliged to help
her carry him home and bury him, that she did not wish to prosecute me for what I had done, but that it was not always possible
to do as one did not wish, that she found me likeable enough in
spite of my hideous appearance and would be happy to hold out
to me a helping hand, and so on, I've forgotten the half of it. Ah
yes, I too needed her, it seemed. She needed me to help her get rid
of her dog, and I needed her, I've forgotten for what. She must
have told me, for that was an insinuation I could not decently pass
over in silence as I had the rest, and I made no bones about telling
her I needed neither her nor anyone else, which was perhaps a
slight exaggeration, for I must have needed my mother, otherwise
why this frenzy of wanting to get to her? That is one of the many
reasons why I avoid speaking as much as possible. For I always
say either too much or too little, which is a terrible thing for a man
with a passion for truth like mine. And I shall not abandon this
subject, to which I shall probably never have occasion to return,
with such a storm blowing up, without making this curious observation, that it often happened to me, before I gave up speaking for
good, to think I had said too little when in fact I had said too
much and in fact to have said too little when I thought
I had said too much. I mean that on reflection, in the long run
rather, my verbal profusion turned out to be penury, and inversely.
So time sometimes turns the tables. In other words, or perhaps
another thing, whatever I said it was never enough and always too
much. Yes, I was never silent, whatever I said I was never silent.
Divine analysis that conduces thus to knowledge of yourself, and
of your fellow-men, if you happen to have any. For to say I needed
no one was not to say too much, but an infinitesimal part of what
I should have said, could not have said, should never have said.
Need of my mother! No, there were no words for the want of need
in which I was perishing. So that she, I mean Sophie, must have
told me the reasons why I needed her, since I had dared to disagree.

And perhaps if I took the trouble I might find them again, but trouble, many thanks, some other time. And now enough of this boulevard, it must have been a boulevard, of all these righteous ones, these guardians of the peace, all these feet and hands, stamping, clutching, clenched in vain, these bawling mouths that never bawl out of season, this sky beginning to drip, enough of being abroad, trapped, visible. Someone was poking the dog, with a malacca. The dog was uniformly yellow, a mongrel I suppose, or a pedigree, I can never tell the difference. His death must have hurt him less than my fall me. And he at least was dead. We slung him across the saddle and set off like an army in retreat, helping each other I suppose, to keep the corpse from falling, to keep the bicycle moving, to keep ourselves moving, through the jeering crowd. The house where Sophie—no, I can't call her that any more, I'll try calling her Lousse, without the Mrs.—the house where Lousse lived was not far away. Oh it was not nearby either, I had my bellyful by the time I got there. That is to say I didn't have it really. You think you have your bellyful but you seldom have it really. It was because I knew I was there that I had my bellyful, a mile more to go and I would only have had my bellyful an hour later. Human nature. Marvellous thing. The house where Lousse lived. Must I describe it? I don't think so. I won't, that's all I know, for the moment. Perhaps later on, if I get to know it. And Lousse? Must I describe her? I suppose so. Let's first bury the dog. It was she dug the hole, under a tree. You always bury your dog under a tree, I don't know why. But I have my suspicions. It was she dug the hole because I couldn't, though I was the gentleman, because of my leg. That is to say I could have dug with a trowel, but not with a spade. For when you dig a grave one leg supports the weight of the body while the other, flexing and unflexing, drives the spade into the earth. Now my sick leg, I forget which, it's immaterial here, was in a condition neither to dig, because it was rigid, nor alone to support me, because it would have collapsed. I had so to speak only one leg at my disposal, I was virtually one-legged, and I would have been happier, livelier, amputated at the groin. And if they had removed a few testicles into the bargain I wouldn't have objected. For from such testicles as mine, dangling

at mid-thigh at the end of a meagre cord, there was nothing more
to be squeezed, not a drop. So that non che la speme il desiderio,
and I longed to see them gone, from the old stand where they bore
false witness, for and against, in the lifelong charge against me.
For if they accused me of having made a balls of it, of me, of them,
they thanked me for it too, from the depths of their rotten bag, the
right lower than the left, or inversely, I forget, decaying circus
clowns. And, worse still, they got in my way when I tried to walk,
when I tried to sit down, as if my sick leg was not enough, and when
I rode my bicycle they bounced up and down. So the best thing for
me would have been for them to go, and I would have seen to it
myself, with a knife or secateur, but for my terror of physical pain
and festered wounds, so that I shook. Yes, all my life I have gone
in terror of festered wounds, I who never festered, I was so acid.
My life, my life, now I speak of it as of something over, now as of
a joke which still goes on, and it is neither, for at the same time
it is over and it goes on, and is there any tense for that? Watch
wound and buried by the watchmaker, before he died, whose ruined
works will one day speak of God, to the worms. But those cullions,
I must be attached to them after all, cherish them as others do
their scars, or the family album. In any case it wasn't their fault
I couldn't dig, but my leg's. It was Lousse dug the hole while I
held the dog in my arms. He was heavy already and cold, but he
had not yet begun to stink. He smelt bad, if you like, but bad like
an old dog, not like a dead dog. He too had dug holes, perhaps at
this very spot. We buried him as he was, no box or wrapping of
any kind, like a Carthusian monk, but with his collar and lead.
It was she put him in the hole, though I was the gentleman. For
I cannot stoop, neither can I kneel, because of my infirmity, and
if ever I stoop, forgetting who I am, or kneel, make no mistake,
it will not be me, but another. To throw him in the hole was all
I could have done, and I would have done it gladly. And yet I
did not do it. All the things you would do gladly, oh without enthusiasm, but gladly, all the things there seems no reason for your
not doing, and that you do not do! Can it be we are not free? It
might be worth looking into. But what was my contribution to this
burial? It was she dug the hole, put in the dog, filled up the hole.

On the whole I was a mere spectator, I contributed my presence. As if it had been my own burial. And it was. It was a larch tree. It is the only tree I can identify, with certainty. Funny she should have chosen, to bury her dog beneath, the only tree I can identify, with certainty. The sea-green needles are like silk and speckled, it always seemed to me, with little red, how shall I say, with little red specks. The dog had ticks in his ears, I have an eye for such things, they were buried with him. When she had finished her grave she handed me the spade and began to muse, or brood. I thought she was going to cry, it was the thing to do, but on the contrary she laughed. It was perhaps her way of crying. Or perhaps I was mistaken and she was really crying, with the noise of laughter. Tears and laughter, they are so much Gaelic to me. She would see him no more, her Teddy she had loved like an only child. I wonder why, since she had obviously made up her mind to bury the dog at home, she had not asked the vet to call and destroy the brute on the premises. Was she really on her way to the vet at the moment her path crossed mine? Or had she said so solely in order to attenuate my guilt? Private calls are naturally more expensive. She ushered me into the drawing-room and gave me food and drink, good things without a doubt. Unfortunately I didn't much care for good things to eat. But I quite liked getting drunk. If she lived in embarrassed circumstances there was no sign of it. That kind of embarrassment I feel at once. Seeing how painful the sitting posture was for me she fetched a chair for my stiff leg. Without ceasing to ply me with delicacies she kept up a chatter of which I did not understand the hundredth part. With her own hand she took off my hat, and carried it away, to hang it up somewhere, on a hat-rack I suppose, and seemed surprised when the lace pulled her up in her stride. She had a parrot, very pretty, all the most approved colours. I understood him better than his mistress. I don't mean I understood him better than she understood him, I mean I understood him better than I understood her. He exclaimed from time to time, Fuck the son of a bitch, fuck the son of a bitch. He must have belonged to an American sailor, before he belonged to Lousse. Pets often change masters. He didn't say much else. No, I'm wrong, he also said, Putain de merde! He must have belonged

to a French sailor before he belonged to the American sailor.
Putain de merde! Unless he had hit on it alone, it wouldn't surprise
me. Lousse tried to make him say, Pretty Polly! I think it was too
late. He listened, his head on one side, pondered, then said, Fuck
the son of a bitch. It was clear he was doing his best. Him too one
day she would bury. In his cage probably. Me too, if I had stayed,
she would have buried. If I had her address I'd write to her, to come
and bury me. I fell asleep. I woke up in a bed, in my skin. They
had carried their impertinence to the point of washing me, to judge
by the smell I gave off, no longer gave off. I went to the door.
Locked. To the window. Barred. It was not yet quite dark. What
is there left to try when you have tried the door and the window?
The chimney perhaps. I looked for my clothes. I found a light
switch and switched it on. No result. What a story! All that left
me cold, or nearly. I found my crutches, against an easy chair. It
may seem strange that I was able to go through the motions I have
described without their help. I find it strange. You don't remember
immediately who you are, when you wake. On a chair I found a
white chamber pot with a roll of toilet-paper in it. Nothing was
being left to chance. I recount these moments with a certain minute-
ness, it is a relief from what I feel coming. I set a pouffe against
the easy chair, sat down in the latter, and on the former laid my
stiff leg. The room was chock-full of pouffes and easy chairs, they
thronged all about me, in the gloom. There were also occasional
tables, footstools, tallboys, etc., in abundance. Strange feeling of
congestion that the night dispersed, though it lit the chandelier,
which I had left turned on. My beard was missing, when I felt for
it with anguished hand. They had shaved me, they had shorn me of
my scant beard. How had my sleep withstood such liberties? My
sleep as a rule so uneasy. To this question I found a number of
replies. But I did not know which of them was right. Perhaps
they were all wrong. My beard grows properly only on my chin
and dewlap. Where the pretty bristles grow on other faces, on mine
there are none. But such as it was they had docked my beard.
Perhaps they had dyed it too, I had no proof they had not. I thought
I was naked, in the easy chair, but I finally realised I was wearing
a nightdress, very flimsy. If they had come and told me I was to

be sacrificed at sunrise I would not have been taken aback. How
foolish one can be. It seemed to me too that I had been perfumed,
lavender perhaps. I said, If only your poor mother could see you
now. I am no enemy of the commonplace. She seemed far away,
my mother, far away from me, and yet I was a little closer to her
than the night before, if my reckoning was accurate. But was it?
If I was in the right town, I had made progress. But was I? If on
the other hand I was in the wrong town, from which my mother
would necessarily be absent, then I had lost ground. I must have
fallen asleep, for all of a sudden there was the moon, a huge moon
framed in the window. Two bars divided it in three segments, of
which the middle remained constant, while little by little the right
gained what the left lost. For the moon was moving from left to
right, or the room was moving from right to left, or both together
perhaps, or both were moving from left to right, but the room not
so fast as the moon, or from right to left, but the moon not so fast
as the room. But can one speak of right and left in such circumstances? That movements of an extreme complexity were taking
place seemed certain, and yet what a simple thing it seemed, that
vast yellow light sailing slowly behind my bars and which little
by little the dense wall devoured, and finally eclipsed. And now its
tranquil course was written on the walls, a radiance scored with
shadow, then a brief quivering of leaves, if they were leaves, then
that too went out, leaving me in the dark. How difficult it is to speak
of the moon and not lose one's head, the witless moon. It must be
her arse she shows us always. Yes, I once took an interest in astronomy, I don't deny it. Then it was geology that killed a few years
for me. The next pain in the balls was anthropology and the other
disciplines, such as psychiatry, that are connected with it, discon-
nected, then connected again, according to the latest discoveries.
What I liked in anthropology was its inexhaustible faculty of
negation, its relentless definition of man, as though he were no
better than God, in terms of what he is not. But my ideas on this
subject were always horribly confused, for my knowledge of men
was scant and the meaning of being beyond me. Oh I've tried
everything. In the end it was magic that had the honour of my ruins,
and still today, when I walk there, I find its vestiges. But mostly

they are a place with neither plan nor bounds and of which I understand nothing, not even of what it is made, still less into what. And
the thing in ruins, I don't know what it is, what it was, nor whether
it is not less a question of ruins than the indestructible chaos of
timeless things, if that is the right expression. It is in any case a
place devoid of mystery, deserted by magic, because devoid of
mystery. And if I do not go there gladly, I go perhaps more gladly
there than anywhere else, astonished and at peace, I nearly said
as in a dream, but no, no. But it is not the kind of place where you
go, but where you find yourself, sometimes, not knowing how, and
which you cannot leave at will, and where you find yourself without
any pleasure, but with more perhaps than in those places you can
escape from, by making an effort, places full of mystery, full of
the familiar mysteries. I listen and the voice is of a world collapsing
endlessly, a frozen world, under a faint untroubled sky, enough to
see by, yes, and frozen too. And I hear it murmur that all wilts
and yields, as if loaded down, but here there are no loads, and the
ground too, unfit for loads, and the light too, down towards an
end it seems can never come. For what possible end to these wastes
where true light never was, nor any upright thing, nor any true
foundation, but only these leaning things, forever lapsing and
crumbling away, beneath a sky without memory of morning or hope
of night. These things, what things, come from where, made of
what? And it says that here nothing stirs, has ever stirred, will
ever stir, except myself, who do not stir either, when I am there,
but see and am seen. Yes, a world at an end, in spite of appearances,
its end brought it forth, ending it began, is it clear enough? And I
too am at an end, when I am there, my eyes close, my sufferings
cease and I end, I wither as the living can not. And if I went on
listening to that far whisper, silent long since and which I still
hear, I would learn still more, about this. But I will listen no longer,
for the time being, to that far whisper, for I do not like it, I fear it.
But it is not a sound like the other sounds, that you listen to,
when you choose, and can sometimes silence, by going away or
stopping your ears, no, but it is a sound which begins to rustle in
your head, without your knowing how, or why. It's with your head
you hear it, not your ears, you can't stop it, but it stops itself, when

it chooses. It makes no difference therefore whether I listen to it
or not, I shall hear it always, no thunder can deliver me, until it
stops. But nothing compels me to speak of it, when it doesn't suit
me. And it doesn't suit me, at the moment. No, what suits me, at
the moment, is to be done with this business of the moon which
was left unfinished, by me, for me. And if I get done with it less
successfully than if I had all my wits about me, I shall none the less
get done with it, as best I can, at least I think so. That moon then,
all things considered, filled me suddenly with amaze, with surprise,
perhaps better. Yes, I was considering it, after my fashion, with
indifference, seeing it again, in a way, in my head, when a great
fright came suddenly upon me. And deeming this deserved to be
looked into I looked into it and quickly made the following discovery, among others, but I confined myself to the following, that
this moon which had just sailed gallant and full past my window
had appeared to me the night before, or the night before that, yes,
more likely, all young and slender, on her back, a shaving. And
then I had said, Now I see, he has waited for the new moon before
launching forth on unknown ways, leading south. And then a little
later, Perhaps I should go to mother tomorrow. For all things hang
together, by the operation of the Holy Ghost, as the saying is. And
if I failed to mention this detail in its proper place, it is because you
cannot mention everything in its proper place, you must choose,
between the things not worth mentioning and those even less so.
For if you set out to mention everything you would never be done,
and that's what counts, to be done, to have done. Oh I know, even
when you mention only a few of the things there are, you do not
get done either, I know, I know. But it's a change of muck. And
if all muck is the same muck that doesn't matter, it's good to have
a change of muck, to move from one heap to another a little further
on, from time to time, fluttering you might say, like a butterfly,
as if you were ephemeral. And if you are wrong, and you are wrong,
I mean when you record circumstances better left unspoken, and
leave unspoken others, rightly, if you like, but how shall I say, for
no good reason, yes, rightly, but for no good reason, as for example
that new moon, it is often in good faith, excellent faith. Had there
then elapsed, between that night on the mountain, that night when

I saw A and C and then made up my mind to go and see my mother, and this other night, more time than I had thought, namely fourteen full days, or nearly? And if so, what had happened to those fourteen days, or nearly, and where had they flown? And what possible chance was there of finding a place for them, no matter what their burden, in the so rigorous chain of events I had just undergone? Was it not wiser to suppose either that the moon seen two nights before, far from being new as I had thought, was on the eve of being full, or else that the moon seen from Lousse's house, far from being full, as it had appeared to me, was in fact merely entering on its first quarter, or else finally that here I had to do with two moons, as far from the new as from the full and so alike in outline that the naked eye could hardly tell between them, and that whatever was at variance with these hypotheses was so much smoke and delusion. It was at all events with the aid of these considerations that I grew calm again and was restored, in the face of nature's pranks, to my old ataraxy, for what it was worth. And it came back also to my mind, as sleep stole over it again, that my nights were moonless and the moon foreign, to my nights, so that I had never seen, drifting past the window, carrying me back to other nights, other moons, this moon I had just seen, I had forgotten who I was (excusably) and spoken of myself as I would have of another, if I had been compelled to speak of another. Yes it sometimes happens and will sometimes happen again that I forget who I am and strut before my eyes, like a stranger. Then I see the sky different from what it is and the earth too takes on false colours. It looks like rest, it is not, I vanish happy in that alien light, which must have once been mine, I am willing to believe it, then the anguish of return, I won't say where, I can't, to absence perhaps, you must return, that's all I know, it's misery to stay, misery to go. The next day I demanded my clothes. The valet went to find out. He came back with the news they had been burnt. I continued my inspection of the room. It was at first sight a perfect cube. Through the lofty window I saw boughs. They rocked gently, but not all the time, shaken now and then by sudden spasms. I noticed the chandelier was burning. My clothes, I said, my crutches, forgetting my crutches were there, against the chair. He left me alone again, leaving the door open. Through the door I saw a big window, bigger than the door which it overlapped entirely, and opaque. The valet came back with the news my clothes had been sent to the dyers, to have the shine taken off. He held my crutches, which should have seemed strange to me, but seemed natural to me, on the contrary. I took hold of one and began to strike the pieces of furniture with it, not very hard, just hard enough to over-turn them, without breaking them. They were fewer than in the night. To tell the truth I pushed them rather than struck them, I thrust at them, I lunged, and that is not pushing either, but it's more like pushing than striking. But recalling who I was I soon threw away my crutch and came to a standstill in the middle of the room, determined to stop asking for things, to stop pretending to be angry. For to want my clothes, and I thought I wanted them, was no reason for pretending to be angry, when they were refused. And alone once more I resumed my inspection of the room and was on the point of endowing it with other properties when the valet came back with the news my clothes had been sent for and I would have them soon. Then he began to straighten the tables and chairs I had overturned and to put them back into place, dusting them as he did so with a feather duster which suddenly appeared in his hand. And so I began to help him as best I could, by way of proving that I bore no grudge against anyone. And though I could not do much, because of my stiff leg, yet I did what I could, that is to say I took each object as he straightened it and proceeded with excruciating meticulousness to restore it to its proper place, stepping back with raised arms the better to assess the result and then springing forward to effect minute improve-ments. And with the tail of my nightdress as with a duster I petulantly flicked them one by one. But of this little game too I soon wearied and suddenly stood stock still in the middle of the room. But seeing him ready to go I took a step forward and said, My bicycle. And I said it again, and again, the same words, until he appeared to understand. I don't know to what race he belonged, he was so tiny and ageless, assuredly not to mine. He was an oriental perhaps, a vague oriental, a child of the Rising Sun. He wore white trousers, a white shirt and a yellow waistcoat, like a

chamois he was, with brass buttons and sandals. It is not often that
I take cognisance so clearly of the clothes that people wear and I
am happy to give you the benefit of it. The reason for that was
perhaps this, that all morning the talk had been of clothes, of mine.
And perhaps I had been saying, to myself, words to this effect,
Look at him, peaceful in his own clothes, and look at me, floating
about inside another man's nightdress, another woman's probably,
for it was pink and transparent and adorned with ribands and frills
and lace. Whereas the room, I saw the room but darkly, at each
fresh inspection it seemed changed, and that is known as seeing
darkly, in the present state of our knowledge. The boughs themselves seemed to shift, as though endowed with an orbital velocity
of their own, and in the big frosted window the door was no longer
inscribed, but had slightly shifted to the right, or to the left, I
forget, so that there now appeared within its frame a panel of white
wall, on which I succeeded in casting faint shadows when I moved.
But that there were natural causes to all these things I am willing
to concede, for the resources of nature are infinite apparently. It
was I who was not natural enough to enter into that order of things,
and appreciate its niceties. But I was used to seeing the sun rise in
the south, used to not knowing where I was going, what I was
leaving, what was going with me, all things turning and twisting
confusedly about me. It is difficult, is it not, to go to one's mother
with things in such a state, more difficult than to the Lousses of
this world, or to its police-stations, or to the other places that are
waiting for me, I know. But the valet having brought my clothes,
in a paper which he unwrapped in front of me, I saw that my hat
was not among them, so that I said, My hat. And when he finally
understood what I wanted he went away and came back a little
later with my hat. Nothing was missing then except the lace to
fasten my hat to my buttonhole, but that was something I could
not hope to make him understand, and so I did not mention it.
An old lace, you can always find an old lace, no lace lasts for ever,
the way clothes do, real clothes. As for the bicycle, I had hopes
that it was waiting for me somewhere below stairs, perhaps even
before the front door, ready to carry me away from these horrible
scenes. And I did not see what good it would do to ask for it again,

to submit him and myself to this fresh ordeal, when it could be avoided. These considerations crossed my mind with a certain rapidity. Now with regard to the pockets, four in all, of my clothes, I verified their contents in front of the valet and discovered that certain things were missing. My sucking-stone in particular was no longer there. But sucking-stones abound on our beaches, when you know where to look for them, and I deemed it wiser to say nothing about it, all the more so as he would have been capable, after an hour's argument, of going and fetching me from the garden a completely unsuckable stone. This was a decision too which I took almost instantaneously. But of the other objects which had disappeared why speak, since I did not know exactly what they were. And perhaps they had been taken from me at the police-station, without my knowing it, or scattered and lost, when I fell, or at some other time, or thrown away, for I would sometimes throw away all I had about me, in a burst of irritation. So why speak of them? I resolved nevertheless to declare loudly that a knife was missing, a noble knife, and I did so to such effect that I soon received a very fine vegetable knife, so-called stainless, but it didn't take me long to stain it, and which opened and shut into the bargain, unlike all the vegetable knives I had ever known, and which had a safety catch, highly dangerous as soon appeared and the cause of innumerable cuts, all over my fingers caught between the handle of so-called genuine Irish horn and the blade red with rust and so blunted that it was less a matter of cuts than of contusions. And if I deal at such length with this knife it is because I have it somewhere still I think, among my possessions, and because having dealt with it here at such length I shall not have to deal with it again, when the moment comes, if it ever comes, to draw up the list of my possessions, and that will be a relief, a welcome relief, when that moment comes, I know. For it is natural I should dilate at lesser length on what I lost than on what I could not lose, that goes without saying. And if I do not always appear to observe this principle it is because it escapes me, from time to time, and vanishes, as utterly as if I had never educed it. Mad words, no matter. For I no longer know what I am doing, nor why, those are things I understand less and less, I don't deny it, for why deny

it, and to whom, to you, to whom nothing is denied? And then
doing fills me with such a, I don't know, impossible to express,
for me, now, after so long, yes, that I don't stop to enquire in
virtue of what principle. And all the less so as whatever I do, that
is to say whatever I say, it will always as it were be the same thing,
yes, as it were. And if I speak of principles, when there are none,
I can't help it, there must be some somewhere. And if always doing
the same thing as it were is not the same as observing the same
principle. I can't help it either. And then how can you know
whether you are observing it or not? And how can you want to
know? No, all that is not worth while, not worth while bothering
about, and yet you do bother about it, your sense of values gone.
And the things that are worth while you do not bother about, you
let them be, for the same reason, or wisely, knowing that all these
questions of worth and value have nothing to do with you, who
don't know what you're doing, nor why, and must go on not knowing it, on pain of, I wonder what, yes, I wonder. For anything
worse than what I do, without knowing what, or why, I have never
been able to conceive, and that doesn't surprise me, for I never
tried. For had I been able to conceive something worse than what
I had I would have known no peace until I got it, if I know anything about myself. And what I have, what I am, is enough, was
always enough for me, and as far as my dear little sweet little
future is concerned I have no qualms, I have a good time coming.
So I put on my clothes, having first made sure they had not been
tampered with, that is to say I put on my trousers, my greatcoat,
my hat, and my boots. My boots. They came up to where my calves
would have been if I had had calves, and partly they buttoned, or
would have buttoned, if they had had buttons, and partly they
laced, and I have them still, I think, somewhere. Then I took my
crutches and left the room. The whole day had gone in this tomfoolery and it was dusk again. Going down the stairs I inspected
the window I had seen through the door. It lit the staircase with
its wild tawny light. Lousse was in the garden, fussing around the
grave. She was sowing grass on it, as if grass wouldn't have sown
itself on it. She was taking advantage of the cool of evening. Seeing
me, she came warmly towards me and gave me food and drink

I ate and drank standing, casting about me in search of my bicycle. She talked and talked. Soon sated, I began the search for my bicycle. She followed me. In the end I found it, half buried in a soft bush. I threw aside my crutches and took it in my hands, by the saddle and the handle-bars, intending to wheel it a little, back and forth, before getting on and leaving for ever this accursed place. But I pushed and pulled in vain, the wheels would not turn. It was as though the brakes were jammed, and heaven knows they were not, for my bicycle had no brakes. And suddenly overcome by a great weariness, in spite of the dying day when I always felt most alive, I threw the bicycle back in the bush and lay down on the ground, on the grass, careless of the dew, I never feared the dew. It was then that Lousse, taking advantage of my weakness, squatted down beside me and began to make me propositions, to which I must confess I listened, absent-mindedly, I had nothing else to do, I could do nothing else, and doubtless she had poisoned my beer with something intended to mollify me, to mollify Molloy, with the result that I was nothing more than a lump of melting wax, so to speak. And from these propositions, which she enunciated slowly and distinctly, repeating each clause several times, I finally elicited the following, or gist. I could not prevent her having a weakness for me, neither could she. I would live in her home, as though it were my own. I would have plenty to eat and drink, to smoke too if I smoked, for nothing, and my remaining days would glide away without a care. I would as it were take the place of the dog I had killed, as it for her had taken the place of a child. I would help in the garden, in the house, when I wished, if I wished. I would not go out on the street, for once out I would never find my way in again. I would adopt the rhythm of life which best suited me, getting up, going to bed and taking my meals at whatsoever hours I pleased. If I did not choose to be clean, to wear nice clothes, to wash and so on, I need not. She would be grieved, but what was her grief, compared to my grief? All she asked was to feel me near her, with her, and the right to contemplate from time to time this extraordinary body both at rest and in motion. Every now and then I interrupted her, to ask what town I was in. But either because she did not understand me, or because she preferred to leave me in ignorance, she did not reply to my question, but went on with her soliloquy, reiterating tirelessly each new proposition, then expounding further, slowly, gently, the benefits for both of us if I would make my home with her. Till nothing was left but this monotonous voice, in the deepening night and the smell of the damp earth and of a strongly scented flower which at the time I could not identify, but which later I identified as spike-lavender. There were beds of it everywhere, in this garden, for Lousse loved spike, she must have told me herself, otherwise I would not have known, she loved it above all other herbs and flowers, because of its smell, and then also because of its spikes, and its colour. And if I had not lost my sense of smell the smell of lavender would always make me think of Lousse, in accordance with the well-known mechanism of association. And she gathered this lavender when it bloomed I presume, left it to dry and then made it up into lavender-bags that she put in her cupboards to perfume her handkerchiefs, her underclothing and house-linen. But none the less from time to time I heard the chiming of the hours, from the clocks and belfries, chiming out longer and longer, then suddenly briefly, then longer and longer again. This will give some idea of the time she took to cozen me, of her patience and physical endurance, for all the time she was squatting or kneeling beside me, whereas I was stretched out at my ease on the grass, now on my back, now on my stomach, now on one side, now on the other. And all the time she never stopped talking, whereas I only opened my mouth to ask, at long intervals, more and more feebly, what town we were in. And sure of her victory at last, or simply feeling she had done all she could and that further insistence was useless, she got up and went away, I don't know where, for I stayed where I was, with regret, mild regret. For in me there have always been two fools, among others, one asking nothing better than to stay where he is and the other imagining that life might be slightly less horrible a little further on. So that I was never disappointed, so to speak, whatever I did, in this domain. And these inseparable fools I indulged turn about, that they might understand their foolishness. And that night there was no question of moon, nor any other light, but it was a night of listening, a night given to the faint soughing

and sighing stirring at night in little pleasure gardens, the shy
sabbath of leaves and petals and the air that eddies there as it does
not in other places, where there is less constraint, and as it does
not during the day, when there is more vigilance, and then something else that is not clear, being neither the air nor what it moves,
perhaps the far unchanging noise the earth makes and which other
noises cover, but not for long. For they do not account for that
noise you hear when you really listen, when all seems hushed. And
there was another noise, that of my life become the life of this
garden as it rode the earth of deeps and wildernesses. Yes, there
were times when I forgot not only who I was, but that I was,
forgot to be. Then I was no longer that sealed jar to which I owed
my being so well preserved, but a wall gave way and I filled with
roots and tame stems for example, stakes long since dead and
ready for burning, the recess of night and the imminence of dawn,
and then the labour of the planet rolling eager into winter, winter
would rid it of these contemptible scabs. Or of that winter I was
the precarious calm, the thaw of the snows which make no difference and all the horrors of it all all over again. But that did not
happen to me often, mostly I stayed in my jar which knew neither
seasons nor gardens. And a good thing too. But in there you have
to be careful, ask yourself questions, as for example whether you
still are, and if no when it stopped, and if yes how long it will still go
on, anything at all to keep you from losing the thread of the dream.
For my part I willingly asked myself questions, one after the other,
just for the sake of looking at them. No, not willingly, wisely, so
that I might believe I was still there. And yet it meant nothing to
me to be still there. I called that thinking. I thought almost without
stopping, I did not dare stop. Perhaps that was the cause of my
innocence. It was a little the worse for wear, a little threadbare
perhaps, but I was glad to have it, yes, I suppose. Thanks I suppose,
as the urchin said when I picked up his marble, I don't know why,
I didn't have to, and I suppose he would have preferred to pick it
up himself. Or perhaps it wasn't to be picked up. And the effort
it cost me, with my stiff leg. The words engraved themselves for
ever on my memory, perhaps because I understood them at once,
a thing I didn't often do. Not that I was hard of hearing, for I had

quite a sensitive ear, and sounds unencumbered with precise meaning were registered perhaps better by me than by most. What was
it then? A defect of the understanding perhaps, which only began
to vibrate on repeated solicitations, or which did vibrate, if you like,
but at a lower frequency, or a higher, than that of ratiocination, if
such a thing is conceivable, and such a thing is conceivable, since
I conceive it. Yes, the words I heard, and heard distinctly, having
quite a sensitive ear, were heard a first time, then a second, and
often even a third, as pure sounds, free of all meaning, and this
is probably one of the reasons why conversation was unspeakably
painful to me. And the words I uttered myself, and which must
nearly always have gone with an effort of the intelligence, were
often to me as the buzzing of an insect. And this is perhaps one
of the reasons I was so untalkative, I mean this trouble I had in
understanding not only what others said to me, but also what I
said to them. It is true that in the end, by dint of patience, we made
ourselves understood, but understood with regard to what, I ask of
you, and to what purpose? And to the noises of nature too, and of
the works of men, I reacted I think in my own way and without
desire of enlightenment. And my eye too, the seeing one, must
have been ill-connected with the spider, for I found it hard to
name what was mirrored there, often quite distinctly. And without
going so far as to say that I saw the world upside down (that would
have been too easy) it is certain I saw it in a way inordinately
formal, though I was far from being an aesthete, or an artist. And
of my two eyes only one functioning more or less correctly, I mis-
judged the distance separating me from the other world, and often
I stretched out my hand for what was far beyond my reach, and
often I knocked against obstacles scarcely visible on the horizon.
But I was like that even when I had my two eyes, it seems to me,
but perhaps not, for it is long since that era of my life, and my recollection of it is more than imperfect. And now I come to think of it,
my attempts at taste and smell were scarcely more fortunate, I smelt
and tasted without knowing exactly what, nor whether it was good,
nor whether it was bad, and seldom twice running the same thing.
I would have been I think an excellent husband, incapable of
wearying of my wife and committing adultery only from absent-

mindedness. Now as to telling you why I stayed a good while with
Lousse, no, I cannot. That is to say I could I suppose, if I took the
trouble. But why should I? In order to establish beyond all question
that I could not do otherwise? For that is the conclusion I would
come to, fatally. I who had loved the image of old Geulincx, dead
young, who left me free, on the black boat of Ulysses, to crawl
towards the East, along the deck. That is a great measure of freedom, for him who has not the pioneering spirit. And from the poop,
poring upon the wave, a sadly rejoicing slave, I follow with my
eyes the proud and futile wake. Which, as it bears me from no
fatherland away, bears me onward to no shipwreck. A good while
then with Lousse. It's vague, a good while, a few months perhaps,
a year perhaps. I know it was warm again the day I left, but that
meant nothing, in my part of the world, where it seemed to be
warm or cold or merely mild at any moment of the year and where
the days did not run gently up and down, no, not gently. Perhaps
things have changed since. So all I know is that it was much the
same weather when I left as when I came, so far as I was capable
of knowing what the weather was. And I had been under the
weather so long, under all weathers, that I could tell quite well
between them, my body could tell between them and seemed even to
have its likes, its dislikes. I think I stayed in several rooms one
after the other, or alternately, I don't know. In my head there are
several windows, that I do know, but perhaps it is always the same
one, open variously on the parading universe. The house was fixed,
that is perhaps what I mean by these different rooms. House and
garden were fixed, thanks to some unknown mechanism of com-
pensation, and I, when I stayed still, as I did most of the time, was
fixed too, and when I moved, from place to place, it was very
slowly, as in a cage out of time, as the saying is, in the jargon of
the schools, and out of space too to be sure. For to be out of one
and not out of the other was for cleverer than me, who was not
clever, but foolish. But I may be quite wrong. And these different
windows that open in my head, when I grope again among those
days, really existed perhaps and perhaps do still, in spite of my
being no longer there, I mean there looking at them, opening them
and shutting them, or crouched in a corner of the room marvelling

at the things they framed. But I will not dwell on this episode, so
ludicrously brief when you think of it and so poor in substance. For
I helped neither in the house nor the garden and knew nothing of
what work was going forward, day and night, nothing save the
sounds that came to me, dull sounds and sharp ones too, and
then often the roar of air being vigorously churned, it seemed to
me, and which perhaps was nothing more than the sound of burning. I preferred the garden to the house, to judge by the long hours
I spent there, for I spent there the greater part of the day and of
the night, whether it was wet or whether it was fine. Men were
always busy there, working at I know not what. For the garden
seemed hardly to change, from day to day, apart from the tiny
changes due to the customary cycle of birth, life and death. And
in the midst of those men I drifted like a dead leaf on springs, or
else I lay down on the ground, and then they stepped gingerly over
me as though I had been a bed of rare flowers. Yes, it was doubtless
in order to preserve the garden from apparent change that they
laboured at it thus. My bicycle had disappeared again. Sometimes
I felt the wish to look for it again, to find it again and find out
what was wrong with it or even go for a little ride on the walks
and paths connecting the different parts of the garden. But instead
of trying to satisfy this wish I stayed where I was looking at it, if
I may say so, looking at it as it shrivelled up and finally disappeared, like the famous fatal skin, only much quicker. For there
seem to be two ways of behaving in the presence of wishes, the
active and the contemplative, and though they both give the same
result it was the latter I preferred, matter of temperament I presume. The garden was surrounded with a high wall, its top bristling
with broken glass like fins. But what must have been absolutely
unexpected was this, that this wall was broken by a wicket-gate
giving free access to the road, for it was never locked, of that I was
all but convinced, having opened and closed it without the least
trouble on more than one occasion, both by day and by night, and
seen it used by others than myself, for the purpose as well of entrance as of exit. I would stick out my nose, then hastily call it
in again. A few further remarks. Never did I see a woman within
these precincts, and by precincts I do not merely mean the garden,

as I probably should, but the house too, but only men, with the
obvious exception of Lousse. What I saw and did not see did not
matter much admittedly, but I mention it all the same. Lousse herself I saw but little, she seldom showed herself to me, out of tact
perhaps, fearing to alarm me. But I think she spied on me a great
deal, hiding behind the bushes, or the curtains, or skulking in the
shadows of a first-floor room, with a spy-glass perhaps. For had
she not said she desired above all to see me, both coming and going
and rooted to the spot. And to get a good view you need the keyhole, the little chink among the leaves, and so on, whatever prevents
you from being seen and from seeing more than a little at a time.
No? I don't know. Yes, she inspected me, little by little, and even
in my very going to bed, my sleeping and my getting up, the
mornings that I went to bed. For in this matter I remained faithful
to my custom, which was to sleep in the morning, when I slept at
all. For it sometimes happened that I did not sleep at all, for
several days, without feeling at all the worse for it. For my waking
was a kind of sleeping. And I did not always sleep in the same
place, but now I slept in the garden, which was large, and now I
slept in the house, which was large too, really extremely spacious.
And this uncertainty as to the hour and place of my sleeping must
have entranced her, I imagine, and made the time pass pleasantly.
But it is useless to dwell on this period of my life. If I go on long
enough calling that my life I'll end up by believing it. It's the principle of advertising. This period of my life. It reminds me, when I
think of it, of air in a water-pipe. So I will only add that this woman
went on giving me slow poison, slipping I know not what poisons
into the drink she gave me, or into the food she gave me, or both,
or one day one, the next the other. That is a grave charge to bring
and I do not bring it lightly. And I bring it without ill-feeling, yes,
I accuse her without ill-feeling of having drugged my food and
drink with noxious and insipid powders and potions. But even
sipid they would have made no difference, I would have swallowed
it all down with the same whole-heartedness. That celebrated whiff
of almonds for example would never have taken away my appetite.
My appetite! What a subject. For conversation. I had hardly any.
I ate like a thrush. But the little I did eat I devoured with a voracity

usually attributed to heavy eaters, and wrongly, for heavy eaters
as a rule eat ponderously and with method, that follows from the
very notion of heavy eating. Whereas I flung myself at the mess,
gulped down the half or the quarter of it in two mouthfuls without
chewing (with what would I have chewed?), then pushed it from
me with loathing. One would have thought I ate to live! Similarly
I would engulf five or six mugs of beer with one swig, then drink
nothing for a week. What do you expect, one is what one is, partly
at least. Nothing or little to be done. Now as to the substances she
insinuated thus into my various systems, I could not say whether
they were stimulants or whether they were not rather depressants.
The truth is, coenaesthetically speaking of course, I felt more or less
the same as usual, that is to say, if I may give myself away, so
terror-stricken that I was virtually bereft of feeling, not to say of
consciousness, and drowned in a deep and merciful torpor shot with
brief abominable gleams, I give you my word. Against such harmony of what avail the miserable molys of Lousse, administered
in infinitesimal doses probably, to draw the pleasure out. Not that
they remained entirely without effect, no, that would be an exaggeration. For from time to time I caught myself making a little
bound in the air, two or three feet off the ground at least, I who
never bounded. It looked like levitation. And it happened too, less
surprisingly, when I was walking, or even propped up against something, that I suddenly collapsed, like a puppet when its strings are
dropped, and lay long where I fell, literally boneless. Yes, that
struck me as less strange, for I was used to collapsing thus, but
with this difference, that I felt it coming, and prepared myself
accordingly, as an epileptic does when he feels the fit coming. I
mean that knowing I was going to fall I lay down, or I wedged
myself where I stood so firmly that nothing short of an earthquake
could have dislodged me, and I waited. But these were precautions
I did not always take, preferring the fall to the trouble of having to
lie down or stand fast. Whereas the falls I suffered when with
Lousse did not give me a chance to circumvent them. But all the
same they surprised me less, they were more in keeping with me,
than the little bounds. For even as a child I do not remember ever
having bounded, neither rage nor pain ever made me bound, even

as a child, however ill-qualified I am to speak of that time. Now with regard to my food, it seems to me I ate it as, when and where it best suited me. I never had to call for it. It was brought to me, wherever I happened to be, on a tray. I can still see the tray, almost at will, it was round, with a low rim, to keep the things from falling off, and coated with red lacquer, cracking here and there. It was small too, as became a tray having to hold a single dish and one slab of bread. For the little I ate I crammed into my mouth with my hands, and the bottles I drank from the bottle were brought to me separately, in a basket. But this basket made no impression on me, good or bad, and I could not tell you what it was like. And many a time, having strayed for one reason or another from the place where the meal had been brought to me, I couldn't find it again, when I felt the desire to eat. Then I searched high and low, often with success, being fairly familiar with the places where it was likely to have been, but often too, in vain. Or I did not search at all, preferring hunger and thirst to the trouble of having to search without being sure of finding, or of having to ask for another tray to be brought, and another basket, or the same, to the place where I was. It was then I regretted my sucking-stone. And when I talk of preferring, for example, or regretting, it must not be supposed that I opted for the least evil, and adopted it, for that would be wrong. But not knowing exactly what I was doing or avoiding, I did it and avoided it all unsuspecting that one day, much later, I would have to go back over all these acts and omissions, dimmed and mellowed by age, and drag them into the eudemonistic slop. But I must say that with Lousse my health got no worse, or scarcely. By which I mean that what was already wrong with me got worse and worse, little by little, as was only to be expected. But there was kindled no new seat of suffering or infection, except of course those arising from the spread of existing plethoras and deficiencies. But I may very well be wrong. For of the disorders to come, as for example the loss of the toes of my left foot, no, I am wrong, my right foot, who can say exactly when on my helpless clay the fatal seeds were sown. So all I can say, and I do my best to say no more, is that during my stay with Lousse no more new symptoms appeared, of a pathological nature, I mean nothing new or strange, nothing I could not have foreseen if I could have, nothing at all comparable to the sudden loss of half my toes. For that is something I could never have foreseen and the meaning of which I have never fathomed, I mean its connection with my other discomforts, from my ignorance of medical matters, I suppose. For all things run together, in the body's long madness, I feel it. But it is useless to drag out this chapter of my, how shall I say, my existence, for it has no sense, to my mind. It is a dug at which I tug in vain, it yields nothing but wind and spatter. So I will confine myself to the following brief additional remarks, and the first of which is this, that Lousse was a woman of extraordinary flatness, physically speaking of course, to such a point that I am still wondering this evening, in the comparative silence of my last abode, if she was not a man rather or at least an androgyne. She had a somewhat hairy face, or am I imagining it, in the interests of the narrative? The poor woman, I saw her so little, so little looked at her. And was not her voice suspiciously deep? So she appears to me today. Don't be tormenting yourself, Molloy, man or woman, what does it matter? But I cannot help asking myself the following question. Could a woman have stopped me as I swept towards mother? Probably. Better still, was such an encounter possible, I mean between me and a woman? Now men, I have rubbed up against a few men in my time, but women? Oh well, I may as well confess it now, yes, I once rubbed up against one. I don't mean my mother, I did more than rub up against her. And if you don't mind we'll leave my mother out of all this. But another who might have been my mother, and even I think my grandmother, if chance had not willed otherwise. Listen to him now talking about chance. It was she made me acquainted with love. She went by the peaceful name of Ruth I think, but I can't say for certain. Perhaps the name was Edith. She had a hole between her legs, oh not the bunghole I had always imagined, but a slit, and in this I put, or rather she put, my so-called virile member, not without difficulty, and I toiled and moiled until I discharged or gave up trying or was begged by her to stop. A mug's game in my opinion and tiring on top of that, in the long run. But I lent myself to it with a good enough grace, knowing it was

love, for she had told me so. She bent over the couch, because of
her rheumatism, and in I went from behind. It was the only position
she could bear, because of her lumbago. It seemed all right to me,
for I had seen dogs, and I was astonished when she confided that
you could go about it differently. I wonder what she meant exactly.
Perhaps after all she put me in her rectum. A matter of complete
indifference to me, I needn't tell you. But is it true love, in the
rectum? That's what bothers me sometimes. Have I never known
true love, after all? She too was an eminently flat woman and she
moved with short stiff steps, leaning on an ebony stick. Perhaps
she too was a man, yet another of them. But in that case surely
our testicles would have collided, while we writhed. Perhaps she
held hers tight in her hand, on purpose to avoid it. She favoured
voluminous tempestuous shifts and petticoats and other undergar-
ments whose names I forget. They welled up all frothing and swish-
ing and then, congress achieved, broke over us in slow cascades.
And all I could see was her taut yellow nape which every now
and then I set my teeth in, forgetting I had none, such is the power
of instinct. We met in a rubbish dump, unlike any other, and yet
they are all alike, rubbish dumps. I don't know what she was doing
there. I was limply poking about in the garbage saying probably,
for at that age I must still have been capable of general ideas, This
is life. She had no time to lose, I had nothing to lose, I would have
made love with a goat, to know what love was. She had a dainty
flat, no, not dainty, it made you want to lie down in a corner and
never get up again. I liked it. It was full of dainty furniture, under
our desperate strokes the couch moved forward on its castors, the
whole place fell about our ears, it was pandemonium. Our com-
merce was not without tenderness, with trembling hands she cut
my toe-nails and I rubbed her rump with winter cream. This idyll
was of short duration. Poor Edith, I hastened her end perhaps. Anyway it was she who started it, in the rubbish dump, when she laid her
hand upon my fly. More precisely, I was bent double over a heap
of muck, in the hope of finding something to disgust me for ever
with eating, when she, undertaking me from behind, thrust her
stick betweens my legs and began to titillate my privates. She gave
me money after each session, to me who would have consented to

know love, and probe it to the bottom, without charge. But she was an idealist. I would have preferred it seems to me an orifice less arid and roomy, that would have given me a higher opinion of love it seems to me. However. Twixt finger and thumb 'tis heaven in comparison. But love is no doubt above such base contingencies. And not when you are comfortable, but when your frantic member casts about for a rubbing-place, and the unction of a little mucous membrane, and meeting with none does not beat in retreat, but retains its tumefaction, it is then no doubt that true love comes to pass, and wings away, high above the tight fit and the loose. And when you add a little pedicure and massage, having nothing to do with the instant of bliss strictly speaking, then I feel no further doubt is justified, in this connection. The other thing that bothers me, in this connection, is the indifference with which I learnt of her death, one black night I was crawling towards her, an indifference softened indeed by the pain of losing a source of revenue. She died taking a warm tub, as her custom was before receiving me. It limbered her up. When I think she might have expired in my arms! The tub overturned and the dirty water spilt all over the floor and down on top of the lodger below, who gave the alarm. Well, well, I didn't think I knew this story so well. She must have been a woman after all, if she hadn't been it would have got around in the neighbourhood. It is true they were extraordinarily reserved, in my part of the world, about everything connected with sexual matters. But things have perhaps changed since my time. And it is quite possible that the fact of having found a man when they should have found a woman was immediately repressed and forgotten, by the few unfortunate enough to know about it. As it is quite possible that everybody knew about it, and spoke about it, with the sole exception of myself. But there is one thing that torments me, when I delve into all this, and that is to know whether all my life has been devoid of love or whether I really met with it, in Ruth. What I do know for certain is that I never sought to repeat the experience, having I suppose the intuition that it had been unique and perfect, of its kind, achieved and inimitable, and that it behoved me to preserve its memory, pure of all pastiche, in my heart, even if it meant my resorting from time to time to the alleged joys of so-called self-abuse. Don't talk to me about the chambermaid, I should never have mentioned her, she was long before, I was sick, perhaps there was no chambermaid, ever, in my life. Molloy, or life without a chambermaid. All of which goes to demonstrate that the fact of having met Lousse and even frequented her, in a way, proved nothing as to her sex. And I am quite willing to go on thinking of her as an old woman, widowed and withered, and of Ruth as another, for she too used to speak of her defunct husband and of his inability to satisfy her legitimate cravings. And there are days, like this evening, when my memory confuses them and I am tempted to think of them as one and the same old hag, flattened and crazed by life. And God forgive me to tell you the horrible truth, my mother's image sometimes mingles with theirs, which is literally unendurable, like being crucified, I don't know why and I don't want to. But I left Lousse at last, one warm airless night, without saying goodbye, as I might at least have done, and without her trying to hold me back, except perhaps by spells. But she must have seen me go, get up, take my crutches and go away, springing on them through the air. And she must have seen the wicket close behind me, for it closed by itself, with the help of a spring, and known me gone, for ever. For she knew the way I had of going to the wicket and peeping out, then quickly drawing back. And she did not try and hold me back but she went and sat down on her dog's grave, perhaps, which was mine too in a way, and which by the way she had not sown with grass, as I had thought, but with all kinds of little many-coloured flowers and herbaceous plants, selected I imagine in such a way that when some went out others lit up. I left her my bicycle which I had taken a dislike to, suspecting it to be the vehicle of some malignant agency and perhaps the cause of my recent misfortunes. But all the same I would have taken it with me if I had known where it was and that it was in running order. But I did not. And I was afraid, if I tried to find out, of wearing out the small voice saying, Get out of here, Molloy, take your crutches and get out of here, and which I had taken so long to understand, for I had been hearing it for a long time. And perhaps I understood it all wrong, but I understood it and that was the novelty. And it seemed to me I was not necessarily

going for good and that I might come back one day, by devious
winding ways, to the place I was leaving. And perhaps my course
it not yet fully run. Outside in the road the wind was blowing, it
was another world. Not knowing where I was nor consequently
what way I ought to go I went with the wind. And when, well
slung between my crutches, I took off, then I felt it helping me,
that little wind blowing from what quarter I could not tell. And
don't come talking at me of the stars, they look all the same to me,
yes, I cannot read the stars, in spite of my astronomical studies.
But I entered the first shelter I came to and stayed there till dawn,
for I knew I was bound to be stopped by the first policeman and
asked what I was doing, a question to which I have never been
able to find the correct reply. But it cannot have been a real shelter
and I did not stay till dawn, for a man came in soon after me and
drove me out. And yet there was room for two. I think he was a
kind of nightwatchman, a man of some kind certainly, he must have
been employed to watch over some kind of public works, digging
I suppose. I see a brazier. There must have been a touch of autumn
in the air, as the saying is. I therefore moved on and ensconced
myself on a flight of stairs, in a mean lodging-house, because there
was no door or it didn't shut, I don't know. Long before dawn
this lodging-house began to empty. People came down the stairs,
men and women. I glued myself against the wall. They paid no
heed to me, nobody interfered with me. In the end I too went away,
when I deemed it prudent, and wandered about the town in search
of a familiar monument, so that I might say, I am in my town,
after all, I have been there all the time. The town was waking,
doors opening and shutting, soon the noise would be deafening.
But espying a narrow alley between two high buildings I looked
about me, then slipped into it. Little windows overlooked it, on
either side, on every floor, facing one another. Lavatory lights I
suppose. There are things from time to time, in spite of everything,
that impose themselves on the understanding with the force of
axioms, for unknown reasons. There was no way out of the alley,
it was not so much an alley as a blind alley. At the end there were
two recesses, no, that's not the word, opposite each other, littered
with miscellaneous rubbish and with excrements, of dogs and

masters, some dry and odourless, others still moist. Ah those papers
never to be read again, perhaps never read. Here lovers must have
lain at night and exchanged their vows. I entered one of the alcoves,
wrong again, and leaned against the wall. I would have preferred
to lie down and there was no proof that I would not. But for the
moment I was content to lean against the wall, my feet far from
the wall, on the verge of slipping, but I had other props, the tips of
my crutches. But a few minutes later I crossed the alley into the
other chapel, that's the word, where I felt I might feel better, and
settled myself in the same hypotenusal posture. And at first I did
actually seem to feel a little better, but little by little I acquired
the conviction that such was not the case. A fine rain was falling
and I took off my hat to give my skull the benefit of it, my skull
all cracked and furrowed and on fire, on fire. But I also took it off
because it was digging into my neck, because of the thrust of the
wall. So I had two good reasons for taking it off and they were
none too many, neither alone would ever have prevailed I feel. I
threw it from me with a careless lavish gesture and back it came,
at the end of its string or lace, and after a few throws came to rest
against my side. At last I began to think, that is to say to listen
harder. Little chance of my being found there, I was in peace for
as long as I could endure peace. For the space of an instant I
considered settling down there, making it my lair and sanctuary,
for the space of an instant. I took the vegetable knife from my
pocket and set about opening my wrist. But pain soon got the better
of me. First I cried out, then I gave up, closed the knife and put
it back in my pocket. I wasn't particularly disappointed, in my
heart of hearts I had not hoped for anything better. So much for
that. And backsliding has always depressed me, but life seems
made up of backsliding, and death itself must be a kind of backsliding, I wouldn't be surprised. Did I say the wind had fallen?
A fine rain falling, somehow that seems to exclude all idea of wind.
My knees are enormous, I have just caught a glimpse of them, when
I got up for a second. My two legs are as stiff as a life-sentence and
yet I sometimes get up. What can you expect? Thus from time to
time I shall recall my present existence compared to which this
is a nursery tale. But only from time to time, so that it may be

said, if necessary, whenever necessary, Is it possible that thing is
still alive? Or again, Oh it's only a diary, it'll soon be over. That my
knees are enormous, that I still get up from time to time, these are
things that do not seem at first sight to signify anything in particular. I record them all the more willingly. In the end I left the im-
passe, where half-standing, half-lying I may have had a little sleep,
my little morning sleep, and I set off, believe it or not, towards
the sun, why not, the wind having fallen. Or rather towards the
least gloomy quarter of the heavens which a vast cloud was shroud-
ing from the zenith to the skylines. It was from this cloud the
above rain was falling. See how all things hang together. And as
to making up my mind which quarter of the heavens was the least
gloomy, it was no easy matter. For at first sight the heavens seemed
uniformly gloomy. But by taking a little pains, for there were
moments in my life when I took a little pains, I obtained a result,
that is to say I came to a decision, in this matter. So I was able to
continue on my way, saying, I am going towards the sun, that is
to say in theory towards the East, or perhaps the South-East, for
I am no longer with Lousse, but out in the heart again of the pre-
established harmony, which makes so sweet a music, which is so
sweet a music, for one who has an ear for music. People were
hastening angrily to and fro, most of them, some in the shelter of
the umbrella, others in that perhaps a little less effective of the
rainproof coat. A few had taken refuge under trees and archways.
And among those who, more courageous or less delicate, came and
went, and among those who had stopped, to avoid getting wet,
many a one must have said, They are right, I am wrong, meaning
by they the category to which he did not belong, or so I imagine.
As many a one too must have said, I am right, they are wrong,
while continuing to storm against the foul weather that was the
occasion of his superiority. But at the sight of a young old man
of wretched aspect, shivering all alone in a narrow doorway, I
suddenly remembered the project conceived the day of my encounter with Lousse and her dog and which this encounter had
prevented me from carrying out. So I went and stood beside him,
with the air, I hoped, of one who says, Here's a clever fellow, let me
follow his example. But before I should make my little speech,

which I wished to seem spontaneous and so did not make at once,
he went out into the rain and away. For this speech was one liable,
in virtue of its content, if not to offend at least to astonish.
And that was why it was important to deliver it at the right
moment and in the right tone. I apologise for these details,
in a moment we'll go faster, much faster. And then perhaps
relapse again into a wealth of filthy circumstance. But which
in its turn again will give way to vast frescoes, dashed off with
loathing. Homo mensura can't do without staffage. There I am
then in my turn alone, in the doorway. I could not hope for anyone
to come and stand beside me, and yet it was a possibility I did not
exclude. That's a fairly good caricature of my state of mind at that
instant. Net result, I stayed where I was. I had stolen from Lousse
a little silver, oh nothing much, massive teaspoons for the most
part, and other small objects whose utility I did not grasp, but
which seemed as if they might have some value. Among these
latter there was one which haunts me still, from time to time. It
consisted of two crosses joined, at their points of intersection, by
a bar, and resembled a tiny sawing-horse, with this difference
however, that the crosses of the true sawing-horse are not perfect
crosses, but truncated at the top, whereas the crosses of the little
object I am referring to were perfect, that is to say composed each
of two identical V's, one upper with its opening above, like all V's
for that matter, and the other lower with its opening below, or more
precisely of four rigorously identical V's, the two I have just named
and then two more, one on the right hand, the other on the left,
having their openings on the right and the left respectively. But
perhaps it is out of place to speak here of right and left, of upper
and lower. For this little object did not seem to have any base
properly so-called, but stood with equal stability on any one of its
four bases, and without any change of appearance, which is not
true of the sawing-horse. This strange instrument I think I still
have somewhere, for I could never bring myself to sell it, even in
my worst need, for I could never understand what possible purpose
it could serve, nor even contrive the faintest hypothesis on the
subject. And from time to time I took it from my pocket and gazed
upon it, with an astonished and affectionate gaze, if I had not been

incapable of affection. But for a certain time I think it inspired me with a kind of veneration, for there was no doubt in my mind that it was not an object of virtue, but that it had a most specific function always to be hidden from me. I could therefore puzzle over it endlessly without the least risk. For to know nothing is nothing, not to want to know anything likewise, but to be beyond knowing anything, to know you are beyond knowing anything, that is when peace enters in, to the soul of the incurious seeker. It is then the true division begins, of twenty-two by seven for example, and the pages fill with the true ciphers at last. But I would rather not affirm anything on this subject. What does seem undeniable to me on the contrary is this, that giving in to the evidence, to a very strong probability rather, I left the shelter of the doorway and began levering myself forward, swinging slowly through the sullen air. There is rapture, or there should be, in the motion crutches give. It is a series of little flights, skimming the ground. You take off, you land, through the thronging sound in wind and limb, who have to fasten one foot to the ground before they dare lift up the other. And even their most joyous hastenings is less aerial than my hobble. But these are reasonings, based on analysis. And though my mind was still taken up with my mother, and with the desire to know if I was near her, it was gradually less so, perhaps because of the silver in my pockets, but I think not, and then too because these were ancient cares and the mind cannot always brood on the same cares, but needs fresh cares from time to time, so as to revert with renewed vigour, when the time comes, to ancient cares. But can one speak here of fresh and ancient cares? I think not. But it would be hard for me to prove it. What I can assert, without fear of—without fear, is that I gradually lost interest in knowing, among other things, what town I was in and if I should soon find my mother and settle the matter between us. And even the nature of that matter grew dim, for me, without however vanishing completely. For it was no small matter and I was bent on it. All my life, I think, I had been bent on it. Yes, so far as I was capable of being bent on anything all a lifetime long, and what a lifetime, I had been bent on settling this matter between my mother and me, but had never succeeded. And while saying to myself that

time was running out, and that soon it would be too late, was perhaps too late already, to settle the matter in question, I felt myself
drifting towards other cares, other phantoms. And far more than
to know what town I was·in, my haste was now to leave it, even
were it the right one, where my mother had waited so long and
perhaps was waiting still. And it seemed to me that if I kept on in
a straight line I was bound to leave it, sooner or later. So I set
myself to this as best I could, making allowance for the drift to
the right of the feeble light that was my guide. And my pertinacity
was such that I did indeed come to the ramparts as night was falling, having described a good quarter of a circle, through bad navigation. It is true I stopped many times, to rest, but not for long,
for I felt harried, wrongly perhaps. But in the country there is
another justice, other judges, at first. And having cleared the ramparts I had to confess the sky was clearing, prior to its winding in
the other shroud, night. Yes, the great cloud was ravelling, discover-
ing here and there a pale and dying sky, and the sun, already down,
was manifest in the livid tongues of fire darting towards the zenith,
falling and darting again, ever more pale and languid, and doomed
no sooner lit to be extinguished. This phenomenon, if I remember
rightly, was characteristic of my region. Things are perhaps different today. Though I fail to see, never having left my region,
what right I have to speak of its characteristics. No, I never escaped,
and even the limits of my region were unknown to me. But I felt
they were far away. But this feeling was based on nothing serious,
it was a simple feeling. For if my region had ended no further than
my feet could carry me, surely I would have felt it changing slowly.
For regions do not suddenly end, as far as I know, but gradually
merge into one another. And I never noticed anything of the kind,
but however far I went, and in no matter what direction, it was always the same sky, always the same earth, precisely, day after day
and night after night. On the other hand, if it is true that regions
gradually merge into one another, and this remains to be proved,
then I may well have left mine many times, thinking I was still
within it. But I preferred to abide by my simple feeling and its
voice that said, Molloy, your region is vast, you have never left it
and you never shall. And wheresoever you wander, within its distant

limits, things will always be the same, precisely. It would thus
appear, if this is so, that my movements owed nothing to the places
they caused to vanish, but were due to something else, to the
buckled wheel that carried me, in unforeseeable jerks, from fatigue
to rest, and inversely, for example. But now I do not wander any
more, anywhere any more, and indeed I scarcely stir at all, and
yet nothing is changed. And the confines of my room, of my bed,
of my body, are as remote from me as were those of my region, in
the days of my splendour. And the cycle continues, joltingly, of
flight and bivouac, in an Egypt without bounds, without infant,
without mother. And when I see my hands, on the sheet, which
they love to floccillate already, they are not mine, less than ever
mine, I have no arms, they are a couple, they play with the sheet,
love-play perhaps, trying to get up perhaps, one on top of the other.
But it doesn't last, I bring them back, little by little, towards me,
it's resting time. And with my feet it's the same, sometimes, when
I see them at the foot of the bed, one with toes, the other without.
And that is more deserving of mention. For my legs, corresponding
here to my arms of a moment ago, are both stiff now and very
sore, and I shouldn't be able to forget them as I can my arms,
which are more or less sound and well. And yet I do forget them
and I watch the couple as they watch each other, a great way off.
But my feet are not like my hands, I do not bring them back to
me, when they become my feet again, for I cannot, but they stay
there, far from me, but not so far as before. End of the recall. But
you'd think that once well clear of the town, and having turned
round to look at it, what there was to see of it, you'd think that
then I should have realised whether it was really my town or not.
But no, I looked at it in vain, and perhaps unquestioningly, and
simply to give the gods a chance, by turning round. Perhaps I only
made a show of looking at it. I didn't feel I missed my bicycle,
no, not really, I didn't mind going on my way the way I said,
swinging low in the dark over the earth, along the little empty
country roads. And I said there was little likelihood of my being
molested and that it was more likely I should molest them, if they
saw me. Morning is the time to hide. They wake up, hale and
hearty, their tongues hanging out for order, beauty and justice,

baying for their due. Yes, from eight or nine till noon is the dangerous time. But towards noon things quiet down, the most implacable are sated, they go home, it might have been better but they've done a good job, there have been a few survivors, but they'll give no more trouble, each man counts his rats. It may begin again in the early afternoon, after the banquet, the celebrations, the congratulations, the orations, but it's nothing compared to the morning, mere fun. Coming up to four or five of course there is the night-shift, the watchmen, beginning to bestir themselves. But already the day is over, the shadows lengthen, the walls multiply, you hug the walls, bowed down like a good boy, oozing with obsequiousness, having nothing to hide, hiding from mere terror, looking neither right nor left, hiding but not provocatively, ready to come out, to smile, to listen, to crawl, nauseating but not pestilent, less rat than toad. Then the true night, perilous too, but sweet to him who knows it, who can open to it like the flower to the sun, who himself is night, day and night. No there is not much to be said for the night either, but compared to the day there is much to be said for it, and notably compared to the morning there is everything to be said for it. For the night purge is in the hands of technicians, for the most part. They do nothing else, the bulk of the population have no part in it, preferring their warm beds, all things considered. Day is the time for lynching, for sleep is sacred, and especially the morning, between breakfast and lunch. My first care then, after a few miles in the desert dawn, was to look for a place to sleep, for sleep too is a kind of protection, strange as it may seem. For sleep, if it excites the lust to capture, seems to appease the lust to kill, there and then and bloodily, any hunter will tell you that. For the monster on the move, or on the watch, lurking in his lair, there is no mercy, whereas he taken unawares, in his sleep, may sometimes get the benefit of milder feelings, which deflect the barrel, sheathe the kris. For the hunter is weak at heart and sentimental, overflowing with repressed treasures of gentleness and compassion. And it is thanks to this sweet sleep of terror or exhaustion that many a foul beast, and worthy of extermination, can live on till he dies in the peace and quiet of our zoological gardens, broken only by the innocent laughter, the knowing laughter, of children and

their elders, on Sundays and Bank Holidays. And I for my part
have always preferred slavery to death, I mean being put to death.
For death is a condition I have never been able to conceive to my
satisfaction and which therefore cannot go down in the ledger of
weal and woe. Whereas my notions on being put to death inspired
me with confidence, rightly or wrongly, and I felt I was entitled
to act on them, in certain emergencies. Oh they weren't notions like
yours, they were notions like mine, all spasm, sweat and trembling,
without an atom of common sense or lucidity. But they were the
best I had. Yes, the confusion of my ideas on the subject of death
was such that I sometimes wondered, believe me or not, if it wasn't
a state of being even worse than life. So I found it natural not to
rush into it and, when I forgot myself to the point of trying, to stop
in time. It's my only excuse. So I crawled into some hole somewhere
I suppose and waited, half sleeping, half sighing, groaning and
laughing, or feeling my body, to see if anything had changed, for
the morning frenzy to abate. Then I resumed my spirals. And as
to saying what became of me, and where I went, in the months and
perhaps the years that followed, no. For I weary of these inventions
and others beckon to me. But in order to blacken a few more pages
may I say I spent some time at the seaside, without incident. There
are people the sea doesn't suit, who prefer the mountains or the
plain. Personally I feel no worse there than anywhere else. Much
of my life has ebbed away before this shivering expanse, to the
sound of the waves in storm and calm, and the claws of the surf.
Before, no, more than before, one with, spread on the sand, or in
a cave. In the sand I was in my element, letting it trickle between
my fingers, scooping holes that I filled in a moment later or that
filled themselves in, flinging it in the air by handfuls, rolling in it.
And in the cave, lit by the beacons at night, I knew what to do in
order to be no worse off than elsewhere. And that my land went
no further, in one direction at least, did not displease me. And to
feel there was one direction at least in which I could go no further,
without first getting wet, then drowned, was a blessing For I have
always said, First learn to walk, then you can take swimming
lessons. But don't imagine my region ended at the coast, that would
be a grave mistake. For it was this sea too, its reefs and distant

islands, and its hidden depths. And I too once went forth on it, in a sort of oarless skiff, but I paddled with an old bit of driftwood. And I sometimes wonder if I ever came back, from that voyage. For if I see myself putting to sea, and the long hours without land-fall, I do not see the return, the tossing on the breakers, and I do not hear the frail keel grating on the shore. I took advantage of being at the seaside to lay in a store of sucking-stones. They were pebbles but I call them stones. Yes, on this occasion I laid in a considerable store. I distributed them equally between my four pockets, and sucked them turn and turn about. This raised a problem which I first solved in the following way. I had say sixteen stones, four in each of my four pockets these being the two pockets of my trousers and the two pockets of my greatcoat. Taking a stone from the right pocket of my greatcoat, and putting it in my mouth, I replaced it in the right pocket of my greatcoat by a stone from the right pocket of my trousers, which I replaced by a stone from the left pocket of my trousers, which I replaced by a stone from the left pocket of my greatcoat, which I replaced by the stone which was in my mouth, as soon as I had finished sucking it. Thus there were still four stones in each of my four pockets, but not quite the same stones. And when the desire to suck took hold of me again, I drew again on the right pocket of my greatcoat, certain of not taking the same stone as the last time. And while I sucked it I rearranged the other stones in the way I have just described. And so on. But this solution did not satisfy me fully. For it did not escape me that, by an extraordinary hazard, the four stones circulating thus might always be the same four. In which case, far from sucking the sixteen stones turn and turn about, I was really only sucking four, always the same, turn and turn about. But I shuffled them well in my pockets, before I began to suck, and again, while I sucked, before transferring them, in the hope of obtaining a more general circulation of the stones from pocket to pocket. But this was only a makeshift that could not long content a man like me. So I began to look for something else. And the first thing I hit upon was that I might do better to transfer the stones four by four, instead of one by one, that is to say, during the sucking, to take the three stones remaining in the right pocket of my greatcoat and replace them by the four in the right pocket of my trousers, and these by the four in the left pocket of my trousers, and these by the four in the left pocket of my greatcoat, and finally these by the three from the right pocket of my greatcoat, plus the one, as soon as I had finished sucking it, which was in my mouth. Yes, it seemed to me at first that by so doing I would arrive at a better result. But on further reflection I had to change my mind and confess that the circulation of the stones four by four came to exactly the same thing as their circulation one by one. For if I was certain of finding each time, in the right pocket of my greatcoat, four stones totally different from their immediate predecessors, the possibility nevertheless remained of my always chancing on the same stone, within each group of four, and consequently of my sucking, not the sixteen turn and turn about as I wished, but in fact four only, always the same, turn and turn about. So I had to seek elsewhere than in the mode of circulation. For no matter how I caused the stones to circulate, I always ran the same risk. It was obvious that by increasing the number of my pockets I was bound to increase my chances of enjoying my stones in the way I planned, that is to say one after the other until their number was exhausted. Had I had eight pockets, for example, instead of the four I did have, then even the most diabolical hazard could not have prevented me from sucking at least eight of my sixteen stones, turn and turn about. The truth is I should have needed sixteen pockets in order to be quite easy in my mind. And for a long time I could see no other conclusion than this, that short of having sixteen pockets, each with its stone, I could never reach the goal I had set myself, short of an extraordinary hazard. And if at a pinch I could double the number of my pockets, were it only by dividing each pocket in two, with the help of a few safety-pins let us say, to quadruple them seemed to be more than I could manage. And I did not feel inclined to take all that trouble for a half-measure. For I was beginning to lose all sense of measure, after all this wrestling and wrangling, and to say, All or nothing. And if I was tempted for an instant to establish a more equitable proportion between my stones and my pockets, by reducing the former to the number of the latter, it was only for an instant. For it would have been an admission of defeat. And sitting on the shore, before the sea, the sixteen stones spread out before my eyes, I gazed at them in anger and perplexity. For just as I had difficulty in sitting on a chair, or in an arm-chair, because of my stiff leg you understand, so I had none in sitting on the ground, because of my stiff leg and my stiffening leg, for it was about this time that my good leg, good in the sense that it was not stiff, began to stiffen. I needed a prop under the ham you understand, and even under the whole length of the leg, the prop of the earth. And while I gazed thus at my stones, revolving interminable martingales all equally defective, and crushing handfuls of sand, so that the sand ran through my fingers and fell back on the strand, yes, while thus I lulled my mind and part of my body, one day suddenly it dawned on the former, dimly, that I might perhaps achieve my purpose without increasing the number of my pockets, or reducing the number of my stones, but simply by sacrificing the principle of trim. The meaning of this illumination, which suddenly began to sing within me, like a verse of Isaiah, or of Jeremiah, I did not penetrate at once, and notably the word trim, which I had never met with, in this sense, long remained obscure. Finally I seemed to grasp that this word trim could not here mean anything else, anything better, than the distribution of the sixteen stones in four groups of four, one group in each pocket, and that it was my refusal to consider any distribution other than this that had vitiated my calculations until then and rendered the problem literally insoluble. And it was on the basis of this interpretation, whether right or wrong, that I finally reached a solution, inelegant assuredly, but sound, sound. Now I am willing to believe, indeed I firmly believe, that other solutions to this problem might have been found, and indeed may still be found, no less sound, but much more elegant, than the one I shall now describe, if I can. And I believe too that had I been a little more insistent, a little more resistant, I could have found them myself. But I was tired, but I was tired, and I contented myself ingloriously with the first solution that was a solution, to this problem. But not to go over the heartbreaking stages through which I passed before I came to it, here it is, in all its hideousness. All (all!) that was necessary was to 'put for example, to begin with, six stones in the right pocket of my great-

coat, or supply-pocket, five in the right pocket of my trousers, and
five in the left pocket of my trousers, that makes the lot, twice five
ten plus six sixteen, and none, for none remained, in the left pocket
of my greatcoat, which for the time being remained empty, empty
of stones that is, for its usual contents remained, as well as occasional objects. For where do you think I hid my vegetable knife,
my silver, my horn and the other things that I have not yet named,
perhaps shall never name. Good. Now I can begin to suck. Watch
me closely. I take a stone from the right pocket of my greatcoat,
suck it, stop sucking it, put it in the left pocket of my greatcoat,
the one empty (of stones). I take a second stone from the right
pocket of my greatcoat, suck it, put it in the left pocket of my
greatcoat. And so on until the right pocket of my greatcoat is
empty (apart from its usual and casual contents) and the six stones
I have just sucked, one after the other, are all in the left pocket of
my greatcoat. Pausing then, and concentrating, so as not to make a
balls of it, I transfer to the right pocket of my greatcoat, in which
there are no stones left, the five stones in the right pocket of my
trousers, which I replace by the five stones in the left pocket of my
trousers, which I replace by the six stones in the left pocket of my
greatcoat. At this stage then the left pocket of my greatcoat is
again empty of stones, while the right pocket of my greatcoat is
again supplied, and in the right way, that is to say with other stones
than those I have just sucked. These other stones I then begin
to suck, one after the other, and to transfer as I go along to
the left pocket of my greatcoat, being absolutely certain, as far
as one can be in an affair of this kind, that I am not sucking the
same stones as a moment before, but others. And when the right
pocket of my greatcoat is again empty (of stones), and the five I
have just sucked are all without exception in the left pocket of my
greatcoat, then I proceed to the same redistribution as a moment
before, or a similar redistribution, that is to say I transfer to the
right pocket of my greatcoat, now again available, the five stones
in the right pocket of my trousers, which I replace by the six stones
in the left pocket of my trousers, which I replace by the five stones
in the left pocket of my greatcoat. And there I am ready to begin
again. Do I have to go on? No, for it is clear that after the next

series, of sucks and transfers, I shall be back where I started, that
is to say with the first six stones back in the supply pocket, the
next five in the right pocket of my stinking old trousers and finally
the last five in left pocket of same, and my sixteen stones will have
been sucked once at least in impeccable succession, not one sucked
twice, not one left unsucked. It is true that the next time I could
scarcely hope to suck my stones in the same order as the first time
and that the first, seventh and twelfth for example of the first
cycle might very well be the sixth, eleventh and sixteenth respectively of the second, if the worst came to the worst. But that was
a drawback I could not avoid. And if in the cycles taken together
utter confusion was bound to reign, at least within each cycle
taken separately I could be easy in my mind, at least as easy as
one can be, in a proceeding of this kind. For in order for each
cycle to be identical, as to the succession of stones in my mouth,
and God knows I had set my heart on it, the only means were
numbered stones or sixteen pockets. And rather than make twelve
more pockets or number my stones, I preferred to make the best
of the comparative peace of mind I enjoyed within each cycle taken
separately. For it was not enough to number the stones, but I would
have had to remember, every time I put a stone in my mouth, the
number I needed and look for it in my pocket. Which would have
put me off stone for ever, in a very short time. For I would never
have been sure of not making a mistake, unless of course I had
kept a kind of register, in which to tick off the stones one by one,
as I sucked them. And of this I believed myself incapable. No, the
only perfect solution would have been the sixteen pockets, sym-
metrically disposed, each one with its stone. Then I would have
needed neither to number nor to think, but merely, as I sucked a
given stone, to move on the fifteen others, each to the next pocket,
a delicate business admittedly, but within my power, and to call
always on the same pocket when I felt like a suck. This would
have freed me from all anxiety, not only within each cycle taken
separately, but also for the sum of all cycles, though they went on
forever. But however imperfect my own solution was, I was pleased
at having found it all alone, yes, quite pleased. And if it was
perhaps less sound than I had thought in the first flush of discovery,

its inelegance never diminished. And it was above all inelegant in
this, to my mind, that the uneven distribution was painful to me,
bodily. It is true that a kind of equilibrium was reached, at a given
moment, in the early stages of each cycle, namely after the third
suck and before the fourth, but it did not last long, and the rest
of the time I felt the weight of the stones dragging me now to one
side, now to the other. So it was something more than a principle
I abandoned, when I abandoned the equal distribution, it was a
bodily need. But to suck the stones in the way I have described,
not haphazard, but with method, was also I think a bodily need.
Here then were two incompatible bodily needs, at loggerheads.
Such things happen. But deep down I didn't give a tinker's curse
about being off my balance, dragged to the right hand and the left,
backwards and forwards. And deep down it was all the same to
me whether I sucked a different stone each time or always the
same stone, until the end of time. For they all tasted exactly the
same. And if I had collected sixteen, it was not in order to ballast
myself in such and such a way, or to suck them turn about, but
simply to have a little store, so as never to be without. But deep
down I didn't give a fiddler's curse about being without, when they
were all gone they would be all gone, I wouldn't be any the worse
off, or hardly any. And the solution to which I rallied in the end
was to throw away all the stones but one, which I kept now in one
pocket, now in another, and which of course I soon lost, or threw
away, or gave away, or swallowed. It was a wild part of the coast.
I don't remember having been seriously molested. The black speck
I was, in the great pale stretch of sand, who could wish it harm?
Some came near, to see what it was, whether it wasn't something
of value from a wreck, washed up by the storm. But when they
saw the jetsam was alive, decently if wretchedly clothed, they turned
away. Old women and young ones, yes, too, come to gather wood,
came and stared, in the early days. But they were always the same
and it was in vain I moved from one place to another, in the end
they all knew what I was and kept their distance. I think one of
them one day, detaching herself from her companions, came and
offered me something to eat and that I looked at her in silence,
until she went away. Yes, it seems to me some such incident

occurred about this time. But perhaps I am thinking of another
stay, at an earlier time, for this will be my last, my last but one, or
two, there is never a last, by the sea. However that may be I see a
young woman coming towards me and stopping from time to time
to look back at her companions. Huddled together like sheep they
watch her recede, urging her on, and laughing no doubt, I seem to
hear laughter far away. Then it is her back I see, as she goes away,
now it is towards me she looks back, but without stopping. But
perhaps I am merging two times in one, and two women, one coming towards me, shyly, urged on by the cries and laughter of her
companions, and the other going away from me, unhesitatingly.
For those who came towards me I saw coming from afar, most
of the time, that is one of the advantages of the seaside. Black
specks in the distance I saw them coming, I could follow all their
manoeuvres, saying, It's getting smaller, or, it's getting bigger.
Yes, to be taken unawares was so to speak impossible, for I
turned often towards the land too. Let me tell you something, my
sight was better at the seaside! Yes, ranging far and wide over
these vast flats, where nothing lay, nothing stood, my good eye
saw more clearly and there were even days when the bad one too
had to look away. And not only did I see more clearly, but I had
less difficulty in saddling with a name the rare things I saw. These
are some of the advantages and disadvantages of the seaside. Or
perhaps it was I who was changing, why not? And in the morning,
in my cave, and even sometimes at night, when the storm raged,
I felt reasonably secure from the elements and mankind. But there
too there is a price to pay. In your box, in your caves, there too
there is a price to pay. And which you pay willingly, for a time,
but which you cannot go on paying forever. For you cannot go
on buying the same thing forever, with your little pittance. And
unfortunately there are other needs than that of rotting in peace,
it's not the word, I mean of course my mother whose image,
blunted for some time past, was beginning now to harrow me again.
So I went back inland, for my town was not strictly speaking on
the sea, whatever may have been said to the contrary. And to get
to it you had to go inland, I at least knew of no other way. For
between my town and the sea there was a kind of swamp which,

as far back as I can remember, and some of my memories have their roots deep in the immediate past, there was always talk of draining, by means of canals I suppose, or of transforming into a vast port and docks, or into a city on piles for the workers, in a word of redeeming somehow or other. And with the same stone they would have killed the scandal, at the gates of their metropolis, of a stinking steaming swamp in which an incalculable number of human lives were yearly engulfed, the statistics escape me for the moment and doubtless always will, so complete is my indifference to this aspect of the question. It is true they actually began to work and that work is still going on in certain areas in the teeth of adversity, setbacks, epidemics and the apathy of the Public Works Department, far from me to deny it. But from this to proclaiming that the sea came lapping at the ramparts of my town, there was a far cry. And I for my part will never lend myself to such a perversion (of the truth), until such time as I am compelled or find it convenient to do so. And I knew this swamp a little, having risked my life in it, cautiously, on several occasions, at a period of my life richer in illusions than the one I am trying to patch together here, I mean richer in certain illusions, in others poorer. So there was no way of coming at my town directly, by sea, but you had to disembark well to the north or the south and take to the roads, just imagine that, for they had never heard of Watt, just imagine that too. And now my progress, slow and painful at all times, was more so than ever, because of my short stiff leg, the same which I thought had long been as stiff as a leg could be, but damn the bit of it, for it was growing stiffer than ever, a thing I would not have thought possible, and at the same time shorter every day, but above all because of the other leg, supple hitherto and now growing rapidly stiff in its turn, but not yet shortening, unhappily. For when the two legs shorten at the same time, and at the same speed, then all is not lost, no. But when one shortens, and the other not, then you begin to be worried. Oh not that I was exactly worried, but it was a nuisance, yes, a nuisance. For I didn't know which foot to land on, when I came down. Let us try and get this dilemma clear. Follow me carefully. The stiff leg hurt me, admittedly, I mean the old stiff leg, and it was the other which I normally used as a pivot, or prop. But now this latter, as a result of its stiffening I suppose, and the ensuing commotion among nerves and sinews, was beginning to hurt me even more than the other. What a story, God send I don't make a balls of it. For the old pain, do you follow me, I had got used to it, in a way, yes, in a kind of way. Whereas to the new pain, though of the same family exactly, I had not yet had time to adjust myself. Nor should it be forgotten that having one bad leg plus another more or less good, I was able to nurse the former, and reduce its sufferings to the minimum, to the maximum, by using the former exclusively, with the help of my crutches. But I no longer had this resource! For I no longer had one bad leg plus another more or less good, but now both were equally bad. And the worse, to my mind, was that which till now had been good, at least comparatively good, and whose change for the worse I had not yet got used to. So in a way, if you like, I still had one bad leg and one good, or rather less bad, with this difference however, that the less bad now was the less good of heretofore. It was therefore on the old bad leg that I often longed to lean, between one crutchstroke and the next. For while still extremely sensitive, it was less so than the other, or it was equally so, if you like, but it did not seem so, to me, because of its seniority. But I couldn't! What? Lean on it. For it was shortening, don't forget, whereas the other, though stiffening, was not yet shortening, or so far behind its fellow that to all intents and purposes, intents and purposes, I'm lost, no matter. If I could even have bent it, at the knee, or even at the hip, I could have made it seem as short as the other, long enough to land on the true short one, before taking off again. But I couldn't. What? Bend it. For how could I bend it, when it was stiff? I was therefore compelled to work the same old leg as heretofore, in spite of its having become, at least as far as the pain was concerned, the worse of the two and the more in need of nursing. Sometimes to be sure, when I was lucky enough to chance on a road conveniently cambered, or by taking advantage of a not too deep ditch or any other breach of surface, I managed to lengthen my short leg, for a short time. But it had done no work for so long that it did not know how to go about it. And I think a pile of dishes would have better sup-

ported me than it, which had so well supported me, when I was a
tiny tot. And another factor of disequilibrium was here involved,
I mean when I thus made the best of the lie of the land, I mean
my crutches, which would have needed to be unequal, one short
and one long, if I was to remain vertical. No? I don't know. In
any case the ways I went were for the most part little forest paths,
that's understandable, where differences of level, though abounding,
were too confused and too erratic to be of any help to me. But did
it make such a difference after all, as far as the pain was concerned,
whether my leg was free to rest or whether it had to work? I think
not. For the suffering of the leg at rest was constant and monotonous. Whereas the leg condemned to the increase of pain inflicted
by work knew the decrease of pain dispensed by work suspended,
the space of an instant. But I am human, I fancy, and my progress
suffered, from this state of affairs, and from the slow and painful
progress it had always been, whatever may have been said to the
contrary, was changed, saving your presence, to a veritable cal-
vary, with no limit to its stations and no hope of crucifixion, though
I say it myself, and no Simon, and reduced me to frequent halts.
Yes, my progress reduced me to stopping more and more often,
it was the only way to progress, to stop. And though it is no part
of my tottering intentions to treat here in full, as they deserve,
these brief moments of the immemorial expiation, I shall nevertheless deal with them briefly, out of the goodness of my heart,
so that my story, so clear till now, may not end in darkness, the
darkness of these towering forests, these giant fronds, where I
hobble, listen, fall, rise, listen and hobble on, wondering sometimes,
need I say, if I shall ever see again the hated light, at least unloved,
stretched palely between the last boles, and my mother, to settle
with her, and if I would not do better, at least just as well, to hang
myself from a bough, with a liane. For, frankly, light meant nothing to me now, and my mother could scarcely be waiting for me
still, after so long. And my legs, my legs. But the thought of suicide
had little hold on me, I don't know why, I thought I did, but I
see I don't. The idea of strangulation in particular, however tempting, I always overcame, after a short struggle. And between you
and me there was never anything wrong with my respiratory tracts,

apart, of course, from the agonies intrinsic to that system. Yes, I
could count the days when I could neither breathe in the blessed
air with its life-giving oxygen nor, when I had breathed it in,
breathe out the bloody stuff, I could have counted them. Ah yes,
my asthma, how often I was tempted to put an end to it, by cutting
my throat. But I never succumbed. The noise betrayed me, I turned
purple. It came on mostly at night, fortunately, or unfortunately,
I could never make up my mind. For if sudden changes of colour
matter less at night, the least unusual noise is then more noticeable,
because of the silence of the night. But these were mere crises, and
what are crises compared to all that never stops, knows neither
ebb nor flow, its surface leaden above infernal depths. Not a word,
not a word against the crises that seized me, wrung me, and finally
threw me away, mercifully, safe from help. And I wrapped my
head in my coat, to stifle the obscene noise of choking, or I disguised it as a fit of coughing, universally accepted and approved
and whose only disadvantage is this, that it is liable to let you in
for pity. And this is perhaps the moment to observe, better late
than never, that when I speak of my progress being slowed down,
consequent on the defection of my good leg, I express only an infinitesimal part of the truth. For the truth is I had other weak points,
here and there, and they too were growing weaker and weaker,
as was only to be expected. But what was not to be expected was
the speed at which their weakness had increased, since my departure from the seaside. For as long as I had remained at the seaside
my weak points, while admittedly increasing in weakness, as was
only to be expected, only increased imperceptibly, in weakness I
mean. So that I would have hesitated to exclaim, with my finger
up my arse-hole for example, Jesus-Christ, it's much worse than
yesterday, I can hardly believe it is the same hole. I apologise for
having to revert to this lewd orifice, 'tis my muse will have it so.
Perhaps it is less to be thought of as the eyesore here called by its
name than as the symbol of those passed over in silence, a distinction due perhaps to its centrality and its air of being a link between
me and the other excrement. We underestimate this little hole, it
seems to me, we call it the arse-hole and affect to despise it. But
is it not rather the true portal of our being and the celebrated

mouth no more than the kitchen-door. Nothing goes in, or so little, that is not rejected on the spot, or very nearly. Almost everything revolts it that comes from without and what comes from within does not seem to receive a very warm welcome either. Are not these significant facts? Time will tell. But I shall do my utmost none the less to keep it in the background in the future. And that will be easy, for the future is by no means uncertain, the unspeakable future. And when it comes to neglecting fundamentals, I think I have nothing to learn, and indeed I confuse them with accidentals. But to return to my weak points, let me say again that at the seaside they had developed normally, yes, I had noticed nothing abnormal. Either because I did not pay enough attention to them, absorbed as I was in the metamorphosis of my excellent leg, or because there was in fact nothing special to report, in this connection. But I had hardly left the shore, harried by the dread of waking one fine day, far from my mother, with my two legs as stiff as my crutches, when they suddenly began to gallop, my weak points did, and their weakness became literally the weakness of death, with all the disadvantages that this entails, when they are not vital points. I fix at this period the dastardly desertion of my toes, so to speak in the thick of the fray. You may object that this is covered by the business of my legs, that it has no importance, since in any case I could not put to the ground the foot in question. Quite, quite. But do you as much as know what foot we're talking about? No. Nor I. Wait till I think. But you are right, that wasn't a weak point properly speaking, I mean my toes, I thought they were in excellent fettle, apart from a few corns, bunions, ingrowing nails and a tendency to cramp. No, my true weak points were elsewhere. And if I do not draw up here and now the impressive list of them it is because I shall never draw it up. No, I shall never draw it up, yes, perhaps I shall. And then I should be sorry to give a wrong idea of my health which, if it was not exactly rude, to the extent of my bursting with it, was at bottom of an incredible robustness. For otherwise how could I have reached the enormous age I have reached. Thanks to moral qualities? Hygienic habits? Fresh air? Starvation? Lack of sleep? Solitude? Persecution? The long silent screams (dangerous to scream)? The daily longing for

the earth to swallow me up? Come come. Fate is rancorous, but
not to that extent. Look at Mammy. What rid me of her, in the
end? I sometimes wonder. Perhaps they buried her alive, it wouldn't
surprise me. Ah the old bitch, a nice dose she gave me, she and her
lousy unconquerable genes. Bristling with boils ever since I was
a brat, a fat lot of good that ever did me. The heart beats, and
what a beat. That my ureters—no, not a word on that subject.
And the capsules. And the bladder. And the urethra. And the
glands. Santa Maria. I give you my word, I cannot piss, my word
of honour, as a gentleman. But my prepuce, sat verbum, oozes
urine, day and night, at least I think it's urine, it smells of kidney.
What's all this, I thought I had lost the sense of smell. Can one
speak of pissing, under these conditions? Rubbish! My sweat too,
and God knows I sweat, has a queer smell. I think it's in my
dribble as well, and heaven knows I dribble. How I eliminate, to
be sure, uremia will never be the death of me. Me too they would
bury alive, in despair, if there was any justice in the world. And
this list of my weak points I shall never draw up, for fear of its
finishing me, I shall perhaps, one day, when the time come for the
inventory of my goods and chattels. For that day, if it ever dawns,
I shall be less afraid, of being finished, than I am today. For today,
if I do not feel precisely at the beginning of my career, I have not
the presumption either to think I am near the end. So I husband
my strength, for the spurt. For to be unable to spurt, when the
hour strikes, no, you might as well give up. But it is forbidden to
give up and even to stop an instant. So I wait, jogging along, for
the bell to say, Molloy, one last effort, it's the end. That's how I
reason, with the help of images little suited to my situation. And
I can't shake off the feeling, I don't know why, that the day will
come for me to say what is left of all I had. But I must first wait,
to be sure there is nothing more I can acquire, or lose, or throw
away, or give away. Then I can say, without fear of error, what is
left, in the end, of my possessions. For it will be the end. And
between now and then I may get poorer, or richer, oh not to the
extent of being any better off, or any worse off, but sufficiently to
preclude me from announcing, here and now, what is left of all
I had, for I have not yet had all. But I can make no sense of this

presentiment, and that I understand is very often the case with
the best presentiments, that you can make no sense of them. So
perhaps it is a true presentiment, apt to be borne out. But can
any more sense be made of false presentiments? I think so, yes,
I think that all that is false may more readily be reduced, to notions
clear and distinct, distinct from all other notions. But I may be
wrong. But I was not given to presentiments, but to sentiments
sweet and simple, to episentiments rather, if I may venture to say
so. For I knew in advance, which made all presentiment superfluous.
I will even go further (what can I lose?), I knew only in advance,
for when the time came I knew no longer, you may have noticed
it, or only when I made a superhuman effort, and when the time
was past I no longer knew either, I regained my ignorance. And all
that taken together, if that is possible, should serve to explain many
things, and notably my astonishing old age, still green in places,
assuming the state of my health, in spite of all I have said about
it, is insufficient to account for it. Simple supposition, committing
me to nothing. But I was saying that if my progress, at this stage,
was becoming more and more slow and painful, this was not due
solely to my legs, but also to innumerable so-called weak points,
having nothing to do with my legs. Unless one is to suppose,
gratuitously, that they and my legs were part of the same syndrome,
which in that case would have been of a diabolical complexity.
The fact is, and I deplore it, but it is too late now to do anything
about it, that I have laid too much stress on my legs, throughout
these wanderings, to the detriment of the rest. For I was no ordinary cripple, far from it, and there were days when my legs were
the best part of me, with the exception of the brain capable of
forming such a judgement. I was therefore obliged to stop more
and more often, I shall never weary of repeating it, and to lie
down, in defiance of the rules, now prone, now supine, now on
one side, now on the other, and as much as possible with the feet
higher than the head, to dislodge the clots. And to lie with the feet
higher than the head, when your legs are stiff, is no easy matter.
But don't worry, I did it. When my comfort was at stake there was
no trouble I would not go to. The forest was all about me and the
boughs, twining together at a prodigious height, compared to mine,

sheltered me from the light and the elements. Some days I advanced
no more than thirty or forty paces, I give you my oath. To say
I stumbled in impenetrable darkness, no, I cannot. I stumbled,
but the darkness was not impenetrable. For there reigned a kind
of blue gloom, more than sufficient for my visual needs. I was
astonished this gloom was not green, rather than blue, but I saw
it blue and perhaps it was. The red of the sun, mingling with the
green of the leaves, gave a blue result, that is how I reasoned. But
from time to time. From time to time. What tenderness in these
little words, what savagery. But from time to time I came on a
kind of crossroads, you know, a star, or circus, of the kind to be
found in even the most unexplored of forests. And turning then
methodically to face the radiating paths in turn, hoping for I
know not what, I described a complete circle, or less than a circle,
or more than a circle, so great was the resemblance between them.
Here the gloom was not so thick and I made haste to leave it. I
don't like gloom to lighten, there's something shady about it. I
had a certain number of encounters in this forest, naturally, where
does one not, but nothing to signify. I notably encountered a charcoal-burner. I might have loved him, I think, if I had been seventy
years younger. But it's not certain. For then he too would have
been younger by as much, oh not quite as much, but much
younger. I never really had much love to spare, but all the same
I had my little quota, when I was small, and it went to the old men,
when it could. And I even think I had time to love one or two, oh
not with true love, no, nothing like the old woman, I've lost her
name again, Rose, no, anyway you see who I mean, but all the
same, how shall I say, tenderly, as those on the brink of a better
earth. Ah I was a precocious child, and then I was a precocious
man. Now they all give me the shits, the ripe, the unripe and the
rotting from the bough. He was all over me, begging me to share
his hut, believe it or not. A total stranger. Sick with solitude
probably. I say charcoal-burner, but I really don't know. I see
smoke somewhere. That's something that never escapes me, smoke.
A long dialogue ensued, interspersed with groans. I could not ask
him the way to my town, the name of which escaped me still. I
asked him the way to the nearest town, I found the necessary words

and accents. He did not know. He was born in the forest probably
and had spent his whole life there. I asked him to show me the
nearest way out of the forest. I grew eloquent. His reply was exceedingly confused. Either I didn't understand a word he said, or
he didn't understand a word I said, or he knew nothing, or he
wanted to keep me near him. It was towards this fourth hypothesis
that in all modesty I leaned, for when I made to go, he held me
back by the sleeve. So I smartly freed a crutch and dealt him a
good dint on the skull. That calmed him. The dirty old brute.
I got up and went on. But I hadn't gone more than a few paces, and
for me at this time a few paces meant something, when I turned
and went back to where he lay, to examine him. Seeing he had not
ceased to breathe I contented myself with giving him a few warm
kicks in the ribs, with my heels. This is how I went about it. I
carefully chose the most favourable position, a few paces from the
body, with my back of course turned to it. Then, nicely balanced
on my crutches, I began to swing, backwards, forwards, feet pressed
together, or rather legs pressed together, for how could I press my
feet together, with my legs in the state they were? But how could
I press my legs together, in the state they were? I pressed them
together, that's all I can tell you. Take it or leave it. Or I didn't
press them together. What can that possibly matter? I swung,
that's all that matters, in an ever-widening arc, until I decided the
moment had come and launched myself forward with all my
strength and consequently, a moment later, backward, which gave
the desired result. Where did I get this access of vigour? From my
weakness perhaps. The shock knocked me down. Naturally. I came
a cropper. You can't have everything, I've often noticed it. I rested
a moment, then got up, picked up my crutches, took up my position
on the other side of the body and applied myself with method to the
same exercise. I always had a mania for symmetry. But I must have
aimed a little low and one of my heels sank in something soft.
However. For if I had missed the ribs, with that heel, I had no
doubt landed in the kidney, oh not hard enough to burst it, no,
I fancy not. People imagine, because you are old, poor, crippled,
terrified, that you can't stand up for yourself, and generally speaking that is so. But given favourable conditions, a feeble and awk-

ward assailant, in your own class what, and a lonely place, and
you have a good chance of showing what stuff you are made of.
And it is doubtless in order to revive interest in this possibility,
too often forgotten, that I have delayed over an incident of no
interest in itself, like all that has a moral. But did I at least eat,
from time to time? Perforce, perforce, roots, berries, sometimes a
little mulberry, a mushroom from time to time, trembling, knowing nothing about mushrooms. What else, ah yes, carobs, so dear
to goats. In a word whatever I could find, forests abound in good
things. And having heard, or more probably read somewhere, in
the days when I thought I would be well advised to educate myself,
or amuse myself, or stupefy myself, or kill time, that when a man
in a forest thinks he is going forward in a straight line, in reality
he is going in a circle, I did my best to go in a circle, hoping in this
way to go in a straight line. For I stopped being half-witted and
became sly, whenever I took the trouble. And my head was a store-
house of useful knowledge. And if I did not go in a rigorously
straight line, with my system of going in a circle, at least I did not
go in a circle, and that was something. And by going on doing this,
day after day, and night after night, I looked forward to getting
out of the forest, some day. For my region was not all forest, far
from it. But there were plains too, mountains and sea, and some
towns and villages, connected by highways and byways. And I
was all the more convinced that I would get out of the forest
some day as I had already got out of it, more than once, and I knew
how difficult it was not to do again what you have done before.
But things had been rather different then. And yet I did not despair
of seeing the light tremble, some day, through the still boughs, the
strange light of the plain, its pale wild eddies, through the bronze-
still boughs, which no breath ever stirred. But it was a day I
dreaded too. So that I was sure it would come sooner or later.
For it was not so bad being in the forest, I could imagine worse,
and I could have stayed there till I died, unrepining, yes, without
pining for the light and the plain and the other amenities of
my region. For I knew them well, the amenities of my region,
and I considered that the forest was no worse. And it was not
only no worse, to my mind, but it was better, in this sense, that

I was there. That is a strange way, is it not, of looking at things. Perhaps less strange than it seems. For being in the forest, a place neither worse nor better than the others, and being free to stay there, was it not natural I should think highly of it, not because of what it was, but because I was there. For I was there. And being there I did not have to go there, and that was not to be despised, seeing the state of my legs and my body in general. That is all I wished to say, and if I did not say it at the outset it is simply that something was against it. But I could not, stay in the forest I mean, I was not free to. That is to say I could have, physically nothing could have been easier, but I was not purely physical, I lacked something, and I would have had the feeling, if I had stayed in the forest, of going against an imperative, at least I had that impression. But perhaps I was mistaken, perhaps I would have been better advised to stay in the forest, perhaps I could have stayed there, without remorse, without the painful impression of committing a fault, almost a sin. For I have greatly sinned, at all times, greatly sinned against my prompters. And if I cannot decently be proud of this I see no reason either to be sorry. But imperatives are a little different, and I have always been inclined to submit to them, I don't know why. For they never led me anywhere, but tore me from places where, if all was not well, all was no worse than anywhere else, and then went silent, leaving me stranded. So I knew my imperatives well, and yet I submitted to them. It had become a habit. It is true they nearly all bore on the same question, that of my relations with my mother, and on the importance of bringing as soon as possible some light to bear on these and even on the kind of light that should be brought to bear and the most effective means of doing so. Yes, these imperatives were quite explicit and even detailed until, having set me in motion at last, they began to falter, then went silent, leaving me there like a fool who neither knows where he is going nor why he is going there. And they nearly all bore, as I may have said already, on the same painful and thorny question. And I do not think I could mention even one having a different purport. And the one enjoining me then to leave the forest without delay was in no way different from those I was used to, as to its meaning. For in its framing I thought I noticed

something new. For after the usual blarney there followed this
solemn warning, Perhaps it is already too late. It was in Latin,
nimis sero, I think that's Latin. Charming things, hypothetical imperatives. But if I had never succeeded in liquidating this matter
of my mother, the fault must not be imputed solely to that voice
which deserted me, prematurely. It was partly to blame, that's all
it can be reproached with. For the outer world opposed my succeeding too, with its wiles, I have given some examples. And even
if the voice could have harried me to the very scene of action, even
then I might well have succeeded no better, because of the other
obstacles barring my way. And in this command which faltered,
then died, it was hard not to hear the unspoken entreaty, Don't
do it, Molloy. In forever reminding me thus of my duty was its
purpose to show me the folly of it? Perhaps. Fortunately it did no
more than stress, the better to mock if you like, an innate velleity.
And of myself, all my life, I think I had been going to my mother,
with the purpose of establishing our relations on a less precarious
footing. And when I was with her, and I often succeeded, I left her
without having done anything. And when I was no longer with her
I was again on my way to her, hoping to do better the next time.
And when I appeared to give up and to busy myself with something else, or with nothing at all any more, in reality I was hatching
my plans and seeking the way to her house. This is taking a queer
turn. So even without this so-called imperative I impugn, it would
have been difficult for me to stay in the forest, since I was forced
to assume my mother was not there. And yet it might have
been better for me to try and stay. But I also said, Yet a little
while, at the rate things are going, and I won't be able to move,
but will have to stay, where I happen to be, unless someone comes
and carries me. Oh I did not say it in such limpid language. And
when I say I said, etc., all I mean is that I knew confusedly things
were so, without knowing exactly what it was all about. And every
time I say, I said this, or, I said that, or speak of a voice saying,
far away inside me, Molloy, and then a fine phrase more or less
clear and simple, or find myself compelled to attribute to others
intelligible words, or hear my own voice uttering to others more or
less articulate sounds, I am merely complying with the convention

that demands you either lie or hold your peace. For what really
happened was quite different. And I did not say, Yet a little while,
at the rate things are going, etc., but that resembled perhaps what
I would have said, if I had been able. In reality I said nothing at
all, but I heard a murmur, something gone wrong with the silence,
and I pricked up my ears, like an animal I imagine, which gives
a start and pretends to be dead. And then sometimes there arose
within me, confusedly, a kind of consciousness, which I express
by saying, I said, etc., or, Don't do it Molloy, or, Is that your
mother's name? said the sergeant, I quote from memory. Or which
I express without sinking to the level of oratio recta, but by means
of other figures quite as deceitful, as for example, It seemed to me
that, etc., or, I had the impression that, etc., for it seemed to me
nothing at all, and I had no impression of any kind, but simply
somewhere something had changed, so that I too had to change, or
the world too had to change, in order for nothing to be changed.
And it was these little adjustments, as between Galileo's vessels,
that I can only express by saying, I feared that, or, I hoped that,
or, Is that your mother's name? said the sergeant, for example,
and that I might doubtless have expressed otherwise and better,
if I had gone to the trouble. And so I shall perhaps some day when
I have less horror of trouble than today. But I think not. So I said,
Yet a little while, at the rate things are going, and I won't be able
to move, but will have to stay, where I happen to be, unless some
kind person comes and carries me. For my marches got shorter
and shorter and my halts in consequence more and more frequent
and I may add prolonged. For the notion of the long halt does not
necessarily follow from that of the short march, nor that of the
frequent halt either, when you come to think of it, unless you give
frequent a meaning it does not possess, and I could never bring
myself to do a thing like that. And it seemed to me all the more
important to get out of this forest with all possible speed as I would
very soon be powerless to get out of anything whatsoever, were it
but a bower. It was winter, it must have been winter, and not only
many trees had lost their leaves, but these lost leaves had gone all
black and spongy and my crutches sank into them, in places right
up to the fork. Strange to say I felt no colder than usual. Perhaps

it was only autumn. But I was never very sensitive to changes of
temperature. And the gloom, if it seemed less blue than before,
was as thick as ever. Which made me say in the end, It is less
blue because there is less green, but it is no less thick thanks to the
leaden winter sky. Then something about the black dripping from
the black boughs, something in that line. The black slush of leaves
slowed me down even more. But leaves or no leaves I would have
abandoned erect motion, that of man. And I still remember the
day when, flat on my face by way of rest, in defiance of the rules,
I suddenly cried, striking my brow, Christ, there's crawling, I never
thought of that. But could I crawl, with my legs in such a state, and
my trunk? And my head. But before I go on, a word about the
forest murmurs. It was in vain I listened, I could hear nothing of
the kind. But rather, with much goodwill and a little imagination,
at long intervals a distant gong. A horn goes well with the forest,
you expect it. It is the huntsman. But a gong! Even a tom-tom,
at a pinch, would not have shocked me. But a gong! It was mortify-
ing, to have been looking forward to the celebrated murmurs if to
nothing else, and to succeed only in hearing, at long intervals, in
the far distance, a gong. For a moment I dared hope it was only
my heart, still beating. But only for a moment. For it does not beat,
not my heart, I'd have to refer you to hydraulics for the squelch
that old pump makes. To the leaves too I listened, before their
fall, attentively in vain. They made no sound, motionless and rigid,
like brass, have I said that before? So much for the forest murmurs. From time to time I blew my horn, through the cloth of my
pocket. Its hoot was fainter every time. I had taken it off my bicycle.
When? I don't know. And now, let us have done. Flat on my belly,
using my crutches like grapnels, I plunged them ahead of me into
the undergrowth, and when I felt they had a hold, I pulled myself
forward, with an effort of the wrists. For my wrists were still quite
strong, fortunately, in spite of my decrepitude, though all swollen
and racked by a kind of chronic arthritis probably. That then
briefly is how I went about it. The advantage of this mode of locomotion compared to others, I mean those I have tried, is this, that
when you want to rest you stop and rest, without further ado. For
standing there is no rest, nor sitting either. And there are men who

move about sitting, and even kneeling, hauling themselves to right
and left, forward and backward, with the help of hooks. But he
who moves in this way, crawling on his belly, like a reptile, no
sooner comes to rest than he begins to rest, and even the very
movement is a kind of rest, compared to other movements, I mean
those that have worn me out. And in this way I moved onward in
the forest, slowly, but with a certain regularity, and I covered my
fifteen paces, day in, day out, without killing myself. And I even
crawled on my back, plunging my crutches blindly behind me into
the thickets, and with the black boughs for sky to my closing eyes.
I was on my way to mother. And from time to time I said, Mother,
to encourage me I suppose. I kept losing my hat, the lace had
broken long ago, until in a fit of temper I banged it down on my
skull with such violence that I couldn't get it off again. And if I
had met any lady friends, if I had had any lady friends, I would
have been powerless to salute them correctly. But there was always
present to my mind, which was still working, if laboriously, the
need to turn, to keep on turning, and every three or four jerks I
altered course, which permitted me to describe, if not a circle, at
least a great polygon, perfection is not of this world, and to hope
that I was going forward in a straight line, in spite of everything,
day and night, towards my mother. And true enough the day came
when the forest ended and I saw the light, the light of the plain,
exactly as I had foreseen. But I did not see it from afar, trembling
beyond the harsh trunks, as I had foreseen, but suddenly I was in
it, I opened my eyes and saw I had arrived. And the reason for
that was probably this, that for some time past I had not opened
my eyes, or seldom. And even my little changes of course were
made blindly, in the dark. The forest ended in a ditch, I don't know
why, and it was in this ditch that I became aware of what had
happened to me. I suppose it was the fall into the ditch that opened
my eyes, for why would they have opened otherwise? I looked at
the plain rolling away as far as the eye could see. No, not quite
so far as that. For my eyes having got used to the light I fancied
I saw, faintly outlined against the horizon, the towers and steeples of
a town, which of course I could not assume was mine, on such slight
evidence. It is true the plain seemed familiar, but in my region all

the plains looked alike, when you knew one you knew them all.
In any case, whether it was my town or not, whether somewhere
under that faint haze my mother panted on, or whether she
poisoned the air a hundred miles away, were ludicrously idle questions for a man in my position, though of undeniable interest on
the plane of pure knowledge. For how could I drag myself over
that vast moor, where my crutches would fumble in vain. Rolling
perhaps. And then? Would they let me roll on to my mother's
door? Fortunately for me at this painful juncture, which I had
vaguely foreseen, but not in all its bitterness, I heard a voice telling
me not to fret, that help was coming. Literally. These words struck
it is not too much to say as clearly on my ear, and on my understanding, as the urchin's thanks I suppose when I stooped and
picked up his marble. Don't fret, Molloy, we're coming. Well, I
suppose you have to try everything once, succour included, to get
a complete picture of the resources of their planet. I lapsed down
to the bottom of the ditch. It must have been spring, a morning
in spring. I thought I heard birds, skylarks perhaps. I had not
heard a bird for a long time. How was it I had not heard any in
the forest? Nor seen any. It had not seemed strange to me. Had
I heard any at the seaside? Mews? I could not remember. I remembered the corn-crakes. The two travellers came back to my memory.
One had a club. I had forgotten them. I saw the sheep again. Or so
I say now. I did not fret, other scenes of my life came back to me.
There seemed to be rain, then sunshine, turn about. Real spring
weather. I longed to go back into the forest. Oh not a real longing.
Molloy could stay, where he happened to be.

II

It is midnight. The rain is beating on the windows. I am calm.
All is sleeping. Nevertheless I get up and go to my desk. I can't
sleep. My lamp sheds a soft and steady light. I have trimmed it.
It will last till morning. I hear the eagle-owl. What a terrible battle-
cry! Once I listened to it unmoved. My son is sleeping. Let him
sleep. The night will come when he too, unable to sleep, will get
up and go to his desk. I shall be forgotten.

My report will be long. Perhaps I shall not finish it. My name
is Moran, Jacques. That is the name I am known by. I am done
for. My son too. All unsuspecting. He must think he's on the
threshold of life, of real life. He's right there. His name is Jacques,
like mine. This cannot lead to confusion.

I remember the day I received the order to see about Molloy.
It was a Sunday in summer. I was sitting in my little garden, in a
wicker chair, a black book closed on my knees. It must have been
about eleven o'clock, still too early to go to church. I was savouring the day of rest, while deploring the importance attached to it,
in certain parishes. To work, even to play on Sunday, was not of
necessity reprehensible, in my opinion. It all depended on the state

of mind of him who worked, or played, and on the nature of his work, of his play, in my opinion. I was reflecting with satisfaction on this, that this slightly libertarian view was gaining ground, even among the clergy, more and more disposed to admit that the sabbath, so long as you go to mass and contribute to the collection, may be considered a day like any other, in certain respects. This did not affect me personally, I've always loved doing nothing. And I would gladly have rested on weekdays too, if I could have afforded it. Not that I was positively lazy. It was something else. Seeing something done which I could have done better myself, if I had wished, and which I did do better whenever I put my mind to it, I had the impression of discharging a function to which no form of activity could have exalted me. But this was a joy in which, during the week, I could seldom indulge.

The weather was fine. I watched absently the coming and going of my bees. I heard on the gravel the scampering steps of my son, caught up in I know not what fantasy of flight and pursuit. I called to him not to dirty himself. He did not answer.

All was still. Not a breath. From my neighbours' chimneys the smoke rose straight and blue. None but tranquil sounds, the clicking of mallet and ball, a rake on pebbles, a distant lawn-mower, the bell of my beloved church. And birds of course, blackbird and thrush, their song sadly dying, vanquished by the heat, and leaving dawn's high boughs for the bushes' gloom. Contentedly I inhaled the scent of my lemon-verbena.

In such surroundings slipped away my last moments of peace and happiness.

A man came into the garden and walked swiftly towards me. I knew him well. Now I have no insuperable objection to a neighbour's dropping in, on a Sunday, to pay his respects, if he feels the need, though I much prefer to see nobody. But this man was not a neighbour. Our dealings were strictly of a business nature and he had journeyed from afar, on purpose to disturb me. So I was disposed to receive him frostily enough, all the more so as he had the impertinence to come straight to where I was sitting, under my Beauty of Bath. With people who took this liberty I had no patience. If they wished to speak to me they had only to ring at

the door of my house. Martha had her instructions. I thought I
was hidden from anybody coming into my grounds and following
the short path which led from the garden-gate to the front door,
and in fact I must have been. But at the noise of the gate being
slammed I turned angrily and saw, blurred by the leaves, this high
mass bearing down on me, across the lawn. 1 neither got up nor
invited him to sit down. He stopped in front of me and we stared
at each other in silence. He was dressed in his heavy, sombre
Sunday best, and at this my displeasure knew no bounds. This
gross external observance, while the soul exults in its rags, has
always appeared to me an abomination. I watched the enormous
feet crushing my daisies. I would gladly have driven him away,
with a knout. Unfortunately it was not he who mattered. Sit down,
I said, mollified by the reflection that after all he was only acting
his part of go-between. Yes, suddenly I had pity on him, pity on
myself. He sat down and mopped his forehead. I caught a glimpse
of my son spying on us from behind a bush. My son was thirteen
or fourteen at the time. He was big and strong for his age. His
intelligence seemed at times a little short of average. My son, in fact.
I called him and ordered him to go and fetch some beer. Peeping
and prying were part of my profession. My son imitated me instinctively. He returned after a remarkably short interval with two
glasses and a quart bottle of beer. He uncorked the bottle and
served us. He was very fond of uncorking bottles. I told him to
go and wash himself, to straighten his clothes, in a word, to get
ready to appear in public, for it would soon be time for mass.
He can stay, said Gaber. I don't wish him to stay, I said. And
turning to my son I told him again to go and get ready. If there
was one thing displeased me, at that time, it was being late for the
last mass. Please yourself, said Gaber. Jacques went away grumbling with his finger in his mouth, a detestable and unhygienic habit,
but preferable, all things considered, to that of the finger in the
nose, in my opinion. If putting his finger in his mouth prevented
my son from putting it in his nose, or elsewhere, he was right to
do it, in a sense.

Here are your instructions, said Gaber. He took a notebook
from his pocket and began to read. Every now and then he closed

the notebook, taking care to leave his finger in it as a marker, and indulged in comments and observations of which I had no need, for I knew my business. When at last he had finished I told him the job did not interest me and that the chief would do better to call on another agent. He wants it to be you, God knows why, said Gaber. I presume he told you why, I said, scenting flattery, for which I had a weakness. He said, replied Gaber, that no one could do it but you. This was more or less what I wanted to hear. And yet, I said, the affair seems childishly simple. Gaber began bitterly to inveigh against our employer, who had made him get up in the middle of the night, just as he was getting into position to make love to his wife. For this kind of nonsense, he added. And he said he had confidence in no one but me? I said. He doesn't know what he says, said Gaber. He added, Nor what he does. He wiped the lining of his bowler, peering inside as if in search of something. In that case it's hard for me to refuse, I said, knowing perfectly well that in any case it was impossible for me to refuse. Refuse! But we agents often amused ourselves with grumbling among ourselves and giving ourselves the airs of free men. You leave today, said Gaber. Today! I cried, but he's out of his mind! Your son goes with you, said Gaber. I said no more. When it came to the point we said no more. Gaber buttoned his notebook and put it back in his pocket, which he also buttoned. He stood up, rubbing his hands over his chest. I could do with another beer, he said. Go to the kitchen, I said, the maid will serve you. Goodbye, Moran, he said.

It was too late for mass. I did not need to consult my watch to know, I could feel mass had begun without me. I who never missed mass, to have missed it on that Sunday of all Sundays! When I so needed it! To buck me up! I decided to ask for a private communion, in the course of the afternoon. I would go without lunch. Father Ambrose was always very kind and accommodating.

I called Jacques. Without result. I said, Seeing me still in conference he has gone to mass alone. This explanation turned out subsequently to be the correct one. But I added, He might have come and seen me before leaving. I liked thinking in monologue and then my lips moved visibly. But no doubt he was afraid of disturbing me and of being reprimanded. For I was sometimes inclined to go too far when I reprimanded my son, who was consequently a little afraid of me. I myself had never been sufficiently chastened. Oh I had not been spoiled either, merely neglected. Whence bad habits ingrained beyond remedy and of which even the most meticulous piety has never been able to break me. I hoped to spare my son this misfortune, by giving him a good clout from time to time, together with my reasons for doing so. Then I said, Is he barefaced enough to tell me, on his return, that he has been to mass if he has not, if for example he has merely run off to join his little friends, behind the slaughter-house? And I determined to get the truth out of Father Ambrose, on this subject. For it was imperative my son should not imagine he was capable of lying to me with impunity. And if Father Ambrose could not enlighten me. I would apply to the verger, whose vigilance it was inconceivable that the presence of my son at twelve o'clock mass had escaped. For I knew for a fact that the verger had a list of the faithful and that, from his place beside the font, he ticked us off when it came to the absolution. It is only fair to say that Father Ambrose knew nothing of these manoeuvres, yes, anything in the nature of surveillance was hateful to the good Father Ambrose. And he would have sent the verger flying about his business if he had suspected him of such a work of supererogation. It must have been for his own edification that the verger kept this register, with such assiduity. Admittedly I knew only what went on at the mass, having no experience personally of the other offices, for the good reason that I never went within a mile of them. But I had heard it said that they were the occasion of exactly the same supervision, at the hands either of the verger himself or, when his duties called him elsewhere, of one of his sons. A strange parish whose flock knew more than its pastor of a circumstance which seemed rather in his province than in theirs.

Such were my thoughts as I waited for my son to come back and Gaber, whom I had not yet heard leave, to go. And tonight I find it strange I could have thought of such things, I mean my son, my lack of breeding, Father Ambrose, Verger Joly with his register, at such a time. Had I not something better to do, after

what I had just heard? The fact is I had not yet begun to take
the matter seriously, And I am all the more surprised as such light-
mindedness was not like me. Or was it in order to win a few more
moments of peace that I instinctively avoided giving my mind to
it? Even if, as set forth in Gaber's report, the affair had seemed un-
worthy of me, the chief's insistence on having me, me Moran,
rather than anybody else, ought to have warned me that it was
no ordinary one. And instead of bringing to bear upon it without
delay all the resources of my mind and of my experience, I sat
dreaming of my breed's infirmities and the singularities of those
about me. And yet the poison was already acting on me, the
poison I had just been given. I stirred restlessly in my arm-chair,
ran my hands over my face, crossed and uncrossed my legs, and
so on. The colour and weight of the world were changing already,
soon I would have to admit I was anxious.

I remembered with annoyance the lager I had just absorbed.
Would I be granted the body of Christ after a pint of Wallenstein?
And if I said nothing? Have you come fasting, my son? He would
not ask. But God would know, sooner or later. Perhaps he would
pardon me. But would the eucharist produce the same effect taken
on top of beer, however light? I could always try. What was the
teaching of the Church on the matter? What if I were about to
commit sacrilege? I decided to suck a few peppermints on the way
to the presbytery.

I got up and went to the kitchen. I asked if Jacques was
back. I haven't seen him, said Martha. She seemed in bad humour.
And the man? I said. What man? she said. The man who came
for a glass of beer, I said. No one came for anything, said Martha.
By the way, I said, unperturbed apparently, I shall not eat lunch
today. She asked if I were ill. For I was naturally a rather heavy
eater. And my Sunday midday meal especially I always liked
extremely copious. It smelt good in the kitchen. I shall lunch a
little later today, that's all, I said. Martha looked at me furiously.
Say four o'clock, I said. In that wizened, grey, skull what
raging and rampaging then, I knew. You will not go out today,
I said coldly, I regret. She flung herself at her pots and pans,
dumb with anger. You will keep all that hot for me, I said,

as best you can. And knowing her capable of poisoning me I added, You can have the whole day off tomorrow, if that is any good to you.

I left her and went out on the road. So Gaber had gone without his beer. And yet he had wanted it badly. It was a good brand, Wallenstein. I stood there on the watch for Jacques. Coming from church he would appear on my right, on my left if he came from the slaughter-house. A neighbour passed. A free-thinker. Well, well, he said, no worship today? He knew my habits, my Sunday habits I mean. Everyone knew them and the chief perhaps better than any, in spite of his remoteness. You look as if you had seen a ghost, said the neighbour. Worse than that, I said, you. I went in, at my back the dutifully hideous smile. I could see him running to his concubine with the news, You know that poor bastard Moran, you should have heard me, I had him lepping! Couldn't speak! Took to his heels!

Jacques came back soon afterwards. No trace of frolic. He said he had been to church alone. I asked him a few pertinent questions concerning the march of the ceremony. His answers were plausible. I told him to wash his hands and sit down to his lunch. I went back to the kitchen. I did nothing but go to and fro. You may dish up, I said. She had wept. I peered into the pots. Irish stew. A nourishing and economical dish, if a little indigestible. All honour to the land it has brought before the world. I shall sit down at four o'clock, I said. I did not need to add sharp. I liked punctuality, all those whom my roof sheltered had to like it too. I went up to my room. And there, stretched on my bed, the curtains drawn, I made a first attempt to grasp the Molloy affair.

My concern at first was only with its immediate vexations and the preparations they demanded of me. The kernel of the affair I continued to shirk. I felt a great confusion coming over me.

Should I set out on my autocycle? This was the question with which I began. I had a methodical mind and never set out on a mission without prolonged reflection as to the best way of setting out. It was the first problem to solve, at the outset of each enquiry, and I never moved until I had solved it to my satisfaction. Sometimes I took my autocycle, sometimes the train, sometimes the motor-coach, just as sometimes too I left on foot, or on my bicycle, silently, in the night. For when you are beset with enemies, as I am, you cannot leave on your autocycle, even in the night, without being noticed, unless you employ it as an ordinary bicycle, which is absurd. But if I was in the habit of first settling this delicate question of transport, it was never without having, if not fully sifted, at least taken into account the factors on which it depended. For how can you decide on the way of setting out if you do not first know where you are going, or at least with what purpose you are going there? But in the present case I was tackling the problem of transport with no other preparation than the languid cognizance I had taken of Gaber's report. I would be able to recover the minutest details of this report when I wished. But I had not yet troubled to do so, I had avoided doing so, saying, The affair is banal. To try and solve the problem of transport under such conditions was madness. Yet that was what I was doing. I was losing my head already.

I liked leaving on my autocycle, I was partial to this way of getting about. And in my ignorance of the reasons against it I decided to leave on my autocycle. Thus was inscribed, on the threshold of the Molloy affair, the fatal pleasure principle.

The sun's beams shone through the rift in the curtains and made visible the sabbath of the motes. I concluded from this that the weather was still fine and rejoiced. When you leave on your autocycle fine weather is to be preferred. I was wrong, the weather was fine no longer, the sky was clouding over, soon it would rain. But for the moment the sun was still shining. It was on this that I went, with inconceivable levity, having nothing else to go on.

Next I attacked, according to my custom, the capital question of the effects to take with me. And on this subject too I should have come to a quite otiose decision but for my son, who burst in wanting to know if he might go out. I controlled myself. He was wiping his mouth with the back of his hand, a thing I do not like to see. But there are nastier gestures, I speak from experience.

Out? I said. Where? Out! Vagueness I abhor. I was beginning to feel hungry. To the Elms, he replied. So we call our little public park. And yet there is not an elm to be seen in it, I have

been told. What for? I said. To go over my botany, he replied.
There were times I suspected my son of deceit. This was one.
I would almost have preferred him to say, For a walk, or, To look
at the tarts. The trouble was he knew far more than I, about
botany. Otherwise I could have set him a few teasers, on his
return. Personally I just liked plants, in all innocence and simplicity.
I even saw in them at times a superfetatory proof of the existence
of God. Go, I said, but be back at half-past four, I want to talk
to you. Yes papa, he said. Yes papa! Ah!

I slept a little. Faster, faster. Passing the church, something
made me stop. I looked at the door, baroque, very fine. I found
it hideous. I hastened on to the presbytery. The Father is sleeping,
said the servant. I can wait, I said. Is it urgent? she said. Yes
and no, I said. She showed me into the sitting-room, bare and
bleak, dreadful. Father Ambrose came in, rubbing his eyes. I
disturb you, Father, I said. He clicked his tongue against the roof
of his mouth, protestingly. I shall not describe our attitudes,
characteristic his of him, mine of me. He offered me a cigar which
I accepted with good grace and put in my pocket, between my
fountain-pen and my propelling-pencil. He flattered himself, Father
Ambrose, with being a man of the world and knowing its ways,
he who never smoked. And everyone said he was most broad. I
asked him if he had noticed my son at the last mass. Certainly, he
said, we even spoke together. I must have looked surprised. Yes,
he said, not seeing you at your place, in the front row, I feared
you were ill. So I called for the dear child, who reassured me. A
most untimely visitor, I said, whom I could not shake off in time.
So your son explained to me, he said. He added, But let us sit
down, we have no train to catch. He laughed and sat down, hitch-
ing up his heavy cassock. May I offer you a little glass of something? he said. I was in a quandary. Had Jacques let slip an allusion
to the lager. He was quite capable of it. I came to ask you a favour,
I said. Granted, he said. We observed each other. It's this, I said,
Sunday for me without the Body and Blood is like—. He raised
his hand. Above all no profane comparisons, he said. Perhaps he
was thinking of the kiss without a moustache or beef without
mustard. I dislike being interrupted. I sulked. Say no more, he

said, a wink is as good as a nod, you want communion. I bowed
my head. It's a little unusual, he said. I wondered if he had fed. I
knew he was given to prolonged fasts, by way of mortification
certainly, and then because his doctor advised it. Thus he killed
two birds with one stone. Not a word to a soul, he said, let it
remain between us and—. He broke off, raising a finger, and his
eyes, to the ceiling. Heavens, he said, what is that stain? I looked
in turn at the ceiling. Damp, I said. Tut tut, he said, how annoying.
The words tut tut seemed to me the maddest I had heard. There
are times, he said, when one feels like weeping. He got up. I'll
go and get my kit, he said. He called that his kit. Alone, my hands
clasped until it seemed my knuckles would crack, I asked the Lord
for guidance. Without result. That was some consolation. As for
Father Ambrose, in view of his alacrity to fetch his kit, it seemed
evident to me he suspected nothing. Or did it amuse him to see
how far I would go? Or did it tickle him to have me commit a
sin? I summarised the situation briefly as follows. If knowing I
have beer taken he gives me the sacrament, his sin, if sin there be,
is as great as mine. I was therefore risking little. He came back with
a kind of portable pyx, opened it, and dispatched me without an
instant's hesitation. I rose and thanked him warmly Pah! he said,
it's nothing. Now we can talk.

I had nothing else to say to him. All I wanted was to return
home as quickly as possible and stuff myself with stew. My soul
appeased, I was ravenous. But being slightly in advance of my
schedule I resigned myself to allowing him eight minutes. They
seemed endless. He informed me that Mrs Clement, the chemist's
wife and herself a highly qualified chemist, had fallen, in her
laboratory, from the top of a ladder, and broken the neck—. The
neck! I cried. Of her femur, he said, can't you let me finish. He
added that it was bound to happen. And I, not to be outdone,
told him how worried I was about my hens, particularly my grey
hen, which would neither brood nor lay and for the past month
and more had done nothing but sit with her arse in the dust, from
morning to night. Like Job, haha, he said. I too said haha. What
a joy it is to laugh, from time to time, he said. Is it not? I
said. It is peculiar to man, he said. So I have noticed, I said.

A brief silence ensued. What do you feed her on? he said. Corn chiefly, I said. Cooked or raw? he said. Both, I said. I added that she ate nothing any more. Nothing! he cried. Next to nothing, I said. Animals never laugh, he said. It takes us to find that funny, I said. What? he said. It takes us to find that funny, I said loudly. He mused. Christ never laughed either, he said, so far as we know. He looked at me. Can you wonder? I said. There it is, he said. He smiled sadly. She has not the pip, I hope, he said. I said she had not, certainly not, anything he liked, but not the pip. He meditated. Have you tried bicarbonate? he said. I beg your pardon? I said. Bicarbonate of soda, he said, have you tried it? Why no, I said. Try it! he cried, flushing with pleasure, have her swallow a few dessertspoonfuls, several times a day, for a few months. You'll see, you won't know her. A powder? I said. Bless my heart to be sure, he said. Many thanks, I said, I'll begin today. Such a fine hen, he said, such a good layer. Or rather tomorrow, I said. I had forgotten the chemist was closed. Except in case of emergency. And now that little cordial, he said. I declined.

This interview with Father Ambrose left me with a painful impression. He was still the same dear man, and yet not. I seemed to have surprised, on his face, a lack, how shall I say, a lack of nobility. The host, it is only fair to say, was lying heavy on my stomach. And as I made my way home I felt like one who, having swallowed a pain-killer, is first astonished, then indignant, on obtaining no relief. And I was almost ready to suspect Father Ambrose, alive to my excesses of the forenoon, of having fobbed me off with unconsecrated bread. Or of mental reservation as he pronounced the magic words. And it was in vile humour that I arrived home, in the pelting rain.

The stew was a great disappointment. Where are the onions? I cried. Gone to nothing, replied Martha. I rushed into the kitchen, to look for the onions I suspected her of having removed from the pot, because she knew how much I liked them. I even rummaged in the bin. Nothing. She watched me mockingly.

I went up to my room again, drew back the curtains on a calamitous sky and lay down. I could not understand what was happening to me. I found it painful at that period not to understand. I tried to pull myself together. In vain. I might have known. My life was running out, I knew not through what breach. I succeeded however in dozing off, which is not so easy, when pain is speculative. And I was marvelling, in that half-sleep, at my half-sleeping, when my son came in, without knocking. Now if there is one thing I abhor, it is someone coming into my room, without knocking. I might just happen to be masturbating, before my cheval-glass. Father with yawning fly and starting eyes, toiling to scatter on the ground his joyless seed, that was no sight for a small boy. Harshly I recalled him to the proprieties. He protested he had knocked twice. If you had knocked a hundred times, I replied, it would not give you the right to come in without being invited. But, he said. But what? I said. You told me to be here at half-past four, he said. There is something, I said, more important in life than punctuality, and that is decorum. Repeat. In that disdainful mouth my phrase put me to shame. He was soaked. What have you been looking at? I said. The liliaceae, papa, he answered. The liliaceae papa! My son had a way of saying papa, when he wanted to hurt me, that was very special. Now listen to me, I said. His face took on an expression of anguished attention. We leave this evening, I said in substance, on a journey. Put on your school suit, the green—. But it's blue, papa, he said. Blue or green, put it on, I said violently. I went on. Put in your little knapsack, the one I gave you for your birthday, your toilet things, one shirt, one pair of socks and seven pairs of drawers. Do you understand? Which shirt, papa? he said. It doesn't matter which shirt, I cried, any shirt! Which shoes am I to wear? he said. You have two pairs of shoes, I said, one for Sundays, and one for weekdays, and you ask me which you are to wear. I sat up. I want none of your lip, I said.

Thus to my son I gave precise instructions. But were they the right ones? Would they stand the test of second thoughts? Would I not be impelled, in a very short time, to cancel them? I who never changed my mind before my son. The worst was to be feared.

Where are we going, papa? he said. How often had I told him not to ask me questions. And where were we going, in point of fact. Do as you're told, I said. I have an appointment with Mr

Py tomorrow, he said. You'll see him another day, I said. But I have an ache, he said. There exist other dentists, I said, Mr Py is not the unique dentist of the northern hemisphere. I added rashly, We are not going into the wilderness. But he's a very good dentist, he said. All dentists are alike, I said. I could have told him to get to hell out of that with his dentist, but no, I reasoned gently with him, I spoke with him as with an equal. I could furthermore have pointed out to him that he was lying when he said he had an ache. He did have an ache, in a bicuspid I believe, but it was over. Py himself had told me so. I have dressed the tooth, he said, your son cannot possibly feel any more pain. I remembered this conversation well. He has naturally very bad teeth, said Py. Naturally, I said, what do you mean, naturally? What are you insinuating? He was born with bad teeth, said Py, and all his life he will have bad teeth. Naturally I shall do what I can. Meaning, I was born with the disposition to do all I can, all my life I shall do all I can, necessarily. Born with bad teeth! As for me, I was down to my incisors, the nippers.

Is it still raining? I said. My son had drawn a small glass from his pocket and was examining the inside of his mouth, prising away his upper lip with his finger. Aaw, he said, without interrupting his inspection. Stop messing about with your mouth! I cried. Go to the window and tell me if it's still raining. He went to the window and told me it was still raining. Is the sky completely overcast? I said. Yes, he said. Not the least rift? I said. No, he said. Draw the curtains, I said. Delicious instants, before one's eyes get used to the dark. Are you still there? I said. He was still there. I asked him what he was waiting for to do as I had told him. If I had been my son I would have left me long ago. He was not worthy of me, not in the same class at all. I could not escape this conclusion. Cold comfort that is, to feel superior to one's son, and hardly sufficient to calm the remorse of having begotten him. May I bring my stamps? he said. My son had two albums, a big one for his collection properly speaking and a small one for the duplicates. I authorised him to bring the latter. When I can give pleasure, without doing violence to my principles, I do so gladly. He withdrew.

I got up and went to the window. I could not keep still. I
passed my head between the curtains. Fine rain, lowering sky. He
had not lied to me. Likely to lift round about eight. Fine sunset,
twilight, night. Waning moon, rising towards midnight. I rang for
Martha and lay down again. We shall dine at home, I said.
She looked at me in astonishment. Did we not always dine at
home? I had not yet told her we were leaving. I would not
tell her till the last moment, one foot in the stirrup as the
saying is. I did not wholly trust her. I would call her at the last
moment and say, Martha, we're leaving, for one day, two days,
three days, a week, two weeks, God knows, goodbye. It was important to leave her in the dark. Then why had I called her? She
would have served us dinner in any case, as she did every day.
I had made the mistake of putting myself in her place. That was
understandable. But to tell her we would dine at home, what a
blunder. For she knew it already, thought she knew, did know.
And as a result of this useless reminder she would sense that something was afoot and spy on us, in the hope of learning what it was.
First mistake. The second, first in time, was my not having enjoined
my son to keep what I had told him to himself. Not that this
would have served any purpose. Nevertheless I should have insisted on it, as due to myself. I was floundering. I so sly as a rule.
I tried to mend matters, saying, A little later than usual, not before
nine. She turned to go, her simple mind already in a turmoil. I
am at home to no one, I said. I knew what she would do, she
would throw a sack over her shoulders and slip off to the bottom
of the garden. There she would call Hannah, the old cook of the
Elsner sisters, and they would whisper together for a long time,
through the railings. Hannah never went out, she did not like
going out. The Elsner sisters were not bad neighbours, as neighbours go. They made a little too much music, that was the only
fault I could find with them. If there is one thing gets on my nerves
it is music. What I assert, deny, question, in the present, I still can.
But mostly I shall use the various tenses of the past. For mostly I
do not know, it is perhaps no longer so, it is too soon to know, I
simply do not know, perhaps shall never know. I thought a little of
the Elsner sisters. Everything remained to be planned and there

I was thinking of the Elsner sisters. They had an aberdeen called Zulu. People called it Zulu. Sometimes, when I was in a good humour, I called, Zulu! Little Zulu! and he would come and talk to me, through the railings. But I had to be feeling gay. I don't like animals. It's a strange thing, I don't like men and I don't like animals. As for God, he is beginning to disgust me. Crouching down I would stroke his ears, through the railings, and utter wheedling words. He did not realise he disgusted me. He reared up on his hind legs and pressed his chest against the bars. Then I could see his little black penis ending in a thin wisp of wetted hair. He felt insecure, his hams trembled, his little paws fumbled for purchase, one after the other. I too wobbled, squatting on my heels. With my free hand I held on to the railings. Perhaps I disgusted him too. I found it hard to tear myself away from these vain thoughts.

I wondered, suddenly rebellious, what compelled me to accept this commission. But I had already accepted it, I had given my word. Too late. Honour. It did not take me long to gild my impotence.

But could I not postpone our departure to the following day? Or leave alone? Ah shilly-shally. But we would wait till the very last moment, a little before midnight. This decision is irrevocable, I said. It was justified moreover by the state of the moon.

I did as when I could not sleep. I wandered in my mind, slowly, noting every detail of the labyrinth, its paths as familiar as those of my garden and yet ever new, as empty as the heart could wish or alive with strange encounters. And I heard the distant cymbals, There is still time, still time. But there was not, for I ceased, all vanished and I tried once more to turn my thoughts to the Molloy affair. Unfathomable mind, now beacon, now sea.

The agent and the messenger. We agents never took anything in writing. Gaber was not an agent in the sense I was. Gaber was a messenger. He was therefore entitled to a notebook. A messenger had to be possessed of singular qualities, good messengers were even more rare than good agents. I who was an excellent agent would have made but a sorry messenger. I often regretted it. Gaber was protected in numerous ways. He used a code incomprehensible to all but himself. Each messenger, before being appointed, had to submit his code to the directorate. Gaber understood nothing about the messages he carried. Reflecting on them he arrived at the most extravagantly false conclusions. Yes, it was not enough for him to understand nothing about them, he had also to believe he understood everything about them. This was not all. His memory was so bad that his messages had no existence in his head, but only in his notebook. He had only to close his notebook to become, a moment later, perfectly innocent as to its contents. And when I say that he reflected on his messages and drew conclusions from them, it was not as we would have reflected on them, you and I, the book closed and probably the eyes too, but little by little as he read. And when he raised his head and indulged in his commentaries, it was without losing a second, for if he had lost a second he would have forgotten everything, both text and gloss. I have often wondered if the messengers were not compelled to undergo a surgical operation, to induce in them such a degree of amnesia. But I think not. For otherwise their memory was good enough. And I have heard Gaber speak of his childhood, and of his family, in extremely plausible terms. To be undecipherable to all but oneself, dead without knowing it to the meaning of one's instructions and incapable of remembering them for more than a few seconds, these are capacities rarely united in the same individual. No less however was demanded of our messengers. And that they were more highly esteemed than the agents, whose qualities were sound rather than brilliant, is shown by the fact that they received a weekly wage of eight pounds as against ours of six pounds ten only, these figures being exclusive of bonuses and travelling expenses. And when I speak of agents and of messengers in the plural, it is with no guarantee of truth. For I had never seen any other messenger than Gaber nor any other agent than myself. But I supposed we were not the only ones and Gaber must have supposed the same. For the feeling that we were the only ones of our kind would, I believe, have been more than we could have borne. And it must have appeared natural, to me, that each agent had his own particular messenger, and to Gaber that each messenger had his own particular agent. Thus I was able to say to Gaber, Let him give this job to someone else, I don't want it, and Gaber was able to reply, He wants it to be you. And these last words, assuming Gaber had not invented them especially to annoy me, had perhaps been uttered by the chief with the sole purpose of fostering our illusion, if it was one. All this is not very clear.

That we thought of ourselves as members of a vast organisation was doubtless also due to the all too human feeling that trouble shared, or is it sorrow, is trouble something, I forget the word. But to me at least, who knew how to listen to the falsetto of reason, it was obvious that we were perhaps alone in doing what we did. Yes, in my moments of lucidity I thought it possible. And, to keep nothing from you, this lucidity was so acute at times that I came even to doubt the existence of Gaber himself. And if I had not hastily sunk back into my darkness I might have gone to the extreme of conjuring away the chief too and regarding myself as solely responsible for my wretched existence. For I knew I was wretched, at six pounds ten a week plus bonuses and expenses. And having made away with Gaber and the chief (one Youdi), could I have denied myself the pleasure of—you know. But I was not made for the great light that devours, a dim lamp was all I had been given, and patience without end, to shine it on the empty shadows. I was a solid in the midst of other solids.

I went down to the kitchen. I did not expect to find Martha there, but I found her there. She was sitting in her rocking-chair, in the chimney-corner, rocking herself moodily. This rocking-chair, she would have you believe, was the only possession to which she clung and she would not have parted with it for an empire. It is interesting to note that she had installed it not in her room, but in the kitchen, in the chimney-corner. Late to bed and early to rise, it was in the kitchen that she benefited by it most. The wage-payers are numerous, and I was one of them, who do not like to see, in the place set aside for toil, the furniture of reclining and repose. The servant wishes to rest? Let her retire to her room. In the kitchen all must be of wood, white and rigid. I should mention that Martha had insisted, before entering my service, that I permit her to keep her rocking-chair in the kitchen. I had refused, indignantly. Then, seeing she was inflexible, I had yielded. I was too kind-hearted.

My weekly supply of lager, half-a-dozen quart bottles, was delivered every Saturday. I never touched them until the next day, for lager must be left to settle after the least disturbance. Of these six bottles Gaber and I, together, had emptied one. There should therefore be five left, plus the remains of a bottle from the previous week. I went into the pantry. The five bottles were there, corked and sealed, and one open bottle three-quarters empty. Martha followed me with her eyes. I left without a word to her and went upstairs. I did nothing but go to and fro. I went into my son's room. Sitting at his little desk he was admiring his stamps, the two albums, large and small, open before him. On my approach he shut them hastily. I saw at once what he was up to. But first I said, Have you got your things ready? He stood up, got his pack and gave it to me. I looked inside. I put my hand inside and felt through the contents, staring vacantly before me. Everything was in. I gave it back to him. What are you doing? I said. Looking at my stamps, he said. You call that looking at your stamps? I said. Yes papa, he said, with unimaginable effrontery. Silence, you little liar! I cried. Do you know what he was doing? Transferring to the album of duplicates, from his good collection properly so-called, certain rare and valuable stamps which he was in the habit of gloating over daily and could not bring himself to leave, even for a few days. Show me your new Timor, the five reis orange, I said. He hesitated. Show it to me! I cried. I had given it to him myself, it had cost me a florin. A bargain, at the time. I've put it in here, he said piteously, picking up the album of duplicates. That was all I wanted to know, to hear him say rather, for I knew it already. Very good, I said. I went to the door. You leave both your albums at home, I said, the small one as well as the large one. Not a word of reproach, a simple prophetic present, on the model of those employed by Youdi. Your son goes with you. I went out. But as with delicate steps, almost mincing, congratulating myself as usual on the resilience of my Wilton, I followed the corridor towards my room, I was struck by a thought which made me go back to my son's room. He was sitting in the same place, but in a slightly different attitude, his arms on the table and his head on his arms. The sight went straight to my heart, but nevertheless I did my duty.

He did not move. To make assurance doubly sure, I said, we shall
put the albums in the safe, until our return. He still did not move.
Do you hear me? I said. He rose with a bound that knocked over
his chair and uttered the furious words, Do what you like with
them! I never want to see them again! Anger should be left to
cool, in my opinion, crisis to pass, before one operates. I took the
albums and withdrew, without a word. He had been lacking in
respect, but this was not the moment to have him admit it. Motionless in the corridor I heard sounds of falling and collision. Another,
less master of himself than I of myself, would have intervened. But
it did not positively displease me that my son should give free vent
to his grief. It purges. Sorrow does more harm when dumb, to my
mind.

The albums under my arm, I returned to my room. I had
spared my son a grave temptation, that of putting in his pocket his
most cherished stamps, in order to gloat on them, during our
journey. Not that his having one or two stamps about him was
reprehensible in itself. But it would have been an act of disobed-
ience. To look at them he would have had to hide from his father.
And when he had lost them, as he inevitably would, he would have
been driven to lie, to account for their disappearance. No, if he
could not really bear to be parted from the gems of his collection,
it would have been better for him to take the entire album. For
an album is less readily lost than a stamp. But I was a better judge
than he of what he could and could not. For I knew what he did
not yet know, among other things, that this ordeal would be of
profit to him. *Sollst entbehren,* that was the lesson I desired to
impress upon him, while he was still young and tender. Magic
words which I had never dreamt, until my fifteenth year, could be
coupled together. And should this undertaking make me odious
in his eyes and not only me, but the very idea of fatherhood, I
would pursue it none the less, with everything in my power. The
thought that between my death and his own, ceasing for an
instant from heaping curses on my memory, he might wonder, in
a flash, whether I had not been right, that was enough for me, that
repaid me for all the trouble I had taken and was still to take. He
would answer in the negative, the first time, and resume his execra-

tions. But the doubt would be sown. He would go back to it. That was how I reasoned.

I still had a few hours left before dinner. I decided to make the most of them. Because after dinner I drowse. I took off my coat and shoes, opened my trousers and got in between the sheets. It is lying down, in the warmth, in the gloom, that I best pierce the outer turmoil's veil, discern my quarry, sense what course to follow, find peace in another's ludicrous distress. Far from the world, its clamours, frenzies, bitterness and dingy light, I pass judgement on it and on those, like me, who are plunged in it beyond recall, and on him who has need of me to be delivered, who cannot deliver myself. All is dark, but with that simple darkness that follows like a balm upon the great dismemberings. From their places masses move, stark as laws. Masses of what? One does not ask. There somewhere man is too, vast conglomerate of all of nature's kingdoms, as lonely and as bound. And in that block the prey is lodged and thinks himself a being apart. Anyone would serve. But I am paid to seek. I arrive, he comes away. His life has been nothing but a waiting for this, to see himself preferred, to fancy himself damned, blessed, to fancy himself everyman, above all others. Warmth, gloom, smells of my bed, such is the effect they sometimes have on me. I get up, go out, and everything is changed. The blood drains from my head, the noise of things bursting, merging, avoiding one another, assails me on all sides, my eyes search in vain for two things alike, each pinpoint of skin screams a different message, I drown in the spray of phenomena. It is at the mercy of these sensations, which happily I know to be illusory, that I have to live and work. It is thanks to them I find myself a meaning. So he whom a sudden pain awakes. He stiffens, ceases to breathe, waits, says, It's a bad dream, or, It's a touch of neuralgia, breathes again, sleeps again, still trembling. And yet it is not unpleasant, before setting to work, to steep oneself again in this slow and massive world, where all things move with the ponderous sullenness of oxen, patiently through the immemorial ways, and where of course no investigation would be possible. But on this occasion, I repeat, on this occasion, my reasons for doing so were I trust more serious and imputable less to pleasure than to business. For it was only by transferring it to this atmosphere, how shall I say, of finality without end, why not, that I could venture to consider the work I had on hand. For where Molloy could not be, nor Moran either for that matter, there Moran could bend over Molloy. And though this examination prove unprofitable and of no utility for the execution of my orders, I should neverthe-less have established a kind of connection, and one not necessarily false. For the falsity of the terms does not necessarily imply that of the relation, so far as I know. And not only this, but I should have invested my man, from the outset, with the air of a fabulous being, which something told me could not fail to help me later on. So I took off my coat and my shoes, I opened my trousers and I slipped in between the sheets, with an easy conscience, knowing only too well what I was doing.

Molloy, or Mollose, was no stranger to me. If I had had colleagues, I might have suspected I had spoken of him to them, as of one destined to occupy us, sooner or later. But I had no colleagues and knew nothing of the circumstances in which I had learnt of his existence. Perhaps I had invented him, I mean found him ready-made in my head. There is no doubt one sometimes meets with strangers who are not entire strangers, through their having played a part in certain cerebral reels. This had never happened to me, I considered myself immune from such exper-iences, and even the simple *déjà vu* seemed infinitely beyond my reach. But it was happening to me then, or I was greatly mistaken. For who could have spoken to me of Molloy if not myself and to whom if not to myself could I have spoken of him? I racked my mind in vain. For in my rare conversations with men I avoided such subjects. If anyone else had spoken to me of Molloy I would have requested him to stop and I myself would not have confided his existence to a living soul for anything in the world. If I had had colleagues things would naturally have been different. Among col-leagues one says things which in any other company one keeps to oneself. But I had no colleagues. And perhaps this accounts for the immense uneasiness I had been feeling ever since the beginning of this affair. For it is no small matter, for a grown man thinking he is done with surprises, to see himself the theatre of such igno-

MOLLOY

miny. I had really good cause to be alarmed.

Mother Molloy, or Mellose, was not completely foreign to me either, it seemed. But she was much less alive than her son, who God knows was far from being so. After all perhaps I knew nothing of mother Molloy, or Mollose, save in so far as such a son might bear, like a scurf of placenta, her stamp.

Of these two names, Molloy and Mollose, the second seemed to me perhaps the more correct. But barely. What I heard, in my soul I suppose, where the acoustics are so bad, was a first syllable, Mol, very clear, followed almost at once by a second, very thick, as though gobbled by the first, and which might have been oy as it might have been ose, or one, or even oc. And if I incline towards ose, it was doubtless that my mind had a weakness for this ending, whereas the others left it cold. But since Gaber had said Molloy, not once but several times, and each time with equal incisiveness, I was compelled to admit that I too should have said Molloy and that in saying Mollose I was at fault. And henceforward, unmindful of my preferences, I shall force myself to say Molloy, like Gaber. That there may have been two different persons involved, one my own Mollose, the other the Molloy of the enquiry, was a thought which did not so much as cross my mind, and if it had I should have driven it away, as one drives away a fly, or a hornet. How little one is at one with oneself, good God. I who prided myself on being a sensible man, cold as crystal and as free from spurious depth.

I knew then about Molloy, without however knowing much about him. I shall say briefly what little I did know about him. I shall also draw attention, in my knowledge of Molloy, to the most striking lacunae.

He had very little room. His time too was limited. He hastened incessantly on, as if in despair, towards extremely close objectives. Now, a prisoner, he hurled himself at I know not what narrow confines, and now, hunted, he sought refuge near the centre.

He panted. He had only to rise up within me for me to be filled with panting.

Even in open country he seemed to be crashing through jungle. He did not so much walk as charge. In spite of this he advanced but slowly. He swayed, to and fro, like a bear.

He rolled his head, uttering incomprehensible words.

He was massive and hulking, to the point of misshapenness.
And, without being black, of a dark colour.

He was forever on the move. I had never seen him rest.
Occasionally he stopped and glared furiously about him.

This was how he came to me, at long intervals. Then I was
nothing but uproar, bulk, rage, suffocation, effort unceasing, frenzied and vain. Just the opposite of myself, in fact. It was a change.
And when I saw him disappear, his whole body a vociferation, I
was almost sorry.

What it was all about I had not the slightest idea.

I had no clue to his age. As he appeared to me, so I felt he
must have always appeared and would continue to appear until the
end, an end indeed which I was hard put to imagine. For being
unable to conceive what had brought him to such a pass, I was
no better able to conceive how, left to his own resources, he could
put an end to it. A natural end seemed unlikely to me, I don't
know why. But then my own natural end, and I was resolved
to have no other, would it not at the same time be his? Modest,
I had my doubts. And then again, what end is not natural, are
they not all by the grace of nature, the undeniably good and the
so-called bad? Idle conjectures.

I had no information as to his face. I assumed it was hirsute,
craggy and grimacing. Nothing justified my doing so.

That a man like me, so meticulous and calm in the main, so
patiently turned towards the outer world as towards the lesser
evil, creature of his house, of his garden, of his few poor possessions, discharging faithfully and ably a revolting function, reining
back his thoughts within the limits of the calculable so great is
his horror of fancy, that a man so contrived, for I was a contri-
vance, should let himself be haunted and possessed by chimeras,
this ought to have seemed strange to me and been a warning to
me to have a care, in my own interest. Nothing of the kind. I saw
it only as the weakness of a solitary, a weakness admittedly to be
deplored, but which had to be indulged in if I wished to remain a
solitary, and I did, I clung to that, with as little enthusiasm as to

my hens or to my faith, but no less lucidly. Besides this took up
very little room in the inenarrable contraption I called my life,
jeopardised it as little as my dreams and was as soon forgotten.
Don't wait to be hunted to hide, that was always my motto. And
if I had to tell the story of my life I should not so much as allude
to these apparitions, and least of all to that of the unfortunate
Molloy. For his was a poor thing, compared to others.

But images of this kind the will cannot revive without doing
them violence. Much of what they had it takes away, much they
never had it foists upon them. And the Molloy I brought to light,
that memorable August Sunday, was certainly not the true denizen
of my dark places, for it was not his hour. But so far as the essential features were concerned, I was easy in my mind, the likeness was there. And the discrepancy could have been still greater
for all I cared. For what I was doing I was doing neither for Molloy,
who mattered nothing to me, nor for myself, of whom I despaired,
but on behalf of a cause which, while having need of us to be
accomplished, was in its essence anonymous, and would subsist,
haunting the minds of men, when its miserable artisans should be
no more. It will not be said, I think, that I did not take my work
to heart. But rather, tenderly, Ah those old craftsmen, their race
is extinct and the mould broken.

Two remarks.

Between the Molloy I stalked within me thus and the true
Molloy, after whom I was so soon to be in full cry, over hill and
dale, the resemblance cannot have been great.

I was annexing perhaps already, without my knowing it, to my
private Molloy, elements of the Molloy described by Gaber.

The fact was there were three, no, four Molloys. He that
inhabited me, my caricature of same, Gaber's and the man of flesh
and blood somewhere awaiting me. To these I would add Youdi's
were it not for Gaber's corpse fidelity to the letter of his messages.
Bad reasoning. For could it seriously be supposed that Youdi had
confided to Gaber all he knew, or thought he knew (all one to
Youdi) about his protégé? Assuredly not. He had only revealed
what he deemed of relevance for the prompt and proper execution
of his orders. I will therefore add a fifth Molloy, that of Youdi.

But would not this fifth Molloy necessarily coincide with the fourth,
the real one as the saying is, him dogged by his shadow? I would
have given a lot to know. There were others too, of course. But
let us leave it at that, if you don't mind, the party is big enough.
And let us not meddle either with the question as to how far these
five Molloys were constant and how far subject to variation. For
there was this about Youdi, that he changed his mind with great
facility.

That makes three remarks. I had only anticipated two.

The ice thus broken, I felt equal to facing Gaber's report and
getting down to the official facts. It seemed as if the enquiry were
about to start at last.

It was then that the sound of a gong, struck with violence,
filled the house. True enough, it was nine o'clock. I got up, adjusted
my clothes and hurried down. To give notice that the soup was in,
nay, that it had begun to coagulate, was always for Martha a little
triumph and a great satisfaction. For as a rule I was at table, my
napkin tucked into my collar, crumbling the bread, fiddling with
the cover, playing with the knife-rest, waiting to be served, a few
minutes before the appointed hour. I attacked the soup. Where is
Jacques? I said. She shrugged her shoulders. Detestable slavish
gesture. Tell him to come down at once, I said. The soup before
me had stopped steaming. Had it ever steamed? She came back.
He won't come down, she said. I laid down my spoon. Tell me,
Martha, I said, what is this preparation? She named it. Have I
had it before? I said. She assured me I had. I then made a joke
which pleased me enormously, I laughed so much I began to hiccup.
It was lost on Martha who stared at me dazedly. Tell him to come
down, I said at last. What? said Martha. I repeated my phrase.
She still looked genuinely perplexed. There are three of us in this
charming home, I said, you, my son and finally myself. What I said
was, Tell him to come down. But he's sick, said Martha. Were he
dying, I said, down he must come. Anger led me sometimes to
slight excesses of language. I could not regret them. It seemed to
me that all language was an excess of language. Naturally I confessed them. I was short of sins.

Jacques was scarlet in the face. Eat your soup, I said, and tell

me what you think of it. I'm not hungry, he said. Eat your soup,
I said. I saw he would not eat it. What ails you? I said. I don't
feel well, he said. What an abominable thing is youth. Try and be
more explicit, I said. I was at pains to use this term, a little difficult
for juveniles, having explained its meaning and application to him
a few days before. So I had high hopes of his telling me he didn't
understand. But he was a cunning little fellow, in his way. Martha!
I bellowed. She appeared. The sequel, I said. I looked more attentively out of the window. Not only had the rain stopped, that I
knew already, but in the west scarves of fine red sheen were mounting in the sky. I felt them rather than saw them, through my little
wood. A great joy, it is hardly too much to say, surged over me
at the sight of so much beauty, so much promise. I turned away
with a sigh, for the joy inspired by beauty is often not unmixed,
and saw in front of me what with good reason I had called the
sequel. Now what have we here? I said. Usually on Sunday evening
we had the cold remains of a fowl, chicken, duck, goose, turkey,
I can think of no other fowl, from Saturday evening. I have always
had great success with my turkeys, they are a better proposition
than ducks, in my opinion, for rearing purposes. More delicate,
possibly, but more remunerative, for one who knows and caters
for their little ways, who likes them in a word and is liked by
them in return. Shepherd's pie, said Martha. I tasted it, from the
dish. And what have you done with yesterday's bird? I said.
Martha's face took on an expression of triumph. She was waiting
for this question, that was obvious, she was counting on it. I
thought, she said, you ought to eat something hot, before you left,
And who told you I was leaving? I said. She went to the door, a
sure sign she was about to launch a shaft. She could only be in-
sulting when in flight. I'm not blind, she said. She opened the door.
More's the pity, she said. She closed the door behind her.

I looked at my son. He had his mouth open and his eyes
closed. Was it you blabbed on us? I said. He pretended not to
know what I was talking about. Did you tell Martha we were
leaving? I said. He said he had not. And why not? I said. I didn't
see her, he said brazenly. But she has just been up to your room,
I said. The pie was already made, he said. At times he was almost

worthy of me. But he was wrong to invoke the pie. But he was still
young and inexperienced and I refrained from humbling him. Try
and tell me, I said, a little more precisely, what it is you feel. I've
a stomach-ache, he said. A stomach-ache! Have you a temperature? I said. I don't know, he said. Find out, I said. He was looking
more and more stupefied. Fortunately I rather enjoyed dotting
my i's. Go and get the minute-thermometer, I said, out of the second
right-hand drawer of my desk, counting from the top, take your
temperature and bring me the thermometer. I let a few minutes
go by and then, without being asked, repeated slowly, word for
word, this rather long and difficult sentence, which contained
no fewer than three or four imperatives. As he went out, having
presumably understood the gist of it, I added jocosely, You know
which mouth to put it in? I was not averse, in conversation with
my son, to jests of doubtful taste, in the interests of his education.
Those whose pungency he could not fully savour at the time, and
they must have been many, he could reflect on at his leisure or
seek in company with his little friends to interpret as best he might.
Which was in itself an excellent exercise. And at the same time I
inclined his young mind towards that most fruitful of dispositions,
horror of the body and its functions. But I had turned my phrase
badly, mouth was not the word I should have used. It was while
examining the shepherd's pie more narrowly that I had this after-
thought. I lifted the crust with my spoon and looked inside. I
probed it with my fork. I called Martha and said, His dog wouldn't
touch it. I thought with a smile of my desk which had only six
drawers in all and for all, three on each side of the space where
I put my legs. Since your dinner is uneatable, I said, be good
enough to prepare a packet of sandwiches, with the chicken you
couldn't finish. My son came back at last. That's all the thanks
you get for having a minute-thermometer. He handed it to me. Did
you have time to wipe it? I said. Seeing me squint at the mercury
he went to the door and switched on the light. How remote Youdi
was at that instant. Sometimes in the winter, coming home harassed
and weary after a day of fruitless errands, I would find my slippers
warming in front of the fire, the uppers turned to the flame. He had
a temperature. There's nothing wrong with you, I said. May I go

up? he said. What for? I said. To lie down, he said. Was not this the providential hindrance for which I could not be held responsible? Doubtless, but I would never dare invoke it. I was not going to expose myself to thunderbolts which might be fatal, simply because my son had the gripes. If he fell seriously ill on the way, it would be another matter. It was not for nothing I had studied the old testament. Have you shat, my child, I said gently. I've tried, he said. Do you want to, I said. Yes, he said. But nothing comes, I said. No, he said. A little wind, I said. Yes, he said. Suddenly I remembered Father Ambrose's cigar. I lit it. We'll see what we can do, I said, getting up. We went upstairs. I gave him an enema, with salt water. He struggled, but not for long. I withdrew the nozzle. Try and hold it, I said, don't stay sitting on the pot, lie flat on your stomach. We were in the bathroom. He lay down on the tiles, his big fat bottom sticking up. Let it soak well in, I said. What a day. I looked at the ash on my cigar. It was firm and blue. I sat down on the edge of the bath. The porcelain, the mirrors, the chromium, instilled a great peace within me. At least I suppose it was they. It wasn't a great peace in any case. I got up, laid down my cigar and brushed my incisors. I also brushed the back gums. I looked at myself, puffing out my lips which normally recede into my mouth. What do I look like? I said. The sight of my moustache, as always, annoyed me. It wasn't quite right. It suited me, without a moustache I was inconceivable. But it ought to have suited me better. A slight change in the cut would have sufficed. But what change ? Was there too much of it, not enough? Now, I said, without ceasing to inspect myself, get back on the pot and strain. Was it not rather the colour? A noise as of a waste recalled me to less elevated preoccupations. He stood up trembling all over. We bent together over the pot which at length I took by the handle and tilted from side to side. A few fibrous shreds floated in the yellow liquid. How can you hope to shit, I said, when you've nothing in your stomach? He protested he had had his lunch. You ate nothing, I said. He said no more. I had scored a hit. You forget we are leaving in an hour or so, I said. I can't, he said. So that, I pursued, you will have to eat something. An acute pain shot through my knee. What's the matter, papa? he said. I let myself fall on the stool, pulled up the leg of my trousers and examined my knee, flexing and unflexing it. Quick the iodex, I said. You're sitting on it, he said. I stood up and the leg of my trousers fell down over my ankle. This inertia of things is enough to drive one literally insane. I let out a bellow which must have been heard by the Elsner sisters. They stop reading, raise their heads, look at each other, listen. Nothing more. Just another cry in the night. Two old hands, veined, ringed, seek each other, clasp. I pulled up the leg of my trousers again, rolled it in a fury round my thigh, raised the lid of the stool, took out the iodex and rubbed it into my knee. The knee is full of little loose bones. Let it soak well in, said my son. He would pay for that later on. When I had finished I put everything back in place, rolled down the leg of my trousers, sat down on the stool again and listened. Nothing more. Unless you'd like to try a real emetic, I said, as if nothing had happened. I'm tired, he said. You go and lie down, I said, I'll bring you something nice and light in bed, you'll have a little sleep and then we'll leave together. I drew him to me. What do you say to that? I said. He said to it, Yes papa. Did he love me then as much as I loved him? You could never be sure with that little hypocrite. Be off with you now, I said, cover yourself up well, I won't be long. I went down to the kitchen, prepared and set out on my handsome lacquer tray a bowl of hot milk and a slice of bread and jam. He asked for a report he'll get his report. Martha watched me in silence, lolling in her rocking-chair. Like a Fate who had run out of thread. I cleaned up everything after me and turned to the door. May I go to bed? she said. She had waited till I was standing up, the laden tray in my hands, to ask me this question. I went out, set down the tray on the chair at the foot of the stairs and went back to the kitchen. Have you made the sandwiches? I said. Meanwhile the milk was getting cold and forming a revolting skin. She had made them. I'm going to bed, she said. Everyone was going to bed. You will have to get up in an hour or so, I said, to lock up. It was for her to decide if it was worthwhile going to bed, under these conditions. She asked me how long I expected to be away. Did she realise I was not setting out alone? I suppose so. When she went up to tell my son to come down,

even if he had told her nothing, she must have noticed the knapsack. I have no idea, I said. Then almost in the same breath, seeing
her so old, worse than old, ageing, so sad and solitary in her everlasting corner, There, there, it won't be long. And I advised her,
in terms for me warm, to have a good rest while I was away and
a good time visiting her friends and receiving them. Stint neither
tea nor sugar, I said, and if by any chance you should happen to
need money, apply to Mr Savory. I carried this sudden cordiality
so far as to shake her by the hand, which she hastily wiped, as
soon as she grasped my intention, on her apron. When I had
finished shaking it, that flabby red hand, I did not let it go. But I
took one finger between the tips of mine, drew it towards me and
gazed at it. And had I had any tears to shed I should have shed
them then, in torrents, for hours. She must have wondered if I was
not on the point of making an attempt on her virtue. I gave her
back her hand, took the sandwiches and left her.

Martha had been a long time in my service. I was often away
from home. I had never taken leave of her in this way, but always
offhandedly, even when a prolonged absence was to be feared,
which was not the case on this occasion. Sometimes I departed
without a word to her.

Before going into my son's room I went into my own. I still
had the cigar in my mouth, but the pretty ash had fallen off. I
reproached myself with this negligence. I dissolved a sleeping-pow-
der in the milk. He asked for a report, he'll get his report. I was
going out with the tray when my eyes fell on the two albums lying
on my desk. I wondered if I might not relent, at any rate so far
as the album of duplicates was concerned. A little while ago he
had come here to fetch the thermometer. He had been a long time.
Had he taken advantage of the opportunity to secure some of his
favourite stamps? I had not time to check them all. I put down the
tray and looked for a few stamps at random, the Togo one mark
carmine with the pretty boat, the Nyassa 1901 ten reis, and several
others. I was very fond of the Nyassa. It was green and showed a
giraffe grazing off the top of a palm-tree. They were all there. That
proved nothing. It only proved that those particular stamps were
there. I finally decided that to go back on my decision, freely taken

and clearly stated, would deal a blow to my authority which it was in no condition to sustain. I did so with sorrow. My son was already sleeping. I woke him. He ate and drank, grimacing with disgust. That was all the thanks I got. I waited until the last drop, the last crumb, had disappeared. He turned to the wall and I tucked him in. I was within a hair's breadth of kissing him. Neither he nor I had uttered a word. We had no further need of words, for the time being. Besides my son rarely spoke to me unless I spoke to him. And when I did so he answered but lamely and as it were with reluctance. And yet with his little friends, when he thought I was out of the way, he was incredibly voluble. That my presence had the effect of dampening this disposition was far from displeasing me. Not one person in a hundred knows how to be silent and listen, no, nor even to conceive what such a thing means. Yet only then can you detect, beyond the fatuous clamour, the silence of which the universe is made. I desired this advantage for my son. And that he should hold aloof from those who pride themselves on their eagle gaze. I had not struggled, toiled, suffered, made good, lived like a Hottentot, so that my son should do the same. I tiptoed out. I quite enjoyed playing my parts through to the bitter end.

Since in this way I shirked the issue, have I to apologise for saying so? I let fall this suggestion for what it is worth. And perfunctorily. For in describing this day I am once more he who suffered it, who crammed it full of futile anxious life, with no other purpose than his own stultification and the means of not doing what he had to do. And as then my thoughts would have none of Molloy, so tonight my pen. This confession has been preying on my mind for some time past. To have made it gives me no relief.

I reflected with bitter satisfaction that if my son lay down and died by the wayside, it would be none of my doing. To every man his own responsibilities. I know of some they do not keep awake.

I said, There is something in this house tying my hands. A man like me cannot forget, in his evasions, what it is he evades. I went down to the garden and moved about in the almost total darkness. If I had not known my garden so well I would have blundered into my shrubberies, or my bee-hives. My cigar had gone out unnoticed. I shook it and put it in my pocket, intending to discard it in the ash-tray, or in the waste-paper basket, later on. But the next day, far from Turdy, I found it in my pocket and indeed not without satisfaction. For I was able to get a few more puffs out of it. To discover the cold cigar between my teeth, to spit it out, to search for it in the dark, to pick it up, to wonder what I should do with it, to shake it needlessly and put it in my pocket, to conjure up the ash-tray and the waste-paper basket, these were merely the principal stages of a sequence which I spun out for a quarter of an hour at least. Others concerned the dog Zulu, the perfumes sharpened tenfold by the rain and whose sources I amused myself exploring, in my head and with my hands, a neighbour's light, another's noise, and so on. My son's window was faintly lit. He liked sleeping with a night-light beside him. I sometimes felt it was wrong of me to let him humour this weakness. Until quite recently he could not sleep unless he had his woolly bear to hug. When he had forgotten the bear (Baby Jack) I would forbid the night-light. What would I have done that day without my son to distract me? My duty perhaps.

Finding my spirits as low in the garden as in the house, I turned to go in, saying to myself it was one of two things, either my house had nothing to do with the kind of nothingness in the midst of which I stumbled or else the whole of my little property was to blame. To adopt this latter hypothesis was to condone what I had done and, in advance, what I was to do, pending my departure. It brought me a semblance of pardon and a brief moment of factitious freedom. I therefore adopted it.

From a distance the kitchen had seemed to be in darkness. And in a sense it was. But in another sense it was not. For gluing my eyes to the window-pane I discerned a faint reddish glow which could not have come from the oven, for I had no oven, but a simple gas-stove. An oven if you like, but a gas-oven. That is to say there was a real oven too in the kitchen, but out of service. I'm sorry, but there it is, in a house without a gas-oven I would not have felt easy. In the night, interrupting my prowl, I like to go up to a window, lit or unlit, and look into the room, to see what is going on. I cover my face with my hands and peer through my fingers. I have terrified more than one neighbour in this way. He rushes

outside, finds no one. For me then from their darkness the darkest
rooms emerge, as if still instant with the vanished day or with the
light turned out a moment before, for reasons perhaps of which
less said the better. But the gloaming in the kitchen was of another
kind and came from the night-light with the red chimney which,
in Martha's room, adjoining the kitchen, burned eternally at the
feet of a litle Virgin carved in wood, hanging on the wall. Weary
of rocking herself she had gone in and lain down on her bed, leaving the door of her room open so as to miss none of the sounds
in the house. But perhaps she had gone to sleep.

I went upstairs again. I stopped at my son's door. I stooped
and applied my ear to the keyhole. Some apply the eye, I the ear,
to keyholes. I heard nothing, to my great surprise. For my son slept
noisily, with open mouth. I took good care not to open the door.
For this silence was of a nature to occupy my mind, for some little
time. I went to my room.

It was then the unheard of sight was to be seen of Moran
making ready to go without knowing where he was going, having
consulted neither map nor time-table, considered neither itinerary
nor halt, heedless of the weather outlook, with only the vaguest
notion of the outfit he would need, the time the expedition was
likely to take, the money he would require and even the very
nature of the work to be done and consequently the means to be
employed. And yet there I was whistling away while I stuffed into
my haversack a minimum of effects, similar to those I had recommended to my son. I put on my old pepper-and-salt shooting-suit
with the knee-breeches, stockings to match and a pair of stout black
boots. I bent down, my hands on my buttocks, and looked at my
legs. Knock-kneed and skeleton thin they made a poor show in
this accoutrement, unknown locally I may add. But when I left at
night, for a distant place, I wore it with pleasure, for the sake of
comfort, though I looked a sight. All I needed was a butterfly-net
to have vaguely the air of a country schoolmaster on convalescent
leave. The heavy glittering black boots, which seemed to implore a
pair of navy-blue serge trousers, gave the finishing blow to this
get-up which otherwise might have appeared, to the uninformed, an
example of well-bred bad taste. On my head, after mature hesita-

tion, I decided to wear my straw boater, yellowed by the rain. It
had lost its band, which gave it an appearance of inordinate height.
I was tempted to take my black cloak, but finally rejected it in
favour of a heavy massive-handled winter umbrella. The cloak is
a serviceable garment and I had more than one. It leaves great
freedom of movement to the arms and at the same time conceals
them. And there are times when a cloak is so to speak indispensable.
But the umbrella too has great merits. And if it had been winter, or
even autumn, instead of summer, I might have taken both. I had
already done so, with most gratifying results.

Dressed thus I could hardly hope to pass unseen. I did not
wish to. Conspicuousness is the A B C of my profession. To call
forth feelings of pity and indulgence, to be the butt of jeers and
hilarity, is indispensable. So many vent-holes in the cask of secrets.
On condition you cannot feel, nor denigrate, nor laugh. This state
was mine at will. And then there was night.

My son could only embarrass me. He was like a thousand
other boys of his age and condition. There is something about a
father that discourages derision. Even grotesque he commands a
certain respect. And when he is seen out with his young hopeful,
whose face grows longer and longer and longer with every step,
then no further work is possible. He is taken for a widower, the
gaudiest colours are of no avail, rather make things worse, he finds
himself saddled with a wife long since deceased, in child-bed as
likely as not. And my antics would be viewed as the harmless
effect of my widowhood, presumed to have unhinged my mind. I
boiled with anger at the thought of him who had shackled me
thus. If he had desired my failure he could not have devised a
better means to it. If I could have reflected with my usual calm
on the work I was required to do, it would perhaps have seemed
of a nature more likely to benefit than to suffer by the presence of
my son. But let us not go back on that. Perhaps I could pass him
off as my assistant, or a mere nephew. I would forbid him to call
me papa, or show me any sign of affection, in public, if he did not
want to get one of those clouts he so dreaded.

And if I whistled fitfully while revolving these lugubrious
thoughts, I suppose it was because I was happy at heart to leave

my house, my garden, my village, I who usually left them with
regret. Some people whistle for no reason at all. Not I. And while
I came and went in my room, tidying up, putting back my clothes
in the wardrobe and my hats in the boxes from which I had taken
them the better to make my choice, locking the various drawers,
while thus employed I had the joyful vision of myself far from
home, from the familiar faces, from all my sheet-anchors, sitting
on a milestone in the dark, my legs crossed, one hand on my thigh,
my elbow in that hand, my chin cupped in the other, my eyes fixed
on the earth as on a chessboard, coldly hatching my plans, for the
next day, for the day after, creating time to come. And then I
forgot that my son would be at my side, restless, plaintive, whining for food, whining for sleep, dirtying his drawers. I opened the
drawer of my night-table and took out a full tube of morphine
tablets, my favourite sedative.

I have a huge bunch of keys, it weighs over a pound. Not a
door, not a drawer in my house but the key to it goes with me,
wherever I go. I carry them in the right-hand pocket of my trousers,
of my breeches in this case. A massive chain, attached to my braces,
prevents me from losing them. This chain, four or five times longer
than necessary, lies, coiled, on the bunch, in my pocket. Its weight
gives me a list to the right, when I am tired, or when I forget to
counteract it, by a muscular effort.

I looked round for the last time, saw that I had neglected
certain precautions, rectified this, took up my haversack, I nearly
wrote my bagpipes, my boater, my umbrella, I hope I'm not forgetting anything, switched off the light, went out into the passage
and locked my door. That at least is clear. Immediately I heard
a strangling noise. It was my son, sleeping. I woke him. We haven't
a moment to lose, I said. Desperately he clung to his sleep. That
was natural. A few hours' sleep however deep are not enough for
an organism in the first stages of puberty suffering from stomach
trouble. And when I began to shake him and help him out of bed,
pulling him first by the arms, then by the hair, he turned away
from me in fury, to the wall, and dug his nails into the mattress.
I had to muster all my strength to overcome his resistance. But I
had hardly freed him from the bed when he broke from my hold,

threw himself down on the floor and rolled about, screaming with anger and defiance. The fun was beginning already. This disgusting exhibition left me no choice but to use my umbrella, holding it by the end with both hands. But a word on the subject of my boater, before I forget. Two holes were bored in the brim, one on either side of course, I had bored them myself, with my little gimlet. And in these holes I had secured the ends of an elastic long enough to pass under my chin, under my jaws rather, but not too long, for it had to hold fast, under my jaws rather. In this way, however great my exertions, my boater stayed in its place, which was on my head. Shame on you, I cried, you ill-bred little pig! I would get angry if I were not careful. And anger is a luxury I cannot afford. For then I go blind, blood veils my eyes and I hear what the great Gustave heard, the benches creaking in the court of assizes. Oh it is not without scathe that one is gentle, courteous, reasonable, patient, day after day, year after year. I threw down my umbrella and ran from the room. On the stairs I met Martha coming up, capless, dishevelled, her clothes in disorder. What's going on? she cried. I looked at her. She went back to her kitchen. Trembling I hastened to the shed, seized my axe, went into the yard and began hacking madly at an old chopping-block that lay there and on which in winter, tranquilly, I split my logs. Finally the blade sank into it so deeply that I could not get it out. The efforts I made to do so brought me, with exhaustion, calm. I went upstairs again. My son was dressing. He was crying. Everybody was crying. I helped him put on his knapsack. I told him not to forget his raincoat. He began to put it in his knapsack. I told him to carry it over his arm, for the moment. It was nearly midnight. I picked up my umbrella. Intact. Get on, I said. He went out of the room which I paused for a moment to survey, before I followed him. It was a shambles. The night was fine, in my humble opinion. Scents filled the air. The gravel crunched under our feet. No, I said, this way. I entered the little wood. My son floundered behind me, bumping into the trees. He did not know how to find his way in the dark. He was still young, the words of reproach died on my lips. I stopped. Take my hand, I said. I might have said, Give me your hand. I said, Take my hand. Strange. But the path was too narrow

for us to walk abreast. So I put my hand behind me and my son
grasped it, gratefully I fancied. So we came to the little wicket-gate.
It was locked. I unlocked it and stood aside, to let my son precede
me. I turned back to look at my house. It was partly hidden by the
little wood. The roof's serrated ridge, the single chimney-stack with
its four flues, stood out faintly against the sky spattered with a
few dim stars. I offered my face to the black mass of fragrant
vegetation that was mine and with which I could do as I pleased
and never be gainsaid. It was full of songbirds, their heads under
their wings, fearing nothing, for they knew me. My trees, my bushes,
my flower-beds, my tiny lawns, I used to think I loved them. If I
sometimes cut a branch, a flower, it was solely for their good, that
they might increase in strength and happiness. And I never did it
without a pang. Indeed if the truth were known, I did not do it
at all, I got Christy to do it. I grew no vegetables. Not far off was
the hen-house. When I said I had turkeys, and so on, I lied. All
I had was a few hens. My grey hen was there, not on the perch with
the others, but on the ground, in a corner, in the dust, at the mercy
of the rats. The cock no longer sought her out to tread her angrily.
The day was at hand, if she did not take a turn for the better, when
the other hens would join forces and tear her to pieces, with their
beaks and claws. All was silent. I have an extremely sensitive ear.
Yet I have no ear for music. I could just hear that adorable murmur
of tiny feet, of quivering feathers and feeble, smothered clucking
that hen-houses make at night and that dies down long before dawn.
How often I had listened to it, entranced, in the evening, saying,
Tomorrow I am free. And so I turned again a last time towards
my little all, before I left it, in the hope of keeping it.

In the lane, having locked the wicket-gate, I said to my son,
Left. I had long since given up going for walks with my son, though
I sometimes longed to do so. The least outing with him was torture,
he lost his way so easily. Yet when alone he seemed to know all the
short cuts. When I sent him to the grocer's, or to Mrs Clement's,
or even further afield, on the road to V for grain, he was back in
half the time I would have taken for the journey myself, and without having run. For I did not want my son to be seen capering
in the streets like the little hooligans he frequented on the sly. No,

I wanted him to walk like his father, with rapid steps, his head up, his breathing even and economical, his arms swinging, looking neither to left nor right, apparently oblivious to everything and in reality missing nothing. But with me he invariably took the wrong turn, a crossing or a simple corner was all he needed to stray from the right road, it of my election. I do not think he did this on purpose. But leaving everything to me he did not heed what he was doing, or look where he was going, and went on mechanically plunged in a kind of dream. It was as though he let himself be sucked in out of sight by every opening that offered. So that we had got into the habit of taking our walks separately. And the only walk we regularly took together was that which led us, every Sunday, from home to church and, mass over, from church to home. Caught up then in the slow tide of the faithful my son was not alone with me. But he was part of that docile herd going yet again to thank God for his goodness and to implore his mercy and forgiveness, and then returning, their souls made easy, to other gratifications.

I waited for him to come back, then spoke the words calculated to settle this matter once and for all. Get behind me, I said, and keep behind me. This solution had its points, from several points of view. But was he capable of keeping behind me? Would not the time be bound to come when he would raise his head and find himself alone, in a strange place, and when I, waking from my reverie, would turn and find him gone? I toyed briefly with the idea of attaching him to me by means of a long rope, its two ends tied about our waists. There are various ways of attracting attention and I was not sure that this was one of the good ones. And he might have undone his knots in silence and escaped, leaving me to go on my way alone, followed by a long rope trailing in the dust, like a burgess of Calais. Until such time as the rope, catching on some fixed or heavy object, should stop me dead in my stride. We should have needed, not the soft silent rope, but a chain, which was not to be dreamt of. And yet I did dream of it, for an instant I amused myself dreaming of it, imagining myself in a world less ill contrived and wondering how, having nothing more than a simple chain, without collar or band or gyves or fetters of any kind, I could chain my son to me in such a way as to prevent him from ever shaking me off again. It was a simple problem of toils and knots and I could have solved it at a pinch. But already I was called elsewhere by the image of my son no longer behind me, but before me. Thus in the rear I could keep my eye on him and intervene, at the least false movement he might make. But apart from having other parts to play, during this expedition, than those of keeper and sick-nurse, the prospect was more than I could bear of being unable to move a step without having before my eyes my son's sullen plump body. Come here! I cried. For on hearing me say we were to go to the left he had gone to the left, as if his dearest wish was to infuriate me. Slumped over my umbrella, my head sunk as beneath a malediction, the fingers of my free hand between two slats of the wicket, I no more stirred than if I had been of stone. So he came back a second time. I tell you to keep behind me and you go before me, I said.

It was the summer holidays. His school cap was green with initials and a boar's head, or a deer's, in gold braid on the front. It lay plumb on his big blond skull as precise as a lid on a pot. There is something about this strict sit of hats and caps that never fails to exasperate me. As for his raincoat, instead of carrying it folded over his arm, or flung across his shoulder, as I had told him, he had rolled it in a ball and was holding it with both hands, on his belly. There he was before me, his big feet splayed, his knees sagging, his stomach sticking out, his chest sunk, his chin in the air, his mouth open, in the attitude of a veritable half-wit. I myself must have looked as if only the support of my umbrella and the wicket were keeping me from falling. I managed finally to articulate, Are you capable of following me? He did not answer. But I seized his thoughts as clearly as if he had spoken them, namely, And you, are you capable of leading me? Midnight struck, from the steeple of my beloved church. It did not matter. I was gone from home. I sought in my mind, where all I need is to be found, what treasured possession he was likely to have about him. I hope, I said, you have not forgotten your scout-knife, we might need it. This knife comprised, apart from the five or six indispensable blades, a cork-screw, a tin-opener, a punch, a screw-driver, a claw, a gouge for removing stones from hooves and I know not what other futilities besides. I had given it to him myself, on the occasion of his first first prize for history and geography, subjects which, at the school he attended, were for obscure reasons regarded as inseparable. The veriest dunce when it came to literature and the so-called exact sciences, he had no equal for the dates of battles, revolutions, restorations and other exploits of the human race, in its slow ascension towards the light, and for the configuration of frontiers and the heights of mountain peaks. He deserved his scout-knife. Don't tell me you've left it behind, I said. Not likely, he said, with pride and satisfaction, tapping his pocket. Then give it to me, I said. Naturally he did not answer. Prompt obedience was contrary to his habits. Give me that knife! I cried. He gave it to me. What could he do, alone with me in the night that tells no tales? It was for his own good, to save him from getting lost. For where a scout's knife is, there will his heart be also, unless he can afford to buy another, which was not the case with my son. For he never had any money in his pocket, not needing it. But every penny he received, and he did not receive many, he deposited first in his savings-box, then in the savings-bank, where they were entered in a book that remained in my possession. He would doubtless at that moment with pleasure have cut my throat, with that selfsame knife I was putting so placidly in my pocket. But he was still a little on the young side, my son, a little on the soft side, for the great deeds of vengeance. But time was on his side and he consoled himself perhaps with that thought, foolish though he was. Be that as it may, he kept back his tears, for which I was obliged to him. I straightened myself and laid my hand on his shoulder, saying, Patience, my child, patience. The awful thing in affairs of this kind is that when you have the will you do not have the way, and vice versa. But of that my unfortunate son could as yet have no suspicion, he must have thought that the rage which distorted his features and made him tremble would never leave him till the day he could vent it as it deserved. And not even then. Yes, he must have felt his soul the soul of a pocket Monte-Cristo, with whose antics as adumbrated in the Schoolboys' Classics he was needless to say familiar. Then with a good clap on that impotent back I said, Off we go. And off indeed I did go, what is more, and my son drew out behind me. I had left, accompanied by my son, in accordance with instructions received.

I have no intention of relating the various adventures which befell us, me and my son, together and singly, before we came to the Molloy country. It would be tedious. But that is not what stops me. All is tedious, in this relation that is forced upon me. But I shall conduct it in my own way, up to a point. And if it has not the good fortune to give satisfaction, to my employer, if there are passages that give offence to him and to his colleagues, then so much the worse for us all, for them all, for there is no worse for me. That is to say, I have not enough imagination to imagine it. And yet I have more than before. And if I submit to this paltry scrivening which is not of my province, it is for reasons very different from those that might be supposed. I am still obeying orders, if you like, but no longer out of fear. No, I am still afraid, but simply from force of habit. And the voice I listen to needs no Gaber to make it heard. For it is within me and exhorts me to continue to the end the faithful servant I have always been, of a cause that is not mine, and patiently fulfil in all its bitterness my calamitous part, as it was my will, when I had a will, that others should. And this with hatred in my heart, and scorn, of my master and his designs. Yes, it is rather an ambiguous voice and not always easy to follow, in its reasonings and decrees. But I follow it none the less, more or less, I follow it in this sense, that I know what it means, and in this sense, that I do what it tells me. And I do not think there are many voices of which as much may be said. And I feel I shall follow it from this day forth, no matter what it commands. And when it ceases, leaving me in doubt and darkness, I shall wait for it to come back, and do nothing, even though the whole world, through the channel of its innumerable authorities speaking with one accord, should enjoin upon me this and that, under pain of unspeakable punishments. But this evening, this morning, I have drunk a little more than usual and tomorrow I may be of a different mind. It also tells me, this voice I am only just beginning to know, that the memory of this work brought scrupulously to a close will help me to endure the long anguish of vagrancy and freedom. Does this mean I shall one day be banished from my house, from my garden, lose my trees, my lawns, my birds of which the least is known to me and the way all its own it has of singing, of flying, of coming up to me or fleeing at my coming, lose and be banished from the absurd comforts of my home where all is snug and neat and all those things at hand without which I could not bear being a man, where my enemies cannot reach me, which it was my life's work to build, to adorn, to perfect, to keep? I am too old to lose all this, and begin again, I am too old! Quiet Moran, quiet. No emotion, please.

I was saying I would not relate all the vicissitudes of the journey from my country to Molloy's, for the simple reason that I do not intend to. And in writing these lines I know in what danger I am of offending him whose favour I know I should court, now more than ever. But I write them all the same, and with a firm hand weaving inexorably back and forth and devouring my page with the indifference of a shuttle. But some I shall relate briefly, because that seems to me desirable, and in order to give some idea of the methods of my full maturity. But before coming to that I shall say what little I knew, on leaving my home, about the Molloy country, so different from my own. For it is one of the features of this penance that I may not pass over what is over and straightway come to the heart of the matter. But that must again be unknown to me which is no longer so and that again fondly believed which then I fondly believed, at my setting out. And if I occasionally break this rule, it is only over details of little importance. And in the main I observe it. And with such zeal that I am far more he who finds than he who tells what he has found, now as then, most of the time, I do not exaggerate. And in the silence of my room, and all over as far as I am concerned, I know scarcely any better where I am going and what awaits me than the night I clung to the wicket, beside my idiot of a son, in the lane. And it would not surprise me if I deviated, in the pages to follow, from the true and exact succession of events. But I do not think even Sisyphus is required to scratch himself, or to groan, or to rejoice, as the fashion is now, always at the same appointed places. And it may even be they are not too particular about the route he takes provided it gets him to his destination safely and on time. And perhaps he thinks each journey is the first. This would keep hope alive, would it not, hellish hope. Whereas to see yourself doing the same thing endlessly over and over again fills you with satisfaction.

By the Molloy country I mean that narrow region whose administrative limits he had never crossed and presumably never would, either because he was forbidden to, or because he had no wish to, or of course because of some extraordinary fortuitous conjunction of circumstances. This region was situated in the north, I mean in relation to mine, less bleak, and comprised a settlement, dignified by some with the name of market-town, by others regarded as no more than a village, and the surrounding country. This market-town, or village, was, I hasten to say, called Bally, and represented, with its dependent lands, a surface area of five or six square miles at the most. In modern countries this is what I think is called a commune, or a canton, I forget, but there exists with us no abstract and generic term for such territorial subdivisions. And to express them we have another system, of singular beauty and simplicity, which consists in saying Bally (since we are talking of Bally) when you mean Bally and Ballyba when you mean Bally plus its domains and Ballybaba when you mean the domains exclusive of Bally itself. I myself for example lived, and come to think of it still live, in Turdy, hub of Turdyba. And in the evening, when I went for a stroll, in the country outside Turdy, to get a breath of fresh air, it was the fresh air of Turdybaba that I got, and no other.

Ballybaba, in spite of its limited range, could boast of a certain diversity. Pastures so-called, a little bogland, a few copses and, as you neared its confines, undulating and almost smiling aspects, as if Ballybaba was glad to go no further.

But the principal beauty of this region was a kind of strangled creek which the slow grey tides emptied and filled, emptied and filled. And the people came flocking from the town, unromantic people, to admire this spectacle. Some said, There is nothing more beautiful than these wet sands. Others, High tide is the best time to see the creek of Ballyba. How lovely then that leaden water, you would swear it was stagnant, if you did not know it was not. And yet others held it was like an underground lake. But all were agreed, like the inhabitants of Blackpool, that their town was on the sea. And they had Bally-on-Sea printed on their notepaper.

The population of Ballyba was small. I confess this thought gave me great satisfaction. The land did not lend itself to cultivation. No sooner did a tilth, or a meadow, begin to be sizeable than it fell foul of a sacred grove or a stretch of marsh from which nothing could be obtained beyond a little inferior turf or scraps of bogoak used for making amulets, paper-knives, napkin-rings, rosaries and other knick-knacks. Martha's madonna, for example, came from Ballyba. The pastures, in spite of the torrential rains, were exceedingly meagre and strewn with boulders. Here only quitchweed grew in abundance, and a curious bitter blue grass fatal to cows and horses, though tolerated apparently by the ass, the goat and the black sheep. What then was the source of Ballyba's prosperity? I'll tell you. No, I'll tell you nothing. Nothing.

That then is a part of what I thought I knew about Ballyba when I left home. I wonder if I was not confusing it with some other place.

Some twenty paces from my wicket-gate the lane skirts the graveyard wall. The lane descends, the wall rises, higher and higher. Soon you are faring below the dead. It is there I have my plot in perpetuity. As long as the earth endures that spot is mine, in theory. Sometimes I went and looked at my grave. The stone was up already. It was a simple Latin cross, white. I wanted to have my name put on it, with the here lies and the date of my birth. Then all it would have wanted was the date of my death. They would not let me. Sometimes I smiled, as if I were dead already.

We walked for several days, by sequestered ways. I did not want to be seen on the highways.

The first day I found the butt of Father Ambrose's cigar. Not only had I not thrown it away, in the ash-tray, in the waste-paper basket, but I had put it in my pocket, when changing my suit. That had happened unbeknown to me. I looked at it in astonishment, lit it, took a few puffs, threw it away. This was the outstanding event of the first day.

I showed my son how to use his pocket-compass. This gave him great pleasure. He was behaving well, better than I had hoped. On the third day I gave him back his knife.

The weather was kind. We easily managed our ten miles a day. We slept in the open. Safety first.

I showed my son how to make a shelter out of branches. He was in the scouts, but knew nothing. Yes, he knew how to make a camp fire. At every halt he implored me to let him exercise this talent. I saw no point in doing so.

We lived on tinned food which I sent him to get in the villages. He was that much use to me. We drank the water of the streams.

All these precautions were assuredly useless. One day in a field I saw a farmer I knew. He was coming towards us. I turned immediately, took my son by the arm and led him away in the direction we were coming from. The farmer overtook us, as I had foreseen. Having greeted me, he asked where we were going. It must have been his field. I replied that we were going home. Fortunately we had not yet left it far behind. Then he asked me where we had been. Perhaps one of his cows had been stolen, or one of his pigs. Out walking, I said. I'd give you a lift and welcome, he said, but I won't be leaving till night. Oh how very unfortunate, I said. If you care to wait, he said, you're very welcome. I declined with thanks. Fortunately it was not yet midday. There was nothing strange in not wanting to wait till night. Well, safe home, he said. We made a wide detour and turned our faces to the north again.

These precautions were doubtless exaggerated. The right thing would have been to travel by night and hide during the day, at least in the early stages. But the weather was so fine I could not bring myself to do it. My pleasure was not my sole consideration, but it was a consideration! Such a thing had never happened to me before, in the course of my work. And our snail's pace! I cannot have been in a hurry to arrive.

I gave fitful thought, while basking in the balm of the warm summer days, to Gaber's instructions. I could not reconstruct them to my entire satisfaction. In the night, under the boughs, screened from the charms of nature, I devoted myself to this problem. The sounds my son made during his sleep hindered me considerably.

Sometimes I went out of the shelter and walked up and down, in the dark. Or I sat down with my back against a trunk, drew my feet up under me, took my legs in my arms and rested my chin on my knee. Even in this posture I could throw no light on the matter. What was I looking for exactly? It is hard to say. I was looking for what was wanting to make Gaber's statement complete. I felt he must have told me what to do with Molloy once he was found. My particular duties never terminated with the running to earth. That would have been too easy. But I had always to deal with the client in one way or another, according to instructions. Such operations took on a multitude of forms, from the most vigorous to the most discreet. The Yerk affair, which took me nearly three months to conclude successfully, was over on the day I succeeded in possessing myself of his tiepin and destroying it. Establishing contact was the least important part of my work. I found Yerk on the third day. I was never required to prove I had succeeded, my word was enough. Youdi must have had some way of verifying. Sometimes I was asked for a report.

On another occasion my mission consisted in bringing the person to a certain place at a certain time. A most delicate affair, for the person concerned was not a woman. I have never had to deal with a woman. I regret it. I don't think Youdi had much interest in them. That reminds me of the old joke about the female soul. Question, Have women a soul? Answer, Yes. Question, Why? Answer, In order that they may be damned. Very witty. Fortunately I had been allowed considerable licence as to the day. The hour was the important thing, not the date. He came to the appointed place and there I left him, on some pretext or other. He was a nice youth, rather sad and silent. I vaguely remember having invented some story about a woman. Wait, it's coming back. Yes, I told him she had been in love with him for six months and greatly desired to meet him in some secluded place. I even gave her name. Quite a well-known actress. Having brought him to the place appointed by her, it was only natural I should withdraw, out of delicacy. I can see him still, looking after me. I fancy he would have liked me for a friend. I don't know what became of him. I lost interest in my patients, once I had finished with them. I may even truthfully say I

never saw one of them again, subsequently, not a single one. No conclusions need be drawn from this. Oh the stories I could tell you if
I were easy. What a rabble in my head, what a gallery of moribunds. Murphy, Watt, Yerk, Mercier and all the others. I would
never have believed that—yes, I believe it willingly. Stories, stories.
I have not been able to tell them. I shall not be able to tell this one.

I could not determine therefore how I was to deal with Molloy,
once I had found him. The directions which Gaber must certainly
have given me with reference to this had gone clean out of my head.
That is what came of wasting the whole of that Sunday on stupid-
ities. There was no good my saying, Let me see now, what is the
usual thing? There were no usual things, in my instructions. Admittedly there was one particular operation that recurred from time
to time, but not often enough to be, with any degree of probability,
the one I was looking for. But even if it had always figured in my instructions, except on one single occasion, then that single occasion
would have been enough to tie my hands, I was so scrupulous.

I told myself I had better give it no more thought, that the first
thing to do was to find Molloy, that then I would devise something,
that there was no hurry, that the thing would come back to me when
I least expected it and that if, having found Molloy, I still did not
know what to do with him, I could always manage to get in touch
with Gaber without Youdi's knowing. I had his address just as he
had mine. I would send him a telegram, How deal with M? To give
me an explicit reply, though in terms if necessary veiled, was not
beyond his powers. But was there a telegraph in Ballyba? But I
also told myself, being only human, that the longer I took to find
Molloy the greater my chances of remembering what I was to do
with him. And we would have peaceably pursued our way on foot,
but for the following incident.

One night, having finally succeeded in falling asleep beside
my son as usual, I woke with a start, feeling as if I had just been
dealt a violent blow. It's all right, I am not going to tell you a
dream properly so called. It was pitch dark in the shelter. I listened
attentively without moving. I heard nothing save the snoring and
gasping of my son. I was about to conclude as usual that it was
just another bad dream when a fulgurating pain went through my

knee. This then was the explanation of my sudden awakening.
The sensation could indeed well be compared to that of a blow,
such as I fancy a horse's hoof might give. I waited anxiously for
it to recur, motionless and hardly breathing, and, of course, sweat-
ing. I acted in a word precisely as one does, if my information
was correct, at such a juncture. And sure enough the pain did
recur a few minutes later, but not so bad as the first time, as the
second rather. Or did it only seem less bad to me because I was
expecting it? Or because I was getting used to it already? I think
not. For it recurred again, several times, and each time less bad
than the time before, and finally subsided altogether so that I was
able to get to sleep again more or less reassured. But before getting
to sleep again I had time to remember that the pain in question
was not altogether new to me. For I had felt it before, in my bathroom, when giving my son his enema. But then it had only attacked
me once and never recurred, till now. And I went to sleep again
wondering, by way of lullaby, whether it had been the same knee
then as the one which had just excruciated me, or the other. And
that is a thing I have never been able to determine. And my son
too, when asked, was incapable of telling me which of my two
knees I had rubbed in front of him, with iodex, the night we left.
And I went to sleep again a little reassured, saying, It's a touch
of neuralgia brought on by all the tramping and trudging and the
chill damp nights, and promising myself to procure a packet of
thermogene wool, with the pretty demon on the outside, at the first
opportunity. Such is the rapidity of thought. But there was more
to come. For waking again towards dawn, this time in consequence
of a natural need, and with a mild erection, to make things more
lifelike, I was unable to get up. That is to say I did get up finally
to be sure, I simply had to, but by dint of what exertions! Unable,
unable, it's easy to talk about being unable, whereas in reality
nothing is more difficult. Because of the will I suppose, which the
least opposition seems to lash into a fury. And this explains no
doubt how it was I despaired at first of ever bending my leg again
and then, a little later, through sheer determination, did succeed
in bending it, slightly. The anchylosis was not total! I am still
talking about my knee. But was it the same one that had waked

me early in the night? I could not have sworn it was. It was not
painful. It simply refused to bend. The pain, having warned me
several times in vain, had no more to say. That is how I saw it.
It would have been impossible for me to kneel, for example, for
no matter how you kneel you must always bend both knees, unless
you adopt an attitude frankly grotesque and impossible to main-
tain for more than a few seconds, I mean with the bad leg stretched
out before you, like a Caucasian dancer. I examined the bad knee
in the light of my torch. It was neither red nor swollen. I fiddled
with the knee-cap. It felt like a clitoris. All this time my son was
puffing like a grampus. He had no suspicion of what life could do
to you. I too was innocent. But I knew it.

The sky was that horrible colour which heralds dawn. Things
steal back into position for the day, take their stand, sham dead.
I sat down cautiously, and I must say with a certain curiosity, on
the ground. Anyone else would have tried to sit down as usual,
off-handedly. Not I. New as this new cross was I at once found the
most comfortable way of being crushed. But when you sit down
on the ground you must sit down tailor-wise, or like a foetus,
these are so to speak the only possible positions, for a beginner.
So that I was not long in letting myself fall back flat on my back.
And I was not long either in making the following addition to the
sum of my knowledge, that when of the innumerable attitudes adopted
unthinkingly by the normal man all are precluded but two or three,
then these are enhanced. I would have sworn just the opposite, but
for this experience. Yes, when you can neither stand nor sit with
comfort, you take refuge in the horizontal, like a child in its
mother's lap. You explore it as never before and find it possessed
of unsuspected delights. In short it becomes infinite. And if in spite
of all you come to tire of it in the end, you have only to stand up,
or indeed sit up, for a few seconds. Such are the advantages of a
local and painless paralysis. And it would not surprise me if the
great classical paralyses were to offer analogous and perhaps even
still more unspeakable satisfactions. To be literally incapable of
motion at last, that must be something! My mind swoons when I
think of it. And mute into the bargain! And perhaps as deaf as a
post! And who knows as blind as a bat! And as likely as not your

memory a blank! And just enough brain intact to allow you to
exult! And to dread death like a regeneration.

I considered the problem of what I should do if my leg did
not get better or got worse. I watched, through the branches, the
sky sinking. The sky sinks in the morning, this fact has been insufficiently observed. It stoops, as if to get a better look. Unless
it is the earth that lifts itself up, to be approved, before it sets out.

I shall not expound my reasoning. I could do so easily, so
easily. Its conclusion made possible the composition of the following passage.

Did you have a good night? I said, as soon as my son opened
his eyes. I could have waked him, but no, I let him wake naturally.
Finally he told me he did not feel well. My son's replies were often
beside the point. Where are we, I said, and what is the nearest
village? He named it. I knew it, I had been there, it was a small
town, luck was on our side. I even had a few acquaintances, among
its inhabitants. What day is it? I said. He specified the day without
a moment's hesitation. And he had only just regained consciousness! I told you he had a genius for history and geography. It was
from him I learned that Condom is on the Baise. Good, I said, off
you go now to Hole, it'll take you—I worked it out—at the most
three hours. He stared at me in astonishment. There, I said, buy
a bicycle to fit you, second-hand for preference. You can go up to
five pounds. I gave him five pounds, in ten-shilling notes. It must
have a very strong carrier, I said, if it isn't very strong get it
changed, for a very strong one. I was trying to be clear. I asked
him if he was pleased. He did not look pleased. I repeated these
instructions and asked him again if he was pleased. He looked if
anything stupefied. A consequence perhaps of the great joy he felt.
Perhaps he could not believe his ears. Do you understand if nothing else? I said. What a boon it is from time to time, a little real
conversation. Tell me what you are to do, I said. It was the only
way of knowing if he understood. Go to Hole, he said, fifteen miles
away. Fifteen miles! I cried. Yes, he said. All right, I said, go on.
And buy a bicycle, he said. I waited. Silence. A bicycle! I cried.
But there are millions of bicycles in Hole! What kind of bicycle?
He reflected. Second-hand, he said, at a venture. And if you can't

find one second-hand? I said. You told me second-hand, he said.
I remained silent for some time. And if you can't find one second-
hand, I said at last, what will you do? You didn't tell me, he said.
What a restful change it is from time to time, a little dialogue.
How much money did I give you? I said. He counted the notes.
Four pounds ten, he said. Count them again, I said. He counted
them again. Four pounds ten, he said. Give it to me, I said. He
gave me the notes and I counted them. Four pounds ten. I gave
you five, I said. He did not answer, he let the figures speak for
themselves. Had he stolen ten shillings and hidden them on his
person? Empty your pockets, I said. He began to empty them. It
must not be forgotten that all this time I was lying down. He did
not know I was ill. Besides I was not ill. I looked vaguely at the
objects he was spreading out before me. He took them out of his
pockets one by one, held them delicately between finger and thumb,
turned them this way and that before my eyes and laid them
finally on the ground beside me. When a pocket was emptied he
pulled out its lining and shook it. Then a little cloud of dust arose.
I was very soon overcome by the absurdity of this verification. I
told him to stop. Perhaps he was hiding the ten shillings up his
sleeve, or in his mouth. I should have had to get up and search
him myself, inch by inch. But then he would have seen I was ill.
Not that I was exactly ill. And why did I not want him to know I
was ill? I don't know. I could have counted the money I had left.
But what use would that have been? Did I even know the amount
I had brought with me? No. To me too I cheerfully applied the
maieutic method. Did I know how much I had spent? No. Usually
I kept the most rigorous accounts when away on business and was
in a position to justify my expenditure down to the last penny.
This time no. For I was throwing my money away with as little
concern as if I had been travelling for my pleasure. Let us suppose
I am wrong, I said, and that I only gave you four pounds ten. He
was calmly picking up the objects littered on the ground and putting
them back in his pockets. How could he be made to understand?
Stop that and listen, I said. I gave him the notes. Count them, I
said. He counted them. How much? I said. Four pounds ten, he
said. Ten what? I said. Ten shillings, he said. You have four

pounds ten shillings? I said. Yes, he said. It was not true, I had
given him five. You agree, I said. Yes, he said. And why do you
think I have given you all that money? I said. His face brightened.
To buy a bicycle, he said, without hesitation. Do you imagine a
second-hand bicycle costs four pounds ten shillings? I said. I don't
know, he said. I did not know either. But that was not the point.
What did I tell you exactly? I said. We racked our brains together.
Second-hand for preference, I said finally, that's what I told you.
Ah, he said. I am not giving this duet in full. Just the main themes.
I didn't tell you second-hand, I said, I told you second-hand for
preference. He had started picking up his things again. Will you
stop that, I cried, and pay attention to what I am saying. He osten-
tatiously let fall a big ball of tangled string. The ten shillings were
perhaps inside it. You see no difference between second-hand and
second-hand for preference, I said, do you? I looked at my watch.
It was ten o'clock. I was only making our ideas more confused.
Stop trying to understand, I said, just listen to what I am going
to say, because I shall not say it twice. He came over to me and
knelt down. You would have thought I was about to breathe my
last. Do you know what a new bicycle is? I said. Yes papa, he said.
Very well, I said, if you can't find a second-hand bicycle buy a new
bicycle. I repeat. I repeated. I who had said I would not repeat.
Now tell me what you are to do, I said. I added, Take your face
away, your breath stinks. I almost added, You don't brush your
teeth and you complain of having abcesses, but I stopped myself
in time. It was not the moment to introduce another theme. I repeated, Tell me what you are to do. He pondered. Go to Hole, he
said, fifteen miles away—. Don't worry about the miles, I said.
You're in Hole. What for ? No, I can't. Finally he understood.
Who is this bicycle for, I said, Goering? He had not yet grasped
that the bicycle was for him. Admittedly he was nearly my size
already. As for the carrier, I might just as well not have mentioned
it. But in the end he had the whole thing off pat. So much so that
he actually asked me what he was to do if he had not enough
money. Come back here, and ask me, I said. I had naturally foreseen, while reflecting on all these matters before my son woke, that
he might have trouble with people asking him how he came by so

much money and he so young. And I knew what he was to do in
that event, namely go and see, or send for, the police-sergeant,
give his name and say it was I, Jacques Moran, ostensibly at home
in Turdy, who had sent him to buy a bicycle in Hole. Here
obviously two distinct operations were involved, the first consisting in foreseeing the difficulty (before my son woke), the second in
overcoming it (at the news that Hole was the nearest locality). But
there was no question of my conveying instructions of such complexity. But don't worry, I said, you've enough and to spare to buy
yourself a good bicycle. I added, And bring it back here as fast as
you can. You had to allow for everything with my son. He could
never have guessed what to do with the bicycle once he had it. He
was capable of hanging about Hole, under God knows what conditions, waiting for further instructions. He asked me what was
wrong. I must have winced. I'm sick of the sight of you, I said,
that's what's wrong. And I asked him what he was waiting for. I
don't feel well, he said. When he asked me how I was I said nothing, and when no one asked him anything he announced he was
not feeling well. Are you not pleased, I said, to have a nice brand-
new bicycle, all your own? I was decidedly set on hearing him say
he was pleased. But I regretted my phrase, it could only add to his
confusion. But perhaps this family chat has lasted long enough.
He left the shelter and when I judged he was at a safe distance I
left it too, painfully. He had gone about twenty paces. Leaning
nonchalantly against a tree-trunk, my good leg boldly folded across
the other, I tried to look light-hearted. I hailed him. He turned.
I waved my hand. He stared at me an instant, then turned away
and went on. I shouted his name. He turned again. A lamp! I cried.
A good lamp! he did not understand. How could he have understood, at twenty paces, he who could not understand at one. He
came back towards me. I waved him away, crying, Go on! Go on!
He stopped and stared at me, his head on one side like a parrot,
utterly bewildered apparently. Foolishly, I made to stoop, to pick
up a stone or a piece of wood or a clod, anything in the way of
a projectile, and nearly fell. I reached up above my head, broke
off a live bough and hurled it violently in his direction. He spun
round and took to his heels. Really there were times I could not

understand my son. He must have known he was out of range,
even of a good stone, and yet he took to his heels. Perhaps he was
afraid I would run after him. And indeed, I think there is something
terrifying about the way I run, with my head flung back, my teeth
clenched, my elbows bent to the full and my knees nearly hitting
me in the face. And I have often caught faster runners than myself
thanks to this way of running. They stop and wait for me, rather
than prolong such a horrible outburst at their heels. As for the
lamp, we did not need a lamp. Later, when the bicycle had taken
its place in my son's life, in the round of his duties and his innocent games, then a lamp would be indispensable, to light his way
in the night. And no doubt it was in anticipation of those happy
days that I had thought of the lamp and cried out to my son to buy
a good one, that later on his comings and goings should not be
hemmed about with darkness and with dangers. And similarly I
might have told him to be careful about the bell, to unscrew the
little cap and examine it well inside, so as to make sure it was a
good bell and in good working order, before concluding the transaction, and to ring it to hear the ring it made. But we would have
time enough, later on, to see to all these things. And it would be
my joy to help my son, when the time came, to fit his bicycle
with the best lamps, both front and rear, and the best bell and the
best brakes that money could buy.

The day seemed very long. I missed my son! I busied myself
as best I could. I ate several times. I took advantage of being alone
at last, with no other witness than God, to masturbate. My son must
have had the same idea, he must have stopped on the way to
masturbate. I hope he enjoyed it more than I did. I circled the
shelter several times, thinking the exercise would benefit my knee.
I moved at quite a good speed and without much pain, but I soon
tired. After ten or eleven steps a great weariness seized hold of my
leg, a heaviness rather, and I had to stop. It went away at once and
I was able to go on. I took a little morphine. I asked myself certain
questions. Why had I not told my son to bring me back something
for my leg? Why had I hidden my condition from him? Was I
secretly glad that this had happened to me, perhaps even to the
point of not wanting to get well? I surrendered myself to the

beauties of the scene, I gazed at the trees, the fields, the sky, the birds, and I listened attentively to the sounds, faint and clear, borne to me on the air. For an instant I fancied I heard the silence mentioned, if I am not mistaken, above. Stretched out in the shelter, I brooded on the undertaking in which I was embarked. I tried again to remember what I was to do with Molloy when I found him. I dragged myself down to the stream. I lay down and looked at my reflection, then I washed my face and hands. I waited for my image to come back, I watched it as it trembled towards an ever increasing likeness. Now and then a drop, falling from my face, shattered it again. I did not see a soul all day. But towards evening I heard a prowling about the shelter. I did not move, and the footsteps died away. But a little later, having left the shelter for some reason or other, I saw a man a few paces off, standing motionless. He had his back to me. He wore a coat much too heavy for the time of the year and was leaning on a stick so massive, and so much thicker at the bottom than at the top, that it seemed more like a club. He turned and we looked at each other for some time in silence. That is to say I looked him full in the face, as I always do, to make people think I am not afraid, whereas he merely threw me a rapid glance from time to time, then lowered his eyes, less from timidity apparently than in order quietly to think over what he had just seen, before adding to it. There was a coldness in his stare, and a thrust, the like of which I never saw. His face was pale and noble, I could have done with it. I was thinking he could not be much over fifty-five when he took off his hat, held it for a moment in his hand, then put it back on his head. No resemblance to what is called raising one's hat. But I thought it advisable to nod. The hat was quite extraordinary, in shape and colour. I shall not attempt to describe it, it was like none I had ever seen. He had a huge shock of dirty snow-white hair. I had time, before he squeezed it in back under his hat, to see the way it swelled up on his skull. His face was dirty and hairy, yes, pale, noble, dirty and hairy. He made a curious movement, like a hen that puffs up its feathers and slowly dwindles till it is smaller than before. I thought he was going to depart without a word to me. But suddenly he asked me to give him a piece of bread. He ac-

companied this humiliating request with a fiery look. His accent
was that of a foreigner or of one who had lost the habit of speech.
But had I not said already with relief, at the mere sight of his back,
He's a foreigner. Would you like a tin of sardines? I said. He asked
for bread and I offered him fish. That is me all over. Bread, he said.
I went into the shelter and took the piece of bread I was keeping
for my son, who would probably be hungry when he came back.
I gave it to him. I expected him to devour it there and then. But
he broke it in two and put the pieces in his coat-pockets. Do you
mind if I look at your stick? I said. I stretched out my hand. He
did not move. I put my hand on the stick, just under his. I could
feel his fingers gradually letting go. Now it was I who held the
stick. Its lightness astounded me. I put it back in his hand. He threw
me a last look and went. It was almost dark. He walked with swift
uncertain step, often changing his course, dragging the stick like a
hindrance. I wished I could have stood there looking after him,
and time at a standstill. I wished I could have been in the middle of
a desert, under the midday sun, to look after him till he was only
a dot, on the edge of the horizon. I stayed out in the air for a long
time. Every now and then I listened. But my son did not come. Beginning to feel cold I went back into the shelter and lay down,
under my son's raincoat. But beginning to feel sleepy I went out
again and lit a big wood-fire, to guide my son towards me. When
the fire kindled I said, Why of course, now I can warm myself! I
warmed myself, rubbing my hands together after having held them
to the flame and before holding them to it again, and turning my
back to the flame and lifting the tail of my coat, and turning as on
a spit. And in the end, overcome with heat and weariness, I lay
down on the ground near the fire and fell asleep, saying, Perhaps a
spark will set fire to my clothes and I wake a living torch. And
saying many other things besides, belonging to separate and
apparently unconnected trains of thought. But when I woke it was
day again and the fire was out. But the embers were still warm. My
leg was no better, but it was no worse either. That is to say it was
perhaps a little worse, without my being in a condition to realize it,
for the simple reason that this leg was becoming a habit, mercifully. But I think not. For at the same time as I listened to my

knee, and then submitted it to various tests, I was on my guard against the effects of this habit and tried to discount them. And it was not so much Moran as another, in the secret of Moran's sensations exclusively, who said, No change, Moran, no change. This may seem impossible. I went into the copse to cut myself a stick. But having finally found a suitable branch, I remembered I had no knife. I went back to the shelter, hoping to find my son's knife among the things he had laid on the ground and neglected to pick up. It was not among them. To make up for this I came across my umbrella and said, Why cut myself a stick when I have my umbrella? And I practised walking with the help of my umbrella. And though in this way I moved no faster and no less painfully, at least I did not tire so quickly. And instead of having to stop every ten steps, to rest, I easily managed fifteen, before having to stop. And even while I rested my umbrella was a help. For I found that when I leaned upon it the heaviness in my leg, due probably to a defect in the bloodstream, disappeared even more quickly than when I stood supported only by my muscles and the tree of life. And thus equipped I no longer confined myself to circling about the shelter, as I had done the previous day, but I radiated from it in every direction. And I even gained a little knoll from which I had a better view of the expanse where my son might suddenly rise into view, at any moment. And in my mind's eye from time to time I saw him, bent over the handlebars or standing on the pedals, drawing near, and I heard him panting and I saw written on the chubby face his joy at being back at last. But at the same time I kept my eye on the shelter, which drew me with an extraordinary pull, so that to cut across from the terminus of one sally to the terminus of the next, and so on, which would have been convenient, was out of the question. But each time I had to retrace my steps, the way I had come, to the shelter, and make sure all was in order, before I sallied forth again. And I consumed the greater part of this second day in these vain comings and goings, these vigils and imaginings, but not all of it. For I also lay down from time to time in the shelter, which I was beginning to think of as my little house, to ruminate in peace on certain things, and notably on my provisions of food which were rapidly running out, so that after a meal devoured at five o'clock I was left with only two tins of sardines, a handful of biscuits and a few apples. But I also tried to remember what I was to do with Molloy, once I found him. And on myself too I pored, on me so changed from what I was. And I seemed to see myself ageing as swiftly as a day-fly. But the idea of ageing was not exactly the one which offered itself to me. And what I saw was more like a crumbling, a frenzied collapsing of all that had always protected me from all I was condemned to be. Or it was like a kind of clawing towards a light and countenance I could not name, that I had once known and long denied. But what words can describe this sensation at first all darkness and bulk, with a noise like the grinding of stones, then suddenly as soft as water flowing. And then I saw a little globe swaying up slowly from the depths, through the quiet water, smooth at first, and scarcely paler than its escorting ripples, then little by little a face, with holes for the eyes and mouth and other wounds, and nothing to show if it was a man's face or a woman's face, a young face or an old face, or if its calm too was not an effect of the water trembling between it and the light. But I confess I attended but absently to these poor figures, in which I suppose my sense of disaster sought to contain itself. And that I did not labour at them more diligently was a further index of the great changes I had suffered and of my growing resignation of being dispossessed of self. And doubtless I should have gone from discovery to discovery, concerning myself, if I had persisted. But at the first faint light, I mean in these wild shadows gathering about me, dispensed by a vision or by an effort of thought, at the first light I fled to other cares. And all had been for nothing. And he who acted thus was a stranger to me too. For it was not my nature, I mean it was not my custom, to conduct my calculations simultaneously, but separately and turn about, pushing each one as far as it would go before turning in desperation to another. Similarly the missing instructions concerning Molloy, when I felt them stirring in the depths of my memory, I turned from them in haste towards other unknowns. And I who a fortnight before would joyfully have reckoned how long I could survive on the provisions that remained, probably with reference to the question of calories and vitamins, and established in my head a series of menus asymptotically approaching nutritional zero, was now content to note feebly that I should soon be dead of inanition, if I did not succeed in renewing my provisions. So much for the second day. But one incident remains to be noted, before I go on to the third.

It was evening. I had lit my fire and was watching it take when I heard myself hailed. The voice, already so near that I started violently, was that of a man. But after this one violent start I collected myself and continued to busy myself with my fire as if nothing had happened, poking it with a branch I had torn from its tree for the purpose a little earlier and stripped of its twigs and leaves and even part of its bark, with my bare nails. I have always loved skinning branches and laying bare the pretty white glossy shaft of sapwood. But obscure feelings of love and pity for the tree held me back most of the time. And I numbered among my familiars the dragon-tree of Teneriffe that perished at the age of five thousand years, struck by lightning. It was an example of longevity. The branch was thick and full of sap and did not burn when I stuck it in the fire. I held it by the thin end. The crackling of the fire, of the writhing brands rather, for fire triumphant does not crackle, but makes an altogether different noise, had permitted the man to come right up to me, without my knowledge. If there is one thing infuriates me it is being taken myself by surprise. I continued then, in spite of my spasm of fright, hoping it had passed unnoticed, to poke the fire as if I were alone. But at the thump of his hand on my shoulder I had no choice but to do what anyone else would have done in my place, and this I achieved by suddenly spinning round in what I trust was a good imitation of fear and anger. There I was face to face with a dim man, dim of face and dim of body, because of the dark. Put it there, he said. But little by little I formed an idea of the type of individual it was. And indeed there reigned between his various parts great harmony and concord, and it could be truly said that his face was worthy of his body, and vice versa. And if I could have seen his arse, I do not doubt I should have found it on a par with the whole. What are you doing in this God-forsaken place, he said, you unexpected pleasure. And moving aside from the fire which was now burning merrily, so that its light fell full on the intruder, I could see he

was precisely the kind of pest I had thought he was, without being
sure, because of the dark. Can you tell me, he said. I shall have
to describe him briefly, though such a thing is contrary to my principles. He was on the small side, but thick-set. He wore a thick
navy-blue suit (double-breasted) of hideous cut and a pair of out-
rageously wide black shoes, with the toe-caps higher than the
uppers. This dreadful shape seems only to occur in black shoes. Do
you happen to know, he said. The fringed extremities of a dark
muffler, seven feet long at least, wound several times round his
neck, hung down his back. He had a narrow-brimmed dark blue
felt hat on his head, with a fish-hook and an artificial fly stuck
in the band, which produced a highly sporting effect. Do you hear
me? he said. But all this was nothing compared to the face which
I regret to say vaguely resembled my own, less the refinement of
course, same little abortive moustache, same little ferrety eyes,
same paraphimosis of the nose, and a thin red mouth that looked
as if it was raw from trying to shit its tongue. Hey you! he said.
I turned back to my fire. It was doing nicely. I threw more wood
on it. Do you hear me talking to you? he said. I went towards the
shelter, he barred my way, emboldened by my limp. Have you a
tongue in your head? he said. I don't know you, I said. I laughed.
I had not intended to be witty. Would you care to see my card?
he said. It would mean nothing to me, I said. He came closer to
me. Get out of my way, I said. It was his turn to laugh. You refuse
to answer? he said. I made a great effort. What do you want to
know? I said He must have thought I was weakening. That's more
like it, he said. I called to my aid the image of my son who might
arrive at any moment. I've already told you, he said. I was trembling all over. Have the goodness to tell me again, I said. To cut a
long story short he wanted to know if I had seen an old man with
a stick pass by. He described him. Badly. The voice seemed to
come to me from afar. No, I said. What do you mean no? he said.
I have seen no one, I said. And yet he passed this way, he said.
I said nothing. How long have you been here? he said. His body
too grew dim, as if coming asunder. What is your business here?
he said. Are you on night patrol? I said. He thrust his hand at
me. I have an idea I told him once again to get out of my way.

I can still see the hand coming towards me, pallid, opening and
closing. As if self-propelled. I do not know what happened then.
But a little later, perhaps a long time later, I found him stretched
on the ground, his head in a pulp. I am sorry I cannot indicate
more clearly how this result was obtained, it would have been
something worth reading. But it is not at this late stage of my
relation that I intend to give way to literature. I myself was un-
scathed, except for a few scratches I did not discover till the
following day. I bent over him. As I did so I realised my leg was
bending normally. He no longer resembled me. I took him by the
ankles and dragged him backwards into the shelter. His shoes
shone with highly polished blacking. He wore fancy socks. The
trousers slid back, disclosing the white hairless legs. His ankles
were bony, like my own. My fingers encircled them nearly. He was
wearing suspenders, one of which had come undone and was hanging loose. This detail went to my heart. Already my knee was
stiffening again. It no longer required to be supple. I went back
to the shelter and took my son's raincoat. I went back to the fire
and lay down, with the coat over me. I did not get much sleep,
but I got some. I listened to the owls. They were not eagle-owls, it
was a cry like the whistle of a locomotive. I listened to a nightin-
gale. And to distant corncrakes. If I had heard of other birds that
cry and sing at night, I should have listened to them too. I
watched the fire dying, my cheek pillowed on my hands. I watched
out for the dawn. It was hardly breaking when I got up and went
to the shelter. His legs too were on the stiff side, but there was
still some play in the hip joints, fortunately. I dragged him into
the copse, with frequent rests on the way, but without letting go
his legs, so as not to have to stoop again to pick them up. Then I
dismantled the shelter and threw the branches over the body. I
packed and shouldered the two bags, took the raincoat and the
umbrella. In a word I struck camp. But before leaving I consulted
with myself to make sure I was forgetting nothing, and without
relying on my intelligence alone, for I felt my pockets and looked
around me. And it was while feeling my pockets that I discovered
something of which my mind had been powerless to inform me,
namely that my keys were no longer there. I was not long in finding

them, scattered on the ground, the ring having broken. And to tell
the truth first I found the chain, then the keys and last the ring,
in two pieces. And since it was out of the question, even with the
help of my umbrella, to stoop each time to pick up a key, I put
down my bags, my umbrella and the coat and lay down flat on my
stomach among the keys which in this way I was able to recover
without much difficulty. And when a key was beyond my reach
I took hold of the grass and dragged myself over to it. And I
wiped each key on the grass, before putting it in my pocket, whether
it needed wiping or not. And from time to time I raised myself on
my hands, to get a better view. And in this way I located a number
of keys at some distance from me, and these I reached by rolling
over and over, like a great cylinder. And finding no more keys, I
said, There is no use my counting them, for I do not know how
many there were. And my eyes resumed their search. But finally
I said, Hell to it, I'll do with those I have. And while looking in
this way for my keys I found an ear which I threw into the copse.
And, to my even greater surprise, I found my straw hat which I
thought was on my head! One of the holes for the elastic had
expanded to the edge of the rim and consequently was no longer
a hole, but a slit. But the other had been spared and the elastic
was still in it. And finally I said, I shall rise now and, from my
full height, run my eyes over this area for the last time. Which I
did. It was then I found the ring, first one piece, then the other.
Then, finding nothing more belonging either to me or to my son, I
shouldered my bags again, jammed the straw-hat hard down on
my skull, folded my son's raincoat over my arm, caught up the
umbrella and went.

But I did not go far. For I soon stopped on the crest of a rise
from where I could survey, without fatigue, the camp-site and the
surrounding country. And I made this curious observation, that
the land from where I was, and even the clouds in the sky, were
so disposed as to lead the eyes gently to the camp, as in a painting
by an old master. I made myself as comfortable as possible.
I got rid of my various burdens and I ate a whole tin of
sardines and one apple. I lay down flat on my stomach on my
son's coat. And now I propped my elbows on the ground and my

jaws between my hands, which carried my eyes towards the horizon, and now I made a little cushion of my two hands on the ground and laid my cheek upon it, five minutes one, five minutes the other, all the while flat on my stomach. I could have made myself a pillow of the bags, but I did not, it did not occur to me. The day passed tranquilly, without incident. And the only thing that relieved the monotony of this third day was a dog. When I first saw him he was sniffing about the remains of my fire, then he went into the copse. But I did not see him come out again, either because my attention was elsewhere, or because he went out the other side, having simply, as it were, gone straight through it. I mended my hat, that is to say with the tin-opener I pierced a new hole beside the old one and made fast the elastic again. And I also mended the ring, twisting the two pieces together, and I slipped on the keys and made fast the long chain again. And to kill time I asked myself a certain number of questions and tried to answer them. For example.

Question. What had happened to the blue felt hat?
Answer.
Question. Would they not suspect the old man with the stick?
Answer. Very probably.
Question. What were his chances of exonerating himself?
Answer. Slight.
Question. Should I tell my son what had happened?
Answer. No, for then it would be his duty to denounce me.
Question. Would he denounce me?
Answer.
Question. How did I feel?
Answer. Much as usual.
Question. And yet I had changed and was still changing?
Answer. Yes.
Question. And in spite of this I felt much as usual?
Answer. Yes.
Question. How was this to be explained?
Answer.

These questions and others too were separated by more or less prolonged intervals of time not only from one another, but also from the answers appertaining to them. And the answers did not always follow in the order of the questions. But while looking for the answer, or the answers, to a given question, I found the answer, or the answers, to a question I had already asked myself in vain, in the sense that I had not been able to answer it, or I found another question, or other questions, demanding in their turn an immediate answer.

Translating myself now in imagination to the present moment, I declare the foregoing to have been written with a firm and even satisfied hand, and a mind calmer than it has been for a long time. For I shall be far away, before these lines are read, in a place where no one will dream of coming to look for me. And then Youdi will take care of me, he will not let me be punished for a fault committed in the execution of my duty. And they can do nothing to my son, rather they will commiserate with him on having had such a father, and offers of help and expressions of esteem will pour in upon him from every side.

So this third day wore away. And about five o'clock I ate my last tin of sardines and a few biscuits, with a good appetite. This left me with only a few apples and a few biscuits. But about seven o'clock my son arrived. The sun was low in the west. I must have dozed a moment, for I did not see him coming, a speck on the horizon, then rapidly bigger and bigger, as I had foreseen. But he was already between me and the camp, making for the latter, when I saw him. A wave of irritation broke over me, I jumped to my feet and began to vociferate, brandishing the umbrella. He turned and I beckoned him to join me, waving the umbrella as if I wanted to hook something with the handle. I thought for a moment he was going to defy me and continue on his way to the camp, to where the camp had been rather, for it was there no more. But finally he came towards me. He was pushing a bicycle which, when he had joined me, he let fall with a gesture signifying he could bear no more. Pick it up, I said, till I look at it. I had to admit it must once have been quite a good bicycle. I would gladly describe it, I would gladly write four thousand words on it alone. And you call that a bicycle? I said. Only half expecting him to answer me I continued to inspect it. But there

was something so strange in his silence that I looked up at him.
His eyes were starting out of his head. What's the matter, I said,
is my fly open? He let go the bicycle again. Pick it up, I said. He
picked it up. What happened to you? he said. I had a fall, I said.
A fall? he said. Yes, a fall, I cried, did you never have a fall? I
tried to remember the name of the plant that springs from the
ejaculations of the hanged and shrieks when plucked. How much
did you give for it? I said. Four pounds, he said. Four pounds!
I cried. If he had said two pounds or even thirty shillings I should
have cried, Two pounds! or Thirty shillings! the same. They asked
four pounds five, he said. Have you the receipt? I said. He did not
know what a receipt was. I described one. The money I spent on
my son's education and he did not know what a simple receipt
was. But I think he knew as well as I. For when I said to him,
Now tell me what a receipt is, he told me very prettily. I really
did not care in the least whether he had been fooled into paying
for the bicycle three or four times what it was worth or whether
on the other hand he had appropriated the best part of the purchase money for his own use. The loss would not be mine. Give
me the ten shillings, I said. I spent them, he said. Enough, enough.
He began explaining that the first day the shops had been closed,
that the second—. I said, Enough, enough. I looked at the carrier.
It was the best thing about that bicycle. It and the pump. Does
it go by any chance? I said. I had a puncture two miles from Hole,
he said, I walked the rest of the way. I looked at his shoes. Pump
it up, I said. I held the bicycle. I forget which wheel it was. As
soon as two things are nearly identical I am lost. The dirty little
twister was letting the air escape between the valve and the connection which he had purposely not screwed tight. Hold the bicycle,
I said, and give me the pump. The tyre was soon hard. I looked
at my son. He began to protest. I soon put a stop to that. Five
minutes later I felt the tyre. It was as hard as ever. I cursed him.
He took a bar of chocolate from his pocket and offered it to me.
I took it. But instead of eating it, as I longed to, and although I
have a horror of waste, I cast it from me, after a moment's hesitation, which I trust my son did not notice. Enough. We went
down the road. It was more like a path. I tried to sit down on the

carrier. The foot of my stiff leg tried to sink into the ground, into the grave. I propped myself up on one of the bags. Keep her steady, I said. I was still too low. I added the other. Its bulges dug into my buttocks. The more things resist me the more rabid I get. With time, and nothing but my teeth and nails, I would rage up from the bowels of the earth to its crust, knowing full well I had nothing to gain. And when I had no more teeth, no more nails, I would dig through the rock with my bones. Here then in a few words is the solution I arrived at. First the bags, then my son's raincoat folded in four, all lashed to the carrier and the saddle with my son's bits of string. As for the umbrella, I hooked it round my neck, so as to have both hands free to hold on to my son by the waist, under the armpits rather, for by this time my seat was higher than his. Pedal, I said. He made a despairing effort, I can well believe it. We fell. I felt a sharp pain in my shin. I was all tangled up in the back wheel. Help! I cried. My son helped me up. My stocking was torn and my leg bleeding. Happily it was the sick leg. What would I have done, with both legs out of action? I would have found a way. It was even perhaps a blessing in disguise. I was thinking of phlebotomy of course. Are you all right? I said. Yes, he said. He would be. With my umbrella I caught him a smart blow on the hamstrings, gleaming between the leg of his shorts and his stocking. He cried out. Do you want to kill us? I said. I'm not strong enough, he said, I'm not strong enough. The bicycle was all right apparently, the back wheel slightly buckled perhaps. I at once saw the error I had made. It was to have settled down in my seat, with my feet clear of the ground, before we moved off. I reflected. We'll try again, I said. I can't, he said. Don't try me too far, I said. He straddled the frame. Start off gently when I tell you, I said. I got up again behind and settled down in my seat, with my feet clear of the ground. Good. Wait till I tell you, I said. I let myself slide to one side till the foot of my good leg touched the ground. The only weight now on the back wheel was that of my sick leg, cocked up rigid at an excruciating angle. I dug my fingers into my son's jacket. Go easy, I said. The wheels began to turn. I followed, half dragged, half hopping. I trembled for my testicles

which swung a little low. Faster! I cried. He bore down on the
pedals. I bounded up to my place. The bicycle swayed, righted
itself, gained speed. Bravo! I cried, beside myself with joy. Hurrah!
cried my son. How I loathe that exclamation! I can hardly set it
down. He was as pleased as I, I do believe. His heart was beating
under my hand and yet my hand was far from his heart. Happily
it was downhill. Happily I had mended my hat, or the wind would
have blown it away. Happily the weather was fine and I no longer
alone. Happily, happily.

In this way we came to Ballyba. I shall not tell of the obstacles we had to surmount, the fiends we had to circumvent, the
misdemeanours of the son, the disintegrations of the father. It was
my intention, almost my desire, to tell of all these things, I rejoiced at the thought that the moment would come when I might
do so. Now the intention is dead, the moment is come and the
desire is gone. My leg was no better. It was no worse either. The
skin had healed. I would never have got there alone. It was thanks
to my son. What? That I got there. He often complained of his
health, his stomach, his teeth. I gave him some morphine. He
looked worse and worse. When I asked him what was wrong he
could not tell me. We had trouble with the bicycle. But I patched
it up. I would not have got there without my son. We were a
long time getting there. Weeks. We kept losing our way, taking
our time. I still did not know what I was to do with Molloy,
when I found him. I thought no more about it. I thought about
myself, much, as we went along, sitting behind my son, looking
over his head, and in the evening, when we camped, while he
made himself useful, and when he went away, leaving me alone.
For he often went away, to spy out the lie of the land and to buy
provisions. I did practically nothing any more. He took good care
of me, I must say. He was clumsy, stupid, slow, dirty, untruthful,
deceitful, prodigal, unfilial, but he did not abandon me. I thought
much about myself. That is to say I often took a quick look at
myself, closed my eyes, forgot, began again. We took a long time
getting to Ballyba, we even got there without knowing it. Stop,
I said to my son one day. I had just caught sight of a shepherd
I liked the look of. He was sitting on the ground stroking his dog.

A flock of black shorn sheep strayed about them, unafraid. What a pastoral land, my God. Leaving my son on the side of the road I went towards them, across the grass. I often stopped and rested, leaning on my umbrella. The shepherd watched me as I came, without getting up. The dog too, without barking. The sheep too. Yes, little by little, one by one, they turned and faced me, watching me as I came. Here and there faint movements of recoil, a tiny foot stamping the ground, betrayed their uneasiness. They did not seem timid, as sheep go. And my son of course watched me as I went, I felt his eyes in my back. The silence was absolute. Profound in any case. All things considered it was a solemn moment. The weather was divine. It was the close of day. Each time I stopped I looked about me. I looked at the shepherd, the sheep, the dog and even at the sky. But when I moved I saw nothing but the ground and the play of my feet, the good one springing forward, holding back, setting itself down, waiting for the other to come up. I came finally to a halt about ten paces from the shepherd. There was no use going any further. How I would love to dwell upon him. His dog loved him, his sheep did not fear him. Soon he would rise, feeling the falling dew. The fold was far, far, he would see from afar the light in his cot. Now I was in the midst of the sheep, they made a circle round me, their eyes converged on me. Perhaps I was the butcher come to make his choice. I took off my hat. I saw the dog's eyes following the movement of my hand. I looked about me again incapable of speech. I did not know how I would ever be able to break this silence. I was on the point of turning away without having spoken. Finally I said, Ballyba, hoping it sounded like a question. The shepherd drew the pipe from his mouth and pointed the stem at the ground. I longed to say, Take me with you, I will serve you faithfully, just for a place to lie and a little food. I had understood, but without seeming to I suppose, for he repeated his gesture, pointing the stem of his pipe at the ground, several times. Bally, I said. He raised one hand, it wavered an instant as if over a map, then stiffened. The pipe still smoked faintly, the smoke hung blue in the air an instant, then vanished. I looked in the direction indicated. The dog too. We were all three turned to the north. The sheep were losing interest in

me. Perhaps they had understood. I heard them straying about
again and grazing. I distinguished at last, at the limit of the plain,
a dim glow, the sum of countless points of light blurred by the
distance, I thought of Juno's milk. It lay like a faint splash on the
sharp dark sweep of the horizon. I gave thanks for evening that
brings out the lights, the stars in the sky and on earth the brave
little lights of men. By day the shepherd would have raised his
pipe in vain, towards the long clear-cut commissure of earth and
sky. But now I felt the man turning towards me again, and the
dog, and the man drawing on his pipe again, in the hope it had
not gone out. And I knew I was all alone gazing at that distant
glow that would get brighter and brighter, I knew that too, then
suddenly go out. And I did not like the feeling of being alone, with
my son perhaps, no, alone, spellbound. And I was wondering
how to depart without self-loathing or sadness, or with as little as
possible, when a kind of immense sigh all round me announced
it was not I who was departing, but the flock. I watched them
move away, the man in front, then the sheep, huddled together,
their heads sunk, jostling one another, breaking now and then into
a little trot, snatching blindly without stopping a last mouthful
from the earth, and last of all the dog, jauntily, waving his long
black plumy tail, though there was no one to witness his contentment, if that is what it was. And so in perfect order, the shepherd
silent and the dog unheeded, the little flock departed. And so no
doubt they would plod on, until they came to the stable or the
fold. And there the shepherd stands aside to let them pass and
he counts them as they go by, though he knows not one is missing.
Then he turns towards his cottage, the kitchen door is open, the
lamp is burning, he goes in and sits down at the table, without
taking off his hat. But the dog stops at the threshold, not knowing
whether he may go in or whether he must stay out, all night.

That night I had a violent scene with my son. I do not remember about what. Wait, it may be important.

No, I don't know. I must have had so many scenes with my
son. At the time it must have seemed a scene like any other,
that's all I know.

I must have got the better of it as I always did, thanks to my

infallible technique, and brought him unerringly to a proper sense
of his iniquities. But the next day I realised my mistake. For
waking early I found myself alone, in the shelter, I who was
always the first to wake. And what is more my instinct told me
I had been alone for some considerable time, my breath no longer
mingling with the breath of my son, in the narrow shelter he had
erected, under my supervision. Not that the fact of his having
disappeared with the bicycle, during the night or with the first
guilty flush of dawn, was in itself a matter for grave anxiety. And
I would have found excellent and honourable reasons for this, if
this had been all. Unfortunately he had taken his knapsack and
his raincoat. And there remained nothing in the shelter, nor outside
the shelter, belonging to him, absolutely nothing. And this was
not yet all, for he had left with a considerable sum of money, he
who was only entitled to a few pence from time to time, for his
savings-box. For since he had been in charge of everything, under
my supervision of course, and notably of the shopping, I was
obliged to place a certain reliance on him in the matter of money.
And he always had a far greater sum in his pocket than was
strictly necessary. And in order to make all this sound more likely
I shall add what follows.

1. I desired him to learn double-entry book-keeping and had
instructed him in its rudiments.

2. I could no longer be bothered with these wretched trifles
which had once been my delight.

3. I had told him to keep an eye out, on his expeditions, for
a second bicycle, light and inexpensive. For I was weary of the
carrier and I also saw the day approaching when my son would
no longer have the strength to pedal for the two of us. And I
believed I was capable, more than that, I knew I was capable, with
a little practice, of learning to pedal with one leg. And then I would
resume my rightful place, I mean in the van. And my son would
follow me. And then the scandal would cease of my son's defy-
ing me, and going left when I told him right, or right when I told
him left, or straight on when I told him right or left as he had been
doing of late, more and more frequently.

That is all I wished to add.

But on examining my pocket-book I found it contained no more than fifteen shillings, which led me to the conclusion that my son had not been content with the sum already in his possession, but had gone through my pockets, before he left, while I slept. And the human breast is so bizarre that my first feeling was of gratitude for his leaving me this little sum, enough to keep me going until help arrived, and I saw in this a kind of delicacy!

I was therefore alone, with my bag, my umbrella (which he might easily have taken too) and fifteen shillings, knowing myself coldly abandoned, with deliberation and no doubt premeditation, in Ballyba it is true, if indeed I was in Ballyba, but still far from Bally. And I remained for several days, I do not know how many, in the place where my son had abandoned me, eating my last provisions (which he might easily have taken too), seeing no living soul, powerless to act, or perhaps strong enough at last to act no more. For I had no illusions, I knew that all was about to end, or to begin again, it little mattered which, and it little mattered how, I had only to wait. And on and off, for fun, and the better to scatter them to the winds, I dallied with the hopes that spring eternal, childish hopes, as for example that my son, his anger spent, would have pity on me and come back to me! Or that Molloy, whose country this was, would come to me, who had not been able to go to him, and grow to be a friend, and like a father to me, and help me do what I had to do, so that Youdi would not be angry with me and would not punish me! Yes, I let them spring within me and grow in strength, brighten and charm me with a thousand fancies, and then I swept them away, with a great disgusted sweep of all my being, I swept myself clean of them and surveyed with satisfaction the void they had polluted. And in the evening I turned to the lights of Bally, I watched them shine brighter and brighter, then all go out together, or nearly all, foul little flickering lights of terrified men. And I said, To think I might be there now, but for my misfortune! And with regard to the Obidil, of whom I have refrained from speaking, until now, and whom I so longed to see face to face, all I can say with regard to him is this, that I never saw him, either face to face or darkly, perhaps there is no such person, that would not greatly surprise me.

And at the thought of the punishments Youdi might inflict upon
me I was seized by such a mighty fit of laughter that I shook, with
mighty silent laughter and my features composed in their wonted
sadness and calm. But my whole body shook, and even my legs,
so that I had to lean against a tree, or against a bush, when the
fit came on me standing, my umbrella being no longer sufficient
to keep me from falling. Strange laughter truly, and no doubt
misnamed, through indolence perhaps, or ignorance. And as for
myself, that unfailing pastime, I must say it was far now from my
thoughts. But there were moments when it did not seem so far
from me, when I seemed to be drawing towards it as the sands
towards the wave, when it crests and whitens, though I must say
this image hardly fitted my situation, which was rather that of
the turd waiting for the flush. And I note here the little beat my
heart once missed, in my home, when a fly, flying low above my
ash-tray, raised a little ash, with the breath of its wings. And I
grew gradually weaker and weaker and more and more content.
For several days I had eaten nothing. I could probably have found
blackberries and mushrooms, but I had no wish for them. I remained all day stretched out in the shelter, vaguely regretting my
son's raincoat, and I crawled out in the evening to have a good
laugh at the lights of Bally. And though suffering a little from wind
and cramps in the stomach I felt extraordinarily content, content
with myself, almost elated, enchanted with my performance. And
I said, I shall soon lose consciousness altogether, it is merely a
question of time. But Gaber's arrival put a stop to these frolics.

It was evening. I had just crawled out of the shelter for my
evening guffaw and the better to savour my exhaustion. He had
already been there for some time. He was sitting on a tree-stump,
half asleep. Well Moran, he said. You recognise me? I said. He
took out and opened his notebook, licked his finger, turned over
the pages till he came to the right page, raised it towards his eyes
which at the same time he lowered towards it. I can see nothing,
he said. He was dressed as when I had last seen him. My strictures
on his Sunday clothes had therefore been unjustified. Unless it
was Sunday again. But had I not always seen him dressed in this
way? Would you have a match? he said. I did not recognise this

far-off voice. Or a torch, he said. He must have seen from my face
that I possessed nothing of a luminous nature. He took a small
electric torch from his pocket and shone it on his page. He read,
Moran, Jacques, home, instanter. He put out his torch, closed his
notebook on his finger and looked at me. I can't walk, I said.
What? he said. I'm sick, I can't move, I said. I can't hear a word
you say, he said. I cried to him that I could not move, that I was
sick, that I should have to be carried, that my son had abandoned
me, that I could bear no more. He examined me laboriously from
head to foot. I executed a few steps leaning on my umbrella to
prove to him I could not walk. He opened his notebook again,
shone the torch on his page, studied it at length and said, Moran,
home, instanter. He closed his notebook, put it back in his pocket,
put his lamp back in his pocket, stood up, drew his hands over
his chest and announced he was dying of thirst. Not a word on how
I was looking. And yet I had not shaved since the day my son
brought back the bicycle from Hole, nor combed my hair, nor
washed, not to mention all the privations I had suffered and the
great inward metamorphoses. Do you recognise me? I cried. Do I
recognise you? he said. He reflected. I knew what he was doing,
he was searching for the phrase most apt to wound me. Ah Moran,
he said, what a man! I was staggering with weakness. If I had
dropped dead at his feet he would have said, Ah poor old Moran,
that's him all over. It was getting darker and darker. I wondered
if it was really Gaber. Is he angry? I said. You wouldn't have a sup
of beer by any chance? he said. I'm asking you if he is angry, I
cried. Angry, said Gaber, don't make me laugh, he keeps rubbing
his hands from morning to night, I can hear them in the outer
room. That means nothing, I said. And chuckling to himself, said
Gaber. He must be angry with me, I said. Do you know what he
told me the other day? said Gaber. Has he changed? I cried.
Changed, said Gaber, no he hasn't changed, why would he have
changed, he's getting old, that's all, like the world. You have a
queer voice this evening, I said. I do not think he heard me. Well,
he said, drawing his hands once more over his chest, downwards,
I'll be going, if that's all you have to say to me. He went, without
saying goodbye. But I overtook him, in spite of my loathing for

him, in spite of my weakness and my sick leg, and held him back
by the sleeve. What did he tell you? I said. He stopped. Moran, he
said, you are beginning to give me a serious pain in the arse. For
pity's sake, I said, tell me what he told you. He gave me a shove.
I fell. He had not intended to make me fall, he did not realise
the state I was in, he had only wanted to push me away. I did not
try to get up. I let out a roar. He came and bent over me. He had a
walrus moustache, chestnut in colour. I saw it lift, the lips open,
and almost at the same time I heard words of solicitude, at a great
distance. He was not brutal, Gaber, I knew him well. Gaber, I said,
it's not much I'm asking you. I remember this scene well. He
wanted to help me up. I pushed him away. I was all right where
I was. What did he tell you? I said. I don't understand, said Gaber.
You were saying a minute ago that he had told you something,
I said, then I cut you short. Short? said Gaber. Do you know what
he told me the other day, I said, those were your very words. His
face lit up. The clod was just about as quick as my son. He said to
me, said Gaber, Gaber, he said—. Louder! I cried. He said to me,
said Gaber, Gaber, he said, life is a thing of beauty, Gaber, and a
joy for ever. He brought his face nearer mine. A joy for ever, he
said, a thing of beauty, Moran, and a joy for ever. He smiled. I
closed my eyes. Smiles are all very nice in their own way, very
heartening, but at a reasonable distance. I said, Do you think he
meant human life? I listened. Perhaps he didn't mean human
life, I said. I opened my eyes. I was alone. My hands were full
of grass and earth I had torn up unwittingly, was still tearing up.
I was literally uprooting. I desisted, yes, the second I realised what
I had done, what I was doing, such a nasty thing, I desisted from
it, I opened my hands, they were soon empty.

    That night I set out for home. I did not get far. But it was a
start. It is the first step that counts. The second counts less. Each
day saw me advance a little further. That last sentence is not
clear, it does not say what I hoped it would. I counted at first
by tens of steps. I stopped when I could go no further and I said,
Bravo, that makes so many tens, so many more than yesterday.
Then I counted by fifteens, by twenties and finally by fifties. Yes,
in the end I could go fifty steps before having to stop, for rest,

leaning on my faithful umbrella. In the beginning I must have
strayed a little in Ballyba, if I really was in Ballyba. Then I followed more or less the same paths we had taken on the way out.
But paths look different, when you go back along them. I ate, in
obedience to the voice of reason, all that nature, the woods, the
fields, the waters had to offer me in the way of edibles. I finished
the morphine.

It was in August, in September at the latest, that I was ordered
home. It was spring when I got there, I will not be more precise.
I had therefore been all winter on the way.

Anyone else would have lain down in the snow, firmly resolved never to rise again. Not I. I used to think that men would
never get the better of me. I still think I am cleverer than things.
There are men and there are things, to hell with animals. And with
God. When a thing resists me, even if it is for my own good, it
does not resist me long. This snow, for example. Though to tell the
truth it lured me more than it resisted me. But in a sense it
resisted me. That was enough. I vanquished it, grinding my teeth
with joy, it is quite possible to grind one's incisors. I forged my
way through it, towards what I would have called my ruin if I
could have conceived what I had left to be ruined. Perhaps I have
conceived it since, perhaps I have not done conceiving it, it takes
time, one is bound to in time, I am bound to. But on the way
home, a prey to the malignancy of man and nature and my own
failing flesh, I could not conceive it. My knee, allowance made for
the dulling effects of habit, was neither more nor less painful than
the first day. The disease, whatever it was, was dormant! How can
such things be? But to return to the flies, I like to think of those
that hatch out at the beginning of winter, within doors, and die
shortly after. You see them crawling and fluttering in the warm
corners, puny, sluggish, torpid, mute. That is you see an odd one
now and then. They must die very young, without having been
able to lay. You sweep them away, you push them into the dust-pan
with the brush, without knowing. That is a strange race of flies. But
I was succumbing to other affections, that is not the word, intestinal
for the most part, I would have described them once, not now,
I am sorry, it would have been worth reading. I shall merely say

that no one else would have surmounted them, without help. But I! Bent double, my free hand pressed to my belly, I advanced, and every now and then I let out a roar, of triumph and distress. Certain mosses I consumed must have disagreed with me. I if I once made up my mind not to keep the hangman waiting, the bloody flux itself would not stop me, I would get there on all fours shitting out my entrails and chanting maledictions. Didn't I tell you it's my brethren that have done for me.

But I shall not dwell upon this journey home, its furies and treacheries. And I shall pass over in silence the fiends in human shape and the phantoms of the dead that tried to prevent me from getting home, in obedience to Youdi's command. But one or two words nevertheless, for my own edification and to prepare my soul to make an end. To begin with my rare thoughts.

Certain questions of a theological nature preoccupied me strangely. As for example.

1. What value is to be attached to the theory that Eve sprang, not from Adam's rib, but from a tumour in the fat of his leg (arse?).

2. Did the serpent crawl or, as Comestor affirms, walk upright?

3. Did Mary conceive through the ear, as Augustine and Adobard assert?

4. How much longer are we to hang about waiting for the antechrist?

5. Does it really matter which hand is employed to absterge the podex?

6. What is one to think of the Irish oath sworn by the natives with the right hand on the relics of the saints and the left on the virile member?

7. Does nature observe the sabbath?

8. Is it true that the devils do not feel the pains of hell?

9. The algebraic theology of Craig. What is one to think of this?

10. Is it true that the infant Saint-Roch refused suck on Wednesdays and Fridays?

11. What is one to think of the excommunication of vermin in the sixteenth century?

12. Is one to approve of the Italian cobbler Lovat who, having

cut off his testicles, crucified himself.

13. What was God doing with himself before the creation?

14. Might not the beatific vision become a source of boredom, in the long run?

15. Is it true that Judas' torments are suspended on Saturdays?

16. What if the mass for the dead were read over the living?

And I recited the pretty quietist Pater, Our Father who art no more in heaven than on earth or in hell, I neither want nor desire that thy name be hallowed, thou knowest best what suits thee. Etc. The middle and the end are very pretty.

It was in this frivolous and charming world that I took refuge, when my cup ran over.

But I asked myself other questions concerning me perhaps more closely. As for example.

1. Why had I not borrowed a few shillings from Gaber?

2. Why had I obeyed the order to go home?

3. What had become of Molloy?

4. Same question for me.

5. What would become of me?

6. Same question for my son.

7. Was his mother in heaven?

8. Same question for my mother.

9. Would I go to heaven ?

10. Would we all meet again in heaven one day, I, my mother, my son, his mother, Youdi, Gaber, Molloy, his mother, Yerk, Murphy, Watt, Camier and the rest?

11. What had become of my hens, my bees? Was my grey hen still living?

12. Zulu, the Elsner sisters, were they still living?

13. Was Youdi's business address still 8, Acacia Square? What if I wrote to him? What if I went to see him? I would explain to him. What would I explain to him? I would crave his forgiveness. Forgiveness for what?

14. Was not the winter exceptionally severe?

15. How long had I gone now without either confession or communion?

16. What was the name of the martyr who, being in prison,

loaded with chains, covered with wounds and vermin, unable to
stir, celebrated the consecration on his stomach and gave himself
absolution?

17. What would I do until my death? Was there no means of
hastening this, without falling into a state of sin?

But before I launch my body properly so-called across these
icy, then, with the thaw, muddy solitudes, I wish to say that I
often thought of my bees, more often than of my hens, and God
knows I thought often of my hens. And I thought above all of
their dance, for my bees danced, oh not as men dance, to amuse
themselves, but in a different way. I alone of all mankind knew
this, to the best of my belief. I had investigated this phenomenon
very fully. The dance was best to be observed among the bees returning to the hive, laden more or less with nectar, and it involved
a great variety of figures and rhythms. These evolutions I finally
interpreted as a system of signals by means of which the incoming
bees, satisfied or dissatisfied with their plunder, informed the outgoing bees in what direction to go, and in what not to go. But the
outgoing bees danced too. It was no doubt their way of saying,
I understand, or, Don't worry about me. But away from the hive,
and busily at work, the bees did not dance. Here their watchword
seemed to be, Every man for himself, assuming bees to be capable
of such notions. The most striking feature of the dance was its
very complicated figures, traced in flight, and I had classified a
great number of these, with their probable meanings. But there
was also the question of the hum, so various in tone in the vicinity
of the hive that this could hardly be an effect of chance. I first concluded that each figure was reinforced by means of a hum peculiar
to it. But I was forced to abandon this agreeable hypothesis. For
I saw the same figure (at least what I called the same figure) accompanied by very different hums. So that I said, The purpose of
the hum is not to emphasise the dance, but on the contrary to
vary it. And the same figure exactly differs in meaning according
to the hum that goes with it. And I had collected and classified a
great number of observations on this subject, with gratifying results.
But there was to be considered not only the figure and the hum,
but also the height at which the figure was executed. And I acquired

the conviction that the selfsame figure, accompanied by the self-same hum, did not mean at all the same thing at twelve feet from the ground as it did at six. For the bees did not dance at any level, haphazard, but there were three or four levels, always the same, at which they danced. And if I were to tell you what these levels were, and what the relations between them, for I had measured them with care, you would not believe me. And this is not the moment to jeopardise my credit. Sometimes you would think I was writing for the public. And in spite of all the pains I have lavished on these problems, I was more than ever stupefied by the complexity of this innumerable dance, involving doubtless other determinants of which I had not the slightest idea. And I said, with rapture, Here is something I can study all my life, and never understand. And all during this long journey home, when I racked my mind for a little joy in store, the thought of my bees and their dance was the nearest thing to comfort. For I was still eager for my little joy, from time to time! And I admitted with good grace the possibility that this dance was after all no better than the dances of the people of the West, frivolous and meaningless. But for me, sitting near my sun-drenched hives, it would always be a noble thing to contemplate, too noble ever to be sullied by the cogitations of a man like me, exiled in his manhood. And I would never do my bees the wrong I had done my God, to whom I had been taught to ascribe my angers, fears, desires, and even my body.

I have spoken of a voice giving me orders, or rather advice. It was on the way home I heard it for the first time. I paid no attention to it.

Physically speaking it seemed to me I was now becoming rapidly unrecognisable. And when I passed my hands over my face, in a characteristic and now more than ever pardonable gesture, the face my hands felt was not my face any more, and the hands my face felt were my hands no longer. And yet the gist of the sensation was the same as in the far-off days when I was well-shaven and perfumed and proud of my intellectual's soft white hands. And this belly I did not know remained my belly, my old belly, thanks to I know not what intuition. And to tell the truth I not only knew who I was, but I had a sharper and clearer sense

of my identity than ever before, in spite of its deep lesions and the
wounds with which it was covered. And from this point of view
I was less fortunate than my other acquaintances. I am sorry if
this last phrase is not so happy as it might be. It deserved, who
knows, to be without ambiguity.

Then there are the clothes that cleave so close to the body
and are so to speak inseparable from it, in time of peace. Yes, I
have always been very sensitive to clothing, though not in the least
a dandy. I had not to complain of mine, tough and of good cut.
I was of course inadequately covered, but whose fault was that?
And I had to part with my straw, not made to resist the rigours
of winter, and with my stockings (two pairs) which the cold and
damp, the trudging and the lack of laundering facilities had literally
annihilated. But I let out my braces to their fullest extent and my
knickerbockers, very baggy as the fashion is, came down to my
calves. And at the sight of the blue flesh, between the knickerbockers and the tops of my boots, I sometimes thought of my son
and the blow I had fetched him, so avid is the mind of the flimsiest
analogy. My boots became rigid, from lack of proper care. So skin
defends itself, when dead and tanned. The air coursed through
them freely, preserving perhaps my feet from freezing. And I had
likewise sadly to part with my drawers (two pairs). They had
rotted, from constant contact with my incontinences. Then the seat
of my breeches, before it too decomposed, sawed my crack from
Dan to Beersheba. What else did I have to discard? My shirt?
Never! But I often wore it inside out and back to front. Let me
see. I had four ways of wearing my shirt. Front to front right side
out, front to front inside out, back to front right side out, back to
front inside out. And the fifth day I began again. It was in the
hope of making it last. Did this make it last? I do not know. It
lasted. To major things the surest road is on the minor pains
bestowed, if you don't happen to be in a hurry. But what else did
I have to discard? My hard collars, yes, I discarded them all, and
even before they were quite worn and torn. But I kept my tie, I even
wore it, knotted round my bare neck, out of sheer bravado I
suppose. It was a spotted tie, but I forget the colour.

When it rained, when it snowed, when it hailed, then I found myself faced with the following dilemma. Was I to go on leaning on my umbrella and get drenched or was I to stop and take shelter under my open umbrella? It was a false dilemma, as so many dilemmas are. For on the one hand all that remained of the canopy of my umbrella was a few flitters of silk fluttering from the stays and on the other I could have gone on, very slowly, using the umbrella no longer as a support, but as a shelter. But I was so accustomed, on the one hand to the perfect watertightness of my expensive umbrella, and on the other hand to being unable to walk without its support, that the dilemma remained entire, for me. I could of course have made myself a stick, out of a branch, and gone on, in spite of the rain, the snow, the hail, leaning on the stick and the umbrella open above me. But I did not, I do not know why. But when the rain descended, and the other things that descend upon us from above, sometimes I pushed on, leaning on the umbrella, getting drenched, but most often I stopped dead, opened the umbrella above me and waited for it to be over. Then I got equally drenched. But that was not the point. And if it had suddenly begun to rain manna I would have waited, stock-still, under my umbrella, for it to be over, before taking advantage of it. And when my arm was weary of holding up the umbrella, then I gave it to the other hand. And with my free hand I slapped and rubbed every part of my body within its reach, in order to keep the blood trickling freely, or I drew it over my face, in a gesture that was characteristic, of me. And the long spike of my umbrella was like a finger. My best thoughts came to me during these halts. But when it was clear that the rain, etc., would not stop all day, or all night, then I did the sensible thing and built myself a proper shelter. But I did not like proper shelters, made of boughs, any more. For soon there were no more leaves, but only the needles of certain conifers. But this was not the real reason why I did not like proper shelters any more, no. But when I was inside them I could think of nothing but my son's raincoat, I literally saw it, I saw nothing else, it filled all space. It was in reality what our English friends call a trench-coat, and I could smell the rubber, though trench-coats are not rubberised as a rule. So I avoided as far as possible having recourse to proper shelters, made of boughs.

preferring the shelter of my faithful umbrella, or of a tree, or of a hedge, or of a bush, or of a ruin.

The thought of taking to the road, to try and get a lift, never crossed my mind.

The thought of turning for help to the villages, to the peasants, would have displeased me, if it had occurred to me.

I reached home with my fifteen shillings intact. No, I spent two. This is how.

I had to suffer other molestations than this, other offences, but I shall not record them. Let us be content with paradigms. I may have to suffer others in the future. This is not certain. But they will never be known. This is certain.

It was evening. I was waiting quietly, under my umbrella, for the weather to clear, when I was brutally accosted from behind. I had heard nothing. I had been in a place where I was all alone. A hand turned me about. It was a big ruddy farmer. He was wearing an oilskin, a bowler hat and wellingtons. His chubby cheeks were streaming, the water was dripping from his bushy moustache. But why describe him? We glared at each other with hatred. Perhaps he was the same who had so politely offered to drive us home in his car. I think not. And yet his face was familiar. Not only his face. He held a lantern in his hand. It was not lit. But he might light it at any moment. In the other he held a spade. To bury me with if necessary. He seized me by the jacket, by the lapel. He had not yet begun to shake me exactly, he would shake me in his own good time, not before. He merely cursed me. I wondered what I could have done, to put him in such a state. I must have raised my eyebrows. But I always raise my eyebrows, they are almost in my hair, my brow is nothing but wales and furrows. I understood finally that I did not own the land. It was his land. What was I doing on his land? If there is one question I dread, to which I have never been able to invent a satisfactory reply, it is the question what am I doing. And on someone else's land to make things worse! And at night! And in weather not fit for a dog! But I did not lose my presence of mind. It is a vow, I said. I have a fairly distinguished voice, when I choose. It must have impressed him. He unhanded me. A pilgrimage, I said, following up my advantage.

He asked me where to. He was lost. To the Turdy Madonna, I said. The Turdy Madonna? he said, as if he knew Turdy like the back of his hand and there were no Madonna in the length and breadth of it. But where is the place in which there is no Madonna? Herself, I said. The black one? he said, to try me. She is not black that I know of, I said. Another would have lost countenance. Not I. I knew my yokels and their weak points. You'll never get there, he said. It's thanks to her I lost my infant boy, I said, and kept his mamma. Such sentiments could not fail to please a cattle breeder. Had he but known! I told him more fully what alas had never happened. Not that I miss Ninette. But she, at least, who knows, in any case, yes, a pity, no matter. She is the Madonna of pregnant women, I said, of pregnant married women, and I have vowed to drag myself miserably to her niche, and thank her. This incident gives but a feeble idea of my ability, even at this late period. But I had gone a little too far, for the vicious look came back into his eye. May I ask you a favour, I said, God will reward you. I added, God sent you to me, this evening. Humbly to ask a favour of people who are on the point of knocking your brains out sometimes produces good results. A little hot tea, I implored, without sugar or milk, to revive me. To grant such a small favour to a pilgrim on the rocks was frankly a temptation difficult to resist. Oh all right, he said, come back to the house, you can dry yourself, before the fire. But I cannot, I cannot, I cried, I have sworn to make a bee-line to her! And to efface the bad impression created by these words I took a florin from my pocket and gave it to him. For your poor-box, I said. And I added, because of the dark, A florin for your poor-box. It's a long way, he said. God will go with you, I said. He thought it over. Well he might. Above all nothing to eat, I said, no really, I must not eat. Ah Moran, wily as a serpent, there was never the like of old Moran. Of course I would have preferred violence, but I dared not take the risk. Finally he took himself off telling me to stay where I was. I do not know what was in his mind. When I judged him at a safe remove I closed the umbrella and set off in the opposite direction, at right angles to the way I was going, in the driving rain. That was how I spent a florin.

Now I may make an end.

I skirted the graveyard. It was night. Midnight perhaps. The lane is steep, I laboured. A little wind was chasing the clouds over the faint sky. It is a great thing to own a plot in perpetuity, a very great thing indeed. If only that were the only perpetuity. I came to the wicket. It was locked. Very properly. But I could not open it. The key went into the hole, but would not turn. Long disuse? A new lock? I burst it open. I drew back to the other side of the lane and hurled myself at it. I had come home, as Youdi had commanded me. In the end I got to my feet. What smelt so sweet? The lilacs? The primroses perhaps. I went towards my hives. They were there, as I feared. I lifted the top off one and laid it on the ground. It was a little roof, with a sharp ridge, and steep overhanging slopes. I put my hand in the hive, moved it among the empty trays, felt along the bottom. It encountered, in a corner, a dry light ball. It crumbled under my fingers. They had clustered together for a little warmth, to try and sleep. I took out a handful. It was too dark to see, I put it in my pocket. It weighed nothing. They had been left out all winter, their honey taken away, without sugar. Yes, now I may make an end. I did not go to the hen-house. My hens were dead too, I knew they were dead. They had not been killed in the same way, except the grey one perhaps, that was the only difference. My bees, my hens, I had deserted them. I went towards the house. It was in darkness. The door was locked. I burst it open. Perhaps I could have opened it, with one of my keys. I turned the switch. No light. I went to the kitchen, to Martha's room. No one. There is nothing more to tell. The house was empty. The company had cut off the light. They have offered to let me have it back. But I told them they could keep it. That is the kind of man I have become. I went back to the garden. The next day I looked at my handful of bees. A little dust of annulets and wings. I found some letters, at the foot of the stairs, in the box. A letter from Savory. My son was well. He would be. Let us hear no more about him. He has come back. He is sleeping. A letter from Youdi, in the third person, asking for a report. He will get his report. It is summer again. This time a year ago I was setting out. I am clearing out. One day I received a visit from Gaber. He wanted the report.

That's funny, I thought I was done with people and talk. Call back, I said. One day I received a visit from Father Ambrose. Is it possible! he said when he saw me. I think he really liked me, in his own way. I told him not to count on me any more. He began to talk. He was right. Who is not right? I left him. I am clearing out. Perhaps I shall meet Molloy. My knee is no better. It is no worse either. I have crutches now. I shall go faster, all will go faster. They will be happy days. I shall learn. All there was to sell I have sold. But I had heavy debts. I have been a man long enough, I shall not put up with it any more, I shall not try any more. I shall never light this lamp again. I am going to blow it out and go into the garden. I think of the long May days, June days, when I lived in the garden. One day I talked to Hanna. She gave me news of Zulu, of the Elsner sisters. She knew who I was, she was not afraid of me. She never went out, she disliked going out. She talked to me from her window. The news was bad, but might have been worse. There was a bright side. They were lovely days. The winter had been exceptionally rigorous, everybody said so. We had there-fore a right to this superb summer. I do not know if we had a right to it. My birds had not been killed. They were wild birds. And yet quite trusting. I recognised them and they seemed to recognise me. But one never knows. Some were missing and some were new. I tried to understand their language better. Without having recourse to mine. They were the longest, loveliest days of all the year. I lived in the garden. I have spoken of a voice telling me things. I was getting to know it better now, to understand what it wanted. It did not use the words that Moran had been taught when he was little and that he in his turn had taught to his little one. So that at first I did not know what it wanted. But in the end I understood this language. I understood it, I understand it, all wrong perhaps. That is not what matters. It told me to write the report. Does this mean I am freer now than I was? I do not know. I shall learn. Then I went back into the house and wrote, It is midnight. The rain is beating on the windows. It was not midnight. It was not raining.

PART II

★

MALONE DIES

I shall soon be quite dead at last in spite of all. Perhaps next month. Then it will be the month of April or of May. For the year is still young, a thousand little signs tell me so. Perhaps I am wrong, perhaps I shall survive Saint John the Baptist's Day and even the Fourteenth of July, festival of freedom. Indeed I would not put it past me to pant on to the Transfiguration, not to speak of the Assumption. But I do not think so, I do not think I am wrong in saying that these rejoicings will take place in my absence, this year. I have that feeling, I have had it now for some days, and I credit it. But in what does it differ from those that have abused me ever since I was born? No, that is the kind of bait I do not rise to any more, my need for prettiness is gone. I could die to-day, if I wished, merely by making a little effort. But it is just as well to let myself die, quietly, without rushing things. Something must have changed. I will not weigh upon the balance any more, one way or the other. I shall be neutral and inert. No difficulty there. Throes are the only trouble,

I must be on my guard against throes. But I am less given to
them now, since coming here. Of course I still have my little fits
of impatience, from time to time, I must be on my guard against
them, for the next fortnight or three weeks. Without exaggeration
to be sure, quietly crying and laughing, without working myself
up into a state. Yes I shall be natural at last, I shall suffer more,
then less, without drawing any conclusions, I shall pay less heed
to myself, I shall be neither hot nor cold any more, I shall be
tepid, I shall die tepid, without enthusiasm. I shall not watch
myself die, that would spoil everything. Have I watched myself
live? Have I ever complained? Then why rejoice now? I am content, necessarily, but not to the point of clapping my hands. I was
always content, knowing I would be repaid. There he is now, my
old debtor. Shall I then fall on his neck? I shall not answer any
more questions. I shall even try not to ask myself any more. While
waiting I shall tell myself stories, if I can. They will not be the
same kind of stories as hitherto, that is all. They will be neither
beautiful nor ugly, they will be calm, there will be no ugliness
or beauty or fever in them any more, they will be almost lifeless,
like the teller. What was that I said? It does not matter. I look
forward to their giving me great satisfaction, some satisfaction.
I am satisfied, there, I have enough, I am repaid, I need nothing
more. Let me say before I go any further that I forgive nobody.
I wish them all an atrocious life and then the fires and ice of
hell and in the execrable generations to come an honoured name.
Enough for this evening.

This time I know where I am going, it is no longer the ancient
night, the recent night. Now it is a game, I am going to play. I
never knew how to play, till now. I longed to, but I knew it was
impossible. And yet I often tried. I turned on all the lights, I took
a good look all round, I began to play with what I saw. People
and things ask nothing better than to play, certain animals too.
All went well at first, they all came to me, pleased that someone
should want to play with them. If I said, Now I need a hunch-
back, immediately one came running, proud as punch of his fine
hunch that was going to perform. It did not occur to him that I
might have to ask him to undress. But it was not long before I

found myself alone, in the dark. That is why I gave up trying to play and took to myself for ever shapelessness and speechlessness, incurious wondering, darkness, long stumbling with outstretched arms, hiding. Such is the earnestness from which, for nearly a century now, I have never been able to depart. From now on it will be different. I shall never do anything any more from now on but play. No, I must not begin with an exaggeration. But I shall play a great part of the time, from now on, the greater part, if I can. But perhaps I shall not succeed any better than hitherto. Perhaps as hitherto I shall find myself abandoned, in the dark, without anything to play with. Then I shall play with myself. To have been able to conceive such a plan is encouraging.

I must have thought about my time-table during the night. I think I shall be able to tell myself four stories, each one on a different theme. One about a man, another about a woman, a third about a thing and finally one about an animal, a bird probably. I think that is everything. Perhaps I shall put the man and the woman in the same story, there is so little difference between a man and a woman, between mine I mean. Perhaps I shall not have time to finish. On the other hand perhaps I shall finish too soon. There I am back at my old aporetics. Is that the word? I don't know. It does not matter if I do not finish. But if I finish too soon? That does not matter either. For then I shall speak of the things that remain in my possession, that is a thing I have always wanted to do. It will be a kind of inventory. In any case that is a thing I must leave to the very last moment, so as to be sure of not having made a mistake. In any case that is a thing I shall certainly do, no matter what happens. It will not take me more than a quarter of an hour at the most. That is to say it could take me longer, if I wished. But should I be short of time, at the last moment, then a brief quarter of an hour would be all I should need to draw up my inventory. My desire is henceforward to be clear, without being finical. I have always wanted that too. It is obvious I may suddenly expire, at any moment. Would it not then be better for me to speak of my possessions without further delay? Would not that be wiser? And then if necessary at the last moment correct any inaccuracies. That is what reason counsels.

But reason has not much hold on me, just now. All things run together to encourage me. But can I really resign myself to the possibility of my dying without leaving an inventory behind? There I am back at my old quibbles. Presumably I can, since I intend to take the risk. All my life long I have put off this reckoning, saying, Too soon, too soon. Well it is still too soon. All my life long I have dreamt of the moment when, edified at last, in so far as one can be before all is lost, I might draw the line and make the tot. This moment seems now at hand. I shall not lose my head on that account. So first of all my stories and then, last of all, if all goes well, my inventory. And I shall begin, that they may plague me no more, with the man and woman. That will be the first story, there is not matter there for two. There will therefore be only three stories after all, that one, then the one about the animal, then the one about the thing, a stone probably. That is all very clear. Then I shall deal with my possessions. If after all that I am still alive I shall take the necessary steps to ensure my not having made a mistake. So much for that. I used not to know where I was going, but I knew I would arrive, I knew there would be an end to the long blind road. What half-truths, my God. No matter. It is playtime now. I find it hard to get used to that idea. The old fog calls. Now the case is reversed, the way well charted and little hope of coming to its end. But I have high hopes. What am I doing now, I wonder, losing time or gaining it? I have also decided to remind myself briefly of my present state before embarking on my stories. I think this is a mistake. It is a weakness. But I shall indulge in it. I shall play with all the more ardour afterwards. And it will be a pendant to the inventory. Aesthetics are therefore on my side, at least a certain kind of aesthetics. For I shall have to become earnest again to be able to speak of my possessions. There it is then divided into five, the time that remains. Into five what? I don't know. Everything divides into itself, I suppose. If I start trying to think again I shall make a mess of my decease. I must say there is something very attractive about such a prospect. But I am on my guard. For the past few days I have been finding something attractive about everything. To return to the five. Present state, three stories, inventory, there.

An occasional interlude is to be feared. A full programme. I shall not deviate from it any further than I must. So much for that. I feel I am making a great mistake. No matter.

Present state. This room seems to be mine. I can find no other explanation to my being left in it. All this time. Unless it be at the behest of one of the powers that be. That is hardly likely. Why should the powers have changed in their attitude towards me? It is better to adopt the simplest explanation, even if it is not simple, even if it does not explain very much. A bright light is not necessary, a taper is all one needs to live in strangeness, if it faithfully burns. Perhaps I came in for the room on the death of whoever was in it before me. I enquire no further in any case. It is not a room in a hospital, or in a madhouse, I can feel that. I have listened at different hours of the day and night and never heard anything suspicious or unusual, but always the peaceful sounds of men at large, getting up, lying down, preparing food, coming and going, weeping and laughing, or nothing at all, no sounds at all. And when I look out of the window it is clear to me from certain signs, that I am not in a house of rest in any sense of the word. No, this is just a plain private room apparently, in what appears to be a plain ordinary house. I do not remember how I got here. In an ambulance perhaps, a vehicle of some kind certainly. One day I found myself here, in the bed. Having probably lost consciousness somewhere, I benefit by a hiatus in my recollections, not to be resumed until I recovered my senses, in this bed. As to the events that led up to my fainting and to which I can hardly have been oblivious, at the time, they have left no discernible trace, on my mind. But who has not experienced such lapses? They are common after drunkenness. I have often amused myself with trying to invent them, those same lost events. But without succeeding in amusing myself really. But what is the last thing I remember, I could start from there, before I came to my senses again here? That too is lost. I was walking certainly, all my life I have been walking, except the first few months and since I have been here. But at the end of the day I did not know where I had been or what my thoughts had been. What then could I be expected to remember, and with what? I remember a

mood. My young days were more varied, such as they come back
to me, in fits and starts. I did not know my way about so well
then. I have lived in a kind of coma. The loss of consciousness
for me was never any great loss. But perhaps I was stunned with
a blow, on the head, in a forest perhaps, yes now that I speak of
a forest I vaguely remember a forest. All that belongs to the past.
Now it is the present I must establish, before I am avenged. It is
an ordinary room. I have little experience of rooms, but this one
seems quite ordinary to me. The truth is, if I did not feel myself
dying, I could well believe myself dead, expiating my sins, or in
one of heaven's mansions. But I feel at last that the sands are
running out, which would not be the case if I were in heaven, or
in hell. Beyond the grave, the sensation of being beyond the grave
was stronger with me six months ago. Had it been foretold to me
that one day I should feel myself living as I do to-day, I should
have smiled. It would not have been noticed, but I would have
known I was smiling. I remember them well, these last few days,
they have left me more memories than the thirty thousand odd
that went before. The reverse would have been less surprising.
When I have completed my inventory, if my death is not ready for
me then, I shall write my memoirs. That's funny, I have made a
joke. No matter. There is a cupboard I have never looked into.
My possessions are in a corner, in a little heap. With my long
stick I can rummage in them, draw them to me, send them back.
My bed is by the window. I lie turned towards it most of the
time. I see roofs and sky, a glimpse of street too, if I crane. I do
not see any fields or hills. And yet they are near. But are they
near? I don't know. I do not see the sea either, but I hear it when
it is high. I can see into a room of the house across the way.
Queer things go on there sometimes, people are queer. Perhaps
these are abnormal. They must see me too, my big shaggy head
up against the window-pane. I never had so much hair as now,
nor so long, I say it without fear of contradiction. But at night
they do not see me, for I never have a light. I have studied the
stars a little here. But I cannot find my way about among them.
Gazing at them one night I suddenly saw myself in London. Is it
possible I got as far as London? And what have stars to do with

that city? The moon on the other hand has grown familiar, I am well familiar now with her changes of aspect and orbit, I know more or less the hours of the night when I may look for her in the sky and the nights when she will not come. What else? The clouds. They are varied, very varied. And all sorts of birds. They come and perch on the window-sill, asking for food! It is touching. They rap on the window-pane, with their beaks. I never give them anything. But they still come. What are they waiting for? They are not vultures. Not only am I left here, but I am looked after! This is how it is done now. The door half opens, a hand puts a dish on the little table left there for that purpose, takes away the dish of the previous day, and the door closes again. This is done for me every day, at the same time probably. When I want to eat I hook the table with my stick and draw it to me. It is on castors, it comes squeaking and lurching towards me. When I need it no longer I send it back to its place by the door. It is soup. They must know I am toothless. I eat it one time out of two, out of three, on an average. When my chamber-pot is full I put it on the table beside the dish. Then I go twenty-four hours without a pot. No, I have two pots. They have thought of everything. I am naked in the bed, in the blankets, whose number I increase and diminish as the seasons come and go. I am never hot, never cold. I don't wash, but I don't get dirty. If I get dirty somewhere I rub the part with my finger wet with spittle. What matters is to eat and excrete. Dish and pot, dish and pot, these are the poles. In the beginning it was different. The woman came right into the room, bustled about, enquired about my needs, my wants. I succeeded in the end in getting them into her head, my needs and my wants. It was not easy. She did not understand. Until the day I found the terms, the accents, that fitted her. All that must be half imagination. It was she who got me this long stick. It has a hook at one end. Thanks to it I can control the furthest recesses of my abode. How great is my debt to sticks! So great that I almost forget the blows they have transferred to me. She is an old woman. I don't know why she is good to me. Yes, let us call it goodness, without quibbling. For her it is certainly goodness. I believe her to be even older than I. But rather less well preserved, in spite of her mobility. Perhaps she goes with the room, in a manner of speaking. In that case she does not call for separate study. But it is conceivable that she does what she does out of sheer charity, or moved with regard to me by a less general feeling of compassion or affection. Nothing is impossible, I cannot keep on denying it much longer. But it is more convenient to suppose that when I came in for the room I came in for her too. All I see of her now is the gaunt hand and part of the sleeve. Not even that, not even that. Perhaps she is dead, having predeceased me, perhaps now it is another's hand that lays and clears my little table. I don't know how long I have been here, I must have said so. All I know is that I was very old already before I found myself here. I call myself an octogenarian, but I cannot prove it. Perhaps I am only a quinquagenarian, or a quadragenarian. It is ages since I counted them, my years I mean. I know the year of my birth, I have not forgotten that, but I do not know what year I have got to now. But I think I have been here for some very considerable time. For there is nothing the various seasons can do to me, within the shelter of these walls, that I do not know. That is not to be learnt in one year or two. In a flicker of my lids whole days have flown. Does anything remain to be said? A few words about myself perhaps. My body is what is called, unadvisedly perhaps, impotent. There is virtually nothing it can do. Sometimes I miss not being able to crawl around any more. But I am not much given to nostalgia. My arms, once they are in position, can exert a certain force. But I find it hard to guide them. Perhaps the red nucleus has faded. I tremble a little, but only a little. The groaning of the bedstead is part of my life, I would not like it to cease, I mean I would not like it to decrease. It is on my back, that is to say prostrate, no, supine, that I feel best, bony. I lie on my back, but my cheek is on the pillow. I have only to open my eyes to have them begin again, the sky and smoke of mankind. My sight and hearing are very bad, on the vast main no light but reflected gleams. All my senses are trained full on me, me. Dark and silent and stale, I am no prey for them. I am far from the sounds of blood and breath, immured. I shall not speak of my sufferings. Cowering deep down among them I feel nothing.

It is there I die, unbeknown to my stupid flesh. That which is seen, that which cries and writhes, my witless remains. Somewhere in this turmoil thought struggles on, it too wide of the mark. It too seeks me, as it always has, where I am not to be found. It too cannot be quiet. On others let it wreak its dying rage, and leave me in peace. Such would seem to be my present state.

The man's name is Saposcat. Like his father's. Christian name? I don't know. He will not need one. His friends call him Sapo. What friends? I don't know. A few words about the boy. This cannot be avoided.

He was a precocious boy. He was not good at his lessons, neither could he see the use of them. He attended his classes with his mind elsewhere, or blank.

He attended his classes with his mind elsewhere. He liked sums, but not the way they were taught. What he liked was the manipulation of concrete numbers. All calculation seemed to him idle in which the nature of the unit was not specified. He made a practice, alone and in company, of mental arithmetic. And the figures then marshalling in his mind thronged it with colours and with forms.

What tedium.

He was the eldest child of poor and sickly parents. He often heard them talk of what they ought to do in order to have better health and more money. He was struck each time by the vagueness of these palavers and not surprised that they never led to anything. His father was a salesman, in a shop. He used to say to his wife, I really must find work for the evenings and the Saturday afternoon. He added, faintly, And the Sunday. His wife would answer, But if you do any more work you'll fall ill. And Mr. Saposcat had to allow that he would indeed be ill-advised to forego his Sunday rest. These people at least are grown up. But his health was not so poor that he could not work in the evenings of the week and on the Saturday afternoon. At what, said his wife, work at what? Perhaps secretarial work of some kind, he said. And who will look after the garden? said his wife. The life of the Saposcats was full of axioms, of which one at least established the criminal absurdity of a garden without roses and with its paths and lawns

uncared for. I might perhaps grow vegetables, he said. They cost
less to buy, said his wife. Sapo marvelled at these conversations.
Think of the price of manure, said his mother. And in the silence
which followed Mr. Saposcat applied his mind, with the earnestness he brought to everything he did, to the high price of manure
which prevented him from supporting his family in greater comfort, while his wife made ready to accuse herself, in her turn, of
not doing all she might. But she was easily persuaded that she
could not do more without exposing herself to the risk of dying
before her time. Think of the doctor's fees we save, said Mr.
Saposcat. And the chemist's bills, said his wife. Nothing remained
but to envisage a smaller house. But we are cramped as it is, said
Mrs. Saposcat. And it was an understood thing that they would
be more and more so with every passing year until the day came
when, the departure of the first-born compensating the arrival of the
new-born, a kind of equilibrium would be attained. Then little by
little the house would empty. And at last they would be all alone,
with their memories. It would be time enough then to move. He
would be pensioned off, she at her last gasp. They would take a
cottage in the country where, having no further need of manure,
they could afford to buy it in cartloads. And their children,
grateful for the sacrifices made on their behalf, would come to
their assistance. It was in this atmosphere of unbridled dream that
these conferences usually ended. It was as though the Saposcats
drew the strength to live from the prospect of their impotence.
But sometimes, before reaching that stage, they paused to consider
the case of their first-born. What age is he now? asked Mr.
Saposcat. His wife provided the information, it being understood
that this was of her province. She was always wrong. Mr. Saposcat
took over the erroneous figure, murmuring it over and over to
himself as though it were a question of the rise in price of some
indispensable commodity, such as butcher's meat. And at the same
time he sought in the appearance of his son some alleviation of
what he had just heard. Was it at least a nice sirloin? Sapo looked
at his father's face, sad, astonished, loving, disappointed, con-
fident in spite of all. Was it on the cruel flight of the years he
brooded, or on the time it was taking his son to command a

salary? Sometimes he stated wearily his regret that his son should not be more eager to make himself useful about the place. It is better for him to prepare his examinations, said his wife. Starting from a given theme their minds laboured in unison. They had no conversation properly speaking. They made use of the spoken word in much the same way as the guard of a train makes use of his flags, or of his lantern. Or else they said, This is where we get down. And their son once signalled, they wondered sadly if it was not the mark of superior minds to fail miserably at the written paper and cover themselves with ridicule at the viva voce. They were not always content to gape in silence at the same landscape. At least his health is good, said Mr. Saposcat. Not all that, said his wife. But no definite disease, said Mr. Saposcat. A nice thing that would be, at his age, said his wife. They did not know why he was committed to a liberal profession. That was yet another thing that went without saying. It was therefore impossible he should be unfitted for it. They thought of him as a doctor for preference. He will look after us when we are old, said Mrs. Saposcat. And her husband replied, I see him rather as a surgeon, as though after a certain age people were inoperable.

What tedium. And I call that playing. I wonder if I am not talking yet again about myself. Shall I be incapable, to the end, of lying on any other subject? I feel the old dark gathering, the solitude preparing, by which I know myself, and the call of that ignorance which might be noble and is mere poltroonery. Already I forget what I have said. That is not how to play. Soon I shall not know where Sapo comes from, nor what he hopes. Perhaps I had better abandon this story and go on to the second, or even the third, the one about the stone. No, it would be the same thing. I must simply be on my guard, reflecting on what I have said before I go on and stopping, each time disaster threatens, to look at myself as I am. That is just what I wanted to avoid. But there seems to be no other solution. After that mud-bath I shall be better able to endure a world unsullied by my presence. What a way to reason. My eyes, I shall open my eyes, look at the little heap of my possessions, give my body the old orders I know it cannot obey, turn to my spirit gone to rack and ruin, spoil my agony the better to live it out, far already from the world that parts at last its labia and lets me go.

I have tried to reflect on the beginning of my story. There are things I do not understand. But nothing to signify. I can go on.

Sapo had no friends—no, that won't do.

Sapo was on good terms with his little friends, though they did not exactly love him. The dolt is seldom solitary. He boxed and wrestled well, was fleet of foot, sneered at his teachers and sometimes even gave them impertinent answers. Fleet of foot? Well well. Pestered with questions one day he cried, Haven't I told you I don't know! Much of his free time he spent confined in school doing impositions and often he did not get home before eight o'clock at night. He submitted with philosophy to these vexations. But he would not let himself be struck. The first time an exasperated master threatened him with a cane, Sapo snatched it from his hand and threw it out of the window, which was closed, for it was winter. This was enough to justify his expulsion. But Sapo was not expelled, either then or later. I must try and discover, when I have time to think about it quietly, why Sapo was not expelled when he so richly deserved to be. For I want as little as possible of darkness in his story. A little darkness, in itself, at the time is nothing. You think no more about it and you go on. But I know what darkness is, it accumulates, thickens, then suddenly bursts and drowns everything.

I have not been able to find out why Sapo was not expelled. I shall have to leave this question open. I try not to be glad. I shall make haste to put a safe remove between him and this incomprehensible indulgence, I shall make him live as though he had been punished according to his deserts. We shall turn our backs on this little cloud, but we shall not let it out of our sight. It will not cover the sky without our knowing, we shall not suddenly raise our eyes, far from help, far from shelter, to a sky as black as ink. That is what I have decided. I see no other solution. It is the best I can do.

At the age of fourteen he was a plump rosy boy. His wrists and ankles were thick, which made his mother say that one day he would be even bigger than his father. Curious deduction. But the most striking thing about him was his big round head horrid with flaxen hair as stiff and straight as the bristles of a brush. Even his teachers could not help thinking he had a remarkable head and they were all the more irked by their failure to get anything into it. His father would say, when in good humour, One of these days he will astonish us all. It was thanks to Sapo's skull that he was enabled to hazard this opinion and, in defiance of the facts and against his better judgment, to revert to it from time to time. But he could not endure the look in Sapo's eyes and went out of his way not to meet it. He has your eyes, his wife would say. Then Mr. Saposcat chafed to be alone, in order to inspect his eyes in the mirror. They were palest blue. Just a shade lighter, said Mrs. Saposcat.

Sapo loved nature, took an interest.

This is awful.

Sapo loved nature, took an interest in animals and plants and willingly raised his eyes to the sky, day and night. But he did not know how to look at all these things, the looks he rained upon them taught him nothing about them. He confused the birds with one another, and the trees, and could not tell one crop from another crop. He did not associate the crocus with the spring nor the chrysanthemum with Michaelmas. The sun, the moon, the planets and the stars did not fill him with wonder. He was sometimes tempted by the knowledge of these strange things, sometimes beautiful, that he would have about him all his life. But from his ignorance of them he drew a kind of joy, as from all that went to swell the murmur, You are a simpleton. But he loved the flight of the hawk and could distinguish it from all others. He would stand rapt, gazing at the long pernings, the quivering poise, the wings lifted for the plummet drop, the wild reascent, fascinated by such extremes of need, of pride, of patience and solitude.

I shall not give up yet. I have finished my soup and sent back the little table to its place by the door. A light has just gone on in one of the two windows of the house across the way. By the two windows I mean those I can see always, without raising my head from the pillow. By this I do not mean the two windows in their entirety, but one in its entirety and part of the other. It is in this

latter that the light has just gone on. For an instant I could see
the woman coming and going. Then she drew the curtain. Until
tomorrow I shall not see her again, her shadow perhaps from
time to time. She does not always draw the curtain. The man has
not yet come home. Home. I have demanded certain movements
of my legs and even feet. I know them well and could feel the
effort they made to obey. I have lived with them that little space
of time, filled with drama, between the message received and the
piteous response. To old dogs the hour comes when, whistled by
their master setting forth with his stick at dawn, they cannot
spring after him. Then they stay in their kennel, or in their
basket, though they are not chained, and listen to the steps
dying away. The man too is sad. But soon the pure air
and the sun console him, he thinks no more about his old
companion, until evening. The lights in his house bid him welcome
home and a feeble barking makes him say, It is time I had him
destroyed. There's a nice passage. Soon it will be even better, soon
things will be better. I am going to rummage a little in my
possessions. Then I shall put my head under the blankets. Then
things will be better, for Sapo and for him who follows him, who
asks nothing but to follow in his footsteps, by clear and endurable
ways.

Sapo's phlegm, his silent ways, were not of a nature to please.
In the midst of tumult, at school and at home, he remained
motionless in his place, often standing, and gazed straight before
him with eyes as pale and unwavering as a gull's. People wondered
what he could brood on thus, hour after hour. His father supposed
him a prey to the first flutterings of sex. At sixteen I was the
same, he would say. At sixteen you were earning your living, said
his wife. So I was, said Mr. Saposcat. But in the view of his
teachers the signs were rather those of besottedness pure and
simple. Sapo dropped his jaw and breathed through his mouth. It
is not easy to see in virtue of what this expression is incompatible
with erotic thoughts. But indeed his dream was less of girls than
of himself, his own life, his life to be. That is more than enough
to stop up the nose of a lucid and sensitive boy, and cause his jaw
temporarily to sag. But it is time I took a little rest, for safety's sake.

I don't like those gull's eyes. They remind me of an old shipwreck, I forget which. I know it is a small thing. But I am easily
frightened now. I know those little phrases that seem so innocuous
and, once you let them in, pollute the whole of speech. *Nothing is
more real than nothing.* They rise up out of the pit and know no
rest until they drag you down into its dark. But I am on my guard
now.

Then he was sorry he had not learnt the art of thinking,
beginning by folding back the second and third fingers the better
to put the index on the subject and the little finger on the verb, in
the way his teacher had shown him, and sorry he could make no
meaning of the babel raging in his head, the doubts, desires,
imaginings and dreads. And a little less well endowed with strength
and courage he too would have abandoned and despaired of ever
knowing what manner of being he was, and how he was going to
live, and lived vanquished, blindly, in a mad world, in the midst
of strangers.

From these reveries he emerged tired and pale, which confirmed his father's impression that he was the victim of lascivious
speculations. He ought to play more games, he would say. We are
getting on, getting on. They told me he would be a good athlete,
said Mr. Saposcat, and now he is not on any team. His studies take
up all his time, said Mrs. Saposcat. And he is always last, said
Mr. Saposcat. He is fond of walking, said Mrs. Saposcat, the long
walks in the country do him good. Then Mr. Saposcat wried his
face, at the thought of his son's long solitary walks and the good
they did him. And sometimes he was carried away to the point
of saying, it might have been better to have put him to a trade.
Whereupon it was usual, though not compulsory, for Sapo to go
away, while his mother exclaimed, Oh Adrian, you have hurt his
feelings!

We are getting on. Nothing is less like me than this patient,
reasonable child, struggling all alone for years to shed a little light
upon himself, avid of the least gleam, a stranger to the joys of
darkness. Here truly is the air I needed, a lively tenuous air, far
from the nourishing murk that is killing me. I shall never go back
into this carcass except to find out its time. I want to be there a

little before the plunge, close for the last time the old hatch on
top of me, say goodbye to the holds where I have lived, go down
with my refuge. I was always sentimental. But between now and
then I have time to frolic, ashore, in the brave company I
have always longed for, always searched for, and which would
never have me. Yes, now my mind is easy, I know the game
is won, I lost them all till now, but it's the last that counts.
A very fine achievement I must say, or rather would, if I did not
fear to contradict myself. Fear to contradict myself! If this continues it is myself I shall lose and the thousand ways that lead
there. And I shall resemble the wretches famed in fable, crushed
beneath the weight of their wish come true. And I even feel a
strange desire come over me, the desire to know what I am doing,
and why. So I near the goal I set myself in my young days and
which prevented me from living. And on the threshold of being
no more I succeed in being another. Very pretty.

The summer holidays. In the morning he took private lessons.
You'll have us in the poorhouse, said Mrs. Saposcat. It's a good
investment, said Mr. Saposcat. In the afternoon he left the house,
with his books under his arm, on the pretext that he worked better
in the open air, no, without a word. Once clear of the town he hid
his books under a stone and ranged the countryside. It was the
season when the labours of the peasants reach their paroxysm and
the long bright days are too short for all there is to do. And often
they took advantage of the moon to make a last journey between
the fields, perhaps far away, and the barn or threshing floor, or to
overhaul the machines and get them ready for the impending
dawn. The impending dawn.

I fell asleep. But I do not want to sleep. There is no time for
sleep in my time-table. I do not want—no, I have no explanations
to give. Coma is for the living. The living. They were always more
than I could bear, all, no, I don't mean that, but groaning with
tedium I watched them come and go, then I killed them, or took
their place, or fled. I feel within me the glow of that old frenzy,
but I know it will set me on fire no more. I stop everything and
wait. Sapo stands on one leg, motionless, his strange eyes closed.
The turmoil of the day freezes in a thousand absurd postures.

The little cloud drifting before their glorious sun will darken the earth as long as I please.

Live and invent. I have tried. I must have tried. Invent. It is not the word. Neither is live. No matter. I have tried. While within me the wild beast of earnestness padded up and down, roaring, ravening, rending. I have done that. And all alone, well hidden, played the clown, all alone, hour after hour, motionless, often standing, spellbound, groaning. That's right, groan. I couldn't play. I turned till I was dizzy, clapped my hands, ran, shouted, saw myself winning, saw myself losing, rejoicing, lamenting. Then suddenly I threw myself on the playthings, if there were any, or on a child, to change his joy to howling, or I fled, to hiding. The grown-ups pursued me, the just, caught me, beat me, hounded me back into the round, the game, the jollity. For I was already in the toils of earnestness. That has been my disease. I was born grave as others syphilitic. And gravely I struggled to be grave no more, to live, to invent, I know what I mean. But at each fresh attempt I lost my head, fled to my shadows as to sanctuary, to his lap who can neither live nor suffer the sight of others living. I say living without knowing what it is. I tried to live without knowing what I was trying. Perhaps I have lived after all, without knowing. I wonder why I speak of all this. Ah yes, to relieve the tedium. Live and cause to live. There is no use indicting words, they are no shoddier than what they peddle. After the fiasco, the solace, the repose, I began again, to try and live, cause to live, be another, in myself, in another. How false all this is. No time now to explain. I began again. But little by little with a different aim, no longer in order to succeed, but in order to fail. Nuance. What I sought, when I struggled out of my hole, then aloft through the stinging air towards an inaccessible boon, was the rapture of vertigo, the letting go, the fall, the gulf, the relapse to darkness, to nothingness, to earnestness, to home, to him waiting for me always, who needed me and whom I needed, who took me in his arms and told me to stay with him always, who gave me his place and watched over me, who suffered every time I left him, whom I have often made suffer and seldom contented, whom I have never seen. There I am forgetting myself again. My concern is not with me, but with another, far beneath me and whom I try to envy, of whose crass adventures I can now tell at last, I don't know how. Of myself I could never tell, any more than live or tell of others. How could I have, who never tried? To show myself now, on the point of vanishing, at the same time as the stranger, and by the same grace, that would be no ordinary last straw. Then live, long enough to feel, behind my closed eyes, other eyes close. What an end.

The market. The inadequacy of the exchanges between rural and urban areas had not escaped the excellent youth. He had mustered, on this subject, the following considerations, some perhaps close to, others no doubt far from, the truth.

In his country the problem—no, I can't do it.

The peasants. His visits to. I can't. Assembled in the farm-yard they watched him depart, on stumbling, wavering feet, as though they scarcely felt the ground. Often he stopped, stood tottering a moment, then suddenly was off again, in a new direction. So he went, limp, drifting, as though tossed by the earth. And when, after a halt, he started off again, it was like a big thistle-down plucked by the wind from the place where it had settled. There is a choice of images.

I have rummaged a little in my things, sorting them out and drawing them over to me, to look at them. I was not far wrong in thinking that I knew them off, by heart, and could speak of them at any moment, without looking at them. But I wanted to make sure. It was well I did. For now I know that the image of these objects, with which I have lulled myself till now, though accurate in the main, was not completely so. And I should be sorry to let slip this unique occasion which seems to offer me the possibility of something suspiciously like a true statement at last. I might feel I had failed in my duty! I want this matter to be free from all trace of approximativeness. I want, when the great day comes, to be in a position to enounce clearly, without addition or omission, all that its interminable prelude had brought me and left me in the way of chattels personal. I presume it is an obsession.

I see then I had attributed to myself certain objects no longer in my possession, as far as I can see. But might they not have

rolled behind a piece of furniture? That would surprise me. A
boot, for example, can a boot roll behind a piece of furniture?
And yet I see only one boot. And behind what piece of furniture?
In this room, to the best of my knowledge, there is only one piece
of furniture capable of intervening between me and my possessions, I refer to the cupboard. But it so cleaves to the wall, to the
two walls, for it stands in the corner, that it seems part of them.
It may be objected that my button-boot, for it was a kind of
button-boot, is in the cupboard. I thought of that. But I have
gone through it, my stick has gone through the cupboard, opening
the doors, the drawers, for the first time perhaps, and rooting
everywhere. And the cupboard, far from containing my boot, is
empty. No, I am now without this boot, just as I am now without
certain other objects of less value, which I thought I had
preserved, among them a zinc ring that shone like silver. I note
on the other hand, in the heap, the presence of two or three
objects I had quite forgotten and one of which at least, the bowl
of a pipe, strikes no chord in my memory. I do not remember ever
having smoked a tobacco-pipe. I remember the soap-pipe with
which, as a child, I used to blow bubbles, an odd bubble. Never
mind, this bowl is now mine, wherever it comes from. A number
of my treasures are derived from the same source. I also discovered a little packet tied up in age-yellowed newspaper. It
reminds me of something, but of what? I drew it over beside the
bed and felt it with the knob of my stick. And my hand understood softness and lightness, better I think than if it had touched
the thing directly, fingering it and weighing it in its palm. I
resolved, I don't know why, not to undo it. I sent it back into the
corner, with the rest. I shall speak of it again perhaps, when the
time comes. I shall say, I can hear myself already, Item, a little
packet, soft, and light as a feather, tied up in newspaper. It will be
my little mystery, all my own. Perhaps it is a lack of rupees. Or
a lock of hair.

I told myself too that I must make better speed. True lives do
not tolerate this excess of circumstance. It is there the demon
lurks, like the gonococcus in the folds of the prostate. My time is
limited. It is thence that one fine day, when all nature smiles and

shines, the rack lets loose its black unforgettable cohorts and sweeps away the blue for ever. My situation is truly delicate. What fine things, what momentous things, I am going to miss through fear, fear of falling back into the old error, fear of not finishing in time, fear of revelling, for the last time, in a last outpouring of misery, impotence and hate. The forms are many in which the unchanging seeks relief from its formlessness. Ah yes, I was always subject to the deep thought, especially in the spring of the year. That one had been nagging at me for the past five minutes. I venture to hope there will be no more, of that depth. After all it is not important not to finish, there are worse things than velleities. But is that the point? Quite likely. All I ask is that the last of mine, as long as it lasts, should have living for its theme, that is all, I know what I mean. If it begins to run short of life I shall feel it. All I ask is to know, before I abandon him whose life has so well begun, that my death and mine alone prevents him from living on, from winning, losing, joying, suffering, rotting and dying, and that even had I lived he would have waited, before he died, for his body to be dead. That is what you might call taking a reef in your sails.

My body does not yet make up its mind. But I fancy it weighs heavier on the bed, flattens and spreads. My breath, when it comes back, fills the room with its din, though my chest moves no more than a sleeping child's. I open my eyes and gaze unblinkingly and long at the night sky. So a tiny tot I gaped, first at the novelties, then at the antiquities. Between it and me the pane, misted and smeared with the filth of years. I should like to breathe on it, but it is too far away. It is such a night as Kaspar David Friedrich loved, tempestuous and bright. That name that comes back to me, those names. The clouds scud, tattered by the wind, across a limpid ground. If I had the patience to wait I would see the moon. But I have not. Now that I have looked I hear the wind. I close my eyes and it mingles with my breath. Words and images run riot in my head, pursuing, flying, clashing, merging, endlessly. But beyond this tumult there is a great calm, and a great indifference, never really to be troubled by anything again. I turn a little on my side, press my mouth against the

pillow, and my nose, crush against the pillow my old hairs now
no doubt as white as snow, pull the blanket over my head. I feel,
deep down in my trunk, I cannot be more explicit, pains that
seem new to me. I think they are chiefly in my back. They have
a kind of rhythm, they even have a kind of little tune. They are
bluish. How bearable all that is, my God. My head is almost
facing the wrong way, like a bird's. I part my lips, now I have the
pillow in my mouth. I have, I have. I suck. The search for myself
is ended. I am buried in the world, I knew I would find my place
there one day, the old world cloisters me, victorious. I am happy,
I knew I would be happy one day. But I am not wise. For the
wise thing now would be to let go, at this instant of happiness.
And what do I do? I go back again to the light, to the fields I so
longed to love, to the sky all astir with little white clouds as
white and light as snowflakes, to the life I could never manage,
through my own fault perhaps, through pride, or pettiness, but
I don't think so. The beasts are at pasture, the sun warms the
rocks and makes them glitter. Yes, I leave my happiness and go
back to the race of men too, they come and go, often with
burdens. Perhaps I have judged them ill, but I don't think so. I
have not judged them at all. All I want now is to make a last
effort to understand, to begin to understand, how such creatures
are possible. No, it is not a question of understanding. Of what
then? I don't know. Here I go none the less, mistakenly. Night,
storm and sorrow, and the catalepsies of the soul, this time I shall
see that they are good. The last word is not yet said between me
and—yes, the last word is said. Perhaps I simply want to hear it
said again. Just once again. No, I want nothing.

 The Lamberts. The Lamberts found it difficult to live, I mean
to make ends meet. There was the man, the woman and two
children, a boy and a girl. There at least is something that admits
of no controversy. The father was known as Big Lambert, and big
he was indeed. He had married his young cousin and was still with
her. This was his third or fourth marriage. He had other children
here and there, grown men and women imbedded deep in life,
hoping for nothing more, from themselves or from others. They
helped him, each one according to his means, or the humour of

the moment, out of gratitude towards him but for whom they had
never seen the light of day, or saying, with indulgence, If it had
not been he it would have been someone else. Big Lambert had
not a tooth in his head and smoked his cigarettes in a cigarette-
holder, while regretting his pipe. He was highly thought of as a
bleeder and disjointer of pigs and greatly sought after, I exaggerate, in that capacity. For his fee was lower than the butcher's, and
he had even been known to demand no more, in return for his
services, than a lump of gammon or a pig's cheek. How plausible
all that is. He often spoke of his father with respect and tenderness. His like will not be seen again, he used to say, once I am
gone. He must have said this in other words. His great days then
fell in December and January, and from February onwards he
waited impatiently for the return of that season, the principal
event of which is unquestionably the Saviour's birth, in a stable,
while wondering if he would be spared till then. Then he would
set forth, hugging under his arm, in their case, the great knives so
lovingly whetted before the fire the night before, and in his pocket,
wrapped in paper, the apron destined to protect his Sunday suit
while he worked. And at the thought that he, Big Lambert, was
on his way towards that distant homestead where all was in readi-
ness for his coming, and that in spite of his great age he was still
needed, and his methods preferred to those of younger men, then
his old heart exulted. From these expeditions he reached home
late in the night, drunk and exhausted by the long road and the
emotions of the day. And for days afterwards he could speak of
nothing but the pig he had just dispatched, I would say into the
other world if I was not aware that pigs have none but this, to
the great affliction of his family. But they did not dare protest, for
they feared him. Yes, at an age when most people cringe and
cower, as if to apologize for still being present, Lambert was
feared and in a position to do as he pleased. And even his young
wife had abandoned all hope of bringing him to heel, by means of
her cunt, that trump card of young wives. For she knew what he
would do to her if she did not open it to him. And he even
insisted on her making things easy for him, in ways that often
appeared to her exorbitant. And at the least show of rebellion

on her part he would run to the wash-house and come back with the battle and beat her until she came round to a better way of thinking. All this by the way. And to return to our pigs, Lambert continued to expatiate, to his near and dear ones, of an evening, while the lamp burned low, on the specimen he had just slaughtered, until the day he was summoned to slaughter another. Then all his conversation was of this new pig, so unlike the other in every respect, so quite unlike, and yet at bottom the same. For all pigs are alike, when you get to know their little ways, struggle, squeal, bleed, squeal, struggle, bleed, squeal and faint away, in more or less the same way exactly, a way that is all their own and could never be imitated by a lamb, for example, or a kid. But once March was out Big Lambert recovered his calm and became his silent self again.

The son, or heir, was a great strapping lad with terrible teeth.

The farm. The farm was in a hollow, flooded in winter and in summer burnt to a cinder. The way to it lay through a fine meadow. But this fine meadow did not belong to the Lamberts, but to other peasants living at a distance. There jonquils and narcissi bloomed in extraordinary profusion, at the appropriate season. And there at nightfall, stealthily, Big Lambert turned loose his goats.

Strange to say this gift that Lambert possessed when it came to sticking pigs seemed of no help to him when it came to rearing them, and it was seldom his own exceeded nine stone. Clapped into a tiny sty on the day of its arrival, in the month of April, it remained there until the day of its death, on Christmas Eve. For Lambert persisted in dreading for his pigs, though every passing year proved him wrong, the thinning effects of exercise. Daylight and fresh air he dreaded for them too. And it was finally a weak pig, blind and lean, that he lay on its back in the box, having tied its legs, and killed, indignantly but without haste, upbraiding it the while for its ingratitude, at the top of his voice. For he could not or would not understand that the pig was not to blame, but he himself, who had coddled it unduly. And he persisted in his error.

Dead world, airless, waterless. That's it, reminisce. Here and there, in the bed of a crater, the shadow of a withered lichen. And

nights of three hundred hours. Dearest of lights, wan, pitted, least
fatuous of lights. That's it, babble. How long can it have lasted?
Five minutes? Ten minutes? Yes, no more, not much more. But
my sliver of sky is silvery with it yet. In the old days I used to
count, up to three hundred, four hundred, and with other things
too, the showers, the bells, the chatter of the sparrows at dawn, or
with nothing, for no reason, for the sake of counting, and then I
divided, by sixty. That passed the time, I was time, I devoured
the world. Not now, any more. A man changes. As he gets on.

In the filthy kitchen, with its earth floor, Sapo had his place,
by the window. Big Lambert and his son left their work, came
and shook his hand, then went away, leaving him with the mother
and the daughter. But they too had their work, they too went
away and left him, alone. There was so much work, so little time,
so few hands. The woman, pausing an instant between two tasks,
or in the midst of one, flung up her arms and, in the same breath,
unable to sustain their great weight, let them fall again. Then she
began to toss them about in a way difficult to describe, and not
easy to understand. The movements resembled those, at once
frantic and slack, of an arm shaking a duster, or a rag, to rid it
of its dust. And so rapid was the trepidation of the limp, empty
hands that there seemed to be four or five at the end of each arm,
instead of the usual one. At the same time angry unanswerable
questions, such as, What's the use? fell from her lips. Her hair
came loose and fell about her face. It was thick, grey and dirty,
for she had no time to tend it, and her face was pale and thin and
as though gouged with worry and its attendant rancours. The
bosom—no, what matters is the head and then the hands it calls
to its help before all else, that clasp, wring, then sadly resume
their labour, lifting the old inert objects and changing their
position, bringing them closer together and moving them further
apart. But this pantomime and these ejaculations were not
intended for any living person. For every day and several times a
day she gave way to them, within doors and without. Then she
little cared whether she was observed or not, whether what she
was doing was urgent or could wait, no, but she dropped everything and began to cry out and gesticulate, the last of all the

living as likely as not and dead to what was going on about her.
Then she fell silent and stood stockstill a moment, before resuming whatever it was she had abandoned or setting about some new
task. Sapo remained alone, by the window, the bowl of goat's
milk on the table before him, forgotten. It was summer. The room
was dark in spite of the door and window open on the great
outer light. Through these narrow openings, far apart, the light
poured, lit up a little space, then died, undiffused. It had no
steadfastness, no assurance of lasting as long as day lasted. But it
entered at every moment, renewed from without, entered and died
at every moment, devoured by the dark. And at the least abate-
ment of the inflow the room grew darker and darker until nothing
in it was visible any more. For the dark had triumphed. And Sapo,
his face turned towards an earth so resplendent that it hurt his
eyes, felt at his back and all about him the unconquerable dark,
and it licked the light on his face. Sometimes abruptly he turned
to face it, letting it envelop and pervade him, with a kind of
relief. Then he heard more clearly the sounds of those at work,
the daughter calling to her goats, the father cursing his mule. But
silence was in the heart of the dark, the silence of dust and the
things that would never stir, if left alone. And the ticking of the
invisible alarm-clock was as the voice of that silence which, like
the dark, would one day triumph too. And then all would be still
and dark and all things at rest for ever at last. Finally he took
from his pocket the few poor gifts he had brought, laid them on
the table and went. But it sometimes happened, before he decided
to go, before he went rather, for there was no decision, that a hen,
taking advantage of the open door, would venture into the room.
No sooner had she crossed the threshold than she paused, one
leg hooked up under her breech, her head on one side, blinking,
anxious. Then, reassured, she advanced a little further, jerkily,
with concertina neck. It was a grey hen, perhaps the grey hen.
Sapo got to know her well and, it seemed to him, to be well
known by her. If he rose to go she did not fly into a flutter. But
perhaps there were several hens, all grey and so alike in other
respects that Sapo's eye, avid of resemblances, could not tell between them. Sometimes she was followed by a second, a third and

even a fourth, bearing no likeness to her, and but little to one
another, in the matter of plumage and entasis. These showed
more confidence than the grey, who had led the way and come to
no harm. They shone an instant in the light, grew dimmer and
dimmer as they advanced, and finally vanished. Silent at first,
fearing to betray their presence, they began gradually to scratch
and cluck, for contentment, and to relax their soughing feathers.
But often the grey hen came alone, or one of the grey hens if
you prefer, for that is a thing that will never be known, though
it might well have been, without much trouble. For all that was
necessary, in order that it might be known whether there was
only one grey hen or more than one, was for someone to be
present when all the hens came running towards Mrs. Lambert as
she cried, Tweet! Tweet!, and banged on an old tin with an old
spoon. But after all what use would that have been? For it was
quite possible there were several grey hens, and yet only one in
the habit of coming to the kitchen. And yet the experiment was
worth making. For it was quite possible there was only one grey
hen, even at feeding-time. Which would have clinched the matter.
And yet that is a thing that will never be known. For among
those who must have known, some are dead and the others have
forgotten. And the day when it was urgent for Sapo to have this
point cleared up, and his mind set at rest, it was too late. Then he
was sorry he had not understood, in time to profit by it, the
importance that those hours were one day to assume, for him,
those long hours in that old kitchen where, neither quite indoors
nor quite out of doors, he waited to be on his feet again, and in
motion, and while waiting noted many things, among them this
big, anxious, ashen bird, poised irresolute on the bright threshold,
then clucking and clawing behind the range and fidgeting her
atrophied wings, soon to be sent flying with a broom and angry
cries and soon to return, cautiously, with little hesitant steps,
stopping often to listen, opening and shutting her little bright black
eyes. And so he went, all unsuspecting, with the fond impression
of having been present at everyday scenes of no import. He
stooped to cross the threshold and saw before him the well, with
its winch, chain and bucket, and often too a long line of tattered

washing, swaying and drying in the sun. He went by the little
path he had come by, along the edge of the meadow in the
shadow of the great trees that bordered the stream, its bed a
chaos of gnarled roots, boulders and baked mud. And so he went,
often unnoticed, in spite of his strange walk, his halts and sudden
starts. Or the Lamberts saw him, from far off or from near by, or
some of them from far off and the others from near by, suddenly
emerge from behind the washing and set off down the path. Then
they did not try to detain him or even call goodbye, unresentful
at his leaving them in a way that seemed so lacking in friendliness,
for they knew he meant no harm. Or if at the time they could
not help feeling a little hurt, this feeling was quite dispelled a
little later, when they found on the kitchen-table the crumpled
paper-bag containing a few little articles of haberdashery. And
these humble presents, but oh how useful, and this oh so delicate
way of giving, disarmed them too at the sight of the bowl of
goat's milk only half emptied, or left untouched, and prevented
them from regarding this as an affront, in the way tradition
required. But it would appear on reflection that Sapo's departure
can seldom have escaped them. For at the least moment within
sight of their land, were it only that of a little bird alighting or
taking to wing, they raised their heads and stared with wide eyes.
And even on the road, of which segments were visible more than
a mile away, nothing could happen without their knowledge, and
they were able not only to identify all those who passed along it
and whose remoteness reduced them to the size of a pin's head,
but also to divine whence they were coming, where they were
going, and for what purpose. Then they cried the news to one
another, for they often worked at a great distance apart, or they
exchanged signals, all erect and turned towards the event, for it
was one, before bowing themselves down to the earth again. And
at the first spell of rest taken in common, about the table or
elsewhere, each one gave his version of what had passed and
listened to those of the others. And if at first they were not in
agreement about what they had seen, they talked it over doggedly
until they were, in agreement I mean, or until they resigned themselves to never being so. It was therefore difficult for Sapo to glide

away unseen, even in the deep shadow of the trees that bordered
the stream, even supposing him to have been capable of gliding,
for his movements were rather those of one floundering in a quag.
And all raised their heads and watched him as he went, then
looked at one another, before stooping to the earth again. And on
each face bent to the earth there played perhaps a little smile, a
little rictus rather, but without malice, each wondering perhaps
if the others felt the same thing and making the resolve to ask
them, at their next meeting. But the face of Sapo as he stumbled
away, now in the shadow of the venerable trees he could not
name, now in the brightness of the waving meadow, so erratic
was his course, the face of Sapo was as always grave, or rather
expressionless. And when he halted it was not the better to think,
or the closer to pore upon his dream, but simply because the voice
had ceased that told him to go on. Then with his pale eyes he
stared down at the earth, blind to its beauty, and to its utility,
and to the little wild many-coloured flowers happy among the
crops and weeds. But these stations were short-lived, for he was
still young. And of a sudden he is off again, on his wanderings,
passing from light to shadow, from shadow to light, unheedingly.

When I stop, as just now, the noises begin again, strangely
loud, those whose turn it is. So that I seem to have again the
hearing of my boyhood. Then in my bed, in the dark, on stormy
nights, I could tell from one another, in the outcry without, the
leaves, the boughs, the groaning trunks, even the grasses and the
house that sheltered me. Each tree had its own cry, just as no
two whispered alike, when the air was still. I heard afar the iron
gates clashing and dragging at their posts and the wind rushing
between their bars. There was nothing, not even the sand on the
paths, that did not utter its cry. The still nights too, still as the
grave as the saying is, were nights of storm for me, clamorous
with countless pantings. These I amused myself with identifying,
as I lay there. Yes, I got great amusement, when young, from
their so-called silence. The sound I liked best had nothing noble
about it. It was the barking of the dogs, at night, in the clusters
of hovels up in the hills, where the stone-cutters lived, like generations of stone-cutters before them. It came down to me where I

lay, in the house in the plain, wild and soft, at the limit of earshot, soon weary. The dogs of the valley replied with their gross bay all fangs and jaws and foam. From the hills another joy came down, I mean the brief scattered lights that sprang up on their slopes at nightfall, merging in blurs scarcely brighter than the sky, less bright than the stars, and which the palest moon extinguished. They were things that scarcely were, on the confines of silence and dark, and soon ceased. So I reason now, at my ease. Standing before my high window I gave myself to them, waiting for them to end, for my joy to end, straining towards the joy of ended joy. But our business at the moment is less with these futilities than with my ears from which there spring two impetuous tufts of no doubt yellow hair, yellowed by wax and lack of care, and so long that the lobes are hidden. I note then, without emotion, that of late their hearing seems to have improved. Oh not that I was ever even incompletely deaf. But for a long time now I have been hearing things confusedly. There I go again. What I mean is possibly this, that the noises of the world, so various in themselves and which I used to be so clever at distinguishing from one another, had been dinning at me for so long, always the same old noises, as gradually to have merged into a single noise, so that all I heard was one vast continuous buzzing. The volume of sound perceived remained no doubt the same, I had simply lost the faculty of decomposing it. The noises of nature, of mankind and even my own, were all jumbled together in one and the same un-bridled gibberish. Enough. I would willingly attribute part of my shall I say my misfortunes to this disordered sense were I not unfortunately rather inclined to look upon it as a blessing. Misfortunes, blessings, I have no time to pick my words, I am in a hurry to be done. And yet no, I am in no hurry. Decidedly this evening I shall say nothing that is not false, I mean nothing that is not calculated to leave me in doubt as to my real intentions. For it is evening, even night, one of the darkest I can remember, I have a short memory. My little finger glides before my pencil across the page and gives warning, falling over the edge, that the end of the line is near. But in the other direction, I mean of course vertically, I have nothing to guide me. I did not want to

write, but I had to resign myself to it in the end. It is in order to
know where I have got to, where he has got to. At first I did not
write, I just said the thing. Then I forgot what I had said. A
minimum of memory is indispensable, if one is to live really.
Take his family, for example, I really know practically nothing
about his family any more. But that does not worry me, there is
a record of it somewhere. It is the only way to keep an eye on
him. But as far as I myself am concerned the same necessity does
not arise, or does it? And yet I write about myself with the same
pencil and in the same exercise-book as about him. It is because
it is no longer I, I must have said so long ago, but another whose
life is just beginning. It is right that he too should have his little
chronicle, his memories, his reason, and be able to recognize the
good in the bad, the bad in the worst, and so grow gently old all
down the unchanging days and die one day like any other day,
only shorter. That is my excuse. But there must be others, no less
excellent. Yes, it is quite dark. I can see nothing. I can scarcely
even see the window-pane, or the wall forming with it so sharp
a contrast that it often looks like the edge of an abyss. I hear the
noise of my little finger as it glides over the paper and then that
so different of the pencil following after. That is what surprises
me and makes me say that something must have changed. Whence
that child I might have been, why not? And I hear also, there we
are at last, I hear a choir, far enough away for me not to hear it
when it goes soft. It is a song I know, I don't know how, and
when it fades, and when it dies quite away, it goes on inside me,
but too slow, or too fast, for when it comes on the air to me again
it is not together with mine, but behind, or ahead. It is a mixed
choir, or I am greatly deceived. With children too perhaps. I
have the absurd feeling it is conducted by a woman. It has been
singing the same song for a long time now. They must be re-
hearsing. It belongs already to the long past, it has uttered for
the last time the triumphal cry on which it ends. Can it be Easter
Week? Thus with the year Seasons return. If it can, could not this
song I have just heard, and which quite frankly is not yet quite
stilled within me, could not this song have simply been to the
honour and glory of him who was the first to rise from the dead,

to him who saved me, twenty centuries in advance? Did I say the first? The final bawl lends colour to this view.

I fear I must have fallen asleep again. In vain I grope, I cannot find my exercise-book. But I still have the pencil in my hand. I shall have to wait for day to break. God knows what I am going to do till then.

I have just written, I fear I must have fallen, etc. I hope this is not too great a distortion of the truth. I now add these few lines, before departing from myself again. I do not depart from myself now with the same avidity as a week ago for example. For this must be going on now for over a week, it must be over a week since I said, I shall soon be quite dead at last, etc. Wrong again. That is not what I said, I could swear to it, that is what I wrote. This last phrase seems familiar, suddenly I seem to have written it somewhere before, or spoken it, word for word. Yes, I shall soon be, etc., that is what I wrote when I realised I did not know what I had said, at the beginning of my say, and subsequently, and that consequently the plan I had formed, to live, and cause to live, at last, to play at last and die alive, was going the way of all my other plans. I think the dawn was not so slow in coming as I had feared, I really do. But I feared nothing, I fear nothing any more. High summer is truly at hand. Turned towards the window I saw the pane shiver at last, before the ghastly sunrise. It is no ordinary pane, it brings me sunset and it brings me sunrise. The exercise-book had fallen to the ground. I took a long time to find it. It was under the bed. How are such things possible? I took a long time to recover it. I had to harpoon it. It is not pierced through and through, but it is in a bad way. It is a thick exercise-book. I hope it will see me out. From now on I shall write on both sides of the page. Where does it come from? I don't know. I found it, just like that, the day I needed it. Knowing perfectly well I had no exercise-book I rummaged in my possessions in the hope of finding one. I was not disappointed, not surprised. If tomorrow I needed an old love-letter I would adopt the same method. It is ruled in squares. The first pages are covered with ciphers and other symbols and diagrams, with here and there a brief phrase. Calculations, I reckon. They seem to stop suddenly, prematurely

at all events. As though discouraged. Perhaps it is astronomy, or
astrology. I did not look closely. I drew a line, no, I did not even
draw a line, and I wrote, Soon I shall be quite dead at last, and
so on, without even going on to the next page, which was blank.
Good. Now I need not dilate on this exercise-book when it comes
to the inventory, but merely say, Item, an exercise-book, giving
perhaps the colour of the cover. But I may well lose it between
now and then, for good and all. The pencil on the contrary is an
old acquaintance, I must have had it about me when I was
brought here. It has five faces. It is very short. It is pointed at
both ends. A Venus. I hope it will see me out. I was saying I did
not depart from myself now with quite the same alacrity. That
must be in the natural order of things, all that pertains to me
must be written there, including my inability to grasp what order
is meant. For I have never seen any sign of any, inside me or
outside me. I have pinned my faith to appearances, believing them
to be vain. I shall not go into the details. Choke, go down, come
up, choke, suppose, deny, affirm, drown. I depart from myself
less gladly. Amen. I waited for the dawn. Doing what? I don't
know. What I had to do. I watched for the window. I gave rein
to my pains, my impotence. And in the end it seemed to me, for
a second, that I was going to have a visit!

The summer holidays were drawing to a close. The decisive
moment was at hand when the hopes reposed in Sapo were to be
fulfilled, or dashed to the ground. He is trained to a hair, said
Mr. Saposcat. And Mrs. Saposcat, whose piety grew warm in
times of crisis, prayed for his success. Kneeling at her bedside, in
her night-dress, she ejaculated, silently for her husband would not
have approved, Oh God grant he pass, grant he pass, grant he
scrape through!

When this first ordeal was surmounted there would be others,
every year, several times a year. But it seemed to the Saposcats
that these would be less terrible than the first which was to give
them, or deny them the right to say, He is doing his medicine, or,
He is reading for the bar. For they felt that a more or less normal
if unintelligent youth, once admitted to the study of these professions, was almost sure to be certified, sooner or later, apt to

exercise them. For they had experience of doctors, and of lawyers, like most people.

One day Mr. Saposcat sold himself a fountain-pen, at a discount. A Bird. I shall give it to him on the morning of the examination, he said. He took off the long cardboard lid and showed the pen to his wife. Leave it in its box! he cried, as she made to take it in her hand. It lay almost hidden in the scrolled leaflet containing the instructions for use. Mr. Saposcat parted the edges of the paper and held up the box for his wife to look inside. But she, instead of looking at the pen, looked at him. He named the price. Might it not be better, she said, to let him have it the day before, to give him time to get used to the nib? You are right, he said, I had not thought of that. Or even two days before, she said, to give him time to change the nib if it does not suit him. A bird, its yellow beak agape to show it was singing, adorned the lid, which Mr. Saposcat now put on again. He wrapped with expert hands the box in tissue-paper and slipped over it a narrow rubber band. He was not pleased. It is a medium nib, he said, and it will certainly suit him.

This conversation was renewed the next day. Mr. Saposcat said, Might it not be better if we just lent him the pen and told him he could keep it for his own, if he passed? Then we must do so at once, said Mrs. Saposcat, otherwise there is no point in it. To which Mr. Saposcat, made, after a silence, a first objection, and then, after a second silence, a second objection. He first objected that his son, if he received the pen forthwith, would have time to break it, or lose it, before the paper. He secondly objected that his son, if he received the pen immediately, and assuming he neither broke nor lost it, would have time to get so used to it and, by comparing it with the pens of his less impoverished friends, so familiar with its defects, that its possession would no longer tempt him. I did not know it was an inferior article, said Mrs. Saposcat. Mr. Saposcat placed his hand on the table-cloth and sat gazing at it for some time. Then he laid down his napkin and left the room. Adrian, cried Mrs. Saposcat, come back and finish your sweet! Alone before the table she listened to the steps on the garden-path, clearer, fainter, clearer, fainter.

The Lamberts. One day Sapo arrived at the farm earlier than usual. But do we know what time he usually arrived? Lengthening, fading shadows. He was surprised to see, at a distance, in the midst of the young stubble, the father's big red and white head. His body was in the hole or pit he had dug for his mule, which had died during the night. Edmund came out of the house, wiping his mouth, and joined him. Lambert then climbed out of the hole and the son went down into it. Drawing closer Sapo saw the mule's black corpse. Then all became clear to him. The mule was lying on its side, as was to be expected. The forelegs were stretched out straight and rigid, the hind drawn up under the belly. The yawning jaws, the wreathed lips, the enormous teeth, the bulging eyes, composed a striking death's-head. Edmund handed up to his father the pick, the shovel and the spade and climbed out of the hole. Together they dragged the mule by the legs to the edge of the hole and heaved it in, on its back. The forelegs, pointing towards heaven, projected above the level of the ground. Old Lambert banged them down with his spade. He handed the spade to his son and went towards the house. Edmund began to fill up the hole. Sapo stood watching him. A great calm stole over him. Great calm is an exaggeration. He felt better. The end of a life is always vivifying. Edmund paused to rest, leaned panting on the spade and smiled. There were great pink gaps in his front teeth. Big Lambert sat by the window, smoking, drinking, watching his son. Sapo sat down before him, laid his hand on the table and his head on his hand, thinking he was alone. Between his head and his hand he slipped the other hand and sat there marble still. Louis began to talk. He seemed in good spirits. The mule, in his opinion, had died of old age. He had bought it, two years before, on its way to the slaughter-house. So he could not complain. After the transaction the owner of the mule predicted that it would drop down dead at the first ploughing. But Lambert was a connoisseur of mules. In the case of mules it is the eye that counts, the rest is unimportant. So he looked the mule full in the eye, at the gates of the slaughter-house, and saw it could still be made to serve. And the mule returned his gaze, in the yard of the slaughter-house. As Lambert unfolded his story the slaughter-

house loomed larger and larger. Thus the site of the transaction
shifted gradually from the road that led to the slaughter-house to
the gates of the slaughter-house and thence to the yard itself.
Yet a little while and he would have contended for the mule with
the knacker. The look in his eye, he said, was like a prayer to
me to take him. It was covered with sores, but in the case of
mules one should never let oneself be deterred by senile sores.
Someone said, He's done ten miles already, you'll never get him
home, he'll drop down dead on the road. I thought I might screw
six months out of him, said Lambert, and I screwed two years. All
the time he told this story he kept his eyes fixed on his son.
There they sat, the table between them, in the gloom, one speaking, the other listening, and far removed, the one from what he
said, the other from what he heard, and far from each other. The
heap of earth was dwindling, the earth shone strangely in the
raking evening light, glowing in patches as though with its own
fires, in the fading light. Edmund stopped often to rest, leaning
on the spade and looking about him. The slaughter-house, said
Lambert, that's where I buy my beasts, will you look at that
loafer. He went out and set to work, beside his son. They worked
together for a time, heedless of each other. Then the son dropped
his shovel, turned aside and moved slowly away, passing from toil
to rest in a single unbroken movement that did not seem of his
doing. The mule was no longer visible. The face of the earth, on
which it had plodded its life away, would see it no more, toiling
before the plough, or the dray. And Big Lambert would soon
be able to plough and harrow the place where it lay, with another
mule, or an old horse, or an old ox, bought at the Knacker's yard,
knowing that the share would not turn up the putrid flesh or be
blunted by the big bones. For he knew how the dead and buried
tend, contrary to what one might expect, to rise to the surface, in
which they resemble the drowned. And he had made allowance
for this when digging the hole. Edmund and his mother passed
each other by in silence. She had been to see a neighbour, to
borrow a pound of lentils for their supper. She was thinking of
the handsome steelyard that had served to weigh them and
wondering if it was true. Before her husband too she rapidly

passed, without a glance, and in his attitude there was nothing to
suggest that he had seen her either. She lit the lamp where it
stood at its usual place on the chimney-piece, beside the alarm-
clock flanked in its turn by a crucifix hanging from a nail. The
clock, being the lowest of the three, had to remain in the middle,
and the lamp and crucifix could not change places because of
the nail from which the latter was hung. She stood with her forehead and her hands pressed against the wall, until she might turn
up the wick. She turned it up and put on the yellow globe which
a large hole defaced. Seeing Sapo she first thought he was her
daughter. Then her thoughts flew to the absent one. She set down
the lamp on the table and the outer world went out. She sat down,
emptied out the lentils on the table and began to sort them. So
that soon there were two heaps on the table, one big heap getting
smaller and one small heap getting bigger. But suddenly with a
furious gesture she swept the two together, annihilating thus in
less than a second the work of two or three minutes. Then she
went away and came back with a saucepan. It won't kill them,
she said, and with the heel of her hand she brought the lentils to
the edge of the table and over the edge into the saucepan, as if
all that mattered was not to be killed, but so clumsily and with
such nervous haste that a great number fell wide of the pan to
the ground. Then she took up the lamp and went out to fetch
wood· perhaps, or a lump of fat bacon. Now that it was dark
again in the kitchen the dark outside gradually lightened and
Sapo, his eye against the window-pane, was able to discern certain
shapes, including that of Big Lambert stamping the ground. To
stop in the middle of a tedious and perhaps futile task was something that Sapo could readily understand. For a great number of
tasks are of this kind, without a doubt, and the only way to end
them is to abandon them. She could have gone on sorting her
lentils all night and never achieved her purpose, which was to
free them from all admixture. But in the end she would have
stopped, saying, I have done all I can do. But she would not have
done all she could have done. But the moment comes when one
desists, because it is the wisest thing to do, discouraged, but not
to the extent of undoing all that has been done. But what if her

purpose, in sorting the lentils, were not to rid them of all that was not lentil, but only of the greater part, what then? I don't know. Whereas there are other tasks, other days, of which one may fairly safely say that they are finished, though I do not see which. She came back holding the lamp high and a little to one side, so as not to be dazzled. In the other hand she held a white rabbit, by the hindlegs. For whereas the mule had been black, the rabbit had been white. It was dead already, it had ceased to be. There are rabbits that die before they are killed, from sheer fright. They have time to do so while being taken out of the hutch, often by the ears, and disposed in the most convenient position to receive the blow, whether on the back of the neck or on some other part. And often you strike a corpse, without knowing it. For you have just seen the rabbit alive and well behind the wire meshing, nibbling at its leaves. And you congratulate yourself on having succeeded with the first blow, and not caused unnecessary suffering, whereas in reality you have taken all that trouble for nothing. This occurs most frequently at night, fright being greater in the night. Hens on the other hand are more stubborn livers and some have been observed, with the head already off, to cut a few last capers before collapsing. Pigeons too are less impressionable and sometimes even struggle, before choking to death. Mrs. Lambert was breathing hard. Little devil! she cried. But Sapo was already far away, trailing his hand in the high waving meadow grasses. Soon afterwards Lambert, then his son, attracted by the savoury smell, entered the kitchen. Sitting at the table, face to face, their eyes averted from each other's eyes, they waited. But the woman, the mother, went to the door and called. Lizzy! she cried, again and again. Then she went back to her range. She had seen the moon. After a silence Lambert declared, I'll kill Whitey tomorrow. Those of course were not the words he used, but that was the meaning. But neither his wife nor his son could approve him, the former because she would have preferred him to kill Blackey, the latter because he held that to kill the kids at such an early stage of their development, either of them, it was all the same to him, would be premature. But Big Lambert told them to hold their tongues and went to the corner to fetch the

case containing the knives, three in number. All he had to do was
to wipe off the grease and whet them a little on one another. Mrs.
Lambert went back to the door, listened, called. In the far
distance the flock replied. She's coming, she said. But a long time
passed before she came. When the meal was over Edmund went
up to bed, so as to masturbate in peace and comfort before his
sister joined him, for they shared the same room. Not that he was
restrained by modesty, when his sister was there. Nor was she,
when her brother was there. Their quarters were cramped, certain
refinements were not possible. Edmund then went up to bed, for
no particular reason. He would have gladly slept with his sister,
the father too, I mean the father would have gladly slept with his
daughter, the time was long past and gone when he would have
gladly slept with his sister. But something held them back. And
she did not seem eager. But she was still young. Incest then was
in the air. Mrs. Lambert, the only member of the household who
had no desire to sleep with anybody, saw it coming with indifference. She went out. Alone with his daughter Lambert sat watching her. She was crouched before the range, in an attitude of
dejection. He told her to eat and she began to eat the remains of
the rabbit, out of the pot, with a spoon. But it is hard to look
steadily for any length of time at a fellow-creature, even when
you are resolved to, and suddenly Lambert saw his daughter at
another place and otherwise engaged than in bringing the spoon
up from the pot into her mouth and down from her mouth into
the pot again. And yet he could have sworn that he had not
taken his eyes off her. He said, To-morrow we'll kill Whitey, you
can hold her if you like. But seeing her still so sad, and her
cheeks wet with tears, he went towards her.

What tedium. If I went on to the stone? No, it would be the
same thing. The Lamberts, the Lamberts, does it matter about
the Lamberts? No, not particularly. But while I am with them the
other is lost. How are my plans getting on, my plans, I had plans
not so long ago. Perhaps I have another ten years ahead of me.
The Lamberts! I shall try and go on all the same, a little longer,
my thoughts elsewhere, I can't stay here. I shall hear myself
talking, afar off, from my far mind, talking of the Lamberts,

talking of myself, my mind wandering, far from here, among its ruins.

Then Mrs. Lambert was alone in the kitchen. She sat down by the window and turned down the wick of the lamp, as she always did before blowing it out, for she did not like to blow out a lamp that was still hot. When she thought the chimney and shade had cooled sufficiently she got up and blew down the chimney. She stood a moment irresolute, bowed forward with her hands on the table, before she sat down again. Her day of toil over, day dawned on other toils within her, on the crass tenacity of life and its diligent pains. Sitting, moving about, she bore them better than in bed. From the well of this unending weariness her sigh went up unendingly, for day when it was night, for night when it was day, and day and night, fearfully, for the light she had been told about, and told she could never understand, because it was not like those she knew, not like the summer dawn she would come again, to her waiting in the kitchen, sitting up straight on the chair, or bowed down over the table, with little sleep, little rest, but more than in her bed. Often she stood up and moved about the room, or out and round the ruinous old house. Five years now it had been going on, five or six, not more. She told herself she had a woman's disease, but half-heartedly. Night seemed less night in the kitchen pervaded with the everyday tribulations, day less dead. It helped her, when things were bad, to cling with her fingers to the worn table at which her family would soon be united, waiting for her to serve them, and to feel about her, ready for use, the life-long pots and pans. She opened the door and looked out. The moon had gone, but the stars were shining. She stood gazing up at them. It was a scene that had sometimes solaced her. She went to the well and grasped the chain. The bucket was at the bottom, the windlass locked. So it was. Her fingers strayed along the sinuous links. Her mind was a press of formless questions, mingling and crumbling limply away. Some seemed to have to do with her daughter, that minor worry, now lying sleepless in her bed, listening. Hearing her mother moving about, she was on the point of getting up and going down to her. But it was only the next day, or the day after, that she decided to tell her what Sapo had told her, namely that he was going away and would not come back. Then, as people do when someone even insignificant dies, they summoned up such memories as he had left them, helping one another and trying to agree. But we all know that little flame and its flickerings in the wild shadows. And agreement only comes a little later, with the forgetting.

Mortal tedium. One day I took counsel of an Israelite on the subject of conation. That must have been when I was still looking for someone to be faithful to me, and for me to be faithful to. Then I opened wide my eyes so that the candidates might admire their bottomless depths and the way they phosphoresced at all we left unspoken. Our faces were so close that I felt on mine the wafts of hot air and sprays of saliva, and he too, no doubt, on his. I can see him still, the fit of laughter past, wiping his eyes and mouth, and myself, with downcast eyes, pained by my wetted trousers and the little pool of urine at my feet. Now that I have no further use for him I may as well give his name, Jackson. I was sorry he had not a cat, or a young dog, or better still an old dog. But all he had to offer in the way of dumb companions was a pink and grey parrot. He used to try and teach it to say, Nihil in intellectu, etc. These first three words the bird managed well enough, but the celebrated restriction was too much for it, all you heard was a series of squawks. This annoyed Jackson, who kept nagging at it to begin all over again. Then Polly flew into a rage and retreated to a corner of its cage. It was a very fine cage, with every convenience, perches, swings, trays, troughs, stairs and cuttle-bones. It was even overcrowded, personally I would have felt cramped. Jackson called me the merino, I don't know why, perhaps because of the French expression. I could not help thinking that the notion of a wandering herd was better adapted to him than to me. But I have never thought anything but wind, the same that was never measured to me. My relations with Jackson were of short duration. I could have put up with him as a friend, but unfortunately he found me disgusting, as did Johnson, Wilson, Nicholson, and Watson, all whoresons. I then tried, for a space, to lay hold of a kindred spirit among the inferior races, red, yellow,

chocolate, and so on. And if the plague-stricken had been less difficult of access I would have intruded on them too, ogling, sidling,
leering, ineffing and conating, my heart palpitating. With the insane
too I failed, by a hair's-breadth. That must have been the way with
me then. But the point is rather what is the way with me now.
When young the old filled me with wonder and awe. Bawling
babies are what dumbfound me now. The house is full of them
finally. Suave mari magno, especially for the old salt. What tedium.
And I thought I had it all thought out. If I had the use of my
body I would throw it out of the window. But perhaps it is the
knowledge of my impotence that emboldens me to that thought.
All hangs together, I am in chains. Unfortunately I do not know
quite what floor I am on, perhaps I am only on the mezzanine.
The doors banging, the steps on the stairs, the noises in the street,
have not enlightened me, on this subject. All I know is that the
living are there, above me and beneath me. It follows at least that
I am not in the basement. And do I not sometimes see the sky
and sometimes, through my window, other windows facing it
apparently? But that proves nothing, I do not wish to prove
anything. Or so I say. Perhaps after all I am in a kind of vault
and this space which I take to be the street in reality no more
than a wide trench or ditch with other vaults opening upon it.
But the noises that rise up from below, the steps that come
climbing towards me? Perhaps there are other vaults even deeper
than mine, why not? In which case the question arises again as to
which floor I am on, there is nothing to be gained by my saying I
am in a basement if there are tiers of basements one on top of
another. But the noises that I say rise up from below, the steps
that I say come climbing towards me, do they really do so? I
have no proof that they do. To conclude from this that I am a prey
to hallucinations pure and simple is however a step I hesitate to
take. And I honestly believe that in this house there are people
coming and going and even conversing, and multitudes of fine
babies, particularly of late, which the parents keep moving about
from one place to another, to prevent their forming the habit of
motionlessness, in anticipation of the day when they will have to
move about unaided. But all things considered I would be hard

set to say for certain where exactly they are, in relation to where exactly I am. And when all is said and done there is nothing more like a step that climbs than a step that descends or even that paces to and fro forever on the same level, I mean for one not only in ignorance of his position and consequently of what he is to expect, in the way of sounds, but at the same time more than half-deaf more than half the time. There is naturally another possibility that does not escape me, though it would be a great disappointment to have it confirmed, and that is that I am dead already and that all continues more or less as when I was not. Perhaps I expired in the forest, or even earlier. In which case all the trouble I have been taking for some time past, for what purpose I do not clearly recall except that it was in some way connected with the feeling that my troubles were nearly over, has been to no purpose whatsoever. But my horse-sense tells me I have not yet quite ceased to gasp. And it summons in support of this view various considerations having to do for example with the little heap of my possessions, my system of nutrition and elimination, the couple across the way, the changing sky, and so on. Whereas in reality all that is perhaps nothing but my worms. Take for example the light that reigns in this den and of which the least that can be said, really the least, is that it is bizarre. I enjoy a kind of night and day, admittedly, often it is even pitch dark, but in rather a different way from the way to which I fancy I was accustomed, before I found myself here. Example, there is nothing like examples, I was once in utter darkness and waiting with some impatience for dawn to break, having need of its light to see to certain little things which it is difficult to see in the dark. And sure enough little by little the dark lightened and I was able to hook with my stick the objects I required. But the light, instead of being the dawn, turned out in a very short time to be the dusk. And the sun, instead of rising higher and higher in the sky as I confidently expected, calmly set, and night, the passing of which I had just celebrated after my fashion, calmly fell again. Now the reverse, as you might say, I mean day closing in the twilight of dawn, I must confess to never having experienced, and that goes to my heart, I mean that I cannot bring myself to declare that I experienced that too. And yet how often I have implored night to fall, all the livelong day, with all my feeble strength, and how often day to break, all the livelong night. But before leaving this subject and entering upon another, I feel it is my duty to say that it is never light in this place, never really light. The light is there, outside, the air sparkles, the granite wall across the way. glitters with all its mica, the light is against my window, but it does not come through. So that here all bathes, I will not say in shadow, nor even in half-shadow, but in a kind of leaden light that makes no shadow, so that it is hard to say from what direction it comes, for it seems to come from all directions at once, and with equal force. I am convinced for example that at the present moment it is as bright under my bed as it is under the ceiling, which admittedly is not saying much, but I need say no more. And does not that amount to simply this, that there is really no colour in this place, except in so far as this kind of grey incandescence may be called a colour? Yes, no doubt one may speak of grey, personally I have no objection, in which case the issue here would lie between this grey and the black that it overlays more or less, I was going to say according to the time of day, but no, it does not always seem to depend on the time of day. I myself am very grey, I even sometimes have the feeling that I emit grey, in the same way as my sheets for example. And my night is not the sky's. Naturally black is black the whole world over. But how is it my little space is not visited by the luminaries I sometimes see shining afar and how is it the moon where Cain toils bowed beneath his burden never sheds its light on my face? In a word there seems to be the light of the outer world, of those who know the sun and moon emerge at such an hour and at such another plunge again below the surface, and who rely on this, and who know that clouds are always to be expected but sooner or later always pass away, and mine. But mine too has its alternations, I will not deny it, its dusks and dawns, but that is what I say, for I too must have lived, once, out there, and there is no recovering from that. And when I examine the ceiling and walls I see there is no possibility of my making light, artificial

light, like the couple across the way for example. But someone
would have to give me a lamp, or a torch, you know, and I don't
know if the air here is of the kind that lends itself to the comedy
of combustion. Mem, look for a match in my possessions, and
see if it burns. The noises too, cries, steps, doors, murmurs, cease
for whole days, their days. Then that silence of which, knowing
what I know, I shall merely say that there is nothing, how shall
I merely say, nothing negative about it. And softly my little space
begins to throb again. You may say it is all in my head, and
indeed sometimes it seems to me I am in a head and that these
eight, no, six, these six planes that enclose me are of solid bone.
But thence to conclude the head is mine, no, never. A kind of air
circulates, I must have said so, and when all goes still I hear it
beating against the walls and being beaten back by them. And
then somewhere in midspace other waves, other onslaughts, gather
and break, whence I suppose the faint sound of aerial surf that is
my silence. Or else it is the sudden storm, analogous to those
outside, rising and drowning the cries of the children, the dying,
the lovers, so that in my innocence I say they cease, whereas in
reality they never cease. It is difficult to decide. And in the skull
is it a vacuum? I ask. And if I close my eyes, close them really,
as others cannot, but as I can, for there are limits to my impotence, then sometimes my bed is caught up into the air and
tossed like a straw by the swirling eddies, and I in it. Fortunately
it is not so much an affair of eyelids, but as it were the soul that
must be veiled, that soul denied in vein, vigilant, anxious, turning
in its cage as in a lantern, in the night without haven or craft
or matter or understanding. Ah yes, I have my little pastimes and
they

What a misfortune, the pencil must have slipped from my
fingers, for I have only just succeeded in recovering it after forty-
eight hours (see above) of intermittent efforts. What my stick lacks
is a little prehensile proboscis like the nocturnal tapir's. I should
really lose my pencil more often, it might do me good, I might be
more cheerful, it might be more cheerful. I have spent two unforgettable days of which nothing will ever be known, it is too
late now, or still too soon, I forget which, except that they have

brought me the solution and conclusion of the whole sorry business,
I mean the business of Malone (since that is what I am called
now) and of the other, for the rest is no business of mine. And
it was, though more unutterable, like the crumbling away of two
little heaps of finest sand, or dust, or ashes, of unequal size, but
diminishing together as it were in ratio, if that means anything,
and leaving behind them, each in its own stead, the blessedness
of absence. While this was going on I was struggling to retrieve
my pencil, by fits and starts. My pencil. It is a little Venus, still
green no doubt, with five or six facets, pointed at both ends and
so short there is just room, between them, for my thumb and the
two adjacent fingers, gathered together in a little vice. I use the
two points turn and turn about, sucking them frequently, I love
to suck. And when they go quite blunt I strip them with my nails
which are long, yellow, sharp and brittle for want of chalk or is
it phosphate. So little by little my little pencil dwindles, inevitably,
and the day is fast approaching when nothing will remain but a
fragment too tiny to hold. So I write as lightly as I can. But the
lead is hard and would leave no trace if I wrote too lightly. But
I say to myself, Between a hard lead with which one dare not
write too lightly, if a trace is to be left, and a soft fat lead which
blackens the page almost without touching it, what possible
difference can there be, from the point of view of durability. Ah
yes, I have my little pastimes. The strange thing is I have another
pencil, made in France, a long cylinder hardly broached, in the
bed with me somewhere I think. So I have nothing to worry about,
on this score. And yet I do worry. Now while I was hunting for
my pencil I made a curious discovery. The floor is whitening. I
struck it several blows with my stick and the sound it gave forth
was at once sharp and dull, wrong in fact. So it was not without
some trepidation that I inspected the other great planes, above
and all about me. And all this time the sand kept trickling away
and I saying to myself, It is gone for ever, meaning of course the
pencil. And I saw that all these superficies, or should I say in-
fraficies, the horizontal as well as the perpendicular, though they
do not look particularly perpendicular from here, had visibly
blanched since my last examination of them, dating from I know

not when. And this is all the more singular as the tendency of
things in general is I believe rather to darken, as time wears on,
with of course the exception of our mortal remains and certain
parts of the body which lose their natural colour and from which
the blood recedes in the long run. Does this mean there is more
light here now, now that I know what is going on? No, I fear
not, it is the same grey as heretofore, literally sparkling at times,
then growing murky and dim, thickening is perhaps the word,
until all things are blotted out except the window which seems in
a manner of speaking to be my umbilicus, so that I say to myself,
When it too goes out I shall know more or less where I am. No,
all I mean is this, that when I open staring wide my eyes I see at
the confines of this restless gloom a gleam and shimmering as of
bones, which was not hitherto the case, to the best of my
knowledge. And I can even distinctly remember the paper-
hangings or wall-paper still clinging in places to the walls and
covered with a writhing mass of roses, violets and other flowers
in such profusion that it seemed to me I had never seen so many
in the whole course of my life, nor of such beauty. But now they
seem to be all gone, quite gone, and if there were no flowers on
the ceiling there was no doubt something else, cupids perhaps,
gone too, without leaving a trace. And while I was busy pursuing
my pencil a moment came when my exercise-book, almost a
child's, fell also to the ground. But it I very soon recovered, slipping
the hook of my stick into one of the rents in the cover and hoisting it gently towards me. And during all this time, so fertile in
incidents and mishaps, in my head I suppose all was streaming
and emptying away as through a sluice, to my great joy, until
finally nothing remained, either of Malone or of the other. And
what is more I was able to follow without difficulty the various
phases of this deliverance and felt no surprise at its irregular
course, now rapid, now slow, so crystal clear was my understanding of the reasons why this could not be otherwise. And I rejoiced
furthermore, quite apart from the spectacle, at the thought that I
now knew what I had to do, I whose every move has always been
a groping, and whose motionlessness too was a kind of groping,
yes, I have greatly groped stockstill. And here again naturally I

was utterly deceived, I mean in imagining I had grasped at last the true nature of my absurd tribulations, but not so utterly as to feel the need to reproach myself with it now. For even as I said, How easy and beautiful it all is!, in the same breath I said, All will grow dark again. And it is without excessive sorrow that I see us again as we are, namely to be removed grain by grain until the hand, wearied, begins to play, scooping us up and letting us trickle back into the same place, dreamily as the saying is. For I knew it would be so, even as I said, At last! And I must say that to me at least and for as long as I can remember the sensation is familiar of a blind and tired hand delving feebly in my particles and letting them trickle between its fingers. And sometimes, when all is quiet, I feel it plunged in me up to the elbow, but gentle, and as though sleeping. But soon it stirs, wakes, fondles, clutches, ransacks, ravages, avenging its failure to scatter me with one sweep. I can understand. But I have felt so many strange things, so many baseless things assuredly, that they are perhaps better left unsaid. To speak for example of the times when I go liquid and become like mud, what good would that do? Or of the others when I would be lost in the eye of a needle, I am so hard and contracted? No, those are well-meaning squirms that get me nowhere. I was speaking then was I not of my little pastimes and I think about to say that I ought to content myself with them, instead of launching forth on all this ballsaching poppycock about life and death, if that is what it is all about, and I suppose it is, for nothing was ever about anything else to the best of my recollection. But what it is all about exactly I could no more say, at the present moment, then take up my bed and walk. It's vague, life and death. I must have had my little private idea on the subject when I began, otherwise I would not have begun, I would have held my peace, I would have gone on peacefully being bored to howls, having my little fun and games with the cones and cylinders, the millet grains beloved of birds and other panics, until someone was kind enough to come and coffin me. But it is gone clean out of my head, my little private idea. No matter, I have just had another. Perhaps it is the same one back again, ideas are so alike, when you get to know them. Be born, that's the brainwave now, that is to say live long enough to get acquainted with free carbonic gas, then say thanks for the nice time and go. That has always been my dream at bottom, all the things that have always been my dream at bottom, so many strings and never a shaft. Yes, an old foetus, that's what I am now, hoar and impotent, mother is done for, I've rotted her, she'll drop me with the help of gangrene, perhaps papa is at the party too, I'll land head-foremost mewling in the charnel-house, not that I'll mewl, not worth it. All the stories I've told myself, clinging to the putrid mucus, and swelling, swelling, saying, Got it at last, my legend. But why this sudden heat, has anything happened, anything changed? No, the answer is no, I shall never get born and therefore never get dead, and a good job too. And if I tell of me and of that other who is my little one, it is as always for want of love, well I'll be buggered, I wasn't expecting that, want of a homuncule, I can't stop. And yet it sometimes seems to me I did get born and had a long life and met Jackson and wandered in the towns, the woods and wildernesses and tarried by the seas in tears before the islands and peninsulas where night lit the little brief yellow lights of man and all night the great white and coloured beams shining in the caves where I was happy, crouched on the sand in the lee of the rocks with the smell of the seaweed and the wet rock and the howling of the wind the waves whipping me with foam or sighing on the beach softly clawing the shingle, no, not happy, I was never that, but wishing night would never end and morning never come when men wake and say, Come on, we'll soon be dead, let's make the most of it. But what matter whether I was born or not, have lived or not, am dead or merely dying, I shall go on doing as I have always done, not knowing what it is I do, nor who I am, nor where I am, nor if I am. Yes, a little creature, I shall try and make a little creature, to hold in my arms, a little creature in my image, no matter what I say. And seeing what a poor thing I have made, or how like myself, I shall eat it. Then be alone a long time, unhappy, not knowing what my prayer should be nor to whom.

I have taken a long time to find him again, but I have found him. How did I know it was he, I don't know. And what can have changed him so? Life perhaps, the struggle to love, to eat, to escape the redressers of wrongs. I slip into him, I suppose in the hope of learning something. But it is a stratum, strata, without debris or vestiges. But before I am done I shall find traces of what was. I ran him down in the heart of the town, sitting on a bench. How did I know it was he? The eyes perhaps. No, I don't know how I knew, I'll take back nothing. Perhaps it is not he. No matter, he is mine now, living flesh and needless to say male, living with that evening life which is like a convalescence, if my memories are mine, and which you savour doddering about in the wake of the fitful sun, or deeper than the dead, in the corridors of the underground railway and the stench of their harassed mobs scurrying from cradle to grave to get to the right place at the right time. What more do I want? Yes, those were the days, quick to night and well beguiled with the search for warmth and reasonably edible scraps. And you imagine it will be so till the end. But suddenly all begins to rage and roar again, you are lost in forests of high threshing ferns or whirled far out on the face of wind-swept wastes, till you begin to wonder if you have not died without knowing and gone to hell or been born again into an even worse place than before. Then it is hard to believe in those brief years when the bakers were often indulgent, at close of day, and baking-apples, I was always a great man for apples, to be had almost for the whinging if you knew your way about, and a little sunshine and shelter for those who direly needed them. And there he is as good as gold on the bench, his back to the river, and dressed as follows, though clothes don't matter, I know, I know, but he'll never have any others, if I know anything about it. He has had them a long time already, to judge by their decay, but no matter, they are the last. But most remarkable of all is his greatcoat, in the sense that it covers him completely and screens him from view. For it is so well buttoned, from top to bottom, by means of fifteen buttons at the very least, set at intervals of three or four inches at the very most, that nothing is to be seen of what goes on inside. And even the two feet, flat on the ground demurely side by side, even they are partly hidden by this coat, in spite of the double flexion of the body.

first at the base of the trunk, where the thighs form a right angle
with the pelvis, and then again at the knees, where the shins
resume the perpendicular. For the posture is completely lacking in
abandon, and but for the absence of bonds you might think he
was bound to the bench, the posture is so stiff and set in the
sharpness of its planes and angles, like that of the Colossus of
Memnon, dearly loved son of Dawn. In other words, when he
walks, or simply stands stockstill, the tails of this coat literally
sweep the ground and rustle like a train, when he walks. And
indeed this coat terminates in a fringe, like certain curtains, and
the thread of the sleeves too is bare and frayed into long waving
strands that flutter in the wind. And the hands too are hidden.
For the sleeves of this vast rag are of a piece with its other parts.
But the collar has remained intact, being of velvet or perhaps shag.
Now as to the colour of this coat, for colour too is an important
consideration, there is no good denying it, all that can be said is
that green predominates. And it might safely be wagered that
this coat, when new, was of a fine plain green colour, what you
might call cab green, for there used to be cabs and carriages
rattling through the town with panels of a handsome bottle green,
I must have seen them myself, and even driven in them, I would
not put it past me. But perhaps I am wrong to call this coat a
greatcoat and perhaps I should rather call it an overcoat or even
cover-me-down, for that is indeed the impression it gives, that it
covers the whole body all over, with the exception obviously of
the head which emerges, lofty and impassive, clear of its embrace.
Yes, passion has marked the face, action too possibly, but it
seems to have ceased from suffering, for the time being. But one
never knows, does one? Now with regard to the buttons of this
coat, they are not so much genuine buttons as little wooden
cylinders two or three inches long, with a hole in the middle for
the thread, for one hole is ample, though two and even four are
more usual, and this because of the inordinate distension of the
button-holes consequent on wear and tear. And cylinders is perhaps an exaggeration, for if some of these little sticks or pegs are
in fact cylindrical, still more have no definable form. But all are
roughly two and a half inches long and thus prevent the lappets

from flying apart, all have this feature in common. Now with regard to the material of this coat, all that can be said is that it looks like felt. And the various dints and bulges inflicted upon it by the spasms and contortions of the body subsist long after the fit is past. So much for this coat. I'll tell myself stories about the boots another time, if I can. The hat, as hard as iron, superbly domed above its narrow guttered rim, is marred by a wide crack or rent extending in front from the crown down and intended probably to facilitate the introduction of the skull. For coat and hat have this much in common, that whereas the coat is too big, the hat is too small. And though the edges of the split brim close on the brow like the jaws of a trap, nevertheless the hat is attached, by a string, for safety, to the topmost button of the coat, because, never mind. And were there nothing more to be said about the structure of this hat, the important thing would still remain unsaid, meaning of course its colour, of which all that can be said is this, that a strong sun full upon it brings out shimmers of buff and pearl grey and that otherwise it verges on black, without however ever really approaching it. And it would not surprise me to learn that this hat once belonged to a sporting gentleman, a turf-man or breeder of rams. And if we now turn to consider this coat and this hat, no longer separately, but in relation to each other, we are very soon agreeably surprised to see how well they are assorted. And it would not surprise me to learn that they had been bought, one at the hatter's, the other at the tailor's, perhaps the same day and by the same toff, for such men exist, I mean fine handsome men six foot tall and over and all in keeping but the head, small from over-breeding. And it is a pleasure to find oneself again in the presence of one of those immutable relations between harmoniously perishing terms and the effect of which is this, that when weary to death one is almost resigned to—I was going to say to the immortality of the soul, but I don't see the connexion. But to pass on now to the garments that really matter, subjacent and even intimate, all that can be said is that this for the moment is delicate ground. For Sapo—no, I can't call him that any more, and I even wonder how I was able to stomach such a name till now. So then for, let me see,

for Macmann, that's not much better but there is no time to lose,
for Macmann might be stark staring naked under this surtout for
all anyone would be any the wiser. The trouble is he does not
stir. Since morning he has been here and now it is evening. The
tugs, their black funnels striped with red, tow to their moorings
the last barges, freighted with empty barrels. The water cradles
already the distant fires of the sunset, orange, rose and green,
quenches them in its ruffles and then in trembling pools spreads
them bright again. His back is turned to the river, but perhaps it
appears to him in the dreadful cries of the gulls that evening
assembles, in paroxysms of hunger, round the outflow of the
sewers, opposite the Bellevue Hotel. Yes, they too, in a last frenzy
before night and its high crags, swoop ravening about the offal.
But his face is towards the people that throng the streets at this
hour, their long day ended and the whole long evening before them.
The doors open and spew them out, each door its contingent. For
an instant they cluster in a daze, huddled on the sidewalk or in
the gutter, then set off singly on their appointed ways. And even
those who know themselves condemned, at the outset, to the
same direction, for the choice of direction at the outset is not
great, take leave of one another and part, but politely, with some
polite excuse, or without a word, for they all know one another's
little ways. And God help him who longs, for once, in his recovered freedom, to walk a little way with a fellow-creature, no
matter which, unless of course by a merciful chance he stumble
on one in the same plight. Then they take a few paces happily
side by side, then part, each one muttering perhaps, Now there
will be no holding him. At this hour then erotic craving accounts
for the majority of couples. But these are few compared to the
solitaries pressing forward through the throng, obstructing the
access to places of amusement, bowed over the parapets, propped
against vacant walls. But soon they come to the appointed place,
at home or at some other home, or abroad, as the saying is, in
a public place, or in a doorway in view of possible rain. And
the first to arrive have seldom long to wait, for all hasten towards
one another, knowing how short the time in which to say all the
things that lie heavy on the heart and conscience and to do all

the things they have to do together, things one cannot do alone.
So there they are for a few hours in safety. Then the drowsiness,
the little memorandum book with its little special pencil, the
yawned goodbyes. Some even take a cab to get more quickly to
the rendezvous or, when the fun is over, home or to the hotel,
where their comfortable bed is waiting for them. Then you see
the last stage of the horse, between its recent career as a pet
horse, or a race-horse, or a pack-horse, or a plough-horse, and
the shambles. It spends most of its time standing still in an attitude
of dejection, its head hanging as low as the shafts and harness
permit, that is to say almost to the cobble-stones. But once in
motion it is transformed, momentarily, perhaps because of the
memories that motion revives, for the mere fact of running
and pulling cannot give it much satisfaction, under such conditions. But when the shafts tilt up, announcing that a fare has,
been taken on board, or when on the contrary the back-hand
begins to gall its spine, according as the passenger is seated facing
the way he is going or, what is perhaps even more restful, with
his back to it, then it rears its head, stiffens its houghs and looks
almost content. And you see the cabman too, all alone on his
box ten feet from the ground, his knees covered at all seasons and
in all weathers with a kind of rug as a rule originally brown, the
same precisely which he has just snatched from the rump of his
horse. Furious and livid perhaps from want of passengers, the
least fare seems to excite him to a frenzy. Then with his huge
exasperated hands he tears at the reins or, half rising and leaning
out over his horse, brings them down with a crack all along its
back. And he launches his equipage blindly through the dark
thronging streets, his mouth full of curses. But the passenger,
having named the place he wants to go and knowing himself as
helpless to act on the course of events as the dark box that
encloses him, abandons himself to the pleasant feeling of being
freed from all responsibility, or he ponders on what lies before
him, or on what lies behind him, saying, Twill not be ever thus,
and then in the same breath, But twas ever thus, for there are not
five hundred different kinds of passengers. And so they hasten,
the horse, the driver and the passenger, towards the appointed

place, by the shortest route or deviously, through the press of other misplaced persons. And each one has his reasons, while wondering from time to time what they are worth, and if they are the true ones, for going where he is going rather than somewhere else, and the horse hardly less darkly than the men, though as a rule it will not know where it is going until it gets there, and not always even then. And if as suggested it is dusk, then another phenomenon to be observed is the number of windows and shopwindows that light up an instant, almost after the fashion of the setting sun, though that all depends on the season. But for Macmann, thank God, he's still there, for Macmann it is a true spring evening, an equinoctial gale howls along the quays bordered by high red houses, many of which are warehouses. Or it is perhaps an evening in autumn and these leaves whirling in the air, whence it is impossible to say, for here there are no trees, are perhaps no longer the first of the year, barely green, but old leaves that have known the long joys of summer and now are good for nothing but to lie rotting in a heap, now that men and beasts have no more need of shade, on the contrary, nor birds of nests to lay and hatch out in, and trees must blacken even where no heart beats, though it appears that some stay green forever, for some obscure reason. And it is no doubt all the same to Macmann whether it is spring or whether it is autumn, unless he prefers summer to winter or inversely, which is improbable. But it must not be thought he will never move again, out of this place and attitude, for he has still the whole of his old age before him, and then that kind of epilogue when it is not very clear what is happening and which does not seem to add very much to what has already been acquired or to shed any great light on its confusion, but which no doubt has its usefulness, as hay is left out to dry before being garnered. He will therefore rise, whether he likes it or not, and proceed by other places to another place, and then by others still to yet another, unless he comes back here where he seems to be snug enough, but one never knows, does one? And so on, on, for long years. Because in order not to die you must come and go, come and go, unless you happen to have someone who brings you food wherever you happen to be, like myself. And you can remain

for two, three and even four days without stirring hand or foot,
but what are four days when you have all old age before you, and
then the lingers of evaporation, a drop in the ocean. It is true you
know nothing of this, you flatter yourself you are hanging by a
thread like all mankind, but that is not the point. For there is no
point, no point in not knowing this or that, either you know all
or you know nothing, and Macmann knows nothing. But he is
concerned only with his ignorance of certain things, of those that
appal him among others, which is only human. But it is bad
policy, for on the fifth day rise you must, and rise in fact you
do, but with how much greater pains than if you had made up
your mind to it the day before, or better still two days before,
and why add to your pains, it's bad policy, assuming you do add
to them, and nothing is less certain. For on the fifth day, when
the problem is how to rise, the fourth and third do not matter
any more, all that matters is how to rise, for you are half out
of your mind. And sometimes you cannot, get to your feet I
mean, and have to drag yourself to the nearest plot of vegetables,
using the tufts of grass and asperities of the earth to drag yourself forward, or to the nearest clump of brambles, where there
are sometimes good things to eat, if acid, and which are superior
to the plots in this, that you can crawl into them and hide, as
you cannot in a plot of ripe potatoes for example, and in this also,
that often you frighten the little wild things away, both furred
and feathered. For it is not as if he possessed the means of
accumulating, in a single day, enough food to keep him alive for
three weeks or a month, and what is a month compared to the
whole of second childishness, a drop in a bucket. But he does not,
possess them I mean, and could not employ them even if he did,
he feels so far from the morrow. And perhaps there is none, no
morrow any more, for one who has waited so long for it in vain.
And perhaps he has come to that stage of his instant when to live
is to wander the last of the living in the depths of an instant
without bounds, where the light never changes and the wrecks
look all alike. Bluer scarcely than white of egg the eyes stare
into the space before them, namely the fulness of the great deep
and its unchanging calm. But at long intervals they close, with

the gentle suddenness of flesh that tightens, often without anger, and closes on itself. Then you see the old lids all red and worn that seem hard set to meet, for there are four, two for each lachrymal. And perhaps it is then he sees the heaven of the old dream, the heaven of the sea and of the earth too, and the spasms of the waves from shore to shore all stirring to their tiniest stir, and the so different motion of men for example, who are not tied together, but free to come and go as they please. And they make full use of it and come and go, their great balls and sockets rattling and clacking like knackers, each on his way. And when one dies the others go on, as if nothing had happened.

I feel

I feel it's coming. How goes it, thanks, it's coming. I wanted to be quite sure before I noted it. Scrupulous to the last, finical to a fault, that's Malone, all over. I mean sure of feeling that my hour is at hand. For I never doubted it would come, sooner or later, except the days I felt it was past. For my stories are all in vain, deep down I never doubted, even the days abounding in proof to the contrary, that I was still alive and breathing in and out the air of earth. At hand, that is in two or three days, in the language of the days when they taught me the names of the days and I marvelled at their being so few and flourished my little fists, crying out for more, and how to tell the time, and what are two or three days, more or less, in the long run, a joke. But not a word and on with the losing game, it's good for the health. And all I have to do is go on as though doomed to see the midsummer moon. For I believe I have now reached what is called the month of May, I don't know why, I mean why I believe that, for May comes from Maia, hell, I remember that too, goddess of increase and plenty, yes, I believe I have entered on the season of increase and plenty, of increase at last, for plenty comes later, with the harvest. So quiet, quiet, I'll be still here at All Saints, in the middle of the chrysanthemums, no, this year I shall not hear them howling over their charnels. But this sensation of dilation is hard to resist. All strains towards the nearest deeps, and notably my feet, which even in the ordinary way are so much further

from me than all the rest, from my head I mean, for that is where
I am fled, my feet are leagues away. And to call them in, to be
cleaned for example, would I think take me over a month, exclusive of the time required to locate them. Strange, I don't feel
my feet any more, my feet feel nothing any more, and a
mercy it is. And yet I feel they are beyond the range
of the most powerful telescope. Is that what is known
as having a foot in the grave? And similarly for the rest.
For a mere local phenomenon is something I would not have
noticed, having been nothing but a series or rather a succession
of local phenomena all my life, without any result. But my fingers
too write in other latitudes and the air that breathes through my
pages and turns them without my knowing, when I doze off, so
that the subject falls far from the verb and the object lands
somewhere in the void, is not the air of this second-last abode,
and a mercy it is. And perhaps on my hands it is the shimmer of
the shadows of leaves and flowers and the brightness of a forgotten sun. Now my sex, I mean the tube itself, and in particular
the nozzle, from which when I was yet a virgin clouts and gouts
of sperm came streaming and splashing up into my face, a continuous flow, while it lasted, and which must still drip a little piss
from time to time, otherwise I would be dead of uraemia, I do
not expect to see my sex again, with my naked eye, not that I
wish to, we've stared at each other long enough, in the eye, but
it gives you some idea. But that is not all and my extremities are
not the only parts to recede, in their respective directions, far
from it. For my arse for example, which can hardly be accused
of being the end of anything, if my arse suddenly started to shit
at the present moment, which God forbid, I firmly believe the
lumps would fall out in Australia. And if I were to stand up
again, from which God preserve me, I fancy I would fill a considerable part of the universe, oh not more than lying down, but
more noticeably. For it is a thing I have often noticed, the best
way to pass unnoticed is to lie down flat and not move. And so
there I am, who always thought I would shrivel and shrivel,
more and more, until in the end I could be almost buried in a
casket, swelling. No matter, what matters is that in spite of my

stories I continue to fit in this room, let us call it a room, that's
all that matters, and I need not worry, I'll fit in it as long as needs
be. And if I ever succeed in breathing my last it will not be in
the street, or in a hospital, but here, in the midst of my possessions, beside this window that sometimes looks as if it were
painted on the wall, like Tiepolo's ceiling at Würzburg, what a
tourist I must have been, I even remember the diaeresis, if it is
one. If only I could be sure, of my deathbed I mean. And yet
how often I have seen this old head swing out through the door,
low, for my big old bones weigh heavy, and the door is low,
lower and lower in my opinion. And each time it bangs against
the jamb, my head does, for I am tall, and the landing is small,
and the man carrying my feet cannot wait, before he starts down
the stairs, for the whole of me to be out, on the landing I mean,
but he has to start turning before that, so as not to bang into the
wall, of the landing I mean. So my head bangs against the jamb,
it's inevitable. And it doesn't matter to my head, in the state it is
in, but the man carrying it says, Eh Bob easy!, out of respect
perhaps, for he doesn't know me, he didn't know me, or for fear
of hurting his fingers. Bang! Easy! Right! The door!, and the
room is vacant at last and ready to receive, after disinfection, for
you can't be too careful, a large family or a pair of turtle doves.
Yes, the event is past, but it's too soon to use it, hence the delay,
that's what I tell myself. But I tell myself so many things, what
truth is there in all this babble? I don't know. I simply believe I
can say nothing that is not true, I mean that has not happened,
it's not the same thing but no matter. Yes, that's what I like about
me, at least one of the things, that I can say, Up the Republic!,
for example, or, Sweetheart!, for example, without having to
wonder if I should not rather have cut my tongue out, or said
something else. Yes, no reflection is needed, before or after, I
have only to open my mouth for it to testify to the old story, my
old story, and to the long silence that has silenced me, so that all
is silent. And if I ever stop talking it will be because there is
nothing more to be said, even though all has not been said, even
though nothing has been said. But let us leave these morbid
matters and get on with that of my demise, in two or three days

if I remember rightly. Then it will be all over with the Murphys,
Merciers, Molloys, Morans and Malones, unless it goes on beyond the grave. But sufficient unto the day, let us first defunge,
then we'll see. How many have I killed, hitting them on the head
or setting fire to them? Off-hand I can only think of four, all
unknowns, I never knew anyone. A sudden wish, I have a sudden
wish to see, as sometimes in the old days, something, anything,
no matter what, something I could not have imagined. There
was the old butler too, in London I think, there's London again, I
cut his throat with his razor, that makes five. It seems to me he
had a name. Yes, what I need now is a touch of the unimaginable,
coloured for preference, that would do me good. For this may
well be my last journey, down the long familiar galleries, with
my little suns and moons that I hang aloft and my pockets full of
pebbles stand for men and their seasons, my last, if I'm lucky.
Then back here, to me, whatever that means, and no more leaving
me, no more asking me for what I haven't got. Or perhaps we'll
all come back, reunited, done with parting, done with prying on
one another, back to this foul little den all dirty white and
vaulted, as though hollowed out of ivory, an old rotten tooth. Or
alone, back alone, as alone as when I went, but I doubt it, I can
hear them from here, clamouring after me down the corridors,
stumbling through the rubble, beseeching me to take them with me.
That settles that. I have just time, if I have calculated right, and
if I have calculated wrong so much the better, I ask nothing
better, besides I haven't calculated anything, don't ask anything
either, just time to go and take a little turn, come back here and
do all I have to do, I forgot what, ah yes, put my possessions
in order, and then something else, I forget what, but it will come
back to me when the time comes. But before I go I should like
to find a hole in the wall behind which so much goes on, such
extraordinary things, and often coloured. One last glimpse and
I feel I could slip away as happy as if I were embarking for—I
nearly said for Cythera, decidedly it is time for this to stop. After
all this window is whatever I want it to be, up to a point, that's
right, don't compromise yourself. What strikes me to begin with
is how much rounder it is than it was, so that it looks like a

bull's-eye, or a porthole. No matter, provided there is something
on the other side. First I see the night, which surprises me, to my
surprise, I suppose because I want to be surprised, just
once more. For in the room it is not night, I know, here it is
never really night, I don't care what I said, but often darker than
now, whereas out there up in the sky it is black night, with few
stars, just enough to show that the black night I see is truly of
mankind and not merely painted on the window-pane, for they
tremble, like true stars, as they would not do if they were painted.
And as if that were not enough to satisfy me it is the outer world,
the other world, suddenly the window across the way lights up,
or suddenly I realize it is lit up, for I am not one of those people
who can take in everything at a single glance, but I have to look
long and fixedly and give things time to travel the long road that
lies between me and them. And that indeed is a happy chance and
augurs well, unless it be devised on purpose to make mock of
me, for I might have found nothing better to speed me from this
place than the nocturnal sky where nothing happens, though it is
full of tumult and violence, nothing unless you have the whole
night before you to follow the slow fall and rise of other worlds,
when there are any, or watch out for the meteors, and I have not
the whole night before me. And it does not matter to me whether
they have risen before dawn, or not yet gone to bed, or risen in
the middle of the night intending perhaps to go back to bed
when they have finished, and it is enough for me to see them
standing up against each other behind the curtain, which is dark,
so that it is a dark light, if one may say so, and dim the shadow
they cast. For they cleave so fast together that they seem a single
body, and consequently a single shadow. But when they totter it
is clear they are twain, and in vain they clasp with the energy of
despair, it is clear we have here two distinct and separate bodies,
each enclosed within its own frontiers, and having no need of
each other to come and go and sustain the flame of life, for each
is well able to do so, independently of the other. Perhaps they are
cold, that they rub against each other so, for friction maintains
heat and brings it back when it is gone. It is all very pretty and
strange, this big complicated shape made up of more than one,

for perhaps there are three of them, and how it sways and totters, but rather poor in colour. But the night must be warm, for of a sudden the curtain lifts on a flare of tender colour, pale blush and white of flesh, then pink that must come from a garment and gold too that I haven't time to understand. So it is not cold they are, standing so lighty clad by the open window. Ah how stupid I am, I see what it is, they must be loving each other, that must be how it is done. Good, that has done me good. I'll see now if the sky is still there, then go. They are right up against the curtain now, motionless. Is it possible they have finished already? They have loved each other standing, like dogs. Soon they will be able to part. Or perhaps they are just having a breather, before they tackle the titbit. Back and forth, back and forth, that must be wonderful. They seem to be in pain. Enough, enough, good-bye.

Caught by the rain far from shelter Macmann stopped and lay down, saying, The surface thus pressed against the ground will remain dry, whereas standing I would get uniformly wet all over, as if rain were a mere matter of drops per hour, like electricity. So he lay down, prostrate, after a moment's hesitation, for he could just as easily have lain down supine or, meeting himself half-way, on one of his two sides. But he fancied that the nape of the neck and the back right down to the loins were more vulnerable than the chest and belly, not realizing, any more than if he had been a crate of tomatoes, that all these parts are intimately and even indissolubly bound up together, at least until death do them part, and to many another too of which he had no conception, and that a drop of water out of season on the coccyx for example may lead to spasms of the risorius lasting for years as when, having waded through a bog, you merely die of pneumonia and your legs none the worse for the wetting, but if anything better, thanks perhaps to the action of the bog-water. It was a heavy, cold and perpendicular rain, which led Macmann to suppose it would be brief, as if there were a relation between violence and duration, and that he would spring to his feet in ten minutes or a quarter of an hour, his front, no, his back, white with, no, front was right, his front white with dust. This is the kind of story he has been telling himself all his life, saying, This cannot possibly last much longer. It was sometime in the afternoon, impossible to say more, for hours and hours past it had been the same leaden light, so it was very probably the afternoon, very. The still air, though not cold as in winter, seemed without promise or memory of warmth. Incommoded by the rain pouring into his hat through the crack, Macmann took it off and laid it on his temple, that is to say turned his head and pressed his cheek to the ground. His hands at the ends of the long outstretched arms clutched the grass, each hand a tuft, with as much energy as if he had been spreadeagled against the face of a cliff. Let us by all means continue this description. The rain pelted down on his back with the sound first of a drum, but in a short time of washing, as when washing is soused gurgling and squelching in a tub, and he distinguished clearly and with interest the difference in noise of the rain falling on him and falling on the earth. For his ear, which is on the same plane as the cheek or nearly, was glued to the earth in a way it seldom is in wet weather, and he could hear the kind of distant roar of the earth drinking and the sighing of the soaked bowed grasses. The idea of punishment came to his mind, addicted it is true to that chimera and probably impressed by the posture of the body and the fingers clenched as though in torment. And without knowing exactly what his sin was he felt full well that living was not a sufficient atonement for it or that this atonement was in itself a sin, calling for more atonement, and so on, as if there could be anything but life, for the living. And no doubt he would have wondered if it was really necessary to be guilty in order to be punished but for the memory, more and more galling, of his having consented to live in his mother, than to leave her. And this again he could not see as his true sin, but as yet another atonement which had miscarried and, far from cleansing him of his sin, plunged him in it deeper than before. And truth to tell the ideas of guilt and punishment were confused together in his mind, as those of cause and effect so often are in the minds of those who continue to think. And it was often in fear and trembling that he suffered, saying, This will cost me dear. But not knowing how to go about it, in order to

think and feel correctly, he would suddenly begin to smile for no
reason, as now, as then, for already it is long since that afternoon,
in March perhaps, or in November perhaps, in October rather,
when the rain caught him far from shelter, to smile and give
thanks for the teeming rain and the promise it contained of stars
a little later, to light his way and enable him to get his bearings,
should he wish to do so. For he did not know quite where he was,
except that he was in a plain, and the mountains not far, nor the
sea, nor the town, and that all he needed was a dust of light and
a few fixed stars to enable him to make definite headway towards
the one, or the other, or the third, or to hold fast where he was,
in the plain, as he might be pleased to decide. For in order to
hold fast in the place where you happen to be you need light
too, unless you go round in circles, which is practically impossible
in the dark, or halt and wait, motionless, for day to dawn again,
and then you die of cold, unless it does not happen to be cold.
But Macmann would have been more than human, after forty or
forty-five minutes of sanguine expectation, seeing the rain persist
as heavy as ever and day recede at last, if he had not begun to
reproach himself with what he had done, namely with having lain
down on the ground instead of continuing on his course, in as
straight a line as possible, in the hope of chancing sooner or
later on a tree, or a ruin. And instead of being astonished at
such long and violent rain, he was astonished at not having understood, from the moment the first timid drops began to fall, that it
was going to rain violently and long and that he must not
stop and lie down, but on the contrary press forward, as fast
as his legs could carry him, for he was no more than human,
than the son and grandson and greatgrandson of humans. But
between him and those grave and sober men, first bearded,
then moustached, there was this difference, that his semen
had never done any harm to anyone. So his link with his
species was through his ascendants only, who were all dead,
in the fond hope they had perpetuated themselves. But the
better late than never thanks to which true men, true links,
can acknowledge the error of their ways and hasten on to the
next, was beyond the power of Macmann, to whom it some-

times seemed that he could grovel and wallow in his mortality
until the end of time and not have done. And without going so
far as that, he who has waited long enough will wait for ever.
And there comes the hour when nothing more can happen and
nobody more can come and all is ended but the waiting that
knows itself in vain. Perhaps he had come to that. And when (for
example) you die, it is too late, you have been waiting too long,
you are no longer sufficiently alive to be able to stop. Perhaps he
had come to that. But apparently not, though acts don't matter,
I know, I know, nor thoughts. For having reproached himself
with what he had done, and with his monstrous error of apprecia-
tion, instead of springing up and hurrying on he turned over on
his back, thus offering all his front to the deluge. And it was then
his hair appeared clearly for the first time since his walks bare-
headed in the smiling haunts of his youth, his hat having remained in the place which his head had just left. For when, lying
on your stomach in a wild and practically illimitable part of the
country, you turn over on your back, then there is a sideways
movement of the whole body, including the head, unless you
make a point of avoiding it, and the head comes to rest at x
inches approximately from where it was before, x being the width
of the shoulders in inches, for the head is right in the middle of
the shoulders. But when you are in a narrow bed, I mean one
just wide enough to contain you, a pallet shall we say, then it is
in vain you turn over on your back, then back over on your
stomach, the head remains always in the same place, unless you
make a point of inclining it to the right or to the left, and some
there doubtless are who go to this trouble, in the hope of finding
a little freshness. He tried to look at the dark streaming mass
which was all that remained of sky and air, but the rain hurt his
eyes and shut them. He opened his mouth and lay for a long time
thus, his mouth open and his hands also and as far apart as
possible from each other. For it is a curious thing, one tends less
to clutch the ground when on one's back than when on one's
stomach, there is a curious remark which might be worth following up. And just as an hour before he had pulled up his sleeves
the better to clutch the grass, so now he pulled them up again

the better to feel the rain pelting down on his palms, also called
the hollows of the hands, or the flats, it all depends. And in the
midst—but I was nearly forgetting the hair, which from the point
of view of colour was to white very much as the hour's gloom to
black and from the point of view of length very long what is more,
very long behind and very long on either side. And on a dry and
windy day it would have gone romping in the grass almost like
grass itself. But the rain glued it to the ground and churned it
up with the earth and grass into a kind of muddy pulp, not a
muddy pulp, a kind of muddy pulp. And in the midst of his
suffering, for one does not remain so long in such a position without being incommoded, he began to wish that the rain would
never cease nor consequently his sufferings or pain, for the cause
of his pain was almost certainly the rain, recumbency in itself
not being particularly unpleasant, as if there existed a relation
between that which suffers and that which causes to suffer. For
the rain could cease without his ceasing to suffer, just as he could
cease to suffer without the rain's ceasing on that account. And on
him already this important quarter-truth was perhaps beginning to
dawn. For while deploring he could not spend the rest of his life
(which would thereby have been agreeably abridged) under this
heavy, cold (without being icy) and perpendicular rain, now
supine, now prone, he was quarter-inclined to wonder if he was
not mistaken in holding it responsible for his sufferings and if in
reality his discomfort was not the effect of quite a different
cause or set of causes. For people are never content to suffer,
but they must have heat and cold, rain and its contrary which is
fine weather, and with that love, friendship, black skin and sexual
and peptic deficiency for example, in short the furies and frenzies
happily too numerous to be numbered of the body including the
skull and its annexes, whatever that means, such as the club-foot,
in order that they may know very precisely what exactly it is that
dares prevent their happiness from being unalloyed. And sticklers
have been met with who had no peace until they knew for certain
whether their carcinoma was of the pylorus or whether on the
contrary it was not rather of the duodenum. But these are flights
for which Macmann was not yet fledged, and indeed he was

rather of the earth earthy and ill-fitted for pure reason, especially
in the circumstances in which we have been fortunate enough to
circumscribe him. And to tell the truth he was by temperament
more reptile than bird and could suffer extensive mutilation and
survive, happier sitting than standing and lying down than sitting,
so that he sat and lay down at the least pretext and only rose
again when the élan vital or struggle for life began to prod him
in the arse again. And a good half of his existence must have been
spent in a motionlessness akin to that of stone, not to say the
three quarters, or even the four fifths, a motionlessness at first
skin-deep, but which little by little invaded, I will not say the vital
parts, but at least the sensibility and understanding. And it
must be presumed that he received from his numerous forbears,
through the agency of his papa and his mama, a cast-iron vegetative
system, to have reached the age he has just reached and which is
nothing or very little compared to the age he will reach, as I know
to my cost, without any serious mishap, I mean one of a nature
to carry him off on the spot. For no one ever came to his help, to
help him avoid the thorns and snares that attend the steps of
innocence, and he could never count on any other craft than his
own, any other strength, to go from morning to evening and then
from evening to morning without mortal hurt. And notably he
never received any gifts of cash, or very seldom, and very paltry,
which would not have mattered if he had been able to earn, in
the sweat of his brow or by making use of his intelligence. But
when given the job of weeding a plot of young carrots for
example, at the rate of threepence or even sixpence an hour, it
often happened that he tore them all up, through absentminded-
ness, or carried away by I know not what irresistible urge that
came over him at the sight of vegetables, and even of flowers,
and literally blinded him to his true interests, the urge to make a
clean sweep and have nothing before his eyes but a patch of
brown earth rid of its parasites, it was often more than he could
resist. Or without going so far as that, suddenly all swam before
his eyes, he could no longer distinguish the plants destined for
the embellishment of the home or the nutrition of man and beast
from the weeds which are said to serve no useful purpose, but

which must have their usefulness too, for the earth to favour
them so, such as squitch beloved of dogs and from which man too
in his turn has succeeded in extracting a brew, and the hoe fell
from his hands. And even with such humble occupations as street-
cleaning to which with hopefulness he had sometimes turned, on
the off chance of his being a born scavenger, he did not succeed
any better. And even he himself was compelled to admit that the
place swept by him looked dirtier at his departure than on his
arrival, as if a demon had driven him to collect, with the broom,
shovel and barrow placed gratis at his disposal by the corporation,
all the dirt and filth which chance had withdrawn from the sight
of the tax-payer and add them thus recovered to those already
visible and which he was employed to remove. With the result that
at the end of the day, throughout the sector consigned to him,
one could see the peels of oranges and bananas, cigarette-butts,
unspeakable scraps of paper, dogs' and horses' excrement and
other muck, carefully concentrated all along the sidewalk or
distributed on the crown of the street, as though in order to in-
spire the greatest possible disgust in the passers-by or provoke
the greatest possible number of accidents, some fatal, by means
of the slip. And yet he had done his honest best to give satisfaction, taking as his model his more experienced colleagues,
and doing as they did. But it was truly as if he were not master
of his movements and did not know what he was doing, while he
was doing it, nor what he had done, once he had done it. For
someone had to say to him, Look at what you have done, sticking
his nose in it so to speak, otherwise he did not realize, but thought
he had done as any man of good will would have done in his
place and with very much the same results, in spite of his lack of
experience. And yet when it came to doing some little thing for
himself, as for example when he had to repair or replace one of
his buttons or pegs, which were not long-lived being mostly of
green wood and exposed to all the rigours of the temperate zone,
then he really exhibited a certain dexterity, without the help of
any other apparatus than his bare hands. And indeed he had
devoted to these little tasks a great part of his existence, that is
to say of the half or quarter of his existence associated with more

or less coordinated movements of the body. For he had to, he
had to, if he wished to go on coming and going on the earth,
which to tell the truth he did not, particularly, but he had to, for
obscure reasons known who knows to God alone, though to tell
the truth God does not seem to need reasons for doing what he
does, and for omitting to do what he omits to do, to the same
degree as his creatures, does he? Such then seemed to be Macmann, seen from a certain angle, incapable of weeding a bed of
pansies or marigolds and leaving one standing and at the same
time well able to consolidate his boots with willow bark and
thongs of wicker, so that he might come and go on the earth
from time to time and not wound himself too sorely on the stones,
thorns and broken glass provided by the carelessness or wicked-
ness of man, with hardly a complaint, for he had to. For he was
incapable of picking his steps and choosing where to put down
his feet (which would have permitted him to go barefoot). And
even had he been so he would have been so to no great purpose,
so little was he master of his movements. And what is the good
of aiming at the smooth and mossy places when the foot, missing
its mark, comes down on the flints and shards or sinks up to the
knee in the cow-pads? But to pass on now to considerations of
another order, it is perhaps not inappropriate to wish Macmann,
since wishing costs nothing, sooner or later a general paralysis at
a pinch the arms if that is conceivable, in a place impermeable as
far as possible to wind, rain, sound, cold, great heat (as in the
seventh century) and daylight, with one or two eiderdowns just
in case and a charitable soul say once a week bearing eating-
apples and sardines in oil for the purpose of postponing as long
as possible the fatal hour, it would be wonderful. But in the meantime in the end, the rain still falling with unabated violence in
spite of his having turned over on his back, Macmann grew restless, flinging himself from side to side as though in a fit of the
fever, buttoning himself and unbuttoning and finally rolling over
and over in the same direction, it little matters which, with a
brief pause after each roll to begin with, and then without break.
And in theory his hat should have followed him, seeing it was
tied to his coat, and the string twisted itself about his neck, but

not at all, for theory is one thing and reality another, and the hat remained where it was, I mean in its place, like a thing forsaken. But perhaps one day a high wind would come and send it, dry and light again, bowling and bounding over the plain until it came to the town, or the ocean, but not necessarily. Now it was not the first time that Macmann rolled upon the ground, but he had always done so without ulterior locomotive motive. Whereas then, as he moved further and further from the place where the rain had caught him far from shelter and which thanks to the hat continued to contrast with the surrounding space, he realized he was advancing with regularity, and even a certain rapidity, along the arc of a gigantic circle probably, for he assumed that one of his extremities was heavier than the other, without knowing quite which, but not by much. And as he rolled he conceived and polished the plan of continuing to roll on all night if necessary, or at least until his strength should fail him, and thus approach the confines of this plain which to tell the truth he was in no hurry to leave, but nevertheless was leaving, he knew it. And without reducing his speed he began to dream of a flat land where he would never have to rise again and hold himslf erect in equilibrium, first on the right foot for example, then on the left, and where he might come and go and so survive after the fashion of a great cylinder endowed with the faculties of cognition and volition. And without exactly building castles in Spain, for that

Quick quick my possessons. Quiet, quiet, twice, I have time, lots of time, as usual. My pencil, my two pencils, the one of which nothing remains between my huge fingers but the lead fallen from the wood and the other, long and round, in the bed somewhere, I was holding it in reserve, I won't look for it, I know it's there somewhere, if I have time when I've finished I'll look for it, if I don't find it I won't have it, I'll make the correction, with the other, if anything remains of it. Quiet, quiet, My exercise-book, I don't see it, but I feel it in my left hand, I don't know where it comes from, I didn't have it when I came here, but I feel it is mine. That's the style, as if I were sweet and seventy. In that case the bed would be mine too, and the little table, the dish, the pots, the cupboard, the blankets. No, nothing of all that is mine. But

the exercise-book is mine, I can't explain. The two pencils then,
the exercise-book and then the stick, which I did not have either
when I came here, but which I consider mine, I must have described it long ago. I am quiet, I have time, but I shall describe
as little as possible. It is with me in the bed, under the blankets,
there was a time I used to rub myself against it, saying, It's a
little woman. But it is so long that it sticks out under the pillow
and finishes far behind me. I continue from memory. It is black
dark. I can hardly see the window. It must be letting in the night
again. Even if I had time to rummage in my possessions, to bring
them over to the bed one by one or tangled together as is often
the way with forsaken things, I would not see anything. And
perhaps indeed I have the time, let us assume I have the time,
and proceed as if I had not. But it cannot be so long since I
checked and went through all my things, in the light, in anticipation of this hour. But since then I must have forgotten it all.
A needle stuck into two corks to prevent it from sticking into me,
for if the point pricks less than the eye, no, that's wrong, for if
point pricks more than the eye, the eye pricks too, that's wrong
too. Round the shank, between the two corks, a wisp of black
thread clings. It is a pretty little object, like a—no, it is like
nothing. The bowl of my pipe, though I never used a tobacco-pipe.
I must have found it somewhere, on the ground, when out walking.
There it was, in the grass, thrown away because it could no longer
serve, the stem having broken off (I suddenly remember that) just
short of the bowl. This pipe could have been repaired, but he
must have said, Bah, I'll buy myself another. But all I found was
the bowl. But all that is mere supposition. Perhaps I thought it
pretty, or felt for it that foul feeling of pity I have so often felt
in the presence of things, especially little portable things in wood
and stone, and which made me wish to have them about me and
keep them always, so that I stooped and picked them up and put
them in my pocket, often with tears, for I wept up to a great
age, never having really evolved in the fields of affection and
passion, in spite of my experiences. And but for the company of
these little objects which I picked up here and there, when out
walking, and which sometimes gave me the impression that they

too needed me, I might have been reduced to the society of nice
people or to the consolations of some religion or other, but I
think not. And I loved, I remember, as I walked along, with
my hands deep in my pockets, for I am trying to speak of the
time when I could still walk without a stick and a fortiori without
crutches, I loved to finger and caress the hard shapely objects that
were there in my deep pockets, it was my way of talking to them
and reassuring them. And I loved to fall asleep holding in my
hand a stone, a horse chestnut or a cone, and I would be still
holding it when I woke, my fingers closed over it, in spite of
sleep which makes a rag of the body, so that it may rest. And
those of which I wearied, or which were ousted by new loves, I
threw away, that is to say I cast round for a place to lay them
where they would be at peace forever, and no one ever find them
short of an extraordinary hazard, and such places are few and
far between, and I laid them there. Or I buried them, or threw
them into the sea, with all my strength as far as possible from the
land, those I knew for certain would not float, evenly briefly. But
many a wooden friend too I have sent to the bottom, weighted
with a stone. Until I realized it was wrong of me. For when the
string is rotted they will rise to the surface, if they have not already
done so, and return to the land, sooner or later. In this way I
disposed of things I loved but could no longer keep, because of
new loves. And often I missed them. But I had hidden them so
well that even I could never find them again. That's the style, as
if I still had time to kill. And so I have, deep down I know it
well. Then why play at being in a hurry? I don't know. Perhaps
I am in a hurry after all, it was the impression I had a short time
ago. But my impressions. And what after all if I were not so
anxious as I make out to recall to mind all that is left to me of
all I ever had, a good dozen objects at least to put it mildly? No
no, I must. Then it's something else. Where were we? My bowl.
So I never got rid of it. I used it as a receptacle, I kept things in
it, I wonder what I could have kept in it, so small a space, and I
made a little cap for it, out of tin. Next. Poor Macmann.
Decidedly it will never have been given to me to finish anything,
except perhaps breathing. One must not be greedy. But is this

how one chokes? Presumably. And the rattle, what about the
rattle? Perhaps it is not de rigueur after all. To have mewled
and not be bloody well able to rattle. How life dulls the power to
protest to be sure. I wonder what my last words will be, written,
the others do not endure, but vanish, into thin air. I shall never
know. I shall not finish this inventory either, a little bird tells
me so, the paraclete perhaps, psittaceously named. Be it so. A
club in any case, I can't help it, I must state the facts, without
trying to understand, to the end. There are moments when I feel
I have been here always, perhaps even was born here. Then it
passes. That would explain many things. Or that I have come
back after a long absence. But I have done with feeling and
hypotheses. This club is mine and that is all about it. It is stained
with blood, but insufficiently, insufficently. I have defended myself,
ill, but I have defended myself. That is what I tell myself sometimes. One boot, originally yellow, I forget for which foot. The
other, its fellow, has gone. They took it away, at the beginning,
before they realized I should never walk again. And they left the
other, in the hope I would be saddened, seeing it there, without
its fellow. Men are like that. Or perhaps it is on top of the cupboard. I have looked for it everywhere, with my stick, but I never
thought of the top of the cupboard. Till now. And as I shall never
look for it any more, or for anything else, either on top of the
cupboard or anywhere else, it is no longer mine. For only those
things are mine the whereabouts of which I know well enough to
be able to lay hold of them, if necessary, that is the definition I
have adopted, to define my possessions. For otherwise there
would be no end to it. But in any case there will be no end to it.
It did not greatly resemble—but it is wrong of me to dwell upon
it—the one I have preserved, the yellow one remarkable for the
number of its eyeholes, I never saw a boot with so many eyeholes,
useless for the most part, having ceased to be holes, and become
slits. All these things are together in the corner in a heap. I could
lay hold of them, even now, in the dark, I need only wish to do
so. I would identify them by touch, the message would flow all
along the stick, I would hook the desired object and bring it over
to the bed, I would hear it coming towards me over the floor,

gliding, jogging, less and less dear, I would hoist it up on the bed
in such a way as not to break the window or damage the ceiling,
and at last I would have it in my hands. If it was my hat I might
put it on, that would remind me of the good old days, though I
remember them sufficiently well. It has lost its brim, it looks like
a bell-glass to put over a melon. In order to put it on and take
it off you have to grasp it like a great ball, between your palms.
It is perhaps the only object in my possession the history of which
I have not forgotten, I mean counting from the day it became
mine. I know in what circumstances it lost its brim, I was there
at the time, it was so that I might keep it on while I slept. I
should rather like it to be buried with me, a harmless whim, but
what steps should I take? Mem, put it on on the off chance, well
wedged down, before it is too late. But all in due time. Should I
go on I wonder. I feel I am perhaps attributing to myself things I
no longer possess and reporting as missing others that are not
missing. And I feel there are others, over there in the corner,
belonging to a third category, that of those of which I know
nothing and with regard to which therefore there is little danger
of my being wrong, or of my being right. And I remind myself
also that since I last went through my possessions much water
has passed beneath Butt Bridge, in both directions. For I have
sufficiently perished in this room to know that some things go out,
and other things come in, through I know not what agency. And
among those that go out there are some that come back, after a
more or less prolonged absence, and others that never come back.
With the result that, among those that come in, some are familiar
to me, others not. I don't understand. And, stranger still, there
exists a whole family of objects, having apparently very little in
common, which have never left me, since I have been here, but
remained quietly in their place, in the corner, as in any ordinary
uninhabited room. Or else they were very quick. How false all that
rings. But there is no guarantee things will be ever thus. I cannot
account in any other way for the changing aspect of my possessions. So that, strictly speaking, it is impossible for me to know,
from one moment to the next, what is mine and what is not,
according to my definition. So I wonder if I should go on, I mean

go on drawing up an inventory corresponding perhaps but faintly
to the facts, and if I should not rather cut it short and devote
myself to some other form of distraction, of less consequence, or
simply wait, doing nothing, or counting perhaps, one, two, three
and so on, until all danger to myself from myself is past at last.
That is what comes of being scrupulous. If I had a penny I
would let it make up my mind. Decidedly the night is long and
poor in counsel. Perhaps I should persist until dawn. All things
considered. Good idea, excellent. If at dawn I am still there I shall
take a decision. I am half asleep. But I dare not sleep. Rectifi-
cations in extremis, in extremissimis, are always possible after all.
But have I not perhaps just passed away? Malone, Malone, no
more of that. Perhaps I should call in all my possessions such as
they are and take them into bed with me. Would that be of any
use? I suppose not. But I may. I have always that resource. When
it is light enough to see. Then I shall have them all round me,
on top of me, under me, in the corner there will be nothing left,
all will be in the bed, with me. I shall hold my photograph in my
hand, my stone, so that they can't get away. I shall put on my
hat. Perhaps I shall have something in my mouth, my scrap of
newspaper perhaps, or my buttons, and I shall be lying on other
treasures still. My photograph. It is not a photograph of me, but
I am perhaps at hand. It is an ass, taken from in front and close
up, at the edge of the ocean, it is not the ocean, but for me it is
the ocean. They naturally tried to make it raise its head, so that
its beautiful eyes might be impressed on the celluloid, but it holds
it lowered. You can tell by its ears that it is not pleased. They
put a boater on its head. The thin hard parallel legs, the little
hooves light and dainty on the sand. The outline is blurred,
that's the operator's giggle shaking the camera. The ocean looks
so unnatural that you'd think you were in a studio, but is it not
rather the reverse I should say? No trace left of any clothes for
example, apart from the boot, the hat and three socks, I counted
them. Where have my clothes disappeared, my greatcoat, my
trousers and the flannel that Mr. Quin gave me, with the remark
that he did not need it any more? Perhaps they were burnt. But
our business is not with what I have no longer, such things do

not count at such a moment, whatever people may say. In any
case I think I'll stop. I was keeping the best for the end, but I
don't feel very well, perhaps I'm going, that would surprise me.
It is a passing weakness, everyone has experienced that. One
weakens, then it passes, one's strength comes back and one
resumes. That is probably what is happening to me. I yawn,
would I yawn if it was serious? Why not? I would gladly eat a
little soup, if there was any left. No, even if there was some left
I would not eat it. So there. It is some days now since my soup
was renewed, did I mention that? I suppose so. It is in vain I
dispatch my table to the door, bring it back beside me, move it
to and fro in the hope that the noise will be heard and correctly
interpreted in the right quarters, the dish remains empty. One of
the pots on the other hand remains full, and the other is filling
slowly. If I ever succeed in filling it I shall empty them both out
on the floor, but it is unlikely. Now that I have stopped eating I
produce less waste and so eliminate less. The pots do not seem to
be mine, I simply have the use of them. They answer to the definition of what is mine, but they are not mine. Perhaps it is the
definition that is at fault. They have each two handles or ears,
projecting above the rim and facing each other, into which I insert
my stick. In this way I move my pots about, lift them up and set
them down. Nothing has been left to chance. Or is it a happy
chance? I can therefore easily turn them upside down, if I am
driven to it, and wait for them to empty, as long as necessary.
After this passing reference to my pots I feel a little more lively.
They are not mine, but I say my pots, as I say my bed, my window, as I say me. Nevertheless I shall stop. It is my possessions
have weakened me, if I start talking about them again I shall
weaken again, for the same causes give rise to the same effects.
I should have liked to speak of the cap of my bicycle-bell, of my
half-crutch, the top half, you'd think it was a baby's crutch. But
I can still do so, what is there to prevent me? I don't know. I can't.
To think I shall perhaps die of hunger, after all, of starvation
rather, after having struggled successfully all my life against that
menace. I can't believe it. There is a providence for impotent old
men, to the end. And when they cannot swallow any more some-

one rams a tube down their gullet, or up their rectum, and fills them full of vitaminized pap, so as not to be accused of murder. I shall therefore die of old age pure and simple, glutted with days as in the days before the flood, on a full stomach. Perhaps they think I am dead. Or perhaps they are dead themselves. I say they, though perhaps I should not. In the beginning, but was it the beginning, I used to see an old woman, then for a time an old yellow arm, then for a time an old yellow hand. But these were probably no more than the agents of a consortium. And indeed the silence at times is such that the earth seems uninhabited. That is what comes of the taste for generalization. You have only to hear nothing for a few days, in your hole, nothing but the sounds of things, and you begin to fancy yourself the last of human kind. What if I started to scream? Not that I wish to draw attention to myself, simply to try and find out if there is someone about. But I don't like screaming. I have spoken softly, gone my ways softly, all my days, as behoves one who has nothing to say, nowhere to go, and so nothing to gain by being seen or heard. Not to mention the possibility of there being not a living soul within a radius of one hundred yards and then such multitudes of people that they are walking on top of one another. They do not dare come near me. In that case I could scream my head off to no purpose. I shall try all the same. I have tried. I heard nothing out of the ordinary. No, I exaggerate, I heard a kind of burning croak deep down in the windpipe, as when one has heartburn. With practice I might produce a groan, before I die. I am not sleepy any more. In any case I must not sleep any more. What tedium. I have missed the ebb. Did I say I only say a small proportion of the things that come into my head? I must have. I choose those that seem somehow akin. It is not always easy. I hope they are the most important. I wonder if I shall ever be able to stop. Perhaps I should throw away my lead. I could never retrieve it now. I might be sorry. My little lead. It is a risk I do not feel inclined to take, just now. What then? I wonder if I could not contrive, wielding my stick like a punt-pole, to move my bed. It may well be on castors, many beds are. Incredible I should never have thought of this, all the time I have been here.

I might even succeed in steering it, it is so narrow, through the
door, and even down the stairs, if there is a stairs that goes down.
To be off and away. The dark is against me, in a sense. But I
can always try and see if the bed will move. I have only to set
the stick against the wall and push. And I can see myself already,
if successful, taking a little turn in the room, until it is light
enough for me to set forth. At least while thus employed I shall
stop telling myself lies. And then, who knows, the physical effort
may polish me off, by means of heart failure.

I have lost my stick, That is the outstanding event of the day,
for it is day again. The bed has not stirred. I must have missed my
point of purchase, in the dark. Sine qua non, Archimedes was
right. The stick, having slipped, would have plucked me from the
bed if I had not let it go. It would of course have been better for
me to relinquish my bed than to lose my stick. But I had not time
to think. The fear of falling is the source of many a folly. It is a
disaster. I suppose the wisest thing now is to live it over again,
meditate upon it and be edified. It is thus that man distinguishes
himself from the ape and rises, from discovery to discovery, ever
higher, towards the light. Now that I have lost my stick I realize
what it is I have lost and all it meant to me. And thence ascend,
painfully, to an understanding of the Stick, shorn of all its accidents, such as I had never dreamt of. What a broadening of the
mind. So that I half discern, in the veritable catastrophe that has
befallen me, a blessing in disguise. How comforting that is.
Catastrophe too in the ancient sense no doubt. To be buried in
lava and not turn a hair, it is then a man shows what stuff he is
made of. To know you can do better next time, unrecognizably
better, and that there is no next time, and that it is a blessing
there is not, there is a thought to be going on with. I thought I
was turning my stick to the best possible account, like a monkey
scratching its fleas with the key that opens its cage. For it is
obvious to me now that by making a more intelligent use of my
stick I might have extracted myself from my bed and perhaps
even got myself back into it, when tired of rolling and dragging
myself about the floor or on the stairs. That would have intro-
duced a little variety into my decomposition. How is it that

never occurred to me? It is true I had no wish to leave my bed.
But can the sage have no wish for something the very possibility
of which he does not conceive? I don't understand. The sage
perhaps. But I? It is day again, at least what passes for such
here. I must have fallen asleep after a brief bout of discouragement, such as I have not experienced for a long time. For why be
discouraged, one of the thieves was saved, that is a generous
percentage. I see the stick on the floor, not far from the bed. That
is to say I see part of it, as of all one sees. It might just as well
be at the equator, or one of the poles. No, not quite, for perhaps
I shall devise a way of retrieving it, I am so ingenious. All is
not then yet quite irrevocably lost. In the meantime nothing is
mine any more, according to my definition, if I remember rightly,
except my exercise-book, my lead and the French pencil, assuming
it really exists. I did well to stop my inventory, it was a happy
thought. I feel less weak, perhaps they fed me while I slept.
I see the pot, the one that is not full, it is lost to me too. I
shall doubtless be obliged to forget myself in the bed, as when I
was a baby. At least I shall not be skelped. But enough about
me. You would think I was relieved to be without my stick. I
think I know how I might retrieve it. But something occurs to me.
Are they depriving me of soup on purpose to help me die? One
judges people too hastily. But in that case why feed me during
my sleep? But there is no proof they have. But if they wished to
help me would it not be more intelligent to give me poisoned
soup, large quantities of poisoned soup? Perhaps they fear an
autopsy. It is obvious they see a long way ahead. That reminds
me that among my possessions I once had a little phial, un-
labelled, containing pills. Laxatives? Sedatives? I forget. To turn
to them for calm and merely obtain a diarrhoea, my, that would
be annoying. In any case the question does not arise I am calm,
insufficiently, I still lack a little calm. But enough about me.
I'll see if there is anything in my little idea, I mean how to
retrieve my stick. The fact is I must be very weak. If there is,
anything in it I mean, I shall try and get myself out of the bed,
for a start. If not I do not know what I shall do. Go and see how
Macmann is getting on perhaps. I have always that resource.

Why this need of activity? I am growing nervous.

One day, much later, to judge by his appearance, Macmann came to again, once again, in a kind of asylum. At first he did not know it was one, being plunged within it, but he was told so as soon as he was in a condition to receive news. They said in substance, You are now in the House of Saint John of God, with the number one hundred and sixty-six. Fear nothing, you are among friends. Friends! Well well. Take no thought for anything, it is we shall think and act for you, from now forward. We like it. Do not thank us therefore. In addition to the nourishment carefully calculated to keep you alive, and even well, you will receive, every Saturday, in honour of our patron, an imperial half-pint of porter and a plug of tobacco. Then followed instructions regarding his duties and prerogatives, for he was credited with a certain number of prerogatives, notwithstanding the bounties showered upon him. Stunned by this torrent of civility, for he had eluded charity all his days, Macmann did not immediately grasp that he was being spoken to. The room, or cell, in which he lay, was thronged with men and women dressed in white. They swarmed about his bed, those in the rear rising on tiptoe and craning their necks to get a better view of him. The speaker was a man, naturally, in the flower and the prime of life, his features stamped with mildness and severity in equal proportions, and he wore a scraggy beard no doubt intended to heighten his resemblance to the Messiah. To tell the truth, yet again, he did not so much read as improvise, or recite, to judge by the paper he held in his hand and on which from time to time he cast an anxious eye. He finally handed this paper to Macmann, together with the stump of an indelible pencil, the point of which he first wetted with his lips, and requested him to sign, adding that it was a mere formality. And when Macmann had obeyed, either because he was afraid of being punished if he refused or because he did not realize the seriousness of what he was doing, the other took back the paper, examined it and said, Mac what? It was then a woman's voice, extraordinarily shrill and unpleasant, was heard to say, Mann, his name is Macmann. This woman was standing behind him, so that he could not see her, and in each hand she clutched a bar

of the bed. Who are you? said the speaker. Someone replied, But
it is Moll, can't you see, her name is Moll. The speaker turned
towards this informant, glared at him for a moment, then dropped
his eyes. To be sure, he said, to be sure, I am out of sorts. He
added, after a pause, Nice name, without its being quite clear
whether this tribute was aimed at the nice name of Moll or at
the nice name of Macmann. Don't push, for Jesus sake! he said,
irritably. Then, suddenly turning, he cried, What in God's name
are you all pushing for for Christ sake? And indeed the room
was filling more and more, under the influx of fresh spectators.
Personally I'm going, said the speaker. Then all retreated, in great
jostle and disorder, each one striving to be first out through the
door, with the sole exception of Moll, who did not stir. But when
all were gone she went to the door and shut it, then came back
and sat down on a chair by the bed. She was a little old woman,
immoderately ill-favoured of both face and body. She seems
called on to play a certain part in the remarkable events which,
I hope, will enable me to make an end. The thin yellow arms
contorted by some kind of bone deformation, the lips so broad
and thick that they seemed to devour half the face, were at first
sight her most revolting features. She wore by way of ear-rings
two long ivory crucifixes which swayed wildly at the least
movement of her head.

I pause to record that I feel in extraordinary form. Delirium
perhaps.

It seemed probable to Macmann that he was committed to
the care and charge of this person. Correct. For it had been
decreed, by those in authority, that one hundred and sixty-six
was Moll's, she having applied for him, formally. She brought
him food (one large dish daily, to first hot, then cold), emptied
his chamber-pot every morning first thing and showed him how to
wash himself, his face and hands every day, and the other parts
of the body successively in the course of the week, Monday the
feet, Tuesday the legs up to the knees, Wednesday the thighs, and
so on, culminating on Sunday with the neck and ears, no, Sunday
he rested from washing. She swept the floor, shook up the bed
from time to time and seemed to take an extreme pleasure in

polishing until they shone the frosted lights of the unique window, which was never opened. She informed Macmann, when he did something, if that thing was permitted or not, and similarly, when he remained inert, whether or not he was entitled to. Does this mean that she stayed with him all the time? Why no, and no doubt she had other attentions to bestow elsewhere, and other instructions to give. But in the early stages, before he had grown used to this new tide in his fortune, she assuredly left him alone as little as possible and even watched over him part of the night. How understanding she was, and how good-natured, appears from the following anecdote. One day, not long after his admission, Macmann realized he was wearing, instead of his usual accoutrement, a long loose smock of coarse linen, or possibly drugget. He at once began to clamour loudly for his clothes, including probably the contents of his pockets, for he cried, My things! My things!, over and over again, tossing about in the bed and beating the blanket with his palms. Then Moll sat down on the edge of the bed and distributed her hands as follows, one on top of one of Macmann's, the other on his brow. She was so small that her feet did not reach to the floor. When he was a little calmer she told him that his clothes had certainly ceased to exist and could not therefore be returned to him. With regard to the objects found in the pockets, they had been assessed as quite worthless and fit only to be thrown away with the exception of a little silver knife-rest which he could have back at any time. But these declarations so distressed him that she hastened to add, with a laugh, that she was only joking and that in reality his clothes, cleaned, pressed, mended, strewn with mothballs and folded away in a cardboard box bearing his name and number, were as safe as if they had been received in deposit by the Bank of England. But as Macmann continued vehemently to demand his things, as if he did not understand a word of what she had just told him, she was obliged to invoke the regulations which tolerated on no account that an inmate should resume contact with the trappings of his derelict days until such time as he might be discharged. But as Macmann continued passionately to clamour for his things, and notably for his hat, she left him, saying he was not reasonable. And she came back a little later, holding with the tips of her fingers the hat in question, retrieved perhaps from the rubbish-heap at the end of the vegetable-garden, for to know everything takes too long, for it was fringed with manure and seemed to be rotting away. And what is more she suffered him to put it on, and even helped him to do so, helping him to sit up in the bed and arranging his pillows in such a way that he might remain propped up without fatigue. And she contemplated with tenderness the old bewildered face relaxing, and in its tod of hair the mouth trying to smile, and the little red eyes turning timidly towards her as if in gratitude or rolling towards the re-covered hat, and the hands raised to set it on more firmly and returning to rest trembling on the blanket. And at last a long look passed between them and Moll's lips puffed and parted in a dreadful smile, which made Macmann's eyes waver like those of an animal glared on by its master and compelled then finally to look away. End of anecdote. This must be the selfsame hat that was abandonend in the middle of the plain, its resemblance to it is so great, allowance being made for the additional wear and tear. Can it be then that it is not the same Macmann at all, after all, in spite of the great resemblance (for those who know the power of the passing years), both physical and otherwise. It is true the Macmanns are legion in the island and pride them-selves, what is more, with few exceptions, on having one and all, in the last analysis, sprung from the same illustrious ball. It is therefore inevitable they should resemble one another, now and then, to the point of being confused even in the minds of those who wish them well and would like nothing better than to tell between them. No matter, any old remains of flesh and spirit do, there is no sense in stalking people. So long as it is what is called a living being you can't go wrong, you have the guilty one. For a long time he did not stir from his bed, not knowing if he could walk, or even stand, and fearing to run foul of the authorities, if he could. Let us then first consider this first phase of Macmann's stay in the House of Saint John of God. We shall then pass on to the second, and even to the third, if necessary.

A thousand little things to report, very strange, in view of my

situation, if I interpret them correctly. But my notes have a
curious tendency, as I realize at last, to annihilate all they purport
to record. So I hasten to turn aside from this extraordinary heat,
to mention only it, which has seized on certain parts of my
economy, I will not specify which. And to think I was expecting
rather to grow cold, if anything!

This first phase, that of the bed, was characterized by the
evolution of the relationship between Macmann and his keeper.
There sprang up gradually between them a kind of intimacy
which, at a given moment, led them to lie together and copulate
as best they could. For given their age and scant experience of
carnal love, it was only natural they should not succeed, at the
first shot, in giving each other the impression they were made for
each other. The spectacle was then offered of Macmann trying to
bundle his sex into his partner's like a pillow into a pillow-slip,
folding it in two and stuffing it in with his fingers. But far from
losing heart they warmed to their work. And though both were
completely impotent they finally succeeded, summoning to their
aid all the resources of the skin, the mucus and the imagination,
in striking from their dry and feeble clips a kind of sombre
gratification. So that Moll exclaimed, being (at that stage) the more
expansive of the two, Oh would we had but met sixty years ago!
But on the long road to this what flutterings, alarms and bashful
fumblings, of which only this, that they gave Macmann some
insight into the meaning of the expression, Two is company. He
then made unquestionable progress in the use of the spoken word
and learnt in a short time to let fall, at the right time, the yesses,
noes, mores and enoughs that keep love alive. It was also the
occasion of his penetrating into the enchanted world of reading,
thanks to the inflammatory letters which Moll brought and put
into his hands. And the memories of school are so tenacious, for
those who have been there, that he was soon able to dispense with
the explanations of his correspondent and understand all unaided,
holding the sheet of paper as far from his eyes as his arms permitted. While he read Moll held a little aloof, with downcast
eyes, saying to herself, Now he's at the part where, and a little
later, Now he's at the part where, and so remained until the

rustle of the sheet going back into the envelope announced that
he had finished. Then she turned eagerly towards him, in time to
see him raise the letter to his lips or press it against his heart,
another reminiscence of the fourth form. Then he gave it back
to her and she put it under his pillow with the others there
already, arranged in chronological order and tied together with a
favour. These letters did not much vary in form and tenor, which
greatly facilitated matters for Macmann. Example. Sweetheart,
Not one day goes by that I do not give thanks to God, on my
bended knees, for having found you, before I die. For we shall
soon die, you and I, that is obvious. That it may be at the same
moment exactly is all I ask. In any case I have the key of the
medicine cupboard. But let us profit first by this superb sundown,
after the long day of storm. Are you not of this opinion? Sweetheart! Ah would we had met but seventy years ago! No, all is
for the best, we shall not have time to grow to loathe each other,
to see our youth slip by, to recall with nausea the ancient
rapture, to seek in the company of third parties, you on the one
hand, I on the other, that which together we can no longer com-
pass, in a word to get to know each other. One must look things
in the face, must one not, sweet pet? When you hold me in your
arms, and I you in mine, it naturally does not amount to much,
compared to the transports of youth, and even middle age. But
all is relative, let us bear that in mind, stags and hinds have their
needs and we have ours. It is even astonishing that you manage so
well, I can hardly get over it, what a chaste and sober life you
must have led. I too, you must have noticed it. Consider moreover
that the flesh is not the end-all and the be-all, especially at our
age, and name me the lovers who can do with their eyes what we
can do with ours, which will soon have seen all there is for them
to see and have often great difficulty in remaining open, and with
their tenderness, without the help of passion, what by this means
alone we realize daily, when separated by our respective obli-
gations. Consider furthermore, since there is nothing more for us
to hide, that I was never beautiful or well-proportioned, but ugly
and even misshapen, to judge by the testimonies I have received.
Papa notably used to say that people would run a mile from me,

I have not forgotten the expression. And you, sweet, even when you were of an age to quicken the pulse of beauty, did you exhibit the other requisites? I doubt it. But with the passing of the years we have become scarcely less hideous than even our best favoured contemporaries and you, in particular, have kept your hair. And thanks to our having never served, never understood, we are not without freshness and innocence, it seems to me. Moral, for us at last it is the season of love, let us make the most of it, there are pears that only ripen in December. Do not fret about our methods, leave all that to me, and I warrant you we'll surprise each other yet. With regard to tetty-beshy I must beg to differ, it is well worth persevering with, in my opinion. Follow my instructions, you'll come back for more. For shame, you dirty old man! It's all these bones that makes it awkward, that I grant you. Well, we must just accept ourselves as we are. And above all *not fret*, these are trifles. Let us think of the hours when, spent, we lie twined together in the dark, our hearts laboring as one, and listen to the wind saying what it is to be abroad, at night, in winter, and what it is to have been what we have been, and sink together, in an unhappiness that has no name. That is how we must look at things. So courage, my sweet old hairy Mac, and oyster kisses just where you think from your own Sucky Moll. P.S. I enquired about the oysters, I have hopes. Such was the rather rambling style of the declarations which Moll, despairing no doubt of giving vent to her feelings by the normal channels, addressed three or four times a week to Macmann, who never answered, I mean in writing, but manifested by every other means in his power how pleased he was to receive them. But towards the close of this idyll, that is to say when it was too late, he began to compose brief rimes of curious structure, to offer to his mistress, for he felt she was drifting away from him. Example.

> *Hairy Mac and Sucky Molly*
> *In the ending days and nights*
> *Of unending melancholy*
> *Love it is at last unites.*

Other example.

> *To the lifelong promised land*
> *Of the nearest cemetery*
> *With his Sucky hand in hand*
> *Love it is at last leads Hairy.*

He had time to compose ten or twelve more or less in this vein,
all remarkable for their exaltation of love regarded as a kind of
lethal glue, a conception frequently to be met with in mystic
texts. And it is extraordinary that Macmann should have succeeded, in so short a time and after such inauspicious beginnings,
in elevating himself to a view of this altitude. And one can only
speculate on what he might have achieved if he had become
acquainted with true sexuality at a less advanced age.

I am lost. Not a word.

Inauspicious beginnings indeed, during which his feeling for
Moll was frankly one of repugnance. Her lips in particular
repelled him, those selfsame lips, or so little changed as to make
no matter, that some months later he was to suck with grunts of
pleasure, so that at the very sight of them he not only closed
his eyes, but covered them with his hands for greater safety. She
it was therefore who at this period exerted herself in tireless
ardours, which may serve to explain why she seemed to weaken
in the end and stand in her turn in need of stimulation. Unless
it was simply a question of health. Which does not exclude a
third hypothesis, namely that Moll, having finally decided that
she had mistaken in Macmann and that he was not the man she
had taken him for, sought a means of putting an end to their
intercourse, but gently, in order not to give him a shock. Unfortunately our concern here is not with Moll, who after all is
only a female, but with Macmann, and not with the close of their
relations, but rather with the beginning. Of the brief period of
plentitude between these two extremes, when between the warming up of the one party and the cooling down of the other there
was established a fleeting equality of temperature, no further
mention will be made. For if it is indispensable to have in order
not to have had and in order to have no longer, there is no
obligation to expatiate upon it. But let us rather let events speak

for themselves, that is more or less the right tone. Example. One day, just as Macmann was getting used to being loved, though without as yet responding as he was subsequently to do, he thrust Moll's face away from his on the pretext of examining her earrings. But as she made to return to the charge he checked her again with the first words that came into his head, namely, Why two Christs?, implying that in his opinion one was more than sufficient. To which she made the absurd reply, Why two ears? But she obtained his forgiveness a moment later, saying, with a smile (she smiled at the least thing), Besides they are the thieves, Christ is in my mouth. Then parting her jaws and pulling down her blobber-lip she discovered, breaking with its solitary fang the monotomy of the gums, a long yellow canine bared to the roots and carved, with the drill probably, to represent the celebrated sacrifice. With the forefinger of her free hand she fingered it. It's loose, she said, one of these fine mornings I'll wake up and find I've swallowed it, perhaps I should have it out. She let go her lip, which sprang back into place with a smack. This incident made a strong impression on Macmann and Moll rose with a bound in his affections. And in the pleasure he was later to enjoy, when he put his tongue in her mouth and let it wander over her gums, this rotten crucifix had assuredly its part. But from these harmless aids what love is free? Sometimes it is an object, a garter I believe or a sweat-absorber for the armpit. And sometimes it is the simple image of a third party. A few words in conclusion on the decline of this liaison. No, I can't.

Weary with my weariness, white last moon, sole regret, not even. To be dead, before her, on her, with her, and turn, dead on dead, about poor mankind, and never have to die any more, from among the living. Not even, not even that. My moon was here below, far below, the little I was able to desire. And one day, soon, soon, one earthlit night, beneath the earth, a dying being will say, like me, in the earthlight, Not even, not even that, and die, without having been able to find a regret.

Moll. I'm going to kill her. She continued to look after Macmann, but she was no longer the same. When she had finished cleaning up she sat down on a chair, in the middle of the room,

and remained without stirring. If he called her she went and
perched on the edge of the bed and even submitted to be titillated.
But it was obvious her thoughts were elsewhere and her only
wish to return to her chair and resume the now familiar gesture
of massaging her stomach, slowly, weighing on it with her two
hands. She was also beginning to smell. She had never smelt
sweet, but between not smelling sweet and giving off the smell she
was giving off now there is a gulf. She was also subject to fits
of vomiting. Turning away, so that her lover should only see her
convulsive back, she vomited at length on the floor. And these
dejections remained sometimes for hours where they fell, until
such time as she had the strength to go and fetch what was
needed to clean up the mess. Half a century younger she might
have been taken for pregnant. At the same time her hair began
to fall out in abundance and she confessed to Macmann that she
did not dare comb it any more, for fear of making it fall out even
faster. He said to himself with satisfaction, She tells me everything. But these were small things compared to the change in
her complexion, now rapidly turning from yellow to saffron. The
sight of her so diminished did not damp Macmann's desire to
take her, all stinking, yellow, bald and vomiting, in his arms. And
he would certainly have done so had she not been opposed to it.
One can understand him (her too). For when one has within reach
the one and only love requited of a life so monstrously prolonged,
it is natural one should wish to profit by it, before it is too late,
and refuse to be deterred by feelings of squeamishness excusable
in the faint-hearted, but which true love disdains. And though all
pointed to Moll's being out of sorts, Macmann could not help
interpreting her attitude as a falling off of her affection for him.
And perhaps indeed there was something of that too. At all
events the more she declined the more Macmann longed to crush
her to his breast, which is at least sufficiently curious and unusual to deserve of mention. And when she turned and looked at
him (and from time to time she did so still), with eyes in which
he fancied he could read boundless regret and love, then a kind
of frenzy seized upon him and he began to belabor with his fists
his chest, his head and even the mattress, writhing and crying out,

in the hope perhaps she would take pity on him and come and comfort him and dry his tears, as on the day when he had demanded his hat. No, it was not that, it was without malice he cried, writhed and beat his breast, for she made no attempt to stop him and even left the room if it went on too long for her liking. Then, all alone and unobserved, he continued to behave as if beside himself, which is proof positive, is it not, that he was disinterested, unless of course he suspected her of having stopped outside the door to listen. And when he grew calm again at last he mourned the long immunity he had lost, from shelter, charity and human tenderness. And he even carried his inconsequence to the length of wondering what right anyone had to take care of him. In a word most evil days, for Macmann. For Moll too probably, naturally, admitted. It was at this time she lost her tooth. It fell unaided from the socket, happily in the daytime, so that she was able to recover it and put it away in a safe place. Macmann said to himself, when she told him, There was a time she would have made me a present of it, or at least shown it to me. But a little later he said, firstly, To have told me, when she need not have, is a mark of confidence and affection, and secondly, But I would have known in any case, when she opened her mouth to speak or smile, and finally, But she does not speak or smile any more. One morning early a man whom he had never seen came and told him that Moll was dead. There's one out of the way at least. My name is Lemuel, he said, though my parents were probably Aryan, and it is in my charge you are from now on. Here is your porridge. Eat it while it is boiling.

A last effort. Lemuel gave the impression of being slightly more stupid than malevolent, and yet his malevolence was considerable. When Macmann, more and more disturbed by his situation apparently and what is more now capable of isolating and expressing well enough to be understood a little of the little that passed through his mind, when Macmann I say asked a question it was seldom he got an immediate answer. When asked for example to state whether Saint John of Gods was a private institution or run by the State, a hospice for the aged and infirm or a madhouse, if once in one might entertain the hope of one

day getting out and, in the affirmative, by means of what steps,
Lemuel remained for a long time plunged in thought, sometimes
for as long as ten minutes or a quarter of an hour, motionless or
if you prefer scratching his head or his armpit, as if such questions
had never crossed his mind, or possibly thinking about something
quite different. And if Macmann, growing impatient or perhaps
feeling he had not made himself clear, ventured to try again, an
imperious gesture bid him be silent. Such was this Lemuel, viewed
from a certain angle. Or he cried, stamping the ground with
indescribable nervousness, Let me think, you shite! It usually
ended by his saying he did not know. But he was subject to almost hypomaniacal fits of good humour. Then he would add, But
I'll enquire. And taking out a note-book as fat as a ship's log he
made note, murmuring, Private or state, mad or like me, how
out, etc. Macmann could then be sure he would never hear any
more about it. May I get up? he said one day. Already in Moll's
lifetime he had expressed the wish to get up and go out into the
fresh air, but timidly, as when one asks for the moon. And he had
then been told that if he was good he might indeed be let up one
day, and out into the pure plateau air, and that on that day, in
the great hall where the staff assembled at dawn before entering
on their duties, there would be seen pinned on the board a note
thus conceived, Let one hundred and sixty-six get up and go out.
For when it came to the regulations Moll was inflexible and their
voice was stronger than the voice of love, in her heart, whenever
they made themselves heard there simultaneously. The oysters for
example, which the Board had refused in a note calling her
attention to the article whereby they were prohibited, but which
she could easily have smuggled in, Macmann never saw sight
or sign of the oysters. But Lemuel was made of sterner stuff, in
this connection, and far from being being a stickler for the statutes
seemed to have little or no acquaintance with them. Indeed the
question might have arisen, in the mind of one looking down
upon the scene, as to whether he had all his wits about him. For
when not rooted to the spot in a daze he was to be seen, with
heavy, furious, reeling tread, stamping up and down for hours on
end, gesticulating and ejaculating unintelligible words. Flayed

alive by memory, his mind crawling with cobras, not daring to
dream or think and powerless not to, his cries were of two kinds,
those having no other cause than moral anguish and those, similar
in every respect, by means of which he hoped to forestall same.
Physical pain, on the contrary, seemed to help him greatly. And
one day rolling up the leg of his trousers, he showed Macmann
his shin covered with bruises, scars and abrasions. Then produc-
ing smartly a hammer from an inner pocket he dealt himself,
right in the middle of his ancient wounds, so violent a blow that
he fell down backwards, or perhaps I should say forwards. But
the part he struck most readily, with his hammer, was the head,
and that is understandable, for it too is a bony part, and sensitive,
and difficult to miss, and the seat of all the shit and misery, so
you rain blows upon it, with more pleasure than on the leg for
example, which never did you any harm, it's only human. Up!
cried Macmann. Let me up! Lemuel came to a standstill. What?
he roared. Up! cried Macmann. Let me up! Let me up!

I have had a visit. Things were going too well. I had forgotten myself, lost myself. I exaggerate. Things were not going
too badly. I was elsewhere. Another was suffering. Then I had
the visit. To bring me back to dying. If that amuses them. The
fact is they don't know, neither do I, but they think they know.
An aeroplane passes, flying low, with a noise like thunder. It is
a noise quite unlike thunder, one says thunder but one does not
think of it, it is just a loud, fleeting noise, nothing more, unlike
any other. It is certainly the first time I have heard it here, to my
knowledge. But I have heard aeroplanes elsewhere and have even
seen them in flight, I saw the very first in flight and then in the
end the latest models, oh not the very latest, the very second-
latest, the very antepenultimate. I was present at one of the first
loopings of the loop, so help me God. I was not afraid. It was
above a racecourse, my mother held me by the hand. She kept
saying, It's a miracle, a miracle. Then I changed my mind. We were
not often of the same mind. One day we were walking along the
road, up a hill of extraordinary steepness, near home I imagine, my
memory is full of steep hills, I get them confused. I said, The sky
is further away than you think, is it not, mama? It was without

malice, I was simply thinking of all the leagues that separated
me from it. She replied, to me her son, It is precisely as far away
as it appears to be. She was right. But at the time I was aghast.
I can still see the spot, opposite Tyler's gate. A market-gardener,
he had only one eye and wore side-whiskers. That's the idea,
rattle on. You could see the sea, the islands, the headlands, the
isthmuses, the coast stretching away to north and south and the
crooked moles of the harbour. We were on our way home from
the butcher's. My mother? Perhaps it is just another story, told
me by some one who found it funny. The stories I was told,
at one time! And all funny, not one not funny. In any case here
I am back in the shit. The aeroplane, on the other hand, has just
passed over at two hundred miles an hour perhaps. It's a good
speed, for the present day. I am with it in spirit, naturally. All
the things I was always with in spirit. In body no. Not such a
fool. Here is the programme anyhow, the end of the programme.
They think they can confuse me and make me lose sight of my
programmes. Proper cunts whoever they are. Here it is. Visit,
various remarks, Macmann continued, agony recalled, Macmann
continued, then mixture of Macmann and agony as long as possible. It does not depend on me, my lead is not inexhaustible,
nor my exercise-book, nor Macmann, nor myself in spite of
appearances. That all may be wiped out at the same instant is
all I ask, for the moment. The visit. I felt a violent blow on the
head. He had perhaps been there for some time. One does not
care to be kept waiting for ever, one draws attention to oneself
as best one can, it's human. I don't doubt he gave me due warning, before he hit me. I don't know what he wanted. He's gone
now. What an idea, all the same, to hit me on the head. The light
has been queer ever since, oh I insinuate nothing, dim and at the
same time radiant, perhaps I have concussion. His mouth opened,
his lips worked, but I heard nothing. He might just as well have
said nothing. And yet I am not deaf, witness the aeroplane, if I
hear nothing it is because there is nothing to hear. But perhaps
life has dulled my irritability to specifically human sounds. I
myself for example make no sound, well well, can't go back on
it now, no, not the tiniest. And yet I pant, cough, moan and gulp

right up against my ear, I could swear to it. In other words I do
not know to what I owe the honour. He seemed vexed. Must I
describe him? Why not? He may be important. I had a clear
view of him. Black suit of antiquated cut, or perhaps come back
into the fashion, black tie, snow-white shirt, heavily starched
clown's cuffs almost entirely covering the hands, oily black hair,
a long, dismal, glabrous, floury face, sombre lacklustre eyes,
medium height and build, block-hat pressed delicately to stomach
with finger-tips, then without warning in a gesture of extraordinary
suddenness and precision slapped on skull. A folding-rule, together with a fin of white handkerchief, emerged from the breast
pocket. I took him at first for the undertaker's man, annoyed at
having called prematurely. He remained some time, seven hours
at least. Perhaps he hoped to have the satisfaction of seeing me
expire before he left, that would probably have saved him time
and trouble. For a moment I thought he was going to finish me
off. What a hope, it would have been a crime. He must have left
at six o'clock, his working day ended. The light is queer ever
since. That it to say he went a first time, came back some hours
later, then left for good. He must have been here from nine to
twelve, then from two to six, now I have it. He kept looking at
his watch, a turnip. Perhaps he will come back to-morrow. It was
in the morning he hit me, about ten o'clock probably. In the
afternoon he did not touch me, though I did not see him immediately, he was already in position when I saw him, standing beside
the bed. I speak of morning and afternoon and of such and such
an hour, if you simply must speak of people you simply must put
yourself in their place, it is not difficult. The only thing you must
never speak of is your happiness, I can think of nothing else for
the moment. Better even not to think of it. Standing by the bed
he watched me. Seeing my lips move, for I tried to speak, he
stooped down to me. I had things to ask him, to give me my
stick for example. He would have refused. Then with clasped
hands and tears in my eyes I would have begged it of him as a
favour. This humiliation has been denied to me thanks to my
aphony. My voice has gone dead, the rest will follow. I could
have written, on a page of my exercise-book, and shown to him,

Please give me back my stick, or, Be so kind as to hand me up
my stick. But I had hidden the exercise-book under the Blanket,
so that he might not take it from me. I did so without thinking
that he had been there for some time (otherwise he would not
have struck me) watching me writing, for I must have been
writing when he came, and that consequently he could easily have
taken my exercise-book if he had wished, and without thinking
either that he was watching me when I slipped it out of sight, and
that consequently the only effect of my precaution was to draw
his attention to the very object I wished to hide from him. There's
reasoning for you. For of all I ever had in this world all has been
taken from me, except the exercise-book, so I cherish it, it's
human. The lead too, I was forgetting the lead, but what is a
lead, without paper? He must have said to himself, over his lunch,
This afternoon I'll take his exercise-book from him, he seems to
cherish it. But when he came back from his lunch the exercise-
book was no longer in the place where he had seen me put it,
he had not thought of that. His umbrella, have I mentioned his
umbrella, the tightest rolled I ever saw? Shifting it every few
minutes from one hand to the other he leaned his weight upon
it, standing beside the bed. Then it bent. He made use of it to
raise my blankets. It was with this umbrella that I thought he was
going to kill me, with its long sharp point, he had only to plunge
it in my heart. Wilful murder, people would have said. Perhaps
he will come back to-morrow, better equipped, or with an
assistant, now that he is familiar with the premises. But if he
watched me I too watched him, I think we gazed at each other
literally for hours, without winking. He probably imagined he
could stare me down, because I am old and helpless. The poor
bastard. It was so long since I had seen a biped of this description
that I had my eyes out on stalks, as the saying is, for fear of not
being able to credit them. I said to myself, One of these days
they'll start grazing the trees. And the face they have! I had
forgotten. At a certain moment, incommoded by the smell probably, he squeezed himself in between the bed and the wall, to
try and open the window. He couldn't. In the morning I didn't
take my eyes off him. But in the afternoon I slept a little. I don't

know what he did while I was asleep, rummaged in my possessions probably, with his umbrella, they are scattered all over the floor now. I thought for a moment he had been sent by the funeral people. Those who have enabled me to live till now will no doubt see to it that I am buried with a minimum of ceremony. Here lies Malone at last, with the dates to give a faint idea of the time he took to be excused and then to distinguish him from his namesakes, numerous in the island and beyond the grave. Funny I never ran into one, to my knowledge, not one. There is still time. Here lies a ne'er-do-well, six feet under hell. But for a moment only, I mean half-an-hour at most. Then I tried him with other functions, all equally disappointing. Strange need to know who people are and what they do for a living and what they want with you. In spite of the ease with which he wore his black and manipulated his umbrella and his consummate mastery of the block-hat, I had for a time the impression he was disguised, but from what if I may say so, and as what? At a given moment, yet another, he took fright, for his breath came faster and he moved away from the bed. It was then I saw he was wearing brown boots, which gave me such a shock as no words can convey. They were copiously caked with fresh mud and I said to myself, Through what sloughs has he had to toil to reach me? I wonder if he was looking for something in particular, it would be so nice to know. I shall tear a page out of my exercise-book and reproduce upon it, from memory, what follows, and show it to him to-morrow, or to-day, or some other day, if he ever comes back. 1. Who are you? 2. What do you do, for a living? 3. Are you looking for something in particular? What else? 4. Why are you so cross? 5. Have I offended you? 6. Do you know anything about me? 7. It was wrong of you to strike me. 8. Give me my stick. 9. Are you your own employer? 10. If not who sends you? 11. Put back my things where you found them. 12. Why has my soup been stopped? 13. For what reason are my pots no longer emptied? 14. Do you think I shall last much longer? 15. May I ask you a favour? 16. Your conditions are mine. 17. Why brown boots and whence the mud? 18. You couldn't by any chance let me have the butt of a pencil? 19. Number your answers. 20.

Don't go, I haven't finished. Will one page suffice? There cannot
be many left. I might as well ask for a rubber while I am about
it. 21. Could you lend me an India rubber? When he had gone I
said to myself, But surely I have seen him somewhere before. And
the people I have seen have seen me too, I can guarantee that.
But of whom may it not be said, I know that man? Drivel, drivel.
And then at evening morning is so far away. I had stopped looking at him. I had got used to him. I was thinking of him, trying
to understand, you can't do that and look at the same time. I
did not even see him go. Oh he did not vanish, after the fashion
of a ghost, no, I heard him, the clank when he took out his watch,
the satisfied thump of the umbrella on the floor, the rightabout,
the rapid steps towards the door, its soft closing and finally, I
am sorry to say, a gay and lively whistle dying away. What have
I omitted? Little things, nothings. They will come back to me
later, make me see more clearly what has happened and say,
Ah if I had only known then, now it is too late. Yes, little by
little I shall see him as he just has been, or as he should have
been for me to be able to say, yet again, Too late, too late.
There's feeling for you. Or he is perhaps just the first of a series
of visitors, all different. They are going to relay one another,
and they are numerous. To-morrow perhaps he will be wearing
leggings, riding-breeches and a check cap, with a whip in his
hand to make up for the umbrella and a horse-shoe in his buttonhole. All the people I have ever caught a glimpse of, at close
quarters or at a distance, may file past from now on, that is
obvious. There may even be women and children, I have caught
a glimpse of a few, they will all be armed with something to lean
on and rummage in my things with, they will all give me a clout
on the head to begin with and then spend the rest of the day
glaring at me in anger and disgust. I shall have to revise my
questionnaire so as to adapt it to all and sundry. Perhaps one, one
day, unmindful of his instructions, will give me my stick. Or I
might be able to catch one, a little girl for example, and half
strangle her, three quarters, until she promises to give me my
stick, give me soup, empty my pots, kiss me, fondle me, smile to
me, give me my hat, stay with me, follow the hearse weeping into

her handkerchief, that would be nice. I am such a good man, at bottom, such a good man, how is it nobody ever noticed it? A little girl would be into my barrow, she would undress before me, sleep beside me, have nobody but me, I would jam the bed against the door to prevent her running away, but then she would throw herself out of the window, when they got to know she was with me they would bring soup for two, I would teach her love and loathing, she would never forget me, I would die delighted, she would close my eyes and put a plug in my arse-hole, as per instructions. Easy, Malone, take it easy, you old whore. That reminds me, how long can one fast with impunity? The Lord Mayor of Cork lasted for ages, but he was young, and then he had political convictions, human ones too probably, just plain human convictions. And he allowed himself a sip of water from time to time, sweetened probably. Water, for pity's sake! How is it I am not thirsty. There must be drinking going on inside me, my secretions. Yes, let us talk a little about me, that will be a rest from all these blackguards. What light! Foretaste of paradise? My head. On fire, full of boiling oil. What shall I die of, in the end? A transport of blood to the brain? That would be the last straw. The pain is almost unbearable, upon my soul it is. Incandescent migraine. Death must take me for someone else. It's the heart's fault, as in the bosom of the match king, Schneider, Schroeder, I forget. It too is burning, with shame, of itself, of me, of them, shame of everything, except of beating apparently. It's nothing, mere nervousness. And who knows, perhaps the first to fail will be my breath, after all. After each avowal, before and during, what swirling murmurs. The window says break of day, rack of tattered rainclouds stampeding. Have a nice time. Far from this molten gloom. Yes, my last gasps are not what they might be, the bellows won't go down, the air is choking me, perhaps it is a little lacking in oxygen. Macmann pygmy beneath the great black gesticulating pines gazes at the distant raging sea. The others are there too, or at their windows, like me, but on their feet, they must be able to move, or to be moved, no, not like me, they can't do anything for anybody, clinging to the shivering poplars, or at their windows, listening. But perhaps I should finish with myself first, in so far naturally as such a thing is possible. The speed I am turning at now makes things difficult admittedly, but it probably can only increase, that is the thing to be considered. Mem, add to the questionnaire, If you happen to have a match try and light it. How is it I heard nothing when he spoke to me and yet heard him leave, whistling? Perhaps he only feigned to speak to me, to try and make me think I had gone deaf. Do I hear anything at the present instant? Let me see. No, the answer is no. Neither the wind, nor the sea, nor the paper, nor the air I exhale with such labour. But this innumerable babble, like a multitude whispering? I don't understand. With my distant hand I count the pages that remain. They will do. This exercise-book is my life, this big child's exercise-book, it has taken me a long time to resign myself to that. And yet I shall not throw it away. For I want to put down in it, for the last time, those I have called to my help, but ill, so that they did not understand, so that they may cease with me. Now rest.

Wearing over his long shirt a great striped cloak reaching down to his ankles Macmann took the air in all weathers, from morning to night. And more than once they had been obliged to go out looking for him with lanterns, to bring him back to his cell, for he had remained deaf to the call of the bell and to the shouts and threats first of Lemuel, then of the other keepers. Then the keepers, in their white clothes, armed with sticks and lanterns, spread out from the buildings and beat the thickets, the copses and the fern-brakes, calling the fugitive by name and threatening him with the direst reprisals if he did not surrender immediately. But they finally remarked that he hid, when he did, always in the same place and that such a deployment of force was unnecessary. From then on it was Lemuel who went out alone, in silence, as always when he knew what he had to do, straight to the bush in which Macmann had made his lair, whenever this was necessary. My God. And often the two of them remained there for some time, in the bush, before going in, huddled together, for the lair was small, saying nothing, perhaps listening to the noises of the night, the owls, the wind in the leaves, the sea when it was high enough to make its voice heard, and then the other night sounds that you cannot tell the meaning of. And it sometimes happened that Macmann, weary of not being alone went away alone and back into his cell and remained there until Lemuel rejoined him, much later. It was a genuine English park, though far from England, extravagantly unformal, luxuriant to the point of wildness, the trees at war with one another, and the bushes, and the wild flowers and weeds, all ravening for earth and light. One evening Macmann went back to his cell with a branch torn from a dead bramble, for use as a stick to support him as he walked. Then Lemuel took it from him and struck him with it over and over again, no, that won't work, then Lemuel called a keeper by the name of Pat, a thorough brute though puny in appearance, and said to him, Pat will you look at that. Then Pat snatched the stick from Macmann who, seeing the turn things were taking, was holding it clutched tight in his two hands, and struck him with it until Lemuel told him to stop, and even for some little time afterwards. All this without a word of explanation. So that a little later Macmann, having brought back from his walk a hyacinth he had torn up bulb and roots in the hope of being able to keep it a little longer thus than if he had simply plucked it, was fiercely reprimanded by Lemuel who wrenched the pretty flower from his hands and threatened to hand him over to Jack again, no, to Pat again, Jack is a different one. And yet the fact of having half demolished the bush, a kind of laurel, in order to hide in it, had never brought upon his head the least reproof. This is not necessarily surprising, there was no proof against him. Had he been questioned about it he would naturally have told the truth, for he did not suspect he had done anything wrong. But they must have assumed he would do nothing but lie and stoutly deny and that it was therefore useless to press him with questions. Besides no questions were ever asked in the House of Saint John of God, but stern measures were simply taken, or not taken, according to the dictates of a peculiar logic. For, when you come to think of it, in virtue of what possible principle of justice can a flower in the hand fasten on the bearer the crime of having gathered it? Or was the mere fact of holding it for all to see in itself a felony, analogous to that of the receiver or fence?

And if so would it not have been preferable to make this known, quite plainly and frankly, to all concerned, so that the sense of guilt, instead of merely following on the guilty act, might precede and accompany it as well? Problem. But nicely posed, I think, very nicely indeed. Thanks to the white cloak with its blue butcher stripes no confusion was possible between the Macmanns on the one hand and the Lemuels, Pats and Jacks on the other. The birds. Numerous and varied in the dense foliage they lived without fear all the year round, or in fear only of their congeners, and those which in summer or in winter flew off to other climes came back the following winter or the following summer, roughly speaking. The air was filled with their voices, especially at dawn and dusk, and those which set off in flocks in the morning, such as the crows and starlings, for distant pastures, came back the same evening all joyous to the sanctuary, where their sentinels awaited them. The gulls were many in stormy weather which paused here on their flight inland. They wheeled long in the cruel air, screeching with anger, then settled in the grass or on the house-tops, mistrustful of the trees. But that is all beside the point, like so many things. All is pretext, Sapo and the birds, Moll, the peasants, those who in the towns seek one another out and fly from one another, my doubts which do not interest me, my situation, my possessions, pretext for not coming to the point, the abandoning, the raising of the arms and going down, without further splash, even though it may annoy the bathers. Yes, there is no good pretending, it is hard to leave everything. The horror-worn eyes linger abject on all they have beseeched so long, in a last prayer, the true prayer at last, the one that asks for nothing. And it is then a little breath of fulfilment revives the dead long-ings and a murmur is born in the silent world, reproaching you affectionately with having despaired too late. The last word in the way of viaticum. Let us try it another way. The pure plateau.

Try and go on. The pure plateau air. Yes, it was a plateau, Moll had not lied, or rather a great mound with gentle slopes. The entire top was occupied by the domain of Saint John and there the wind blew almost without ceasing, causing the stoutest trees to bend and groan, breaking the boughs, tossing the bushes,

lashing the ferns to fury, flattening the grass and whirling leaves
and flowers far away, I hope I have not forgotten anything. Good.
A high wall encompassed it about, without however shutting off
the view, unless you happened to be in its lee. How was this
possible? Why thanks to the rising ground to be sure, culminating
in a summit called the Rock, because of the rock that was on it.
From here a fine view was to be obtained of the plain, the sea,
the mountains, the smoke of the town and the buildings of the
institution, bulking large in spite of their remoteness and all astir
with little dots or flecks forever appearing and disappearing, in
reality the keepers coming and going, perhaps mingled with I was
going to say with the prisoners! For seen from this distance the
striped cloak had no stripes, nor indeed any great resemblance
to a cloak at all. So that one could only say, when the first shock
of surprise was past, Those are men and women, you know,
people, without being able to specify further. A stream at long
intervals bestrid—but to hell with all this fucking scenery. Where
could it have risen anyway, tell me that. Underground perhaps.
In a word a little Paradise for those who like their nature sloven.
Macmann sometimes wondered what was lacking to his happiness.
The right to be abroad in all weathers morning, noon and night,
trees and bushes with outstretched branches to wrap him round
and hide him, food and lodging such as they were free of all
charge, superb views on every hand out over the lifelong enemy,
a minimum of persecution and corporal punishment, the song of
the birds, no human contact except with Lemuel, who went out
of his way to avoid him, the faculties of memory and reflection
stunned by the incessant walking and high wind, Moll dead, what
more could he wish? I must be happy, he said, it is less pleasant
than I should have thought. And he clung closer and closer to the
wall, but not too close, for it was guarded, seeking a way out into
the desolation of having nobody and nothing, the wilds of the
hunted, the scant bread and the scant shelter and the black joy
of the solitary way, in helplessness and will-lessness, through all
the beauty, the knowing and the loving. Which he stated by
saying, for he was artless, I have had enough, without pausing a
moment to reflect on what it was he had enough of or to com-

pare it with what it had been he had had enough of, until he
lost it, and would have enough of again, when he got it back
again, and without suspecting that the thing so often felt to be
excessive, and honoured by such a variety of names, was perhaps
in reality always one and the same. But there was one reflecting
in his place and setting down coldly the sign of equality where it
was needed, as if that could make any difference. So he had only
to go on gasping, in his artless way, Enough! Enough!, as he
crept along by the wall under the cover of the bushes, searching
for a breach through which he might slip out, under cover of
night, or a place with footholds where he might climb over. But
the wall was unbroken and smooth and topped uninterruptedly
with broken glass, of a bottle green. But let us cast a glance at
the main entrance, wide enough to admit two large vehicles
abreast and flanked by two charming lodges covered with
Virginia creeper and occupied by large deserving families, to
judge by the swarms of little brats playing nearby, pursuing one
another with cries of joy, rage and grief. But space hemmed him
in on every side and held him in its toils, with the multitude of
other faintly stirring, faintly struggling things, such as the children, the lodges and the gates, and like a sweat of things the
moments streamed away in a great chaotic conflux of oozings and
torrents, and the trapped huddled things changed and died each
one according to its solitude. Beyond the gate, on the road,
shapes passed that Macmann could not understand, because of
the bars, because of all the trembling and raging behind him and
beside him, because of the cries, the sky, the earth enjoining him to
fall and his long blind life. A keeper came out of one of the lodges,
in obedience to a telephone-call probably, all in white, a long
black object in his hand, a key, and the children lined up along
the drive. Suddenly there were women. All fell silent. The heavy
gates swung open, driving the keeper before them. He backed
away, then suddenly turned and fled to his doorstep. The road
appeared, white with dust, bordered with dark masses, stretched
a little way and ran up dead, against a narrow grey sky. Macmann let go the tree that hid him and turned back up the hill,
not running, for he could hardly walk, but as fast as he could,

bowed and stumbling, helping himself forward with the boles
and boughs that offered. Little by little the haze formed again,
and the sense of absence, and the captive things began to murmur again, each one to itself, and it was as if nothing had ever
happened or would ever happen again.

Others besides Macmann strayed from morning to night,
stooped under the heavy cloak, in the rare glades, among the
trees that hid the sky and in the high ferns where they looked
like swimmers. They seldom came near to one another, because
they were few and the park was vast. But when chance brought
one or more together, near enough for them to realize it had done
so, then they hastened to turn back or, without going to such
extremes, simply aside, as if ashamed to be seen by their fellows.
But sometimes they brushed against one another without seeming to notice it, their heads buried in the ample hood.

Macmann carried with him and contemplated from time to
time the photograph that Moll had given him, it was perhaps
rather a daguerreotype. She was standing beside a chair and
squeezing in her hands her long plaits. Traces were visible, behind her, of a kind of trellis with clambering flowers, roses
probably, they sometimes like to clamber. When giving this keep-
sake to Macmann she had said, I was fourteen, I well remember
the day, a summer day, it was my birthday, afterwards they took
me to see Punch and Judy. Macmann remembered those words.
What he liked best in this picture was the chair, the seat of which
seemed to be made of straw. Diligently Moll pressed her lips
together, in order to hide her great buck-teeth. The roses must
have been pretty, they must have scented the air. In the end
Macmann tore up this photograph and threw the bits in the air,
one windy day. Then they scattered, though all subjected to the
same conditions, as though with alacrity.

When it rained, when it snowed

On. One morning Lemuel, putting in the prescribed appearance in the great hall before setting out on his rounds, found
pinned on the board a notice concerning him. Group Lemuel,
excursion to the islands, weather permitting, with Lady Pedal,
leaving one p.m. His colleagues observed him, sniggering and

poking one another in the ribs. But they did not dare say anything. One woman however did pass a witty remark, to good effect. Lemuel was not liked, that was clear. But would he have wished to be, that is less clear. He initialled the notice and went away. The sun was dragging itself up, dispatching on its way what perhaps would be, thanks to it, a glorious May or April day, April more likely, it is doubtless the Easter week-end, spent by Jesus in hell. And it may well have been in honour of this latter that Lady Pedal had organized, for the benefit of Lemuel's group, this outing to the islands which was going to cost her dear, but she was well off and lived for doing good and bringing a little happiness into the lives of those less fortunate than herself, who was all right in her head and to whom life had always smiled or, as she had it herself, returned her smile, enlarged as in a convex mirror, or a concave, I forget. Taking advantage of the terrestrial atmosphere that dimmed its brightness Lemuel glared with loathing at the sun. He had reached his room, on the fourth or fifth floor, whence on countless occasions he could have thrown himself in perfect safety out of the window if he had been less weak-minded. The long silver carpet was in position, ending in a point, trembling across the calm repoussé sea. The room was small and absolutely empty, for Lemuel slept on the bare boards and even off them ate his lesser meals, now at one place, now at another. But what matter about Lemuel and his room? On. Lady Pedal was not the only one to take an interest in the inmates of Saint John of God's, known pleasantly locally as the Johnny Goddams, or the Goddam Johnnies, not the only one to treat them on an average once every two years to excursions by land and sea through scenery renowned for its beauty or grandeur and even to entertainments on the premises such as whole evenings of prestidigitation and ventriloquism in the moonlight on the terrace, no, but she was seconded by other ladies sharing her way of thinking and similarly blessed in means and leisure. But what matter about Lady Pedal? On. Carrying in one hand two buckets wedged the one within the other Lemuel proceeded to the vast kitchen, full of stir and bustle at that hour. Six excursion soups, he growled. What? said the cook. Six excursion soups!

roared Lemuel, dashing his buckets against the oven, without however relinquishing the handles, for he retained enough presence of mind to dread the thought of having to stoop and pick them up again. The difference between an excursion soup and a common or house soup was simply this, that the latter was uniformly liquid whereas the former contained a piece of fat bacon intended to keep up the strength of the excursionist until his return. When his bucket had been filled Lemuel withdrew to a secluded place, rolled up his sleeve to the elbow, fished up from the bottom of the bucket one after another the six pieces of bacon, his own and the five others, ate all the fat off them, sucked the rinds and threw them back in the soup. Strange when you come to think of it, but after all not so strange really, that they should have issued six extra or excursion soups at his mere demand, without requiring a written order. The cells of the five were far apart and so astutely disposed that Lemuel had never been able to determine how best, that is to say with the minimum of fatigue and annoyance, to visit them in turn. In the first a young man, dead young, seated in an old rocking-chair, his shirt rolled up and his hands on his thighs, would have seemed asleep had not his eyes been wide open. He never went out, unless commanded to do so, and then someone had to accompany him, in order to make him move forward. His chamber-pot was empty, whereas in his bowl the soup of the previous day had congealed. The reverse would have been less surprising. But Lemuel was used to this, so used that he had long since ceased to wonder on what this creature fed. He emptied the bowl into his empty bucket and from his full bucket filled it with fresh soup. Then he went, a bucket in each hand, whereas up to now a single hand had been enough to carry the two buckets. Because of the excursion he locked the door behind him, an unnecessary precaution. The second cell, four or five hundred paces distant from the first, contained one whose only really striking features were his stature, his stiffness and his air of perpetually looking for something while at the same time wondering what that something could possibly be. Nothing in his person gave any indication of his age, whether he was marvellously well-preserved or on the contrary prematurely de-

cayed. He was called the Saxon, though he was far from being
any such thing. Without troubling to take off his shirt he had
swathed himself in his two blankets as in swaddlings and over
and above this rough and ready cocoon he wore his cloak. He
gathered it shiveringly about him, with one hand, for he needed
the other to help him in his investigation of all that aroused his
suspicions. Good-morning, good-morning, good-morning, he said,
with a strong foreign accent and darting fearful glances all about
him, fucking awful business this, no, yes? Sudden starts instantly
repressed dislodged him imperceptibly from his coign of maximum vantage in the centre of the room. What! he exclaimed. His
soup, examined drop by drop, had been transferred in its entirety
to his pot. Anxiously he watched Lemuel performing his office,
filling and emptying. Dreamt all night of that bloody man Quin
again, he said. It was his habit to go out from time to time, into
the air. But after a few steps he would halt, totter, turn and hasten
back into his cell, aghast at such depths of opacity.

   In the third a small thin man was pacing up and down, his
cloak folded over his arm, an umbrella in his hand. Fine head of
white flossy hair. He was asking himself questions in a low voice,
reflecting, replying. The door had hardly opened when he made a
dart to get out, for he spent his days ranging about the park in
all directions. Without putting down his buckets Lemuel sent him
flying with a toss of his shoulder. He lay where he had fallen,
clutching his cloak and umbrella. Then, having recovered from
his surprise, he began to cry. In the fourth a misshapen giant,
bearded, occupied to the exclusion of all else in scratching himself, intermittently. Sprawling on his pillow on the floor under
the window, his head sunk, his mouth open, his legs wide apart,
his knees raised, leaning with one hand on the ground while the
other came and went under his shirt, he awaited his soup. When
his bowl had been filled he stopped scratching and stretched out
his hand towards Lemuel, in the daily disappointed hope of being
spared the trouble of getting up. He still loved the gloom and
secrecy of the ferns, but never sought them out. The youth then,
the Saxon, the thin one and the giant. I don't know if they have
changed, I don't remember. May the others forgive me. In the

fifth Macmann, half asleep.

A few lines to remind me that I too subsist. He has not come back. How long ago is it now? I don't know. Long. And I? Indubitably going, that's all that matters. Whence this assurance? Try and think. I can't. Grandiose suffering. I am swelling. What if I should burst? The ceiling rises and falls, rises and falls, rhythmically, as when I was a foetus. Also to be mentioned a noise of rushing water, phenomenon mutatis mutandis perhaps analogous to that of the mirage, in the desert. The window. I shall not see it again. Why? Because, to my grief, I cannot turn my head. Leaden light again, thick, eddying, riddled with little tunnels through to brightness, perhaps I should say air, sucking air. All is ready. Except me. I am being given, if I may venture the expression, birth to into death, such is my impression. The feet are clear already, of the great cunt of existence. Favourable presentation I trust. My head will be the last to die. Haul in your hands. I can't. The render rent. My story ended I'll be living yet. Promising lag. That is the end of me. I shall say I no more.

Surrounded by his little flock which after nearly two hours of efforts he had succeeded in assembling, single-handed, Pat having refused to help him, Lemuel stood on the terrace waiting for Lady Pedal to arrive. Cords tethered by the ankles the thin one to the youth, the Saxon to the giant, and Lemuel held Macmann by the arm. Of the five it was Macmann, furious at having been shut up in his cell all morning and at a loss to understand what was wanted of him, whose resistance had been the most lively. He had notably refused to stir a step without his hat, with such fierce determination that Lemuel had finally consented to his keeping it on, provided it was hidden by the hood. In spite of this Macmann continued peevish and agitated, trying to free his arm and saying over and over again, Let me go! Let me go! The youth, tormented by the sun, was grabbing feebly at the thin one's umbrella, saying, Pasol! Pasol! The thin one retaliated with petulant taps on his hands and arms. Naughty! he cried. Help! The giant had thrown his arms round the Saxon's neck and hung there, his legs limp. The Saxon, tottering, too proud to collapse,

demanded to be enlightened in tones without anger. Who is this
shite anyhow, he said, any of you poor buggers happen to know?
The director, or his delegate, also present, said dreamily from
time to time, Now, now, please. They were alone on the great
terrace. Can it be she fears a change of weather? said the
director. He added, turning towards Lemuel, I am asking you a
question. The sky was cloudless, the air still. Where is the beautiful young man with the Messiah beard? But in that case would
she not have telephoned? said the director.

The waggonette. Up on the box, beside the coachman, Lady
Pedal. On one of the seats, set parallel to the wheels, Lemuel,
Macmann, the Saxon and the giant. In the other, facing them
the youth, the thin one and the two colossi dressed in sailor-suits.
As they passed through the gates the children cheered. A sudden
descent, long and steep, sent them plunging towards the sea.
Under the drag of the brakes the wheels slid more than they
rolled and the stumbling horses reared against the thrust. Lady
Pedal clung to the box, her bust flung back. She was a huge, big,
tall, fat woman. Artificial daisies with brilliant yellow disks
gushed from her broad-brimmed straw hat. At the same time
behind the heavily spotted fall-veil her plump red face appeared
to pullulate. The passengers, yielding with unanimous inertia to
the tilt of the seats, sprawled pell-mell beneath the box. Sit back!
cried Lady Pedal. Nobody stirred. What good would that do?
said one of the sailors. None, said the other. Should they not all
get down, said Lady Pedal to the coachman, and walk? When
they were safely at the bottom of the hill at last Lady Pedal
turned affably to her guests. Courage my hearties! she said, to
show she was not superior. The waggonette jolted on with gathering speed. The giant lay on the boards, between the seats. Are you
the one in charge? said Lady Pedal. One of the sailors leaned
towards Lemuel and said, She wants to know if you're the one in
charge. Fuck off, said Lemuel. The Saxon uttered a roar which
Lady Pedal, on the qui vive for the least sign of animation, was
pleased to interpret as a manifestation of joy. That's the spirit!
she cried. Sing! Make the most of this glorious day! Banish your
cares, for an hour or so! And she burst forth:

Oh the jolly jolly spring
Blue and sun and nests and flowers
Alleluiah Christ is King
Oh the happy happy hours
Oh the jolly jolly —

She broke off, discouraged. What is the matter with them? she said. The youth, less youthful now, doubled in two, his head swathed in the skirts of his cloak, seemed to be vomiting. His legs, monstrously bony and knock-kneed, were knocking together at the knees. The thin one, shivering, though in theory the Saxon is the shiverer, had resumed his dialogue. Motionless and concentrated between the voices he reinforced these with passionate gestures amplified by the umbrella. And you? . . . Thanks . . . And you? . . . THANKS! . . . True . . . Left . . . Try . . . Back . . . Where? . . . On . . . No! . . . Right . . . Try . . . Do you smell the sea, said Lady Pedal, I do. Macmann made a bid for freedom. In vain. Lemuel produced a hatchet from under his cloak and dealt himself a few smart blows on the skull, with the heel, for safety. Nice jaunt we're having, said one of the sailors. Swell, said the other. Sun azure. Ernest, hand out the buns, said Lady Pedal.

The boat. Room, as in the waggonette, for twice as many, three times, four times, at a pinch. A land receding, another approaching, big and little islands. No sound save the oars, the rowlocks, the blue sea against the keel. In the stern-sheets Lady Pedal, sad. What beauty! she murmured. Alone, not understood, good, too good. Taking off her glove she trailed in the transparent water her sapphire-laden hand. Four oars, no rudder, the oars steer. My creatures, what of them? Nothing. They are there, each as best he can, as best he can be somewhere. Lemuel watches the mountains rising behind the steeples beyond the harbour, no they are no more

No, they are no more than hills, they raise themselves gently, faintly blue, out of the confused plain. It was there somewhere he was born, in a fine house, of loving parents. Their slopes are covered with ling and furze, its hot yellow bells, better

known as gorse. The hammers of the stone-cutters ring all day
like bells.

The island. A last effort. The islet. The shore facing the open
sea is jagged with creeks. One could live there, perhaps happy,
if life was a possible thing, but nobody lives there. The deep
water comes washing into its heart, between high walls of rock.
One day nothing will remain of it but two islands, separated by
a gulf, narrow at first, then wider and wider as the centuries slip
by, two islands, two reefs. It is difficult to speak of man, under
such conditions. Come, Ernest, said Lady Pedal, let us find a
place to picnic. And you, Maurice, she added, stay by the dinghy.
She called that a dinghy. The thin one chafed to run about, but
the youth had thrown himself down in the shade of a rock, like
Sordello, but less noble, for Sordello resembled a lion at rest, and
clung to it with both hands. The poor creatures, said Lady Pedal,
let them loose. Maurice made to obey. Keep off, said Lemuel.
The giant had refused to leave the boat, so that the Saxon could
not leave it either. Macmann was not free either, Lemuel held him
by the waist, perhaps lovingly. Well, said Lady Pedal, you are the
one in charge. She moved away with Ernest. Suddenly she turned
and said, You know, on the island, there are Druid

remains. She looked at them in turn. When we have had our
tea, she said, we shall hunt for them, what do you say? Finally
she moved away again, followed by Ernest carrying the hamper
in his arms. When she had disappeared Lemuel released Macmann, went up behind Maurice who was sitting on a stone filling
his pipe and killed him with the hatchet. We're getting on, getting
on. The youth and the giant took no notice. The thin one broke
his umbrella against the rock, a curious gesture. The Saxon cried,
bending forward and slapping his thighs, Nice work, sir, nice
work! A little later Ernest came back to fetch them. Going to
meet him Lemuel killed him in his turn, in the same way as
the other. It merely took a little longer. Two decent, quiet,
harmless men, brothers-in-law into the bargain, there are billions
of such brutes. Macmann's huge head. He has put his hat on
again. The voice of Lady Pedal, calling. She appeared, joyous.
Come along, she cried, all of you, before the tea gets cold. But at

the sight of the late sailors she fainted, which caused her to fall. Smash her! screamed the Saxon. She had raised her veil and was holding in her hand a tiny sandwich. She must have broken something in her fall, her hip perhaps, old ladies often break their hips, for no sooner had she recovered her senses than she began to moan and groan, as if she were the only being on the face of the earth deserving of pity. When the sun had vanished, behind the hills, and the lights of the land began to glitter, Lemuel made Macmann and the two others get into the boat and got into it himself. Then they set out, all six, from the shore.

Gurgles of outflow.

This tangle of grey bodies is they. Silent, dim, perhaps clinging to one another, their heads buried in their cloaks, they lie together in a heap, in the night. They are far out in the bay. Lemuel has shipped his oars, the oars trail in the water. The night is strewn with absurd

absurd lights, the stars, the beacons, the buoys, the lights of earth and in the hills the faint fires of the blazing gorse. Macmann, my last, my possessions, I remember, he is there too, perhaps he sleeps. Lemuel

Lemuel is in charge, he raises his hatchet on which the blood will never dry, but not to hit anyone, he will not hit anyone, he will not hit anyone any more, he will not touch anyone any more, either with it or with it or with it or with

or with it or with his hammer or with his stick or with his fist or in thought in dream I mean never he will never

or with his pencil or with his stick or

or light light I mean

never there he will never

never anything

there

any more

PART III

★

THE UNNAMABLE

Where now? Who now? When now? Unquestioning. I, say I. Unbelieving. Questions, hypotheses, call them that. Keep going, going on, call that going, call that on. Can it be that one day, off it goes on, that one day I simply stayed in, in where, instead of going out, in the old way, out to spend day and night as far away as possible, it wasn't far. Perhaps that is how it began. You think you are simply resting, the better to act when the time comes, or for no reason, and you soon find yourself powerless ever to do anything again. No matter how it happened. It, say it, not knowing what. Perhaps I simply assented at last to an old thing. But I did nothing. I seem to speak, it is not I, about me, it is not about me. These few general remarks to begin with. What am I to do, what shall I do, what should I do, in my situation, how proceed? By aporia pure and simple? Or by affirmations and negations invalidated as uttered, or sooner or later? Generally speaking. There must be other shifts. Otherwise it would be quite hopeless. But it is quite hopeless. I should mention before going any further, any further on, that I say aporia without knowing what it means. Can one be ephectic otherwise than unawares? I don't know. With

the yesses and noes it is different, they will come back to me as
I go along and how, like a bird, to shit on them all without
exception. The fact would seem to be, if in my situation one may
speak of facts, not only that I shall have to speak of things of
which I cannot speak, but also, which is even more interesting, but
also that I, which is if possible even more interesting, that I shall
have to, I forget, no matter. And at the same time I am obliged
to speak. I shall never be silent. Never.

I shall not be alone, in the beginning. I am of course alone.
Alone. That is soon said. Things have to be soon said. And how
can one be sure, in such darkness? I shall have company. In the
beginning. A few puppets. Then I'll scatter them, to the winds, if
I can. And things, what is the correct attitude to adopt towards
things? And, to begin with, are they necessary? What a question.
But I have few illusions, things are to be expected. The best is
not to decide anything, in this connection, in advance. If a thing
turns up, for some reason or another, take it into consideration.
Where there are people, it is said, there are things. Does this mean
that when you admit the former you must also admit the latter?
Time will tell. The thing to avòid, I don't know why, is the spirit
of system. People with things, people without things, things without people, what does it matter, I flatter myself it will not take
me long to scatter them, whenever I choose, to the winds. I don't
see how. The best would be not to begin. But I have to begin.
That is to say I have to go on. Perhaps in the end I shall smother
in a throng. Incessant comings and goings, the crush and bustle of
a bargain sale. No, no danger. Of that.

Malone is there. Of his mortal liveliness little trace remains.
He passes before me at doubtless regular intervals, unless it is I
who pass before him. No, once and for all, I do not move. He
passes, motionless. But there will not be much on the subject of
Malone, from whom there is nothing further to be hoped. Personally I do not intend to be bored. It was while watching him pass
that I wondered if we cast a shadow. Impossible to say. He passes
close by me, a few feet away, slowly, always in the same direction.
I am almost sure it is he. The brimless hat seems to me conclusive.
With his two hands he props up his jaw. He passes without a word.

Perhaps he does not see me. One of these days I'll challenge him.
I'll say, I don't know, I'll say something, I'll think of something
when the time comes. There are no days here, but I use the expression. I see him from the waist up, he stops at the waist, as far
as I am concerned. The trunk is erect. But I do not know whether
he is on his feet or on his knees. He might also be seated. I see
him in profile. Sometimes I wonder if it is not Molloy. Perhaps it
is Molloy, wearing Malone's hat. But it is more reasonable to
suppose it is Malone, wearing his own hat. Oh look, there is the
first thing, Malone's hat. I see no other clothes. Perhaps Molloy is
not here at all. Could he be, without my knowledge? The place is
no doubt vast. Dim intermittent lights suggest a kind of distance.
To tell the truth I believe they are all here, at least from Murphy
on, I believe we are all here, but so far I have only seen Malone.
Another hypothesis, they were here, but are here no longer. I shall
examine it after my fashion. Are there other pits, deeper down?
To which one accedes by mine? Stupid obsession with depth. Are
there other places set aside for us and this one where I am, with
Malone, merely their narthex? I thought I had done with prelimin-
aries. No, no, we have all been here forever, we shall all be here
forever, I know it.

No more questions. Is not this rather the place where one
finishes vanishing? Will the day come when Malone will pass
before me no more? Will the day come when Malone will pass
before the spot where I was? Will the day come when another will
pass before me, before the spot where I was? I have no opinion,
on these matters.

Were I not devoid of feeling his beard would fill me with pity.
It hangs down, on either side of his chin, in two twists of unequal
length. Was there a time when I too revolved thus? No, I have
always been sitting here, at this selfsame spot, my hands on my
knees, gazing before me like a great horn-owl in an aviary. The
tears stream down my cheeks from my unblinking eyes. What makes
me weep so? From time to time. There is nothing saddening here.
Perhaps it is liquefied brain. Past happiness in any case has clean
gone from my memory, assuming it was ever there. If I accomplish other natural functions it is unawares. Nothing ever troubles

me. And yet I am troubled. Nothing has ever changed since I have
been here. But I dare not infer from this that nothing ever will
change. Let us try and see where these considerations lead. I have
been here, ever since I began to be, my appearances elsewhere
having been put in by other parties. All has procceded, all this
time, in the utmost calm, the most perfect order, apart from one or
two manifestations the meaning of which escapes me. No, it is not
that their meaning escapes me, my own escapes me just as much.
Here all things, no, I shall not say it, being unable to. I owe my
existence to no one, these faint fires are not of those that illuminate
or burn. Going nowhere, coming from nowhere, Malone passes.
These notions of forbears, of houses where lamps are lit at night,
and other such, where do they come to me from? And all these
questions I ask myself. It is not in a spirit of curiosity. I cannot
be silent. About myself I need know nothing. Here all is clear.
No, all is not clear. But the discourse must go on. So one invents
obscurities. Rhetoric. These lights for instance, which I do not
require to mean anything, what is there so strange about them, so
wrong? Is it their irregularity, their instability, their shining strong
one minute and weak the next, but never beyond the power of one
or two candles? Malone appears and disappears with the punctuality of clockwork, always at the same remove, the same velocity,
in the same direction, the same attitude. But the play of the lights
is truly unpredictable. It is only fair to say that to eyes less knowing
than mine they would probably pass unseen. But even to mine
do they not sometimes do so? They are perhaps unwavering and
fixed and my fitful perceiving the cause of their inconstancy. I
hope I may have occasion to revert to this question. But I shall
remark without further delay, in order to be sure of doing so,
that I am relying on these lights, as indeed on all other similar
sources of credible perplexity, to help me continue and perhaps
even conclude. I resume, having no alternative. Where was I? Ah
yes, from the unexceptionable order which has prevailed here up
to date may I infer that such will always be the case? I may of
course. But the mere fact of asking myself such a question gives
me to reflect. It is in vain I tell myself that its only purpose is to
stimulate the lagging discourse, this excellent explanation does not

satisfy me. Can it be I am the prey of a genuine preoccupation, of a need to know as one might say? I don't know. I'll try it another way. If one day a change were to take place, resulting from a principle of disorder already present, or on its way, what then? That would seem to depend on the nature of the change. No, here all change would be fatal and land me back, there and then, in all the fun of the fair. I'll try it another way. Has nothing really changed since I have been here? No, frankly, hand on heart, wait a second, no, nothing, to my knowledge. But, as I have said, the place may well be vast, as it may well measure twelve feet in diameter. It comes to the same thing, as far as discerning its limits is concerned. I like to think I occupy the centre, but nothing is less certain. In a sense I would be better off at the circumference, since my eyes are always fixed in the same direction. But I am certainly not at the circumference. For if I were it would follow that Molloy, wheeling about me as he does, would issue from the enceinte at every revolution, which is manifestly impossible. But does he in fact wheel, does he not perhaps simply pass before me in a straight line? No, he wheels, I feel it, and about me, like a planet about its sun. And if he made a noise, as he goes, I would hear him all the time, on my right hand, behind my back, on my left hand, before seeing him again. But he makes none, for I am not deaf, of that I am convinced, that is to say half-convinced. From centre to circumference in any case it is a far cry and I may well be situated somewhere between the two. It is equally possible, I do not deny it, that I too am in perpetual motion, accompanied by Malone, as the earth by its moon. In which case there would be no further grounds for my complaining about the disorder of the lights, this being due simply to my insistence on regarding them as always the same lights and viewed always from the same point. All is possible, or almost. But the best is to think of myself as fixed and at the centre of this place, whatever its shape and extent may be. This is also probably the most pleasing to me. In a word, no change apparently since I have been here, disorder of the lights perhaps an illusion, all change to be feared, incomprehensible uneasiness.

That I am not stone deaf is shown by the sounds that reach me. For though the silence here is almost unbroken, it is not completely so. I remember the first sound heard in this place, I have often heard it since. For I am obliged to assign a beginning to my residence here, if only for the sake of clarity. Hell itself, although eternal, dates from the revolt of Lucifer. It is therefore permissible, in the light of this distant analogy, to think of myself as being here forever, but not as having been here forever. This will greatly help me in my relation. Memory notably, which I did not think myself entitled to draw upon, will have its word to say, if necessary. This represents at least a thousand words I was not counting on. I may well be glad of them. So after a long period of immaculate silence a feeble cry was heard, by me. I do not know if Malone heard it too. I was surprised, the word is not too strong. After so long a silence a little cry, stifled outright. What kind of creature uttered it and, if it is the same, still does, from time to time? Impossible to say. Not a human one in any case, there are no human creatures here, or if there are they have done with crying. Is Malone the culprit? Am I? Is it not perhaps a simple little fart, they can be rending? Deplorable mania, when something happens, to inquire what. If only I were not obliged to manifest. And why speak of a cry? Perhaps it is something breaking, some two things colliding. There are sounds here, from time to time, let that suffice. This cry to begin with, since it was the first. And others, rather different. I am getting to know them. I do not know them all. A man may die at the age of seventy without ever having had the possibility of seeing Halley's comet.

It would help me, since to me too I must attribute a beginning, if I could relate it to that of my abode. Did I wait somewhere for this place to be ready to receive me? Or did it wait for me to come and people it? By far the better of these hypotheses, from the point of view of usefulness, is the former, and I shall often have occasion to fall back on it. But both are distasteful. I shall say therefore that our beginnings coincide, that this place was made for me, and I for it, at the same instant. And the sounds I do not yet know have not yet made themselves heard. But they will change nothing. The cry changed nothing, even the first time. And my surprise? I must have been expecting it.

It is no doubt time I gave a companion to Malone. But first

I shall tell of an incident that has only occurred once, so far. I await its recurrence without impatience. Two shapes then, oblong like man, entered into collision before me. They fell and I saw them no more. I naturally thought of the pseudocouple Mercier-Camier. The next time they enter the field, moving slowly towards each other, I shall know they are going to collide, fall and disappear, and this will perhaps enable me to observe them better. Wrong. I continue to see Malone as darkly as the first time. My eyes being fixed always in the same direction I can only see, I shall not say clearly, but as clearly as the visibility permits, that which takes place immediately in front of me, that is to say, in the case before us, the collision, followed by the fall and disappearance. Of their approach I shall never obtain other than a confused glimpse, out of the corner of the eye, and what an eye. For their path too must be a curve, two curves, and meeting I need not say close beside me. For the visibility, unless it be the state of my eyesight, only permits me to see what is close beside me. I may add that my seat would appear to be somewhat elevated, in relation to the surrounding ground, if ground is what it is. Perhaps it is water or some other liquid. With the result that, in order to obtain the optimum view of what takes place in front of me, I should have to lower my eyes a little. But I lower my eyes no more. In a word, I only see what appears immediately in front of me, I only see what appears close beside me, what I best see I see ill.

Why did I have myself represented in the midst of men, the light of day? It seems to me it was none of my doing. We won't go into that now. I can see them still, my delegates. The things they have told me! About men, the light of day. I refused to believe them. But some of it has stuck. But when, through what channels, did I communicate with these gentlemen? Did they intrude on me here? No, no one has ever intruded on me here. Elsewhere then. But I have never been elsewhere. But it can only have been from them I learnt what I know about men and the ways they have of putting up with it. It does not amount to much. I could have dispensed with it. I don't say it was all to no purpose. I'll make use of it, if I'm driven to it. It won't be the first time.

What puzzles me is the thought of being indebted for this information to persons with whom I can never have been in contact. Can it be innate knowledge? Like that of good and evil. This seems improbable to me. Innate knowledge of my mother, for example, is that conceivable? Not for me. She was one of their favourite subjects, of conversation. They also gave me the low-down on God. They told me I depended on him, in the last analysis. They had it on the reliable authority of his agents at Bally I forget what, this being the place, according to them, where the inestimable gift of life had been rammed down my gullet. But what they were most determined for me to swallow was my fellow-creatures. In this they were without mercy. I remember little or nothing of these lectures. I cannot have understood a great deal. But I seem to have retained certain descriptions, in spite of myself. They gave me courses on love, on intelligence, most precious, most precious. They also taught me to count, and even to reason. Some of this rubbish has come in handy on occasions, I don't deny it, on occasions which would never have arisen if they had left me in peace. I use it still, to scratch my arse with. Low types they must have been, their pockets full of poison and antidote. Perhaps all this instruction was by correspondence. And yet I seem to know their faces. From photographs perhaps. When did all this nonsense stop? And has it stopped? A few last questions. Is it merely a lull? There were four or five of them at me, they called that presenting their report. One in particular, Basil I think he was called, filled me with hatred. Without opening his mouth, fastening on me his eyes like cinders with all their seeing, he changed me a little more each time into what he wanted me to be. Is he still glaring at me, from the shadows? Is he still usurping my name, the one they foisted on me, up there in their world, patiently, from season to season? No no, here I am in safety, amusing myself wondering who can have dealt me these insignificant wounds.

The other advances full upon me. He emerges as from heavy hangings, advances a few steps, looks at me, then backs away. He is stooping and seems to be dragging invisible burdens. What I see best is his hat. The crown is all worn through, like the sole of an old boot, giving vent to a straggle of grey hairs. He raises his eyes and I feel the long imploring gaze, as if I could do something for him. Another impression, no doubt equally false, he brings me presents and dare not give them. He takes them away again, or he lets them fall, and they vanish. He does not come often, I cannot be more precise, but regularly assuredly. His visit has never coincided, up to now, with the transit of Malone. But perhaps some day it will. That would not necessarily be a violation of the order prevailing here. For if I can work out to within a few inches the orbit of Malone, assuming perhaps erroneously that he passes before me at a distance of say three feet, with regard to the other's career I must remain in the dark. For I am incapable not only of measuring time, which in itself is sufficient to vitiate all calculation in this connection, but also of comparing their respective velocities. So I cannot tell if I shall ever have the good fortune to see the two of them at once. But I am inclined to think I shall. For if I were never to see the two of them at once, then it would follow, or should follow, that between their respective appearances the interval never varies. No, wrong. For the interval may vary considerably, and indeed it seems to me it does, without ever being abolished. Nevertheless I am inclined to think, because of this erratic interval, that my two visitors may some day meet before my eyes, collide and perhaps even knock each other down. I have said that all things here recur sooner or later, no, I was going to say it, then thought better of it. But is it not possible that this does not apply to encounters? The only encounter I ever witnessed, a long time ago now, has never yet been re-enacted. It was perhaps the end of something. And I shall perhaps be delivered of Malone and the other, not that they disturb me, the day I see the two of them at one and the same time, that is to say in collision. Unfortunately they are not the only disturbers of my peace. Others come towards me, pass before me, wheel about me. And no doubt others still, invisible so far. I repeat they do not disturb me. But in the long run it might become wearisome. I don't see how. But the possibility must be taken into account. One starts things moving without a thought of how to stop them. In order to speak. One starts speaking as if it were possible to stop at will. It is better so. The search for the means to put an end to things, an end to speech, is what enables the discourse to continue. No, I must not try to think, simply utter. Method or no method I shall have to banish them in the end, the beings, things, shapes, sounds and lights with which my haste to speak has encumbered this place. In the frenzy of utterance the concern with truth. Hence the interest of a possible deliverance by means of encounter. But not so fast. First dirty, then make clean.

Perhaps it is time I paid a little attention to myself, for a change. I shall be reduced to it sooner or later. At first sight it seems impossible. Me, utter me, in the same foul breath as my creatures? Say of me that I see this, feel that, fear, hope, know and do not know? Yes, I will say it, and of me alone. Impassive, still and mute, Malone revolves, a stranger forever to my infirmities, one who is not as I can never not be. I am motionless in vain, he is the god. And the other? I have assigned him eyes that implore me, offerings for me, need of succour. He does not look at me, does not know of me, wants for nothing. I alone am man and all the rest divine.

Air, the air, is there anything to be squeezed from that old chestnut? Close to me it is grey, dimly transparent, and beyond that charmed circle deepens and spreads its fine impenetrable veils. Is it I who cast the faint light that enables me to see what goes on under my nose? There is nothing to be gained, for the moment, by supposing so. There is no night so deep, so I have heard tell, that it may not be pierced in the end, with the help of no other light than that of the blackened sky, or of the earth itself. Nothing nocturnal here. This grey, first murky, then frankly opaque, is luminous none the less. But may not this screen which my eyes probe in vain, and see as denser air, in reality be the enclosure wall, as compact as lead? To elucidate this point I would need a stick or pole, and the means of plying it, the former being of little avail without the latter, and vice versa. I could also do, incidentally, with future and conditional participles. Then I would dart it, like a javelin, straight before me and know, by the sound made, whether that which hems me round, and blots out my world, is the old void, or a plenum. Or else, without letting it go, I would wield it like a sword and thrust it through empty air, or against the barrier. But the days of sticks are over, here I can count on my body alone, my body incapable of the smallest movement and whose very eyes can no longer close as they once could, (according to Basil and his crew,) to rest me from seeing, to rest me from waking, to darken me to sleep, and no longer look away, or down, or up open to heaven, but must remain forever fixed and staring on the narrow space before them where there is nothing to be seen, 99 per cent of the time. They must be as red as live coals. I sometimes wonder if the two retinae are not facing each other. And come to think of it this grey is shot with rose, like the plumage of certain birds, among which I seem to remember the cockatoo.

Whether all grow black, or all grow bright, or all remain grey, it is grey we need, to begin with, because of what it is, and of what it can do, made of bright and black, able to shed the former, or the latter, and be the latter or the former alone. But perhaps I am the prey, on the subject of grey, in the grey, to delusions.

How, in such conditions, can I write, to consider only the manual aspect of that bitter folly? I don't know. I could know. But I shall not know. Not this time. It is I who write, who cannot raise my hand from my knee. It is I who think, just enough to write, whose head is far. I am Matthew and I am the angel, I who came before the cross, before the sinning, came into the world, came here.

I add this, to be on the safe side. These things I say, and shall say, if I can, are no longer, or are not yet, or never were, or never will be, or if they were, if they are, if they will be, were not here, are not here, will not be here, but elsewhere. But I am here. So I am obliged to add this. I who am here, who cannot speak, cannot think, and who must speak, and therefore perhaps think a little, cannot in relation only to me who am here, to here where I am, but can a little, sufficiently, I don't know how, unimportant, in relation to me who was elsewhere, who shall be elsewhere, and to those places where I was, where I shall be. But I have never been elsewhere, however uncertain the future. And the simplest therefore is to say that what I say, what I shall say, if I can, relates to the place where I am, to me who am there, in spite of my inability to think of these, or to speak of them, because of the compulsion I am under to speak of them, and therefore perhaps think of them a little. Another thing. What I say, what I may say, on this subject, the subject of me and my abode, has already been said since, having always been here, I am here still. At last a piece of reasoning that pleases me, and worthy of my situation. So I have no cause for anxiety. And yet I am anxious. So I am not heading for disaster, I am not heading anywhere, my adventures are over, my say said, I call that my adventures. And yet I feel not. And indeed I greatly fear, since my speech can only be of me and here, that I am once more engaged in putting an end to both. Which would not matter, far from it, but for the obligation, once rid of them, to begin again, to start again from nowhere, from no one and from nothing and win to me again, to me here again, by fresh ways to be sure, or by the ancient ways, unrecognisable at each fresh faring. Whence a certain confusion in the exordia, long enough to situate the condemned and prepare him for execution. And yet I do not despair of one day sparing me, without going silent. And that day, I don't know why, I shall be able to go silent, and make an end, I know it. Yes, the hope is there, once again, of not making me, not losing me, of staying here, where I said I have always been, but I had to say something quick, of ending here, it would be wonderful. But is it to be wished? Yes, it is to be wished, to end would be wonderful, no matter who I am, no matter where I am.

I hope this preamble will soon come to an end and the statement begin that will dispose of me. Unfortunately I am afraid, as always, of going on. For to go on means going from here, means finding me, losing me, vanishing and beginning again, a stranger first, then little by little the same as always, in another place, where I shall say I have always been, of which I shall know nothing, being incapable of seeing, moving, thinking, speaking, but of which little by little, in spite of these handicaps, I shall begin to know something, just enough for it to turn out to be the same place as always, the same which seems made for me and does not want me, which I seem to want and do not want, take your choice, which spews me out or swallows me up, I'll never know, which is perhaps merely the inside of my distant skull where once I wandered, now am fixed, lost for tininess, or straining against the walls, with my head, my hands, my feet, my back, and ever murmuring my old stories, my old story, as if it were the first time. So there is nothing to be afraid of. And yet I am afraid, afraid of what my words will do to me, to my refuge, yet again. Is there really nothing new to try? I mentioned my hope, but it is not serious. If I could speak and yet say nothing, really nothing? Then I might escape being gnawed to death as by an old satiated rat, and my little tester-bed along with me, a cradle, or be gnawed to death not so fast, in my old cradle, and the torn flesh have time to knit, as in the Caucasus, before being torn again. But it seems impossible to speak and yet say nothing, you think you have succeeded, but you always overlook something, a little yes, a little no, enough to exterminate a regiment of dragoons. And yet I do not despair, this time, while saying who I am, where I am, of not losing me, of not going from here, of ending here. What prevents the miracle is the spirit of method to which I have perhaps been a little too addicted. The fact that Prometheus was delivered twenty-nine thousand nine hundred and seventy years after having purged his offence leaves me naturally as cold as camphor. For between me and that miscreant who mocked the gods, invented fire, denatured clay and domesticated the horse, in a word obliged humanity, I trust there is nothing in common. But the thing is worth mentioning. In a word, shall I be able to speak of me and of this place without putting an end to us, shall I ever be able to go silent, is there any connection between these two questions? Nothing like issues. There are a few to be going on with, perhaps one only.

All these Murphys, Molloys and Malones do not fool me. They have made me waste my time, suffer for nothing, speak of them when, in order to stop speaking, I should have spoken of me and of me alone. But I just said I have spoken of me, am speaking of me. I don't care a curse what I just said. It is now I shall speak of me, for the first time. I thought I was right in enlisting these sufferers of my pains. I was wrong. They never suffered my pains, their pains are nothing, compared to mine, a mere tittle of mine, the tittle I thought I could put from me, in order to witness it. Let them be gone now, them and all the others, those I have used and those I have not used, give me back the pains I lent them and vanish, from my life, my memory, my terrors and shames. There, now there is no one here but me, no one wheels about me, no one comes towards me, no one has ever met anyone before my eyes, these creatures have never been, only I and this black void have ever been. And the sounds? No, all is silent. And the lights, on which I had set such store, must they too go out? Yes, out with them, there is no light here. No grey either, black is what I should have said. Nothing then but me, of which I know nothing, except that I have never uttered, and this black, of which I know nothing either, except that it is black, and empty. That then is what, since I have to speak, I shall speak of, until I need speak no more. And Basil and his gang? Inexistent, invented to explain I forget what. Ah yes, all lies, God and man, nature and the light of day, the heart's outpourings and the means of understanding, all invented, basely, by me alone, with the help of no one, since there is no one, to put off the hour when I must speak of me. There will be no more about them.

I, of whom I know nothing, I know my eyes are open, because of the tears that pour from them unceasingly. I know I am seated, my hands on my knees, because of the pressure against my rump, against the soles of my feet, against the palms of my hands, against my knees. Against my palms the pressure is of my knees, against my knees of my palms, but what is it that presses against my rump, against the soles of my feet? I don't know. My spine is not supported. I mention these details to make sure I am not lying on my back, my legs raised and bent, my eyes closed. It is well to establish the position of the body from the outset, before passing on to more important matters. But what makes me say I gaze straight before me, as I have said? I feel my back straight, my neck stiff and free of twist and up on top of it the head, like the ball of the cup-and-ball in its cup at the end of the stick. These comparisons are uncalled for. Then there is the way of flowing of my tears which flow all over my face, and even down along the neck, in a way it seems to me they could not do if the face were bowed, or lifted up. But I must not confuse the unbowed head with the level gaze, nor the vertical with the horizontal plane. This question in any case is secondary, since I see nothing. Am I clothed? I have often asked myself this question, then suddenly started talking about Malone's hat, or Molloy's greatcoat, or Murphy's suit. If I am, I am but lightly. For I feel my tears coursing over my chest, my sides, and all down my back. Ah yes, I am truly bathed in tears. They gather in my beard and from there, when it can hold no more— no, no beard, no hair either, it is a great smooth ball I carry on my shoulders, featureless, but for the eyes, of which only the sockets remain. And were it not for the distant testimony of my palms, my soles, which I have not yet been able to quash, I would gladly give myself the shape, if not the consistency, of an egg, with two holes no matter where to prevent it from bursting, for the consistency is more like that of mucilage. But softly, softly, otherwise I'll never arrive. In the matter of clothes then I can think of nothing for the moment but possibly puttees, with perhaps a few rags clinging to me here and there. No more obscenities either. Why should I have a sex, who have no longer a nose? All those things have fallen, all the things that stick out, with my eyes, my hair, without leaving a trace, fallen so far, so deep, that I heard nothing, perhaps are falling still, my hair slowly like soot still, of the fall of my ears heard nothing. Mean words, and needless, from the mean old spirit, I invented love, music, the smell of flowering currant, to escape from me. Organs, a without, it's easy to imagine, a god, it's unavoidable, you imagine them, it's easy, the worst is dulled, you doze away, an instant. Yes, God, fomenter of calm, I never believed, not a second. No more pauses either. Can I keep nothing then, nothing of what has borne my poor thoughts, bent beneath my words, while I hid? I'll dry these streaming sockets too, bung them up, there, it's done, no more tears, I'm a big talking ball, talking about things that do not exist, or that exist perhaps, impossible to know, beside the point. Ah yes, quick let me change my tune. And after all why a ball, rather than something else, and why big? Why not a cylinder, a small cylinder? An egg, a medium egg? No no, that's the old nonsense, I always knew I was round, solid and round, without daring to say so, no asperities, no apertures, invisible perhaps, or as vast as Sirius in the Great Dog, these expressions mean nothing. All that matters is that I am round and hard, there must be reasons for that, for my being round and hard rather than of some irregular shape and subject to the dents and bulges incident to shock, but I have done with reasons. All the rest I renounce, including this ridiculous black which I thought for a moment worthier than grey to enfold me. What rubbish all this stuff about light and dark. And how I have luxuriated in it. But do I roll, in the manner of a true ball? Or am I in equilibrium somewhere, on one of my numberless poles? I feel strongly tempted to inquire. What reams of discourse I could elicit from this seemingly so legitimate preoccupation. But which would not be credited to me. No, between me and the right to silence, the living rest, stretches the same old lesson, the one I once knew by heart and would not say, I don't know why, perhaps for fear of silence, or thinking any old thing would do, and so for preference lies, in order to remain hidden, no importance. But now I shall say my old lesson, if I can remember it. Under the skies, on the roads, in the towns, in the woods, in the hills, in the plains, by the shores, on the seas, behind my mannikins, I was not always sad, I wasted my time, abjured my rights, suffered for nothing, forgot my lesson. Then a little hell after my own heart, not too cruel, with a few nice damned to foist my groans on, something sighing off and on and the distant gleams of pity's fires biding their hour to promote us to ashes. I speak, speak, because I must, but I do not listen, I seek my lesson, my life I used to know and would not confess, hence possibly an occasional slight lack of limpidity. And perhaps now again I shall do no more than seek my lesson, to the self-accompaniment of a tongue that is not mine. But instead of saying what I should not have said, and what I shall say no more, if I can, and what I shall say perhaps, if I can, should I not rather say some other thing, even though it be not yet the right thing? I'll try, I'll try in another present, even though it be not yet mine, without pauses, without tears, without eyes, without reasons. Let it be assumed then that I am at rest, though this is unimportant, at rest or forever moving, through the air or in contact with other surfaces, or that I sometimes move, sometimes rest, since I feel nothing, neither quietude nor change, nothing that can serve as a point of departure towards an opinion

on this subject, which would not greatly matter if I possessed some
general notions, and then the use of reason, but there it is, I feel
nothing, know nothing, and as far as thinking is concerned I do
just enough to preserve me from going silent, you can't call that
thinking. Let us then assume nothing, neither that I move, nor
that I don't, it's safer, since the thing is unimportant, and pass on
to those that are. Namely? This voice that speaks, knowing that it
lies, indifferent to what it says, too old perhaps and too abased
ever to succeed in saying the words that would be its last, knowing
itself useless and its uselessness in vain, not listening to itself but
to the silence that it breaks and whence perhaps one day will
come stealing the long clear sigh of advent and farewell, is it one?
I'll ask no more questions, there are no more questions, I know
none any more. It issues from me, it fills me, it clamours against
my walls, it is not mine, I can't stop it, I can't prevent it, from
tearing me, racking me, assailing me. It is not mine, I have none,
I have no voice and must speak, that is all I know, it's round that
I must revolve, of that I must speak, with this voice that is not
mine, but can only be mine, since there is no one but me, or if
there are others, to whom it might belong, they have never come
near me. I won't delay just now to make this clear. Perhaps they
are watching me from afar, I have no objection, as long as I don't
see them, watching me like a face in the embers which they know
is doomed to crumble, but it takes too long, it's getting late, eyes
are heavy and tomorrow they must rise betimes. So it is I who
speak, all alone, since I can't do otherwise. No, I am speechless.
Talking of speaking, what if I went silent? What would happen
to me then? Worse than what is happening? But fie these are
questions again. That is typical. I know no more questions and they
keep on pouring out of my mouth. I think I know what it is, it's
to prevent the discourse from coming to an end, this futile discourse which is not credited to me and brings me not a syllable
nearer silence. But now I am on my guard, I shall not answer them
any more, I shall not pretend any more to answer them. Perhaps
I shall be obliged, in order not to peter out, to invent another
fairy-tale, yet another, with heads, trunks, arms, legs and all that
follows, let loose in the changeless round of imperfect shadow and

dubious light. But I hope and trust not. But I always can if necessary. For while unfolding my facetiae, the last time that happened
to me, or to the other who passes for me, I was not inattentive.
And it seemed to me then that I heard a murmur telling of another
and less unpleasant method of ending my troubles and that I even
succeeded in catching, without ceasing for an instant to emit my
he said, and he said to himself, and he asked, and he answered,
a certain number of highly promising formulae and which indeed
I promised myself to turn to good account at the first opportunity,
that is to say as soon as I had finished with my troop of lunatics.
But all has gone clean from my head. For it is difficult to speak,
even any old rubbish, and at the same time focus one's attention
on another point, where one's true interest lies, as fitfully defined
by a feeble murmur seeming to apologise for not being dead. And
what it seemed to me I heard then, concerning what I should do,
and say, in order to have nothing further to do, nothing further
to say, it seemed to me I only barely heard it, because of the
noise I was engaged in making elsewhere, in obedience to the unintelligible terms of an incomprehensible damnation. And yet I was
sufficiently impressed by certain expressions to make a vow, while
continuing my yelps, never to forget them and, what is more, to
ensure they should engender others and finally, in an irresistible
torrent, banish from my vile mouth all other utterance, from my
mouth spent in vain with vain inventions all other utterance but
theirs, the true at last, the last at last. But all is forgotten and I
have done nothing, unless what I am doing now is something, and
nothing could give me greater satisfaction. For if I could hear such
a music at such a time, I mean while floundering through a ponderous chronicle of moribunds in their courses, moving, clashing,
writhing or fallen in short-lived swoons, with how much more
reason should I not hear it now, when supposedly I am burdened
with myself alone. But this is thinking again. And I see myself slipping, though not yet at the last extremity, towards the resorts of
fable. Would it not be better if I were simply to keep on saying
bababababa, for example, while waiting to ascertain the true function
of this venerable organ? Enough questions, enough reasoning, I
resume, years later, meaning I suppose that I went silent, that I

can go silent. And now this noise again. That is all rather obscure.
I say years, though here there are no years. What matter how
long? Years is one of Basil's ideas. A short time, a long time, it's
all the same. I kept silence, that's all that counts, if that counts,
I have forgotten if that is supposed to count. And now it is taken
from me again. Silence, yes, but what silence! For it is all very
fine to keep silence, but one has also to consider the kind of silence
one keeps. I listened. One might as well speak and be done with
it. What liberty! I strained my ear towards what must have been
my voice still, so weak, so far, that it was like the sea, a far calm
sea dying—no, none of that, no beach, no shore, the sea is enough,
I've had enough of shingle, enough of sand, enough of earth,
enough of sea too. Decidedly Basil is becoming important, I'll call
him Mahood instead, I prefer that, I'm queer. It was he told me
stories about me, lived in my stead, issued forth from me, came
back to me, entered back into me, heaped stories on my head. I
don't know how it was done. I always liked not knowing, but
Mahood said it wasn't right. He didn't know either, but it worried
him. It is his voice which has often, always, mingled with mine,
and sometimes drowned it completely. Until he left me for good,
or refused to leave me any more, I don't know. Yes, I don't know
if he's here now or far away, but I don't think I am far wrong
in saying that he has ceased to plague me. When he was away I
tried to find myself again, to forget what he had said, about me,
about my misfortunes, fatuous misfortunes, idiotic pains, in the
light of my true situation, revolting word. But his voice continued
to testify for me, as though woven into mine, preventing me from
saying who I was, what I was, so as to have done with saying, done
with listening. And still today, as he would say, though he plagues
me no more his voice is there, in mine, but less, less. And being
no longer renewed it will disappear one day, I hope, from mine,
completely. But in order for that to happen I must speak, speak.
And at the same time, I do not deceive myself, he may come back
again, or go away again and then come back again. Then my
voice, the voice, would say, That's an idea, now I'll tell one of
Mahood's stories, I need a rest. Yes, that's how it would happen.
And it would say, Then refreshed, set about the truth again, with

redoubled vigour. To make me think I was a free agent. But it would not be my voice, not even in part. That is how it would be done. Or quietly, stealthily, the story would begin, as if nothing had happened and I still the teller and the told. But I would be fast asleep, my mouth agape, as usual, I would look the same as usual. And from my sleeping mouth the lies would pour, about me. No, not sleeping, listening, in tears. But now, is it I now, I on me? Sometimes I think it is. And then I realise it is not. I am doing my best, and failing again, yet again. I don't mind failing, it's a pleasure, but I want to go silent. Not as just now, the better to listen, but peacefully, victorious, without ulterior object. Then it would be a life worth having, a life at last. My speech-parched voice at rest would fill with spittle, I'd let it flow over and over, happy at last, dribbling with life, my pensum ended, in the silence. I spoke, I must have spoken, of a lesson, it was pensum I should have said, I confused pensum with lesson. Yes, I have a pensum to discharge, before I can be free, free to dribble, free to speak no more, listen no more, and I've forgotten what it is. There at last is a fair picture of my situation. I was given a pensum, at birth perhaps, as a punishment for having been born perhaps, or for no particular reason, because they dislike me, and I've forgotten what it is. But was I ever told? Squeeze, squeeze, not too hard, but squeeze a little longer, this is perhaps about you, and your goal at hand. After ten thousand words? Well let us say one goal, after it there will be others. Speak, yes, but to me, I have never spoken enough to me, never listened enough to me, never replied enough to me, never had pity enough on me, I have spoken for my master, listened for the words of my master never spoken, Well done, my child, well done, my son, you may stop, you may go, you are free, you are acquitted, you are pardoned, never spoken. My master. There is a vein I must not lose sight of. But for the moment my concern—but before I forget, there may be more than one, a whole college of tyrants, differing in their views as to what should be done with me, in conclave since time began or a little later, listening to me from time to time, then breaking up for a meal or a game of cards—my concern is with the pensum of which I think I may safely say, without loss of face,

that it is in some way related to that lesson too hastily proclaimed,
too hastily denied. For all I need say is this, that if I have a pensum
to perform it is because I could not say my lesson, and that when
I have finished my pensum I shall still have my lesson to say,
before I have the right to stay quiet in my corner, alive and dribbling, my mouth shut, my tongue at rest, far from all disturbance,
all sound, my mind at peace, that is to say empty. But this does
not get me very far. For even should I hit upon the right pensum,
somewhere in this churn of words at last, I would still have to
reconstitute the right lesson, unless of course the two are one and
the same, which obviously is not impossible either. Strange notion
in any case, and eminently open to suspicion, that of a task to be
performed, before one can be at rest. Strange task, which consists
in speaking of oneself. Strange hope, turned towards silence and
peace. Possessed of nothing but my voice, the voice, it may seem
natural, once the idea of obligation has been swallowed, that I
should interpret it as an obligation to say something. But is it
possible? Bereft of hands, perhaps it is my duty to clap or, striking
the palms together, to call the waiter, and of feet, to dance the
Carmagnole. But let us first suppose, in order to get on a little,
then we'll suppose something else, in order to get on a little further,
that it is in fact required of me that I say something, something
that is not to be found in all I have said up to now. That seems a
reasonable assumption. But thence to infer that the something
required is something about me suddenly strikes me as unwar-
ranted. Might it not rather be the praise of my master, intoned, in
order to obtain his forgiveness? Or the admission that I am
Mahood after all and these stories of a being whose identity he
usurps, and whose voice he prevents from being heard, all lies
from beginning to end? And what if Mahood were my master?
I'll leave it at that, for the time being. So many prospects in so
short a time, it's too much. Decidedly it seems impossible, at this
stage, that I should dispense with questions, as I promised myself
I would. No, I merely swore I'd stop asking them. And perhaps
before long, who knows, I shall light on the happy combination
which will prevent them from ever arising again in my—let us not
be over-nice—mind. For what I am doing is not being done without

a minimum of mind. Not mine perhaps, granted, with pleasure,
but I draw on it, at least I try and look as if I did. Rich matter
there, to be exploited, fatten you up, suck it to the core, keep you
going for years, tasty into the bargain, I quiver at the thought,
give you my word, spoken in jest, quiver and hurry on, all life
before me, on and forget, what I was saying, just now, something
important, it's gone, it'll come back, no regrets, as good as new,
unrecognisable, let's hope so, some day when I feel more on for
high-class nuts to crack. On. The master. I never paid him enough
attention. No more perhapses either, that old trick is worn to a
thread. I'll forbid myself everything, then go on as if I hadn't.
The master. A few allusions here and there, as to a satrap, with a
view to enlisting sympathy. They clothed me and gave me money,
that kind of thing, the light touch. Then no more. Or Moran's
boss, I forget his name. Ah yes, certain things, things I invented,
hoping for the best, full of doubts, croaking with fatigue, I remember certain things, not always the same. But to investigate this
matter seriously, I mean with as much futile ardour as that of
the underling, which I hoped was mine, close to mine, the road
to mine, no, that never occurred to me. And if it occurs to me
now it is because I have despaired of mine. A moment of discouragement, to strike while hot. My master then, assuming he is
solitary, in my image, wishes me well, poor devil, wishes my good,
and if he does not seem to do very much in order not to be disappointed it is because there is not very much to be done or, better
still, because there is nothing to be done, otherwise he would have
done it, my great and good master, that must be it, long ago, poor
devil. Another supposition, he has taken the necessary steps, his
will is done as far as I am concerned (for he may have other
protégés) and all is well with me without my knowing it. Cases
one and two. I'll consider the former first, if I can. Then I'll admire
the latter, if my eyes are still open. This sounds like one of Malone's
anecdotes. But quick, consider, before you forget. There he is then,
the unfortunate brute, quite miserable because of me, for whom
there is nothing to be done, and he so anxious to help, so used to
giving orders and to being obeyed. There he is, ever since I came
into the world, possibly at his instigation, I wouldn't put it past

him, commanding me to be well, you know, in every way, no
complaints at all, with as much success as if he were shouting at
a lump of inanimate matter. If he is not pleased with this panegyric
I hope I may be—I nearly said hanged, but that I hope in any
case, without restriction, I nearly said con, that would cut my
cackle. Ah for a neck! I want all to be well with you, do you hear
me, that's what he keeps on dinning at me. To which I reply, in
a respectful attitude, I too, your Lordship. I say that to cheer him
up, he sounds so unhappy. I am good-hearted, on the surface. No,
we have no conversation, never a mum of his mouth to me. He's
out of luck, that's certain, perhaps he didn't choose me. What he
means by good, my good, is another problem. He is capable of
wanting me to be happy, such a thing has been known, it appears.
Or to serve a purpose. Or the two at once! A little more explicit-
ness on his part, since the initiative belongs to him, might be a
help, as well from his point of view as from the one he attributes
to me. Let the man explain himself and have done with it. It's none
of my business to ask him questions, even if I knew how to reach
him. Let him inform me once and for all what exactly it is he wants
from me, for me. What he wants is my good, I know that, at least
I say it, in the hope of bringing him round to a more reasonable
frame of mind, assuming he exists and, existing, hears me. But
what good, there must be more than one. The supreme perhaps.
In a word let him enlighten me, that's all I ask, so that I may at
least have the satisfaction of knowing in what sense I leave to be
desired. If he wants me to say something, for my good naturally,
he has only to tell me what it is and I'll let it out with a roar
straight away. It's true he may have already told me a hundred
times. Well, let him make it a hundred and one, this time I'll try
and pay attention. But perhaps I malign him unjustly, my good
master, perhaps he is not solitary like me, not free like me, but
associated with others, equally good, equally concerned with my
welfare, but differing as to its nature. Every day, up above, I
mean up above me, from one set hour to another set hour, everything there being set and settled except what is to be done with
me, they assemble to discuss me. Or perhaps it's a meeting of
deputies, with instructions to elaborate a tentative agreement. The

fact of my continuing, while they are thus engaged, to be what I have always been is naturally preferable to a lame resolution, voted perhaps by a majority of one, or drawn from an old hat. They too are unhappy, all this time, each one to the best of his capacity, because all is not well with me. And now enough of that. If that doesn't mollify them so much the worse for me, I can still conceive of such a thing. But one more suggestion before I forget and go on to serious matters. Why don't they wash their hands of me and set me free? That might do me good. I don't know. Perhaps then I could go silent, for good and all. Idle talk, idle talk, I am free, abandoned. All for nothing again. Even Mahood has left me, I'm alone. All this business of a labour to accomplish, before I can end, of words to say, a truth to recover, in order to say it, before I can end, of an imposed task, once known, long neglected, finally forgotten, to perform, before I can be done with speaking, done with listening, I invented it all, in the hope it would console me, help me to go on, allow me to think of myself as somewhere on a road, moving, between a beginning and an end, gaining ground, losing ground, getting lost, but somehow in the long run making headway. All lies. I have nothing to do, that is to say nothing in particular. I have to speak, whatever that means. Having nothing to say, no words but the words of others, I have to speak. No one compels me to, there is no one, it's an accident, a fact. Nothing can ever exempt me from it, there is nothing, nothing to discover, nothing to recover, nothing that can lessen what remains to say, I have the ocean to drink, so there is an ocean then. Not to have been a dupe, that will have been my best possession, my best deed, to have been a dupe, wishing I wasn't, thinking I wasn't, knowing I was, not being a dupe of not being a dupe. For any old thing, no, that doesn't work, that should work, but it doesn't. Labyrinthine torment that can't be grasped, or limited, or felt, or suffered, no, not even suffered, I suffer all wrong too, even that I do all wrong too, like an old turkey-hen dying on her feet, her back covered with chickens and the rats spying on her. Next instalment, quick. No cries, above all no cries, be urbane, a credit to the art and code of dying, while the others cackle, I can hear them from here, like the crackling of thorns, no, I forgot, it's impossible, it's myself I hear, howling behind my dissertation. So not any old thing. Even Mahood's stories are not any old thing, though no less foreign, to what, to that unfamiliar native land of mine, as unfamiliar as that other where men come and go, and feel at home, on tracks they have made themselves, in order to visit one another with the maximum of convenience and dispatch, in the light of a choice of luminaries pissing on the darkness turn about, so that it is never dark, never deserted, that must be terrible. So be it. Not any old thing, but as near as no matter. Mahood. Before him there were others, taking themselves for me, it must be a sinecure handed down from generation to generation, to judge by their family air. Mahood is no worse than his predecessors. But before executing his portrait, full length on his surviving leg, let me note that my next vice-exister will be a billy in the bowl, that's final, with his bowl on his head and his arse in the dust, plump down on thousand-breasted Tellus, it'll be softer for him. Faith that's an idea, yet another, mutilate, mutilate, and perhaps some day, fifteen generations hence, you'll succeed in beginning to look like yourself, among the passers-by. In the meantime it's Mahood, this caricature is he. What if we were one and the same after all, as he affirms, and I deny? And I been in the places where he says I have been, instead of having stayed on here, trying to take advantage of his absence to unravel my tangle? Here, in my domain, what is Mahood doing in my domain, and how does he get here? There I am launched again on the same old hopeless business, there we are face to face, Mahood and I, if we are twain, as I say we are. I never saw him, I don't see him, he has told me what he is like, what I am like, they have all told me that, it must be one of their principal functions. It isn't enough that I should know what I'm doing, I must also know what I'm looking like. This time I am short of a leg. And yet it appears I have rejuvenated. That's part of the programme. Having brought me to death's door, senile gangrene, they whip off a leg and yip off I go again, like a young one, scouring the earth for a hole to hide in. A single leg and other distinctive stigmata to go with it, human to be sure, but not exaggeratedly, lest I take fright and refuse to nibble. He'll resign himself in the end, he'll own up in the end,

that's the watchword. Let's try him this time with a hairless wedge-
head, he might fancy that, that kind of talk. With the solitary leg
in the middle, that might appeal to him. The poor bastards. They
could clap an artificial anus in the hollow of my hand and still I
wouldn't be there, alive with their life, not far short of a man,
just barely a man, sufficiently a man to have hopes one day of
being one, my avatars behind me. And yet sometimes it seems to
me I am there, among the incriminated scenes, tottering under
the attributes peculiar to the lords of creation, dumb with howling
to be put out of my misery, and all round me the spinach blue
rustling with satisfaction. Yes, more than once I almost took myself
for the other, all but suffered after his fashion, the space of an
instant. Then they uncorked the champagne. One of us at last!
Green with anguish! A real little terrestrial! Choking in the
chlorophyll! Hugging the slaughterhouse walls! Paltry priests of
the irrepressible ephemeral, how they must hate me. Come, my
lambkin, join in our gambols, it's soon over, you'll see, just time
to frolic with a lambkinette, that's jam. Love, there's a carrot never
fails, I always had to thread some old bodkin. And that's the kind
of jakes in which I sometimes dreamt I dwelt, and even let down
my trousers. Mahood himself nearly codded me more than once.
I've been he an instant, hobbling through a nature which, it is
only fair to say, was on the barren side and, what is more, it is
only just to add, tolerably deserted to begin with. After each thrust
of my crutches I stopped, to devour a narcotic and measure the
distance gone, the distance yet to go. My head is there too, broad
at the base, its slopes denuded, culminating in a ridge or crowning
glory strewn with long waving hairs like those that grow on naevi.
No denying it, I'm confoundedly well informed. You must allow
it was tempting. I say an instant, perhaps it was years. Then I withdrew my adhesion, it was getting too much of a good thing. I had
already advanced a good ten paces, if one may call them paces,
not in a straight line I need hardly say, but in a sharp curve which,
if I continued to follow it, seemed likely to restore me to my
point of departure, or to one adjacent. I must have got embroiled
in a kind of inverted spiral, I mean one the coils of which,
instead of widening more and more, grew narrower and narrower

and finally, given the kind of space in which I was supposed to evolve, would come to an end for lack of room. Faced then with the material impossibility of going any further I should no doubt have had to stop, unless of course I elected to set off again at once in the opposite direction, to unscrew myself as it were, after having screwed myself to a standstill, which would have been an experience rich in interest and fertile in surprises if I am to believe what I once was told, in spite of my protests, namely that there is no road so dull, on the way out, but it has quite a different aspect, quite a different dullness, on the way back, and vice versa. No good wriggling, I'm a mine of useless knowledge. But a difficulty arises here. For if by dint of winding myself up, if I may venture that ellipse, it doesn't often happen to me now, if by dint of winding myself up, I don't seem to have gained much time, if by dint of winding myself up I must inevitably find myself stuck in the end, once launched in the opposite direction should I not normally unfold ad infinitum, with no possibility of ever stopping, the space in which I was marooned being globular, or is it the earth, no matter, I know what I mean. But where is the difficulty? There was one a moment ago, I could swear to it. Not to mention that I could quite easily at any moment, literally any, run foul of a wall, a tree or similar obstacle, which of course it would be prohibited to circumvent, and thereby have an end put to my gyrations as effectively as by the kind of cramp just mentioned. But obstacles, it appears, can be removed in the fullness of time, but not by me, me they would stop dead forever, if I lived among them. But even without such aids it seems to me that once beyond the equator you would start turning inwards again, out of sheer necessity, I somehow have that feeling. At the particular moment I am referring to, I mean when I took myself for Mahood, I must have been coming to the end of a world tour, perhaps not more than two or three centuries to go. My state of decay lends colour to this view, perhaps I had left my leg behind in the Pacific, yes, no perhaps about it, I had, somewhere off the coast of Java and its jungles red with rafflesia stinking of carrion, no, that's the Indian Ocean, what a gazetteer I am, no matter, somewhere round there. In a word I was returning to the fold, admittedly reduced, and doubtless fated to

be even more so, before I could be restored to my wife and parents,
you know, my loved ones, and clasp in my arms, both of which I
had succeeded in preserving, my little ones born in my absence. I
found myself in a kind of vast yard or campus, surrounded by high
walls, its surface an amalgam of dirt and ashes, and this seemed
sweet to me after the vast and heaving wastes I had traversed, if
my information was correct. I almost felt out of danger! At the
centre of this enclosure stood a small rotunda, windowless, but well
furnished with loopholes. Without being quite sure I had seen it
before, I had been so long from home, I kept saying to myself,
Yonder is the nest you should never have left, there your dear
absent ones are awaiting your return, patiently, and you too must
be patient. It was swarming with them, grandpa, grandma, little
mother and the eight or nine brats. With their eyes glued to the
slits and their hearts going out to me they surveyed my efforts.
This yard so long deserted was now enlivened, for them, by me.
So we turned, in our respective orbits, I without, they within. At
night, keeping watch by turns, they observed me with the help of
a searchlight. So the seasons came and went. The children increased
in stature, the periods of Ptomaine grew pale, the ancients glowered
at each other, muttering, to themselves, I'll bury you yet, or, You'll
bury me yet. Since my arrival they had a subject of conversation,
and even of discussion, the same as of old, at the moment of
my setting forth, perhaps even an interest in life, the same as of old.
Time hung less heavy on their hands. What about throwing him a
few scraps? No no, it might upset him. They did not want to check
the impetus that was sweeping me towards them. You wouldn't
know him! True, papa, and yet you can't mistake him. They who
in the ordinary way never answered when spoken to, my elders,
my wife, she who had chosen me, rather than one of her suitors.
A few more summers and he'll be in our midst. Where am I going to
put him? In the basement? Perhaps after all I am simply in the basement. What possesses him to be stopping all the time? Oh he was
always like that, ever since he was a mite, always stopping, wasn't
he, Granny? Yes indeed, never easy, always stopping. According
to Mahood I never reached them, that is to say they all died first,
the whole ten or eleven of them, carried off by sausage-poisoning,

in great agony. Incommoded first by their shrieks, then by the stench of decomposition, I turned sadly away. But not so fast, otherwise we'll never arrive. It's no longer I in any case. He'll never reach us if he doesn't get a move on. He looks as if he had slowed down, since last year. Oh the last laps won't take him long. My missing leg didn't seem to affect them, perhaps it was already missing when I left. What about throwing him a sponge? No no, it might confuse him. In the evening, after supper, while my wife kept her eye on me, gaffer and gammer related my life history, to the sleepy children. Bedtime story atmosphere. That's one of Mahood's favourite tricks, to produce ostensibly independent testimony in support of my historical existence. The instalment over, all joined in a hymn, Safe in the arms of Jesus, for example, or, Jesus lover of my soul, let me to thy bosom fly, for example. Then they went to bed, with the exception of the one on watch duty. My parents differed in their views on me, but they were agreed I had been a fine baby, at the very beginning, the first fortnight or three weeks. And yet he was a fine baby, with these words they invariably closed their relations. Often they fell silent, engulfed in their memories. Then it was usual for one of the children to launch, by way of envoy, the consecrated phrase, And yet he was a fine baby. A burst of clear and innocent laughter, from the mouths of those whom sleep had not yet overcome, greeted this premature conclusion. And the narrators themselves, torn from their melancholy thoughts, could scarce forbear to smile. Then they all rose, with the exception of my mother whose knees couldn't support her, and sang, Gentle Jesus, meek and mild, for example, or Jesus, my one, my all, hear me when I call, for example. He too must have been a fine baby. Finally my wife announced the latest news, for them to take to bed with them. He's backing away again, or, He's stopped to scratch himself, or, You should have seen him hopping sidelong, or, Oh look children, quick he's down on his hands and knee, admittedly that must have been worth seeing. It was then customary that someone should ask her if I was approaching none the less, if in spite of everything I was making headway, they couldn't bear the thought of going to bed, those who were still awake, without the assurance that I wasn't losing

ground. Ptoto set their minds at rest. I had moved, no further
proof was needed. I had been drawing near for so long now that
provided I remained in motion there could be no cause for anxiety.
I was launched, there was no reason why I should suddenly begin
to retreat, I just wasn't made that way. Then having kissed all
round and wished one another happy dreams they retired, with
the exception of the watch. What about hailing him? Poor Papa,
he burned to encourage me vocally. Stick it, lad, it's your last
winter. But in view of the trouble I was having, the trouble I was
taking, they held him back, pointing out that the moment was ill-
chosen to give me a shock. But what were my own feelings at this
period? What was I thinking of? With what? Was I having difficulty with my morale? The answer to all that is this, I quote
Malone, that I was entirely absorbed in the business on hand and
not at all concerned to know precisely, or even approximately,
what it consisted in. The only problem for me was how to continue,
since I could not do otherwise, to the best of my declining powers,
in the motion which had been imparted to me. This obligation, and
the quasi-impossibility of fulfilling it, engrossed me in a purely
mechanical way, excluding notably the free play of the intelligence
and sensibility, so that my situation rather resembled that of an
old broken-down cart- or bat-horse unable to receive the least
information either from its instinct or from its observation as to
whether it is moving towards the stable or away from it, and
not greatly caring either way. The question, among others, of how
such things are possible had long since ceased to preoccupy me.
This touching picture of my situation I found by no means un-
attractive and as I recall it I find myself wondering again if I
was not in fact the creature revolving in that yard, as Mahood
assured me. Well supplied with pain-killers I drew upon them
freely, without however permitting myself the lethal dose that
would have cut short my functions, whatever they may have been.
Having somehow or other remarked the habitation and even admitted to myself that I had perhaps seen it before, I gave it no
further thought, nor to the near and dear ones that filled it to
overflowing, in a mounting fever of impatience. Though now close
at hand, as the crow flies, to my goal, I did not quicken my step.

I could have no doubt, but I had to husband my strength, if I was ever to arrive. I had no wish to arrive, but I had to do my utmost, in order to arrive. A desirable goal, no, I never had time to dwell on that. To go on, I still call that on, to go on and get on has been my only care, if not always in a straight line, at least in obedience to the figure assigned to me, there was never any room in my life for anything else. Still Mahood speaking. Never once have I stopped. My halts do not count. Their purpose was to enable me to go on. I did not use them to brood on my lot, but to rub myself as best I might with Elliman's Embrocation, for example, or to give myself an injection of laudanum, no easy matters for a man with only one leg. Often the cry went up, He's down! But in reality I had sunk to the ground of my own free will, in order to be rid of my crutches and have both hands available to minister to myself in peace and comfort. Admittedly it is difficult, for a man with but one leg, to sink to earth in the full force of the expression, particularly when he is weak in the head and the sole surviving leg flaccid for want of exercise, or from excess of it. The simplest thing then is to fling away the crutches and collapse. That is what I did. They were therefore right in saying I had fallen, they were not far wrong. Oh I have also been known to fall involuntarily, but not often, an old warrior like me, you can imagine. But have it any way you like. Up or down, taking my anodynes, waiting for the pain to abate, panting to be on my way again, I stopped, if you insist, but not in the sense they meant when they said, He's down again, he'll never reach us. When I penetrate into that house, if I ever do, it will be to go on turning, faster and faster, more and more convulsive, like a constipated dog, or one suffering from worms, overturning the furniture, in the midst of my family all trying to embrace me at once, until by virtue of a supreme spasm I am catapulted in the opposite direction and gradually leave backwards, without having said good-evening. I must really lend myself to this story a little longer, there may possibly be a grain of truth in it. Mahood must have remarked that I remained sceptical, for he casually let fall that I was lacking not only a leg, but an arm also. With regard to the homologous crutch, I seemed to have retained sufficient armpit to hold and manoeuvre

it, with the help of my unique foot to kick the end of it forward as
occasion required. But what shocked me profoundly, to such a
degree that my mind (Mahood dixit) was assailed by insuperable
doubts, was the suggestion that the misfortune experienced by my
family and brought to my notice first by the noise of their agony,
then by the smell of their corpses, had caused me to turn back.
From that moment on I ceased to go along with him. I'll explain
why, that will permit me to think of something else and in the first
place of how to get back to me, back to where I am waiting for
me, I'd just as soon not, but it's my only chance, at least I think
so, the only chance I have of going silent, of saying something at
last that is not false, if that is what they want, so as to have nothing more to say. My reasons. I'll give three or four, that ought to
be enough for me. First this family of mine, the mere fact of having
a family should have put me on my guard. But my good-will at
certain moments is such, and my longing to have floundered however briefly, however feebly, in the great life torrent streaming
from the earliest protozoa to the very latest humans, that I, no,
parenthesis unfinished. I'll begin again. My family. To begin with
it had no part or share in what I was doing. Having set forth from
that place, it was only natural I should return to it, given the accuracy of my navigation. And my family could have moved to other
quarters during my absence, and settled down a hundred leagues
away, without my deviating by as much as a hair's-breadth from
my course. As for the screams of pain and wafts of decomposition,
assuming I was capable of noticing them, they would have seemed
to me quite in the natural order of things, such as I had come to
know it. If before such manifestations I had been compelled each
time to turn aside, I should not have got very far. Washed on the
surface only by the rains, my head cracking with unutterable im-
precations, it was from myself I should have had to turn aside, before all else. After all perhaps I was doing so, that would account for
my vaguely circular motion. Lies, lies, mine was not to know, nor
to judge, nor to rail, but to go. That the bacillus botulinus should
have exterminated my entire kith and kin, I shall never weary of
repeating this, was something I, could readily admit, but only on
condition that my personal behaviour had not to suffer by it. Let

us rather consider what really took place, if Mahood was telling the truth. And why should he have lied to me, he so anxious to obtain my adhesion, to what now that I come to think of it, to his conception of me? Why? For fear of paining me perhaps. But I am there to be pained, that is what my tempters have never grasped. What they all wanted, each according to his particular notion of what is endurable, was that I should exist and at the same time be only moderately, or perhaps I should say finitely pained. They have even killed me off, with the friendly remark that having reached the end of my endurance I had no choice but to disappear. The end of my endurance! It was one second they should have schooled me to endure, after that I would have held out for all eternity, whistling a merry tune. The hard knocks they invented for me! But the bouquet was this story of Mahood's in which I appear as upset at having been delivered so economically of a pack of blood relations, not to mention the two cunts into the bargain, the one for ever accursed that ejected me into this world and the other, infundibuliform, in which, pumping my likes, I tried to take my revenge. To tell the truth, let us be honest at least, it is some considerable time now since I last knew what I was talking about. It is because my thoughts are elsewhere. I am therefore forgiven. So long as one's thoughts are somewhere everything is permitted. On then, without misgiving, as if nothing had happened. And let us consider what really took place, if Mahood was telling the truth when he represented me as rid at one glorious sweep of parents, wife and heirs. I've plenty of time to blow it all skyhigh, this circus where it is enough to breathe to qualify for asphyxiation, I'll find a way out of it, it won't be like the other times. But I should not like to defame my defamer. For when he made me turn and set off in the other direction, before I had exhausted the possibilities of the one I was pursuing, he had not in mind a shrinking of the spirit, not for a moment, but a purely physiological commotion, followed by a simple desire to vomit, corresponding respectively to the howls of my family as they grudgingly succumbed and the subsequent stench, this latter compelling me to beat in retreat under penalty of losing consciousness entirely. This version of the facts having been restored, it only remains to say it is no

better than the other and no less incompatible with the kind of
creature I might just conceivably have been if they had known how
to take me. So let us consider now what really occurred. Finally
I found myself, without surprise, within the building, circular in
form as already stated, its ground-floor consisting of a single room
flush with the arena, and there completed my rounds, stamping
under foot the unrecognisable remains of my family, here a face,
there a stomach, as the case might be, and sinking into them with
the ends of my crutches, both coming and going. To say I did so
with satisfaction would be stretching the truth. For my feeling was
rather one of annoyance at having to flounder in such muck just
at the moment when my closing contortions called for a firm and
level surface. I like to fancy, even if it is not true, that it was in
mother's entrails I spent the last days of my long voyage, and set
out on the next. No, I have no preference, Isolde's breast would
have done just as well, or papa's private parts, or the heart of one
of the little bastards. But is it certain? Would I have not been more
likely, in a sudden access of independence, to devour what remained
of the fatal corned-beef? How often did I fall during these final
stages, while the storms raged without? But enough of this nonsense. I was never anywhere but here, no one ever got me out of
here. Enough of acting the infant who has been told so often
how he was found under a cabbage that in the end he remembers
the exact spot in the garden and the kind of life he led there before
joining the family circle. There will be no more from me about
bodies and trajectories, sky and earth, I don't know what it all is.
They have told me, explained to me, described to me, what it all
is, what it looks like, what it's all for, one after the other, thousands of times, in thousands of connections, until I must have begun
to look as if I understood. Who would ever think, to hear me, that
I've never seen anything, never heard anything but their voices?
And man, the lectures they gave me on men, before they even
began trying to assimilate me to him! What I speak of, what I speak
with, all comes from them. It's all the same to me, but it's no
good, there's no end to it. It's of me now I must speak, even if I
have to do it with their language, it will be a start, a step towards
silence and the end of madness, the madness of having to speak

and not being able to, except of things that don't concern me, that
don't count, that I don't believe, that they have crammed me full
of to prevent me from saying who I am, where I am, and from
doing what I have to do in the only way that can put an end to it,
from doing what I have to do. How they must hate me!
Ah a nice state they have me in, but still I'm not their
creature, not quite, not yet. To testify to them, until I die, as if
there was any dying with that tomfoolery, that's what they've sworn
they'll bring me to. Not to be able to open my mouth without proclaiming them, and our fellowship, that's what they imagine they'll
have me reduced to. It's a poor trick that consists in ramming a
set of words down your gullet on the principle that you can't bring
them up without being branded as belonging to their breed. But
I'll fix their gibberish for them. I never understood a word of it
in any case, not a word of the stories it spews, like gobbets in a
vomit. My inability to absorb, my genius for forgetting, are more
than they reckoned with. Dear incomprehension, it's thanks to you
I'll be myself, in the end. Nothing will remain of all the lies they
have glutted me with. And I'll be myself at last, as a starveling
belches his odourless wind, before the bliss of coma. But who, they?
Is it really worth while inquiring? With my cogged means? No,
but that's no reason not to. On their own ground, with their own
arms, I'll scatter them, and their miscreated puppets. Perhaps I'll
find traces of myself by the same occasion. That's decided then.
What is strange is that they haven't been pestering me for some
time past, yes, they've inflicted the notion of time on me too. What
conclusion, using their methods, am I to draw from this? Mahood
is silent, that is to say his voice continues, but is no longer renewed.
Do they consider me so plastered with their rubbish that I can
never extricate myself, never make a gesture but their cast must
come to life? But within, motionless, I can live, and utter me, for
no ears but my own. They loaded me down with their trappings
and stoned me through the carnival. I'll sham dead now, whom
they couldn't bring to life, and my monster's carapace will rot off
me. But it's entirely a matter of voices, no other metaphor is appropriate. They've blown me up with their voices, like a balloon,
and even as I collapse it's them I hear. Who, them? And why

nothing more from them lately? Can it be they have abandoned
me, saying, Very well, there's nothing to be done with him, let's
leave it at that, he's not dangerous. Ah but the little murmur of
unconsenting man, to murmur what it is their humanity stifles, the
little gasp of the condemned to life, rotting in his dungeon garrotted
and racked, to gasp what it is to have to celebrate banishment,
beware. No, they have nothing to fear, I am walled round with
their vociferations, none will ever know what I am, none will ever
hear me say it, I won't say it, I can't say it, I have no language but
theirs, no, perhaps I'll say it, even with their language, for me alone,
so as not to have not lived in vain, and so as to go silent, if that
is what confers the right to silence, and it's unlikely, it's they who
have silence in their gift, they who decide, the same old gang,
among themselves, no matter, to hell with silence, I'll say what I
am, so as not to have not been born for nothing, I'll fix their jargon
for them, then any old thing, no matter what, whatever they want,
with a will, till time is done, at least with a good grace. First I'll
say what I'm not, that's how they taught me to proceed, then what
I am, it's already under way, I have only to resume at the point
where I let myself be cowed. I am neither, I needn't say, Murphy,
nor Watt, nor Mercier, nor—no, I can't even bring myself to name
them, nor any of the others whose very names I forget, who told
me I was they, who I must have tried to be, under duress, or
through fear, or to avoid acknowledging me, not the slightest connection. I never desired, never sought, never suffered, never partook in any of that, never knew what it was to have, things, adver-
saries, mind, senses. But enough of this. There is no use denying,
no use harping on the same old thing I know so well, and so
easy to say, and which simply amounts in the end to speaking yet again in the way they intend me to speak, that is
to say about them, even with execration and disbelief. Perhaps
they exist in the way they have decreed will be mine, it's possible,
I don't know and I'm not interested. If they had taught me how to
wish I'd wish they did. There's no getting rid of them without
naming them and their contraptions, that's the thing to keep in
mind. I might as well tell another of Mahood's stories and no more
about it, to be understood in the way I was given to understand it,

namely as being about me. That's an idea. To heighten my disgust.
I'll recite it. This will leave me free to consider how I may best
proceed with my own affair, beginning again at the point where
I had to interrupt it, under duress, or through fear, or through
ignorance. It will be the last story. I'll try and look as if I was
telling it willingly, to keep them quiet in case they should feel like
refreshing my memory, on the subject of my behaviour above in
the island, among my compatriots, contemporaries, coreligionists
and companions in distress. This will leave me free to consider
how to set about showing myself forth. No one will be any the
wiser. But who are these maniacs let loose on me from on high
for what they call my good, let us first try and throw a little light
on that. To tell the truth—no, first the story. The island, I'm on
the island, I've never left the island, God help me. I was under
the impression I spent my life in spirals round the earth. Wrong,
it's on the island I wind my endless ways. The island, that's all
the earth I know. I don't know it either, never having had the
stomach to look at it. When I come to the coast I turn back inland.
And my course is not helicoidal, I got that wrong too, but a succession of irregular loops, now sharp and short as in the waltz,
now of a parabolic sweep that embraces entire boglands, now between the two, somewhere or other, and invariably unpredictable in
direction, that is to say determined by the panic of the moment.
But at the period I refer to now this active life is at an end, I do
not move and never shall again, unless it be under the impulsion
of a third party. For of the great traveller I had been, on my hands
and knees in the later stages, then crawling on my belly or rolling
on the ground, only the trunk remains (in sorry trim), surmounted
by the head with which we are already familiar, this is the part of
myself the description of which I have best assimilated and retained.
Stuck like a sheaf of flowers in a deep jar, its neck flush with my
mouth, on the side of a quiet street near the shambles, I am at rest
at last. If I turn, I shall not say my head, but my eyes, free to roll
as they list, I can see the statue of the apostle of horse's meat, a
bust. His pupilless eyes of stone are fixed upon me. That makes
four, with those of my creator, omnipresent, do not imagine I flatter
myself I am privileged. Though not exactly in order I am tolerated

by the police. They know I am speechless and consequently incapable of taking unfair advantage of my situation to stir up the
population against its governors, by means of burning oratory
during the rush hour or subversive slogans whispered, after nightfall, to belated pedestrians the worse for drink. And since I have
lost all my members, with the exception of the one-time virile,
they know also that I shall not be guilty of any gestures liable to
be construed as inciting to alms, a prisonable offence. The fact is
I trouble no one, except possibly that category of hypersensitive
persons for whom the least thing is an occasion for scandal and
indignation. But even here the risk is negligible, such people avoiding the neighbourhood for fear of being overcome at the sight of
the cattle, fat and fresh from their pastures, trooping towards the
humane killer. From this point of view the spot is well chosen, from
my point of view. And even those sufficiently unhinged to be
affected by the spectacle I offer, I mean upset and temporarily
diminished in their capacity for work and aptitude for happiness,
need only look at me a second time, those who can bring themselves to do it, to have immediately their minds made easy. For
my face reflects nothing but the satisfaction of one savouring a
well-earned rest. It is true my mouth was hidden, most of the
time, and my eyes closed. Ah yes, sometimes it's in the past, sometimes in the present. And alone perhaps the state of my skull,
covered with pustules and bluebottles, these latter naturally abounding in such a neighbourhood, preserved me from being an object
of envy for many, and a source of discontent. I hope this gives a
fair picture of my situation. Once a week I was taken out of my
receptacle, so that it might be emptied. This duty fell to the pro-
prietress of the chop-house across the street and she performed it
punctually and without complaint, beyond an occasional good-
natured reflection to the effect that I was a nasty old pig, for she
had a kitchen-garden. Without perhaps having exactly won her
heart it was clear I did not leave her indifferent. And before putting
me back she took advantage of the circumstance that my mouth
was accessible to stick into it a chunk of lights or a marrow-bone.
And when snow fell she covered me with a tarpaulin still water-
tight in places. It was under its shelter, snug and dry, that I became

acquainted with the boon of tears, while wondering to what I
was indebted for it, not feeling moved. And this not merely once,
but every time she covered me, that is to say twice or three times
a year. Yes, it was fatal, no sooner had the tarpaulin settled over
me, and the precipitate steps of my benefactress died away, than
the tears began to flow. Is this, was this to be interpreted as an
effect of gratitude? But in that case should not I have felt grateful? Besides I realised darkly that if she took care of me thus, it
was not solely out of goodness, or else I had not rightly understood the meaning of goodness, when it was explained to me. It
must not be forgotten that I represented for this woman an undeniable asset. For quite apart from the services I rendered to her
lettuce, I constituted for her establishment a kind of landmark, not
to say an advertisement, far more effective than for example a chef
in cardboard, pot-bellied in profile and full face wafer thin. That
she was well aware of this is shown by the trouble she had taken
to festoon my jar with Chinese lanterns, of a very pretty effect in
the twilight, and a fortiori in the night. And the jar itself, so that the
passer-by might consult with greater ease the menu attached to it,
had been raised on a pedestal at her own expense. It is thus I learnt
that her turnips in gravy are not so good as they used to be, but
that on the other hand her carrots, equally in gravy, are even
better than formerly. The gravy has not varied. This is the kind
of language I can almost understand, these the kind of clear and
simple notions on which it is possible for me to build, I ask for no
other spiritual nourishment. A turnip, I know roughly what a turnip
is like, a carrot too, particularly the Flakkee, or Colmar Red. I
seem to grasp at certain moments the nuance that divides bad
from worse. And if I do not always feel the full force of yesterday and today, this does not detract very much from the satisfaction I feel at having penetrated the gist of the matter. Of her
salad, for example, I never heard anything but praise. Yes, I
represent for her a tidy little capital and, if I should ever happen
to die, I am convinced she would be genuinely annoyed. This should
help me to live. I like to fancy that when the fatal hour of reckoning comes, if it ever does, and my debt to nature is paid off at last,
she will do her best to prevent the removal, from where it now

stands, of the old vase in which I shall have accomplished my
vicissitudes. And perhaps in the place now occupied by my head
she will set a melon, or a vegetable-marrow, or a big pineapple
with its little tuft, or better still, I don't know why, a swede, in
memory of me. Then I shall not vanish quite, as is so often the
way with people when buried. But it is not to speak of her that I
have started lying again. *De nobis ipsis silemus,* decidedly that
should have been my motto. Yes, they gave me some lessons in
pigsty Latin too, it looks well, sprinkled through the perjury. It is
perhaps worth noting that snow alone, provided of course it is
heavy, entitles me to the tarpaulin. No other form of filthy weather
lets loose in her the maternal instinct, in my favour. I have tried
to make her understand, dashing my head angrily against the neck
of the jar, that I should like to be shrouded more often. At the
same time I let my spittle flow over, in an attempt to show my
displeasure. In vain. I wonder what explanation she can have found
to account for this behaviour. She must have talked it over with
her husband and probably been told that I was merely stifling,
that is just the reverse of the truth. But credit where credit is due,
we made a balls of it between us, I with my signs and she with
her reading of them. This story is no good, I'm beginning almost
to believe it. But let us see how it is supposed to end, that will sober
me. The trouble is I forget how it goes on. But did I ever know?
Perhaps it stops there, perhaps they stopped it there, saying, who
knows, There you are now, you don't need us any more. This in
fact is one of their favourite devices, to stop suddenly at the least
sign of adhesion from me, leaving me high and dry, with nothing
for my renewal but the life they have imputed to me. And it is
only when they see me stranded that they take up again the thread
of my misfortunes, judging me still insufficiently vitalised to bring
them to a successful conclusion alone. But instead of making the
junction, I have often noticed this, I mean instead of resuming me
at the point where I was left off, they pick me up at a much later
stage, perhaps thereby hoping to induce in me the illusion that I
had got through the interval all on my own, lived without help of
any kind for quite some time, and with no recollection of by what
means or in what circumstances, or even died, all on my own, and

come back to earth again, by way of the vagina like a real live baby, and reached a ripe age, and even senility, without the least assistance from them and thanks solely to the hints they had given me. To saddle me with a lifetime is probably not enough for them, I have to be given a taste of two or three generations. But it's not certain. Perhaps all they have told me has reference to a single existence, the confusion of identities being merely apparent and due to my inaptitude to assume any. If I ever succeed in dying under my own steam, then they will be in a better position to decide if I am worthy to adorn another age, or to try the same one again, with the benefit of my experience. I may therefore perhaps legitimately suppose that the one-armed one-legged wayfarer of a moment ago and the wedge-headed trunk in which I am now marooned are simply two phases of the same carnal envelope, the soul being notoriously immune from deterioration and dismemberment. Having lost one leg, what indeed more likely than that I should mislay the other? And similarly for the arms. A natural transition in sum. But what then of that other old age they bestowed upon me, if I remember right, and that other middle age, when neither legs nor arms were lacking, but simply the power to profit by them? And of that kind of youth in which they had to give me up for dead? If I have a warm place, it is not in their hearts. Oh I don't say they haven't done all they could to be agreeable to me, to get me out of here, on no matter what pretext, in no matter what disguise. All I reproach them with is their insistence. For beyond them is that other who will not give me quittance until they have abandoned me as inutilisable and restored me to myself. Then at last I can set about saying what I was, and where, during all this long lost time. But who is he, if my guess is right, who is waiting for that, from me? And who these others whose designs are so different? And into whose hands I play when I ask myself such questions? But do I, do I? In the jar did I ask myself questions? And in the arena? I have dwindled, I dwindle. Not so long ago, with a kind of shrink of my head and shoulders, as when one is scolded, I could disappear. Soon, at my present rate of decrease, I may spare myself this effort. And spare myself the trouble of closing my eyes, so as not to see the day, for they are blinded by the jar a few inches away. And I have only to let my head fall forward against the wall to be sure that the light from above, which at night is that of the moon, will not be reflected there either, in those little blue mirrors, I used to look at myself in them, to try and brighten them. Wrong again, wrong again, this effort and this trouble will not be spared me. For the woman, displeased at seeing me sink lower and lower, has raised me up by filling the bottom of my jar with sawdust which she changes every week, when she makes my toilet. It is softer than the stone, but less hygienic. And I had got used to the stone. Now I'm getting used to the sawdust. It's an occupation. I could never bear to be idle, it saps one's energy. And I open and close my eyes, open and close, as in the past. And I move my head in and out, in and out, as heretofore. And often at dawn, having left it out all night, I bring it in, to mock the woman and lead her astray. For in the morning, when she has rattled up her shutters, the first look of her eyes still moist with fornication is for the jar. And when she does not see my head she comes running to find out what has happened. For either I have escaped during the night or else I have shrunk again. But just before she reaches me I up with it like a jack-in-the-box, the old eyes glaring up at her. I mentioned I cannot turn my head, and this is true, my neck having stiffened prematurely. But this does not mean it is always facing in the same direction. For with a kind of tossing and writhing I succeed in imparting to my trunk the degree of rotation required, and not merely in one direction, but in the other also. My little game, which I should have thought inoffensive, has cost me dear, and yet I could have sworn I was insolvable. It is true one does not know one's riches until they are lost and I probably have others still that only await the thief to be brought to my notice. And today, if I can still open and close my eyes, as in the past, I can no longer, because of my roguish character, move my head in and out, as in the good old days. For a collar, fixed to the mouth of the jar, now encircles my neck, just below the chin. And my lips which used to be hidden, and which I sometimes pressed against the freshness of the stone, can now be seen by all and sundry. Did I say I catch flies? I snap them up, clack! Does this mean I still have my teeth? To have lost one's limbs and preserved one's dentition, what a mockery! But to revert now to the gloomy side of this affair, I may say that this collar, or ring, of cement, makes it very awkward for me to turn, in the way I have said. I take advantage of this to learn to stay quiet. To have forever before my eyes, when I open them, approximately the same set of hallucinations exactly, is a joy I might never have known, but for my cang. There is really only one thing that worries me, and that is the prospect of being throttled if I should ever happen to shorten further. Asphyxia! I who was always the respiratory type, witness this thorax still mine, together with the abdomen. I who murmured, each time I breathed in, Here comes more oxygen, and each time I breathed out, There go the impurities, the blood is bright red again. The blue face! The obscene protrusion of the tongue! The tumefaction of the penis! The penis, well now, that's a nice surprise, I'd forgotten I had one. What a pity I have no arms, there might still be something to be wrung from it. No, 'tis better thus. At my age, to start manstuprating again, it would be indecent. And fruitless. And yet one can never tell. With a yo heave ho, concentrating with all my might on a horse's rump, at the moment when the tail rises, who knows, I might not go altogether empty-handed away. Heaven, I almost felt it flutter! Does this mean they did not geld me? I could have sworn they had gelt me. But perhaps I am getting mixed up with other scrota. Not another stir out of it in any case. I'll concentrate again. A Clydesdale. A Suffolk stallion. Come come, a little cooperation please, finish dying, it's the least you might do, after all the trouble they've taken to bring you to life. The worst is over. You've been sufficiently assassinated, sufficiently suicided, to be able now to stand on your own feet, like a big boy. That's what I keep telling myself. And I add, quite carried away, Slough off this mortal inertia, it is out of place, in this society. They can't do everything. They have put you on the right road, led you by the hand to the very brink of the precipice, now it's up to you, with an unassisted last step, to show them your gratitude. I like this colourful language, these bold metaphors and apostrophes. Through the splendours of nature they dragged a paralytic and now there's nothing more to admire it's my duty to jump, that it may be said, There goes another who has lived. It does not seem to occur to them that I was never there, that this glassy eye, this fallen chap and the foam at the mouth owe nothing to the Bay of Naples, or Aubervilliers. The last step! I who could never manage the first. But perhaps they would consider themselves sufficiently rewarded if I simply waited for the wind to blow me over. That by all means, it's in my repertory. The trouble is there is no wind equal to it. The cliff would have to cave in under me. If only I were alive inside one might look forward to heart-failure, or to a nice little infarctus somewhere or other. It's usually with sticks they put me out of their agony, the idea being to demonstrate, to the backers, and bystanders, that I had a beginning, and an end. Then planting the foot on my chest, where all is as usual, to the assembly. Ah if you had seen him fifty years ago, what push, what go! Knowing perfectly well they have to begin me all over again. But perhaps I exaggerate my need of them. I accuse myself of inertia, and yet I move, at least I did, can I by any chance have missed the tide? Let us consider the head. There something seems to stir, from time to time, no reason therefore to despair of a fit of apoplexy. What else? The organs of digestion and evacuation, though sluggish, are not wholly inactive, as is shown by the attentions I receive. It's encouraging. While there's life there's hope. The flies, considered as traumatic agents, hardly call for mention. I suppose they might bring me typhus. No, that's rats. I have seen a few, but they are not yet reduced to me. A lowly tapeworm? Not interesting. It is clear in any case that I have lost heart too lightly, it is quite possible I have all that is required to give them satisfaction. But already I'm beginning to be there no more, in that calamitous street they made so clear to me. I could describe it, I could have, a moment ago, as if I had been there, in the form they chose for me, diminished certainly, not the man I was, not much longer for this world, but the eyes still open to impressions, and one ear, sufficiently, and the head sufficiently obedient, to provide me at least with a vague idea of the elements to be eliminated from the setting in order for all to be empty and silent. That was always the way. Just at the moment when the world is assembled at last, and it begins to dawn on me how I can leave it, all fades

and disappears. I shall never see this place again, where my jar
stands on its pedestal, with its garland of many-coloured lanterns,
and me inside it, I could not cling to it. Perhaps they will have me
struck by lightning, for a change, or poleaxed, one merry bank-
holiday evening, then bundled in my shroud and whisked away,
out of sight and mind. Or removed alive, for a change, shifted and
deposited elsewhere, on the off chance. And at my next appearance,
if I ever appear again, all will be new, new and strange. But little
by little I'll get used to it, admonished by them, used to the scene,
used to me, and little by little the old problem will raise its horrid
head, how to live, with their kind of life, for a single second, young
or old, without aid and assistance. And thus reminded of other
attempts, in other circumstances, I shall start asking myself questions, prompted by them, like those I have been asking, concerning me, and them, and these sudden shifts of time and age, and
how to succeed at last where I had always failed, so that they may
be pleased with me, and perhaps leave me in peace at last, and free
to do what I have to do, namely try and please the other, if that
is what I have to do, so that he may be pleased with me, and leave
me in peace at last, and give me quittance, and the right to rest,
and silence, if that is in his gift. It's a lot to expect of one creature,
it's a lot to ask, that he should first behave as if he were not, then
as if he were, before being admitted to that peace where he neither
is, nor is not, and where the language dies that permits of such
expressions. Two falsehoods, two trappings, to be borne to the end,
before I can be let loose, alone, in the unthinkable unspeakable,
where I have not ceased to be, where they will not let me be. It
will perhaps be less restful than I appear to think, alone there at
last, and never importuned. No matter, rest is one of their words,
think is another. But here at last, it seems to me, is food for
delirium. What a shame if I should pitch on something and never
notice it, another candle throw its little light and I be none the wiser.
Yes, I feel the moment has come for me to look back, if I can, and
take my bearings, if I am to go on. If only I knew what I have
been saying. Bah, no need to worry, it can only have been one thing,
the same as ever. I have my faults, but changing my tune is not one
of them. I have only to go on, as if there was something to be done,

something begun, somewhere to go. It all boils down to a question
of words, I must not forget this, I have not forgotten it. But I must
have said this before, since I say it now. I have to speak in a
certain way, with warmth perhaps, all is possible, first of the
creature I am not, as if I were he, and then, as if I were he, of the
creature I am. Before I can, etc. It's a question of voices, of voices
to keep going, in the right manner, when they stop, on purpose, to
put me to the test, as now the one whose burden is roughly to the
effect that I am alive. Warmth, ease, conviction, the right manner,
as if it were my own voice, pronouncing my own words, words
pronouncing me alive, since that's how they want me to be, I don't
know why, with their billions of quick, their trillions of dead, that's
not enough for them, I too must contribute my little convulsion,
mewl, howl, gasp and rattle, loving my neighbour and blessed with
reason. But what is the right manner, I don't know. It is they who
dictate this torrent of balls, they who stuffed me full of these groans
that choke me. And out it all pours unchanged, I have only to
belch to be sure of hearing them, the same old sour teachings I
can't change a tittle of. A parrot, that's what they're up against, a
parrot. If they had told me what I have to say, in order to meet
with their approval, I'd be bound to say it, sooner or later. But
God forbid, that would be too easy, my heart wouldn't be in it,
I have to puke my heart out too, spew it up whole along with the
rest of the vomit, it's then at last I'll look as if I mean what I'm
saying, it won't be just idle words. Well, don't lose hope, keep your
mouth open and your stomach turned, perhaps you'll come out
with it one of these days. But the other voice, of him who does not
share this passion for the animal kingdom, who is waiting to hear
from me, what is its burden? Nice point, too nice for me. For on
the subject of me properly so called, I know what I mean, so
far as I know I have received no information up to date. May one
speak of a voice, in these conditions? Probably not. And yet I do.
The fact is all this business about voices requires to be revised,
corrected and then abandoned. Hearing nothing I am none the
less a prey to communications. And I speak of voices! After all,
why not, so long as one knows it's untrue. But there are limits,
it appears. Let them come. So nothing about me. That is to say

no connected statement. Faint calls, at long intervals. Hear me! Be yourself again! Someone has therefore something to say to me. But never the least news concerning me, beyond the insinuation that I am not in a condition to receive any, since I am not there, which I knew already. I have naturally remarked, in a moment of exceptional receptivity, that these exhortations are conveyed to me by the same channel as that used by Malone and Co. for their transports. That's suspicious, or rather would be if I still hoped to obtain, from these revelations to come, some truth of more value than those I have been plastered with ever since they took it into their heads I had better exist. But this fond hope, which buoyed me up as recently as a moment ago, if I remember right, has now passed from me. Two labours then, to be distinguished perhaps, as the mine from the quarry, on the plane of the effort required, but identically deficient in charm and interest. I. Who might that be? The galley-man, bound for the Pillars of Hercules, who drops his sweep under cover of night and crawls between the thwarts, towards the rising sun, unseen by the guard, praying for storm. Except that I've stopped praying for anything. No no, I'm still a suppliant. I'll get over it, between now and the last voyage, on this leaden sea. It's like the other madness, the mad wish to know, to remember, one's transgressions. I won't be caught at that again, I'll leave it to this year's damned. And now let us think no more about it, think no more about anything, think no more. He alone or they a many, all solicit me in the same tongue, the only one they taught me. They told me there were others, I don't regret not knowing them. The moment the silence is broken in this way it can only mean one thing. Orders, prayers, threats, praise, reproach, reasons. Praise, yes, they gave me to understand I was making progress. Well done, sonny, that will be all for today, run along now back to your dark and see you tomorrow. And there I am, with my white beard, sitting among the children, babbling, cringing from the rod. I'll die in the lower third, bowed down with years and impositions, four foot tall again, like when I had a future, bare-legged in my old black pinafore, wetting my drawers. Pupil Mahood, for the twenty-five thousandth time, what is a mammal? And I'll fall down dead, worn out by the rudiments.

But I'll have made progress, they told me so, only not enough,
not enough. Ah! Where was I, in my lessons? That is what has
had a fatal effect on my development, my lack of memory, no
doubt about it. Pupil Mahood, repeat after me, Man is a higher
mammal. I couldn't. Always talking about mammals, in this men-
agerie. Frankly, between ourselves, what the hell could it matter
to pupil Mahood, that man was this rather than that? Presumably
nothing has been lost in any case, since here it all comes slobbering out again, let loose by the nightmare. I'll have my bellyful of
mammals, I can see that from here, before I wake. Quick, give
me a mother and let me suck her white, pinching my tits. But it's
time I gave this solitary a name, nothing doing without proper
names. I therefore baptise him Worm. It was high time. Worm.
I don't like it, but I haven't much choice. It will be my name too,
when the time comes, when I needn't be called Mahood any more,
if that happy time ever comes. Before Mahood there were others
like him, of the same breed and creed, armed with the same prong.
But Worm is the first of his kind. That's soon said. I must not
forget I don't know him. Perhaps he too will weary, renounce the
task of forming me and make way for another, having laid the
foundations. He has not yet been able to speak his mind, only
murmur, I have not ceased to hear his murmur, all the while the
others discoursed. He has survived them all, Mahood too, if
Mahood is dead. I can hear him yet, faithful, begging me to still
this dead tongue of the living. I imagine that is what he says, in
his unchanging tone. If I could be silent I would better understand
what he wants of me, wants me to be, wants me to say. Why
doesn't he thunder it at me and get it over? Too easy, it is I who
must be silent, hold my breath. But there is something wrong here.
For if Mahood were silent, Worm would be silent too. That the
impossible should be asked of me, good, what else could be asked
of me? But the absurd! Of me whom they have reduced to reason.
It is true poor Worm is not to blame for this. That's soon said.
But let me complete my views, before I shit on them. For if I am
Mahood, I am Worm too, plop. Or if I am not yet Worm, I shall
be when I cease to be Mahood, plop. On now to serious matters.
No, not yet. Another of Mahood's yarns perhaps, to perfect my

besotment. No, not worth the trouble, it will come at its appointed hour, the record is in position from time immemorial. Yes, the big words must out too, all be taken as it comes. The problem of liberty too, as sure as fate, will come up for my consideration at the pre-established moment. But perhaps I have been too hasty in oppos-ing these two fomenters of fiasco. Is it not the fault of one that I cannot be the other? Accomplices therefore. That's the way to reason, warmly. Or is one to postulate a tertius gaudens, meaning myself, responsible for the double failure? Shall I come upon my true countenance at last, bathing in a smile? I have the feeling I shall be spared this spectacle. At no moment do I know what I'm talking about, nor of whom, nor of where, nor how, nor why, but I could employ fifty wretches for this sinister operation and still be short of a fifty-first, to close the circuit, that I know, without know-ing what it means. The essential is never to arrive anywhere, never to be anywhere, neither where Mahood is, nor where Worm is, nor where I am, it little matters thanks to what dispensation. The essential is to go on squirming forever at the end of the line, as long as there are waters and banks and ravening in heaven a sport-ing God to plague his creature, per pro his chosen shits. I've swal-lowed three hooks and am still hungry. Hence the howls. What a joy to know where one is, and where one will stay, without being there. Nothing to do but stretch out comfortably on the rack, in the blissful knowledge you are nobody for all eternity. A pity I should have to give tongue at the same time, it prevents it from bleeding in peace, licking the lips. Well I suppose one can't have everything, so late in the proceedings. They'll surely bring me to the surface one day or another and all then sink their differences and agree it was not worth while going to so much trouble for such a paltry kill, for such paltry killers. What silence then! And now let's see what news there is of Worm, just to please the old bastard. I'll soon know if the other is still after me. But even if he isn't nothing will come of it, he won't catch me, I won't be delivered from him, I mean Worm, I swear it, the other never caught me, I was never delivered from him, it's past history, up to the present. I am he who will never be caught, never delivered, who crawls be-tween the thwarts, towards the new day that promises to be glorious,

festooned with lifebelts, praying for rack and ruin. The third line
falls plumb from the skies, it's for her majesty my soul, I'd have
hooked her on it long ago if I knew where to find her. That brings
us up to four, gathered together. I knew it, there might be a hundred of us and still we'd lack the hundred and first, we'll always
be short of me. Worm, I nearly said Watt, Worm, what can I say
of Worm, who hasn't the wit to make himself plain, what to still
this gnawing of termites in my Punch and Judy box, what that might
not just as well be said of the other? Perhaps it's by trying to be
Worm that I'll finally succeed in being Mahood, I hadn't thought
of that. Then all I'll have to do is be Worm. Which no doubt I
shall achieve by trying to be Jones. Then all I'll have to do is be
Jones. Stop, perhaps he'll spare me that, have compassion and let
me stop. The dawn will not be always rosy. Worm, Worm, it's
between the three of us now, and the devil take the hindmost.
It seems to me besides that I must have already made, contrary
to what it seems to me I must have already said, some efforts in
this direction. I should have noted them, if only in my head. But
Worm cannot note. There at least is a first affirmation, I mean
negation, on which to build. Worm cannot note. Can Mahood note?
That's it, weave, weave. Yes, it is the characteristic, among others,
of Mahood to note, even if he does not always succeed in doing
so, certain things, perhaps I should say all things, so as to turn
them to account, for his governance. And indeed we have seen
him do so, in the yard, in his jar, in a sense. I knew I had only
to try and talk of Worm to begin talking of Mahood, with more
felicity and understanding than ever. How close to me he suddenly
seems, squinting up at the medals of the hippophagist Ducroix.
It is the hour of the apéritif, already people pause, to read the
menu. Charming hour of the day, particularly when, as sometimes
happens, it is also that of the setting sun whose last rays, raking
the street from end to end, lend to my cenotaph an interminable
shadow, astraddle of the gutter and the sidewalk. There was a time
I used to contemplate it, when I was freer to turn my head than
now, since being put in the collar. Then over there, far from me,
I knew my head was lying, and people treading on it, and on my
flies, which went on gliding none the less, prettily on the dark

ground. And I saw the people coming towards me, all along my
shadow, followed by long faithful trembling shadows. For sometimes I confuse myself with my shadow, and sometimes don't.
And sometimes I don't confuse myself with my jar, and sometimes
do. It all depends what mood we're in. And often I went on looking without flinching until, ceasing to be, I ceased to see. Delicious
instant truly, coinciding from time to time, as already observed,
with that of the apéritif. But this joy, which for my part I should
have thought harmless, and without danger for the public, is something I have to go without now that the collar holds my face turned
towards the railings, just above the menu, for it is important that
the prospective customer should be able to compose his meal
without the risk of being run over. The meat, in this quarter, has
a high reputation, and people come from a distance, from great
distances, on purpose to relish it. Which having done they hurry
away. By ten o'clock in the evening all is silent, as the grave, as
they say. Such is the fruit of my observations accumulated over a
long period of years and constantly subjected to a process of in-
duction. Here all is killing and eating. This evening there is tripe.
It's a winter dish, or a late autumn one. Soon Marguerite will
come and light me up. She is late. Already more than one passer-
by has flashed his lighter under my nose the better to decipher
what I shall now describe, by way of elegant variation, as the bill
of fare. Please God nothing has happened to my protectress. I
shall not hear her coming, I shall not hear her steps, because of
the snow. I spent all morning under my cover. When the first frosts
come she makes me a nest of rags, well tucked in all round me,
to preserve me from chills. It's snug. I wonder will she powder
my skull this evening, with her great puff. It's her latest invention.
She's always thinking of something new, to relieve me. If only
the earth would quake! The shambles swallow me up! Through
the railings, at the end of a vista between two blocks of buildings,
the sky appears to me. A bar moves over and shuts it off, whenever
I please. If I could raise my head I'd see it streaming into the main
of the firmament. What is there to add, to these particulars? The
evening is still young, I know that, don't let us go just yet, not yet
say goodbye once more forever, to this heap of rubbish. What

about trying to cogitate, while waiting for something intelligible to take place? Just this once. Almost immediately a thought presents itself, I should really concentrate more often. Quick let me record it before it vanishes. How is it the people do not notice me? I seem to exist for none but Madeleine. That a passer-by pressed for time, in headlong flight or hot pursuit, should have no eyes for me, that I can conceive. But the idlers come to hear the cattle's bellows of pain and who, time obviously heavy on their hands, pace up and down waiting for the slaughter to begin? The hungry compelled by the position of the menu, and whether they like it or not, to post themselves literally face to face with me, in the full blast of my breath? The children on their way to and from their playgrounds beyond the gates, all out for a bit of fun? It seems to me that even a human head, recently washed and with a few hairs on top, should be quite a popular curiosity in the position occupied by mine. Can it be out of discretion, and a reluctance to hurt, that they affect to be unaware of my existence? But this is a refinement of feeling which can hardly be attributed to the dogs that come pissing against my abode, apparently never doubting that it contains some flesh and bones. It follows therefore that I have no smell either. And yet if anyone should have a smell, it is I. How, under these conditions, can Mahood expect me to behave normally? The flies vouch for me, if you like, but how far? Would they not settle with equal appetite on a lump of cowshit? No, as long as this point is not cleared up to my satisfaction, or as long as I am not distinguished by some sense organs other than Madeleine's, it will be impossible for me to believe, sufficiently to pursue my act, the things that are told about me. I should further remark, with regard to this testimony which I consider indispensable, that I shall soon be in no fit condition to receive it, so greatly have my faculties declined, in recent times. It is obvious we have here a principle of change pregnant with possibilities. But say I succeed in dying, to adopt the most comfortable hypothesis, without having been able to believe I ever lived, I know to my cost it is not that they wish for me. For it has happened to me many times already, without their having granted me as much as a brief sick-leave among the worms, before resurrecting me. But who knows, this time, what the future holds in store. That qua sentient and thinking being I should be going downhill fast is in any case an excellent thing. Perhaps some day some gentleman, chancing to pass my way with his sweetheart on his arm, at the precise moment when my last is favouring me with a final smack of the flight of time, will exclaim, loud enough for me to hear, Oh I say, this man is ailing, we must call an ambulance! Thus with a single stone, when all hope seemed lost, the two rare birds. I shall be dead, but I shall have lived. Unless one is to suppose him victim of a hallucination. Yes, to dispel all doubt his betrothed would need to say, You are right, my love, he looks as if he were going to throw up. Then I'd know for certain and giving up the ghost be born at last, to the sound perhaps of one of those hiccups which mar alas too often the solemnity of the passing. When Mahood I once knew a doctor who held that scientifically speaking the latest breath could only issue from the fundament and this therefore, rather than the mouth, the orifice to which the family should present the mirror, before opening the will. However this may be, and without dwelling further on these macabre details, it is certain I was grievously mistaken in supposing that death in itself could be regarded as evidence, or even a strong presumption, in support of a preliminary life. And I for my part have no longer the least desire to leave this world, in which they keep trying to foist me, without some kind of assurance that I was really there, such as a kick in the arse, for example, or a kiss, the nature of the attention is of little importance, provided I cannot be suspected of being its author. But let two third parties remark me, there, before my eyes, and I'll take care of the rest. How all becomes clear and simple when one opens an eye on the within, having of course previously exposed it to the without, in order to benefit by the contrast. I should be sorry, though exhausted personally, to abandon prematurely this rich vein. For I shall not come back to it in a hurry, ah no. But enough of this cursed first person, it is really too red a herring, I'll get out of my depth if I'm not careful. But what then is the subject? Mahood? No, not yet. Worm? Even less. Bah, any old pronoun will do, provided one sees through it. Matter of habit. To be adjusted later. Where was I? Ah yes, the bliss of what

is clear and simple. The next thing is somehow to connect this with
the unhappy Madeleine and her great goodness. Attentions such
as hers, the pertinacity with which she continues to acknowledge
me, do not these sufficiently attest my real presence here, in the
Rue Brancion, never heard of in my island home? Would she rid
me of my paltry excrements every Sunday, make me a nest at the
approach of winter, protect me from the snow, change my sawdust,
rub salt into my scalp, I hope I'm not forgetting anything, if I were
not there? Would she have put me in a cang, raised me on a
pedestal, hung me with lanterns, if she were not convinced of my
substantiality? How happy I should be to submit to this evidence
and to the execution upon me of the sentence it entails. Unfortunately I regard it as highly subject to caution, not to say unal-
lowable. For what is one to think of the redoubled attentions she
has been lavishing on me for some time past? How different from
the serenity of our early relations, when I saw her only once a week.
No, there is no getting away from it, this woman is losing faith
in me. And she is trying to put off the moment when she must
finally confess her error by coming every few minutes to see if I
am still more or less imaginable in situ. Similarly the belief in
God, in all modesty be it said, is sometimes lost following a period
of intensified zeal and observance, it appears. Here I pause to make
a distinction (I must be still thinking). That the jar is really standing where they say, all right, I wouldn't dream of denying it, after
all it's none of my business, though its presence at such a place,
about the reality of which I do not propose to quibble either, does
not strike me as very credible. No, I merely doubt that I am in it.
It is easier to raise a shrine than bring the deity down to haunt it.
But what's all this confusion now? That's what comes of distinc-
tions. No matter. She loves me, I've always felt it. She needs me.
Her chop-house, her husband, her children if she has any, are not
enough, there is in her a void that I alone can fill. It is not surprising then she should have visions. There was a time I thought
she was perhaps a near relation, mother, sister, daughter, or such-
like, perhaps even a wife, and that she was sequestrating me. That
is to say Mahood, seeing how little impressed I was by his chief
witness, whispered this suggestion in my ear, adding, I didn't say

anything. I must admit it is not so preposterous as it looks at first sight, it even accounts for certain bizarreries which had not yet struck me at the time of its formulation, among others my inexistence in the eyes of those who are not in the know, that is to say all mankind. But assuming I was being stowed away in a public place, why go to such trouble to draw attention to my head, artistically illuminated from dusk to midnight? You may of course retort that results are all that count. Another thing however. This woman has never spoken to me, to the best of my knowledge. If I have said anything to the contrary I was mistaken. If I say anything to the contrary again I shall be mistaken again. Unless I am mistaken now. Into the dossier with it in any case, in support of whatever thesis you fancy. Never an affectionate word, never a reprimand. For fear of bringing me to the public notice? Or lest the illusion should be dispelled? I shall now sum up. The moment is at hand when my only believer must deny me. Nothing has happened. The lanterns have not been lit. Is it the same evening? Perhaps dinner is over. Perhaps Marguerite has come and gone, come again and gone again, without my having noticed her. Perhaps I have blazed with all my usual brilliance, for hours on end, all unsuspecting. And yet something has changed. It is not a night like other nights. Not because I see no stars, it is not often I see a star, away up in the depths of the sliver of sky I command. Not because I don't see anything, not even the railings, that has often happened. Not because of the silence either, it is a silent place, at night. And I am half-deaf. It is not the first time I have strained my ears in vain for the stables' muffled sounds. All of a sudden a horse will neigh. Then I'll know that nothing has changed. Or I'll see the lantern of the watchman, swinging knee-high in the yard. I must be patient. It is cold, this morning it snowed. And yet I don't feel the cold on my head. Perhaps I am still under the tarpaulin, perhaps she flung it over me again, for fear of more snow in the night, while I was meditating. But the sensation I so love, of the tarpaulin weighing on my head, is lacking too. Has my head lost all feeling? Or did I have a stroke, while I was meditating? I don't know. I shall be patient, asking no more questions, on the qui vive. Hours have passed, it must be day again, nothing has happened, I hear nothing. I placed them before their responsibilities, perhaps they have let me go. For this feeling of being entirely enclosed, and yet nothing touching me, is new. The sawdust no longer presses against my stumps, I don't know where I end. I left it yesterday, Mahood's world, the street, the chop-house, the slaughter, the statue and, through the railings, the sky like a slate-pencil. I shall never hear again the lowing of the cattle, nor the clinking of the forks and glasses, nor the angry voices of the butchers, nor the litany of the dishes and the prices. There will never be another woman wanting me in vain to live, my shadow at evening will not darken the ground. The stories of Mahood are ended. He has realised they could not be about me, he has abandoned, it is I who win, who tried so hard to lose, in order to please him, and be left in peace. Having won, shall I be left in peace? It doesn't look like it, I seem to be going on talking. In any case all these suppositions are probably erroneous. I shall no doubt be launched again, girt with better arms, against the fortress of mortality. What is more important is that I should know what is going on now, in order to announce it, as my function requires. It must not be forgotten, sometimes I forget, that all is a question of voices. I say what I am told to say, in the hope that some day they will weary of talking at me. The trouble is I say it wrong, having no ear, no head, no memory. Now I seem to hear them say it is Worm's voice beginning, I pass on the news, for what it is worth. Do they believe I believe it is I who am speaking? That's theirs too. To make me believe I have an ego all my own, and can speak of it, as they of theirs. Another trap to snap me up among the living. It's how to fall into it they can't have explained to me sufficiently. They'll never get the better of my stupidity. Why do they speak to me thus? Is it possible certain things change on their passage through me, in a way they can't prevent? Do they believe I believe it is I who am asking these questions? That's theirs too, a little distorted perhaps. I don't say it's not the right method. I don't say they won't catch me in the end. I wish they would, to be thrown away. It's this hunt that is tiring, this unending being at bay. Images, they imagine that by piling on the images they'll entice me in the end. Like the mother who whistles to prevent baby's bladder from bursting, there's another. They, yes, now they're all in the same galley. Worm to play, his lead, I wish him a happy time. To think I thought he was against what they were trying to do with me! To think I saw in him, if not me, a step towards me! To get me to be he, the anti-Mahood, and then to say, But what am I doing but living, in a kind of way, the only possible way, that's the combination. Or by the absurd prove to me that I am, the absurd of not being able. Unfortunately it is no help my being forewarned, I never remain so for long. In any case I wish him every success, in his courageous undertaking. And I am even prepared to collaborate with him, as with Mahood and Co., to the best of my ability, being unable to do otherwise, and knowing my ability. Worm, to say he does not know what he is, where he is, what is happening, is to underestimate him. What he does not know is that there is anything to know. His senses tell him nothing, nothing about himself, nothing about the rest, and this distinction is beyond him. Feeling nothing, knowing nothing, he exists nevertheless, but not for himself, for others, others conceive him and say, Worm is, since we conceive him, as if there could be no being but being conceived, if only by the beer. Others. One alone, then others. One alone turned towards the all-impotent, all-nescient, that haunts him, then others. Towards him whom he would nourish, he the famished one, and who, having nothing human, has nothing else, has nothing, is nothing. Come into the world unborn, abiding there unliving, with no hope of death, epicentre of joys, of griefs, of calm. Who seems the truest possession, because the most unchanging. The one outside of life we always were in the end, all our long vain life long. Who is not spared by the mad need to speak, to think, to know where one is, where one was, during the wild dream, up above, under the skies, venturing forth at night. The one ignorant of himself and silent, ignorant of his silence and silent, who could not be and gave up trying. Who crouches in their midst who see themselves in him and in their eyes stares his unchanging stare. Thanks for these first notions. And it's not all. He who seeks his true countenance, let him be of good cheer, he'll find it, convulsed with anguish, the eyes out on stalks. He who longs to have lived, while he was alive, let him be reassured, life will tell him how. That's all very comforting. Worm, be Worm, you'll see, it's impossible, what a velvet glove, a little worn at the knuckles with all the hard hitting. Bah, let's turn the black eye. And the starching begin at last, of this old clout so patiently pawed in vain, as limp and drooping still as the first day. But it is solely a question of voices, no other image is appropriate. Let it go through me at last, the right one, the last one, his who has none, by his own confession. Do they think they'll lull me, with all this hemming and hawing? What can it matter to me, that I succeed or fail? The undertaking is none of mine, if they want me to succeed I'll fail, and vice versa, so as not to be rid of my tormentors. Is there a single word of mine in all I say? No, I have no voice, in this matter I have none. That's one of the reasons why I confused myself with Worm. But I have no reasons either, no reason, I'm like Worm, without voice or reason, I'm Worm, no, if I were Worm I wouldn't know it, I wouldn't say it, I wouldn't say anything, I'd be Worm. But I don't say anything, I don't know anything, these voices are not mine, nor these thoughts, but the voices and thoughts of the devils who beset me. Who make me say that I can't be Worm, the inexpugnable. Who make me say that I am he perhaps, as they are. Who make me say that since I can't be he I must be he. That since I couldn't be Mahood, as I might have been, I must be Worm, as I cannot be. But is it still they who say that when I have failed to be Worm I'll be Mahood, automatically, on the rebound? As if, and a little silence, as if I were big enough now to take a hint and understand, certain things, but they're wrong, I need explanations, of everything, and even then, I don't understand, that's how I'll sicken them in the end, by my stupidity, so they say, to lull me, to make me think I'm stupider than I am. And is it still they who say that when I surprise them all and am Worm at last, then at last I'll be Mahood, Worm proving to be Mahood the moment one is he? Ah if they could only begin, and do what they want with me, and succeed at last, in doing what they want with me, I'm ready to be whatever they want, I'm tired of being matter, matter, pawed and pummelled endlessly in vain. Or give me up and leave me lying in a heap, in such a heap that none would ever be found again to try and fashion it. But they are not of the same mind, they are all of the same kidney and yet they don't know what they want to do with me, they don't know where I am, or what I'm like, I'm like dust, they want to make a man out of dust. Listen to them, losing heart! That's to lull me, till I imagine I hear myself saying, myself at last, to myself at last, that it can't be they, speaking thus, that it can only be I, speaking thus. Ah if I could only find a voice of my own, in all this babble, it would be the end of their troubles, and of mine. That's why there are all these little silences, to try and make me break them. They think I can't bear silence, that some day, somehow, my horror of silence will force me to break it. That's why they are always leaving off, to try and drive me to extremities. But they dare not be silent for long, the whole fabrication might collapse. It's true I dread these gulfs they all bend over, straining their ears for the murmur of a man. It isn't silence, it's pitfalls, into which nothing would please me better than to fall, with the little cry that might be taken for human, like a wounded wistiti, the first and last, and vanish for good and all, having squeaked. Well, if they ever succeed in getting me to give a voice to Worm, in a moment of euphory, perhaps I'll succeed in making it mine, in a moment of confusion. There we have the stake. But they won't. Did they ever get Mahood to speak? It seems to me not. I think Murphy spoke now and then, the others too perhaps, I don't remember, but it was clumsily done, you could see the ventriloquist. And now I feel it's about to begin. They must consider me sufficiently stupefied, with all their balls about being and existing. Yes, now that I've forgotten who Worm is, where he is, what he's like, I'll begin to be he. Anything rather than these college quips. Quick, a place. With no way in, no way out, a safe place. Not like Eden. And Worm inside. Feeling nothing, knowing nothing, capable of nothing, wanting nothing. Until the instant he hears the sound that will never stop. Then it's the end, Worm no longer is. We know it, but we don't say it, we say it's the awakening, the beginning of Worm, for now we must speak, and speak of Worm. It's no longer he, but let us proceed as if it were still he, he at last, who hears, and trembles, and is delivered over, to affliction and the struggle to withstand it, the starting eye, the labouring mind. Yes, let us call that thing Worm, so as to exclaim, the sleight of hand accomplished, Oh look, life again, life everywhere and always, the life that's on every tongue, the only possible! Poor Worm, who thought he was different, there he is in the madhouse for life. Where am I? That's my first question, after an age of listening. From it, when it hasn't been answered, I'll rebound towards others, of a more personal nature, much later. Perhaps I'll even end up, before regaining my coma, by thinking of myself as living, technically speaking. But let us proceed with method. I shall do my best, as always, since I cannot do otherwise. I shall submit, more corpse-obliging than ever. I shall transmit the words as received, by the ear, or roared through a trumpet into the arsehole, in all their purity, and in the same order, as far as possible. This infinitesimal lag, between arrival and departure, this trifling delay in evacuation, is all I have to worry about. The truth about me will boil forth at last, scalding, provided of course they don't start stuttering again. I listen. Enough procrastination. I'm Worm, that is to say I am no longer he, since I hear. But I'll forget that in the heat of misery, I'll forget I am no longer Worm, but a kind of tenth-rate Toussaint L'Ouverture, that's what they're counting on. Worm then I catch this sound that will never stop, monotonous beyond words and yet not altogether devoid of a certain variety. At the end of I know not what eternity, they don't say, this has sufficiently exasperated my intelligence for it to grasp that the nuisance is a voice and that the realm of nature, in which I flatter myself I have a foot already, has other noises to offer which are even more unpleasant and may be relied on to make themselves heard before long. Don't tell me after that I had no predispositions for man's estate. What a weary way since that first disaster, what nerves torn from the heart of insentience, with the appertaining terror and the cerebellum on fire. It took him a long time to adapt himself to this excoriation. To realise pooh it's nothing. A mere bagatelle. The common lot. A harmless joke. That will not last for ever. For me to gather while I may. They mentioned roses. I'll smell them before I'm finished. Then they'll put the accent on the thorns. What prodigious variety! The thorns they'll have to come and stick into me, as into their unfortunate Jesus. No, I need nobody, they'll start sprouting under my arse, unaided, some day I feel myself soaring above my condition. A billybowl of thorns and the air perfume-laden. But not so fast. I still leave much to be desired, I have no technique, none. For example, in case you don't believe me, I don't yet know how to move, either locally, in relation to myself, or bodily, in relation to the rest of the shit. I don't know how to want to, I want to in vain. What doesn't come to me from me has come to the wrong address. Similarly my understanding is not yet sufficiently well-oiled to function without the pressure of some critical circumstance, such as a violent pain felt for the first time. Some nice point in semantics, for example, of a nature to accelerate the march of the hours, could not retain my attention. For others the time-abolishing joys of impersonal and disinterested speculation. I only think, if that is the name for this vertiginous panic as of hornets smoked out of their nest, once a certain degree of terror has been exceeded. Does this mean I am less exposed to doing so, by the grace of inurement? To argue so would be to underestimate the extent of the repertory in which I am plunged and which, it appears, is nothing compared to what is in store for me at the conclusion of the novitiate. These lights gleaming low afar, then rearing up in a blaze and sweeping down upon me, blinding, to devour me, are merely one example. My familiarity with them avails me nothing, they invariably give me to reflect. Each time, at the last moment, just as I begin to scorch, they go out, smoking and hissing, and yet each time my phlegm is shattered. And in my head, which I am beginning to locate to my satisfaction, above and a little to the right, the sparks spirt and dash themselves out against the walls. And sometimes I say to myself I am in a head, it's terror makes me say it, and the longing to be in safety, surrounded on all sides by massive bone. And I add that I am foolish to let myself be frightened by another's thoughts, lacerating my sky with harmless fires and assailing me with noises signifying nothing. But one thing at a time. And often all sleeps, as when I was really Worm, except this voice which has denatured me, which never stops, but often grows confused and falters, as if it were going to abandon me. But it is merely a passing

weakness, unless it is done on purpose, to teach me hope. Strange
thing, ruined as I am and still young in this abjection they have
brought me to, I sometimes seem to remember what I was like when
I was Worm, and not yet delivered into their hands. That's to
tempt me into saying, I am indeed Worm after all, and into thinking that after all he may have become the thing that I have become.
But it doesn't work. But they will devise another means, less
childish, of getting me to admit, or pretend to admit, that I am
he whose name they call me by, and no other. Or they'll wait,
counting on my weariness, as they press me ever harder, to wipe
him from my memory who cannot be brought to the pass they
have brought me to, not to mention yesterday, not to mention tomorrow. And yet it seems to me I remember, and shall never
forget, what I was like when I was he, before all became confused.
But that is of course impossible, since Worm could not know what
he was like, or who he was, that's how they want me to reason.
And it seems to me too, which is even more deplorable, that I
could become Worm again, if I were left in peace. This transmis-
sion is really excellent. I wonder if it's going to get us somewhere.
If only they would stop talking for nothing, pending their stopping
everything. Nothing? That's soon said. It is not for me to judge.
What would I judge with? It's more provocation. They want me
to lose patience and rush, suddenly beside myself, to their rescue.
How transparent that all is! Sometimes I say to myself, they say
to me, Worm says to me, the subject matters little, that my pur-
veyors are more than one, four or five. But it's more likely the
same foul brute all the time, amusing himself pretending to be a
many, varying his register, his tone, his accent and his drivel.
Unless it comes natural to him. A bare and rusty hook I might
accept. But all these titbits! But there are long silences too, at long
intervals, during which, hearing nothing, I say nothing. That is to
say I hear murmuring, if I listen hard enough, but it's not for me,
it's for them alone, they are putting their heads together again.
I don't hear what they say, all I know is they are still there, they
haven't done, with me. They have moved a little aside. Secrets.
Or if there is only one it is he alone, taking counsel with himself,
muttering and chewing his moustache, getting ready for a fresh

flow of inanity. To think of me eavesdropping, me, when silence falls! Ah a nice state they have me in. But it's with the hope there is no one left. But this is not the time to speak of that. Good. Of what is it the time to speak? Of Worm, at last. Good. We must first, to begin with, go back to his beginnings and then, to go on with, follow him patiently through the various stages, taking care to show their fatal concatenation, which have made him what I am. The whole to be tossed off with bravura. Then notes from day to day, until I collapse. And finally, to wind up with, song and dance of thanksgiving by victim, to celebrate his nativity. Please God nothing goes wrong. Mahood I couldn't die. Worm will I ever get born? It's the same problem. But perhaps not the same personage after all. The scytheman will tell, it's all one to him. But let us go back as planned, afterwards we'll fall forward as projected. The reverse would be more like it. But not by much. Upstream, downstream, what matter, I begin by the ear, that's the way to talk. Before that it was the night of time. Whereas ever since, what radiance! Now at least I know where I am, as far as my origins go, I mean my origins considered as a subject of conversation, that's what counts. The moment one can say, Someone is on his way, all is well. Perhaps I have still a thousand years to go. No matter. He's on his way. I begin to be familiar with the premises. I wonder if I couldn't sneak out by the fundament, one morning, with the French breakfast. No, I can't move, not yet. One minute in a skull and the next in a belly, strange, and the next nowhere in particular. Perhaps it's Botal's Foramen, when all about me palpitates and labours. Bait, bait. Can it be I have a friend among them, shaking his head in sorrow and saying nothing or only, from time to time, Enough, enough. One can be before beginning, they have set their hearts on that. They want me roots and all. This onward-rushing time is the same which used to sleep. And this silence they yelp against in vain and which one day will be restored, the same as in the past. Perhaps a little the worse for wear. Agreed, agreed, I who am on my way, words bellying out my sails, am also that unthinkable ancestor of whom nothing can be said. But perhaps I shall speak of him some day, and of the impenetrable age when I was he, some day when they fall silent, convinced at last I shall

never get born, having failed to be conceived. Yes, perhaps I shall
speak of him, for an instant, like the echo that mocks, before
being restored to him, the one they could not part me from. And
indeed they are weakening already, it's perceptible. But it's a feint,
to have me rejoice without cause, after their fashion, and accept
their terms, for the sake of peace at any price. But I can do nothing,
that is what they seem to forget at each instant. I can't rejoice
and I can't grieve, it's in vain they explained to me how it's done,
I never understood. And what terms? I don't know what it is they
want. I say what it is, but I don't know. I emit sounds, better and
better it seems to me. If that's not enough for them I can't help
it. If I speak of a head, referring to me, it's because I hear it being
spoken of. But why keep on saying the same thing? They hope
things will change one day, it's natural. That one day on my windpipe, or some other section of the conduit, a nice little abscess will
form, with an idea inside, point of departure for a general infection.
This would enable me to jubilate like a normal person, knowing
why. And in no time I'd be a network of fistulae, bubbling with
the blessed pus of reason. Ah if I were flesh and blood, as they are
kind enough to posit, I wouldn't say no, there might be something
in their little idea. They say I suffer like true thinking flesh, but
I'm sorry, I feel nothing. Mahood I felt a little, now and then, but
what good did that do them? No, they'd be better advised to try
something else. I felt the cang, the flies, the sawdust under my
stumps, the tarpaulin on my skull, when they were mentioned to
me. But can that be called a life which vanishes when the subject
is changed? I don't see why not. But they must have decreed it
can't. They are too hard to please, they ask too much. They want
me to have a pain in the neck, irrefragable proof of animation,
while listening to talk of the heavens. They want me to have a mind
where it is known once and for all that I have a pain in the neck,
that flies are devouring me and that the heavens can do nothing
to help. Let them scourge me without ceasing and evermore, more
and more lustily (in view of the habituation factor), in the end I
might begin to look as if I had grasped the meaning of life. They
might even take a breather from time to time, without my ceasing
to howl. For they would have warned me, before they started,

You must howl, do you hear, otherwise it proves nothing. And worn out at last, or feeble with old age, and my cries having ceased for want of nourishment, they could pronounce me dead with every appearance of veracity. And without ever having had to move I would have gained my rest and heard them say, striking softly together their dry old hands as if to shake off the dust, He'll never move again. No, that would be too simple. We must have the heavens and God knows what besides, lights, luminaries, the three-monthly ray of hope and the gleam of consolation. But let us close this parenthesis and, with a light heart, open the next. The noise. How long did I remain a pure ear? Up to the moment when it could go on no longer, being too good to last, compared to what was coming. These millions of different sounds, always the same, recurring without pause, are all one requires to sprout a head, a bud to begin with, finally huge, its function first to silence, then to extinguish when the eye joins in, and worse than the evil, its treasure-house. But no lingering on this thin ice. The mechanism matters little, provided I succeed in saying, before I go deaf, It's a voice, and it speaks to me. In inquiring, boldly, if it is not mine. In deciding, it doesn't matter how, that I have none. In blowing darkly hot and cold, with concomitant identical sensations. It's a starting-point, he's off, they don't see me, but they hear me, panting, riveted, they don't know I'm riveted. He knows they are words, he is not sure they are not his, that's how it begins, with such a start no one ever looked back, one day he'll make them his, when he thinks he is alone, far from all men, out of range of every voice, and come to the light of day they keep telling him of. Yes, I know they are words, there was a time I didn't, as I still don't know if they are mine. Their hopes are therefore founded. In their shoes I'd be content with my knowing what I know, I'd demand no more of me than to know that what I hear is not the innocent and necessary sound of dumb things constrained to endure, but the terror-stricken babble of the condemned to silence. I would have pity, give me quittance, not harry me into appearing my own destroyer. But they are severe, greedy, no less, perhaps more, than when I was playing Mahood. Instead of drawing in their horns! It's true I have not spoken yet. In at one ear and incontinent out

through the mouth, or the other ear, that's possible too. No sense
in multiplying the occasions of error. Two holes and me in the
middle, slightly choked. Or a single one, entrance and exit, where
the words swarm and jostle like ants, hasty, indifferent, bringing
nothing, taking nothing away, too light to leave a mark. I shall
not say I again, ever again, it's too farcical. I shall put in
it's place, whenever I hear it, the third person, if I think of it.
Anything to please them. It will make no difference. Where I am
there is no one but me, who am not. So much for that. Words, he
says he knows they are words. But how can he know, who has never
heard anything else? True. Not to mention other things, many
others, to which the abundance of matter has unfortunately up to
now prohibited the least allusion. For example, to begin with,
his breathing. There he is now with breath in his nostrils,
it only remains for him to suffocate. The thorax rises and
falls, the wear and tear are in full spring, the rot spreads downwards, soon he'll have legs, the possibility of crawling. More lies,
he doesn't breathe yet, he'll never breathe. Then what is this faint
noise, as of air stealthily stirred, recalling the breath of life, to those
whom it corrodes? It's a bad example. But these lights that go out
hissing? Is it not more likely a great crackle of laughter, at the
sight of his terror and distress? To see him flooded with light, then
suddenly plunged back in darkness, must strike them as irresistibly
funny. But they have been there so long now, on every side, they
may have made a hole in the wall, a little hole, to glue their eyes
to, turn about. And these lights are perhaps those they shine upon
him, from time to time, in order to observe the progress he is
making. But this question of lights deserves to be treated in a
section apart, it is so intriguing, and at length, composedly, and so
it will be, at the first opportunity, when time is not so short, and
the mind more composed. Resolution number twenty-three. And
in the meantime the conclusion to be drawn? That the only noises
Worm has had till now are those of mouths? Correct. Not forgetting the groaning of the air beneath the burden. He's coming, that's
the main thing. When on earth later on the storms rage, drowning
momentarily the free expression of opinion, he'll know what is
afoot, that the end of the world is not at hand. No, in the place

where he is he cannot learn, the head cannot work, he knows no more than on the first day, he merely hears, and suffers, uncomprehending, that must be possible. A head has grown out of his ear, the better to enrage him, that must be it. The head is there, glued to the ear, and in it nothing but rage, that's all that matters, for the time being. It's a transformer in which sound is turned, without the help of reason, to rage and terror, that's all that is required, for the moment. The circumvolutionisation will be seen too later, when they get him out. Why then the human voice, rather than a hyena's howls or the clanging of a hammer? Answer, so that the shock may not be too great, when the writhings of true lips meet his gaze. Between them they find a rejoinder to everything. And how they enjoy talking, they know there is no worse torment, for one not in the conversation. They are numerous, all round, holding hands perhaps, an endless chain, taking turns to talk. They wheel, in jerks, so that the voice always comes from the same quarter. But often they all speak at once, they all say simultaneously the same thing exactly, but so perfectly together that one would take it for a single voice, a single mouth, if one did not know that God alone can fill the rose of the winds, without moving from his place. One, but not Worm, who says nothing, knows nothing, yet. Similarly turn about they benefit by the peephole, those who care to. While one speaks another peeps, the one no doubt whose voice is next due and whose remarks may possibly have reference to what he may possibly have seen, this depending on whether what he has seen has aroused his interest to the extent of appearing worthy of remark, even indirectly. But what hope has sustained them, all the time they have been thus employed? For it is difficult not to suppose them sustained by some form of hope. And what is the nature of the change they are on the look out for, gluing one eye to the hole and closing the other. They have no pedagogic purpose in view, that's definite. There is no question of imparting to him any instruction whatsoever, for the moment. This catechist's tongue, honeyed and perfidious, is the only one they know. Let him move, try and move, that's all they ask, for the moment. No matter where he goes, being at the centre, he will go towards them. So he is at the centre,

there is a clue of the highest interest, it matters little to what.
They look, to see if he has stirred. He is nothing but a shapeless
heap, without a face capable of reflecting the niceties of a torment,
but the disposition of which, its greater or lesser degree of crouch
and huddledness, is no doubt expressive, for specialists, and enables
them to assess the chances of its suddenly making a bound, or
dragging its coils faintly away, as if stricken to death. Somewhere
in the heap an eye, a wild equine eye, always open, they must have
an eye, they see him possessed of an eye. No matter where he goes
he will go towards them, towards their song of triumph, when they
know he has moved, or towards their sudden silence, when they
know he has moved, to make him think he did well to move, or
towards the voice growing softer, as if receding, to make him
think he is drawing away from them, but not yet far enough,
whereas he is drawing nearer, nearer and nearer. No, he can't
think anything, can't judge of anything, but the kind of flesh he
has is good enough, will try and go where peace seems to be,
drop and lie when it suffers no more, or less, or can go no further.
Then the voice will begin again, low at first, then louder, coming
from the quarter they want him to retreat from, to make him think
he is pursued and struggle on, towards them. In this way they'll
bring him to the wall, and even to the precise point where they
have made other holes through which to pass their arms and seize
him. How physical this all is! And then, unable to go any further,
because of the obstacle, and unable to go any further in any case,
and not needing to go any further for the moment, because of the
great silence which has fallen, he will drop, assuming he had risen,
but even a reptile can drop, after a long flight, the expression may
be used without impropriety. He will drop, it will be his first
corner, his first experience of the vertical support, the vertical
shelter, reinforcing those of the ground. That must be something,
while waiting for oblivion, to feel a prop and buckler, not only for
one of one's six planes, but for two, for the first time. But Worm
will never know this joy but darkly, being less than a beast, before
he is restored, more or less, to that state in which he was before
the beginning of his prehistory. Then they will lay hold of him
and gather him into their midst. For if they could make a small

hole for the eye, then bigger ones for the arms, they can make one bigger still for the transit of Worm, from darkness to light. But what is the good of talking about what they will do as soon as Worm sets himself in motion, so as to gather him without fail into their midst, since he cannot set himself in motion, though he often desires to, if when speaking of him one may speak of desire, and one may not, one should not, but there it is, that is the way to speak of him, that is the way to speak to him, as if he were alive, as if he could understand, as if he could desire, even if it serves no purpose, and it serves none. And it is a blessing for him he cannot stir, even though he suffers because of it, for it would be to sign his life-warrant, to stir from where he is, in search of a little calm and something of the silence of old. But perhaps one day he will stir, the day when the little effort of the early stages, infinitely weak, will have become, by dint of repetition, a great effort, strong enough to tear him from where he lies. Or perhaps one day they will leave him in peace, letting go their hands, filling up the holes and departing, towards more profitable occupations, in Indian file. For a decision must be reached, the scales must tilt, to one side or the other. No, one can spend one's life thus, unable to live, unable to bring to life, and die in vain, having done nothing, been nothing. It is strange they do not go and fetch him in his den, since they seem to have access to it. They dare not, the air in the midst of which he lies is not for them, and yet they want him to breathe theirs. They could set a dog on him perhaps, with instructions to drag him out. But no dog would survive there either, not for one second. With a long pole perhaps, with a hook at the end. But the place where he lies is vast, that's interesting, he is far, too far for them to reach him even with the longest pole. That tiny blur, in the depths of the pit, is he. There he is now in a pit, no avenue will have been left unexplored. They say they see him, the blur is what they see, they say the blur is he, perhaps it is. They say he hears them, they don't know, perhaps he does, yes, he hears, nothing else is certain. Worm hears, though hear is not the word, but it will do, it will have to do. They look down upon him then, according to the latest news, he'll have to climb to reach them. Bah, the latest news, the latest news is not the last. The slopes are

gentle that meet where he lies, they flatten out under him, it is not
a meeting, it is not a pit, that didn't take long, soon we'll have him
perched on an eminence. They don't know what to say, to be able
to believe in him, what to invent, to be reassured, they see nothing,
they see grey, like still smoke, unbroken, where he might be, if
he must be somewhere, where they have decreed he is, into
which they launch their voices, one after another, in the hope of
dislodging him, hearing him stir, seeing him loom within reach of
their gaffs, hooks, barbs, grapnels, saved at last, home at last.
And now that's enough about them, their usefulness is over, no,
not yet, let them stay, they may still serve, stay where they are,
turning in a ring, launching their voices, through the hole, there
must be a hole for the voices too. But is it them he hears? Are
they really necessary that he may hear, they and kindred puppets?
Enough concessions, to the spirit of geometry. He hears, that's all
about it, he who is alone, and mute, lost in the smoke, it is not
real smoke, there is no fire, no matter, strange hell that has no
heating, no denizens, perhaps it's paradise, perhaps it's the light
of paradise, and the solitude, and this voice the voice of the blest
interceding invisible, for the living, for the dead, all is possible. It
isn't the earth, that's all that counts, it can't be the earth, it can't
be a hole in the earth, inhabited by Worm alone, or by others if
you like, huddled in a heap like him, mute, immovable, and this
voice the voice of those who mourn them, envy them, call on
them and forget them, that would account for its incoherence, all
is possible. Yes, so much the worse, he knows it is a voice, how is
not known, nothing is known, he understands nothing it says, just
a little, almost nothing, it's inexplicable, but it's necessary, it's
preferable, that he should understand just a little, almost nothing,
like a dog that always gets the same filth flung to it, the same
orders, the same threats, the same cajoleries. That settles that, the
end is in sight. But the eye, let's leave him his eye too, it's to see
with, this great wild black and white eye, moist, it's to weep with,
it's to practise with, before he goes to Killarney. What does he do
with it, he does nothing with it, the eye stays open, it's an eye
without lids, no need for lids here, where nothing happens, or so
little, if he could blink he might miss the odd sight, if he could

close it, the kind he is, he'd never open it again. Tears gush from
it practically without ceasing, why is not known, nothing is known,
whether it's with rage, or whether it's with grief, the fact is there,
perhaps it's the voice that makes it weep, with rage, or some other
passion, or at having to see, from time to time, some sight or other,
perhaps that's it, perhaps he weeps in order not to see, though it
seems difficult to credit him with an initiative of this complexity.
The rascal, he's getting humanised, he's going to lose if he doesn't
watch out, if he doesn't take care, and with what could he take care,
with what could he form the faintest conception of the condition
they are decoying him into, with their ears, their eyes, their tears
and a brainpan where anything may happen. That's his strength,
his only strength, that he understands nothing, can't take thought,
doesn't know what they want, doesn't know they are there, feels
nothing, ah but just a moment, he feels, he suffers, the noise makes
him suffer, and he knows, he knows it's a voice, and he understands, a few expressions here and there, a few intonations, ah it
looks bad, bad, no, perhaps not, for it's they describe him thus,
without knowing, thus because they need him thus, perhaps he
hears nothing, suffers nothing, and this eye, more mere imagination.
He hears, true, though it's they again who say it, but this can't
be denied, this is better not denied. Worm hears, that's all can be
said for certain, whereas there was a time he didn't, the same Worm,
according to them, he has therefore changed, that's grave, gravid,
who knows to what lengths he may be carried, no, he can be relied
on. The eye too, of course, is there to put him to flight, make him
take fright, badly enough to break his bonds, they call that bonds,
they want to deliver him, ah mother of God, the things one has
to listen to, perhaps it's tears of mirth. Well, no matter, let's drive
on now to the end of the joke, we must be nearly there, and see
what they have to offer him, in the way of bugaboos. Who, we?
Don't all speak at once, there's no sense in that either. All will come
right, later on in the evening, everyone gone and silence restored. In
the meantime no sense in bickering about pronouns and other parts
of blather. The subject doesn't matter, there is none. Worm being
in the singular, as it turned out, they are in the plural, to avoid
confusion, confusion is better avoided, pending the great confound-

ing. Perhaps there is only one of them, one would do the trick
just as well, but he might get mixed up with his victim, that would
be abominable, downright masturbation. We're getting on. Nothing
much then in the way of sights for sore eyes. But who can be sure
who has not been there, has not lived there, they call that living,
for them the spark is present, ready to burst into flame, all it needs
is preaching on, to become a living torch, screams included. Then
they may go silent, without having to fear an embarrassing silence,
when steps are heard on graves as the saying is, genuine hell.
Decidedly this eye is hard of hearing. Noises travel, traverse walls,
but may the same be said of appearances? By no means, generally
speaking. But the present case is rather special. But what appearances, it is always well to try and find out what one is talking about,
even at the risk of being deceived. This grey to begin with, meant
to be depressing no doubt. And yet there is yellow in it, pink too
apparently, it's a nice grey, of the kind recommended as going with
everything, urinous and warm. In it the eye can see, otherwise why
the eye, but dimly, that's right, no superfluous particulars, later
to be controverted. A man would wonder where his kingdom ended,
his eye strive to penetrate the gloom, and he crave for a stick, an
arm, fingers apt to grasp and then release, at the right moment, a
stone, stones, or for the power to utter a cry and wait, counting the
seconds, for it to come back to him, and suffer, certainly, at having
neither voice nor other missile, nor limbs submissive to him, bending and unbending at the word of command, and perhaps even
regret being a man, under such conditions, that is to say a head
abandoned to its ancient solitary resources. But Worm suffers only
from the noise which prevents him from being what he was before,
admire the nuance. If it's the same Worm, and they have set their
hearts on it. And if it is not it makes no difference, he suffers as
he has always suffered, from this noise that prevents nothing, that
must be feasible. In any case this grey can hardly be said to add
to his misery, brightness would be better suited for that purpose,
since he cannot close his eye. He cannot avert it either, nor lower it,
nor lift it up, it remains trained on the same tiny field, a stranger
forever to the boons and blessings of accommodation. But perhaps
one day brightness will come, little by little, or rapidly, or in a

sudden flood, and then it is hard to see how Worm could stay,
and it is also hard to see how he could go. But impossible situations cannot be prolonged, unduly, the fact is well known, either
they disperse, or else they turn out to be possible after all, it's
only to be expected, not to mention other possibilities. Let there
then be light, it will not necessarily be disastrous. Or let there be
none, we'll manage without it. But these lights, in the plural, which
rear aloft, swell, sweep down and go out hissing, reminding one of
the naja, perhaps the moment has come to throw them into the
balance and have done with this tedious equipoise, at last. No,
the moment has not yet come, to do that. Ha. None of your hoping
here, that would spoil everything. Let others hope for him, outside,
in the cool, in the light, if they have a wish to, or if they are
obliged to, or if they are paid to, yes, they must be paid to hope,
they hope nothing, they hope things will continue as they are,
it's a soft job, their thoughts wander as they call on Jude, it's
praying they are, praying for Worm, praying to Worm, to have
pity, pity on them, pity on Worm, they call that pity, merciful
God, the things one has to put up with, fortunately it all means
nothing to him. Currish obscurity, to thy kennel, hell-hound! Grey,
What else? Calm, calm, there must be something else, to go with
this grey, which goes with everything. There must be something
of everything here, as in every world, a little of everything.
Mighty little, it seems. Beside the point in any case. What balls
is going on before this impotent crystalline, that's all that needs
to be imagined. A face, how encouraging that would be, if it
could be a face, every now and then, always the same, methodically varying its expressions, doggedly demonstrating all a true
face can do, without every ceasing to be recognisable as such,
passing from unmixed joy to the sullen fixity of marble, via the
most characteristic shades of disenchantment, how pleasant that
would be. Worth ten of Saint Anthony's pig's arse. Passing by at
the right distance, the right level, say once a month, that's not
exorbitant, full face and profile, like criminals. It might even
pause, open its mouth, raises its eyebrows, bless its soul, stutter,
mutter, howl, groan and finally shut up, the chaps clenched to
cracking point, or fallen, to let the dribble out. That would be

nice. A presence at last. A visitor, faithful, with his visiting-day, his visiting-hour, never staying too long, it would be wearisome, or too little, it would not be enough, but just the necessary time for hope to be born, grow, languish and die, say five minutes. And even should the notion of time dawn on his darkness, at this punctual image of the countenance everlasting, who could blame him? Involving very naturally that of space, they have taken to going hand in hand, in certain quarters, it's safer. And the game would be won, lost and won, he'd be somehow suddenly among us, among the rendezvous, and people saying, Look at old Worm, waiting for his sweetheart, and the flowers, look at the flowers, you'd think he was asleep, you know old Worm, waiting for his love, and the daisies, look at the daisies, you'd think he was dead. That would be worth seeing. Fortunately it's all a dream. For here there is no face, nor anything resembling one, nothing to reflect the joy of living and succedanea, nothing for it but to try something else. Some simple thing, a box, a piece of wood, to come to rest before him for an instant, once a year, once every two years, a ball, revolving one knows not how about one knows not what, about him, every two years, every three years, frequency unimportant in the early stages, without stopping, it needn't stop, that would be better than nothing, he'd hear it approaching, hear it receding, it would be an event, he might learn to count, the minutes, the hours, to fret, be brave, have patience, lose patience, turn his head, roll his eye, a big stone, and faithful, that would be better than nothing, pending the hearts of flesh. And even should his start off, his heart that is, on its waltz, in his ear, tralatralay pom pom, again, tralatralay pom pom, re mi re do bang bang, who could reprehend him? Unfortunately we must stick to the facts, for what else is there, to stick to, to cling to, when all founders, but the facts, when there are any, still floating, within reach of the heart, happy expression that, of the heart crying out, The facts are there, the facts are there, and then more calmly, when the danger is past, the continuation, namely, in the case before us, Here there is no wood, nor any stone, or if there is, the facts are there, it's as if there wasn't, the facts are there, no vegetables, no minerals, only Worm, kingdom unknown, Worm is there, as it were, as it were.

But not too fast, it's too soon, to return, to where I am, empty-handed, in triumph, to where I'm waiting, calm, passably calm, knowing, thinking I know, that nothing has befallen me, nothing will befall me, nothing good, nothing bad, nothing to be the death of me, nothing to be the life of me, it would be premature. I see me, I see my place, there is nothing to show it, nothing to distinguish it, from all the other places, they are mine, all mine, if I wish, I wish none but mine, there is nothing to mark it, I am there so little, I see it, I feel it round me, it enfolds me, it covers me, if only this voice would stop, for a second, it would seem long to me, a second of silence. I'd listen, I'd know if it was going to start again, or if it was stilled for ever, what would I know it with, I'd know. And I'd keep on listening, to try and advance in their good graces, keep my place in their favour, and be ready, in case they judged fit to take me in hand again, or I'd stop, stop listening, is it possible that one day I shall stop listening, without having to fear the worst, namely, I don't know, what can be worse than this, a woman's voice perhaps, I hadn't thought of that, they might engage a soprano. But let us leave these dreams and try again. If only I knew what they want, they want me to be Worm, but I was, I was, what's wrong, I was, but ill, it must be that, it can only be that, what else can it be, but that, I didn't report in the light, the light of day, in their midst, to hear them say, Didn't we tell you you were alive and kicking? I have endured, that must be it, I shouldn't have endured, but I feel nothing, yes, yes, this voice, I have endured it, I didn't fly from it, I should have fled, Worm should have fled, but where, how, he's riveted, Worm should have dragged himself away, no matter where, towards them, towards the azure, but how could he, he can't stir, it needn't be bonds, there are no bonds here, it's as if he were rooted, that's bonds if you like, the earth would have to quake, it isn't earth, one doesn't know what it is, it's like sargasso, no, it's like molasses, no, no matter, an eruption is what's needed, to spew him into the light. But what calm, apart from the discourse, not a breath, it's suspicious, the calm that precedes life, no no, not all this time, it's like slime, paradise, it would be paradise, but for this noise, it's life trying to get in, no, trying to get him out, or little

bubbles bursting all around, no, there's no air here, air is to make
you choke, light is to close your eyes, that's where he must go,
where it's never dark, but here it's never dark either, yes, here
it's dark, it's they who make this grey, with their lamps. When
they go, when they go silent, it will be dark, not a sound, not a
glimmer, but they'll never go, yes, they'll go, they'll go silent perhaps and go, one day, one evening, slowly, sadly, in Indian file,
casting long shadows, towards their master, who will punish them,
or who will spare them, what else is there, up above, for those
who lose, punishment, pardon, so they say. What have you done
with your material? We have left it behind. But commanded to
say whether yes or no they filled up the holes, have you filled
up the holes yes or no, they will say yes and no, or some yes,
others no, at the same time, not knowing what answer the master
wants, to his question. But both are defendable, both yes and no,
for they filled up the holes, if you like, and if you don't like they
didn't, for they didn't know what to do, on departing, whether
to fill up the holes or, on the contrary, leave them gaping wide.
So they fixed their lamps in the holes, their long lamps, to prevent
them from closing of themselves, it's like potter's clay, their powerful lamps, lit and trained on the within, to make him think they
are still there, notwithstanding the silence, or to make him think
the grey is natural, or to make him go on suffering, for he does
not suffer from the noise alone, he suffers from the grey too, from
the light, he must, it's preferable, or to make it possible for them to
come back, if the master commands them to, without his knowing
they have gone, as if he could know, or for no other reason than
their ignorance of what to do, whether to fill up the holes or let
them fill up of themselves, it's like shit, there we have it at last,
there it is at last, the right word, one has only to seek, seek in
vain, to be sure of finding in the end, it's a question of elimination. Enough now about holes. The grey means nothing, the grey
silence is not necessarily a mere lull, to be got through somehow,
it may be final, or it may not. But the lamps unattended will not
burn on forever, on the contrary, they will go out, little by little,
without attendants to charge them anew, and go silent, in the end.
Then it will be black. But it is with the black as with the grey,

the black proves nothing either, as to the nature of the silence
which it inspissates (as it were). For they may come back, long
after the lights are spent, having pleaded for years in vain before
the master and failed to convince him there is nothing to be done,
with Worm, for Worm. Then all will start over again, obviously.
So it will never be known, Worm will never know, let the silence
be black, or let it be grey, it can never be known, as long as it
lasts, whether it is final, or whether it is a mere lull, and what a
lull, when he must listen, strain his ears for the murmurs of
olden silences, hold himself ready for the next instalment, under
pain of supplementary thunderbolts. But Worm must not be confused with another. Though this has no importance, as it happens.
For he who has once had to listen will listen always, whether he
knows he will never hear anything again, or whether he does not.
In other words, they like other words, no doubt about it, silence
once broken will never again be whole. Is there then no hope?
Good gracious, no, heavens, what an idea! Just a faint one perhaps, but which will never serve. But one forgets. And if there is
only one he will depart all alone, towards his master, and his long
shadow will follow him, across the desert, it's a desert, that's
news, Worm will see the light in a desert, the light of day, the
desert day, the day they catch him, it's the same as everywhere else, they say not, they say it's purer, clearer, fat
lot of difference that will make, oh it is not necessarily the Sahara,
or Gobi, there are others, it's the ozone that matters, in the beginning, yes indeed, in the end too, it sterilises. But this livid eye,
what use is it to him? To see the light, they call that seeing, no
objection, since it causes him suffering, they call that suffering,
they know how to cause suffering, the master explained to them,
Do this, do that, you'll see him squirm, you'll hear him weep. He
weeps, it's a fact, oh not a very firm one, to be made the most
of quick. As for the squirming, nothing doing. But there is always
this to be said, things are only beginning, though long since begun,
they will not lose heart, they'll remember the motto of William
the Silent and keep on talking, that's what they're paid for, not
for results. Enough about them, they can speak of nothing else,
all is theirs, but for them there would be nothing, not even Worm,

he's an idea they have, a word they use, when speaking of them, enough about them. But this grey, this light, if he could escape from this light, which makes him suffer, is it not obvious it would make him suffer more and more, in whatever direction he went, since he is at the centre, and drive him back there, after forty or fifty vain excursions? No, that is not obvious. For it is obvious the light would lessen as he went towards it, they would see to that, to make him think he was on the right road and so bring him to the wall. Then the blaze, the capture and the paean. As long as he suffers there's hope, even though they need none, to make him suffer. But how can they know he suffers? Do they see him? They say they do. But it's impossible. Hear him? Certainly not. He makes no noise, A little with his whining perhaps. In any case they are easy, rightly or wrongly, in their minds, he suffers, and thanks to them. Oh not yet sufficiently, but gently does it, an excess of severity at this stage might darken his understanding forever. Another thing. The problem is delicate. The dulling effect of habit, how do they deal with that? They can combat it of course, raising the voice, increasing the light. But suppose, instead of suffering less, as time flies, he continues to suffer as much, precisely, as the first day. That must be possible. And but suppose, instead of suffering less than the first day, or no less, he suffers more and more, as time flies, and the metamorphosis is accomplished, of unchanging future into unchangeable past. Eh? Another thing, but of a different order. The affair is thorny. Is not a uniform suffering preferable to one which, by its ups and downs, is liable at certain moments to encourage the view that perhaps after all it is not eternal? That must depend on the object pursued. Namely? A little fit of impatience, on the part of the patient. Thank you. That is the immediate object. Afterwards there will be others. Afterwards he'll be given lessons in keeping quiet. But for the moment let him toss and turn at least, roll on the ground, damn it all, since there's no other remedy, anything at all, to relieve the monotony, damn it all, look at the burnt alive, they don't have to be told, when not lashed to the stake, to rush about in every direction, without method, crackling, in search of a little cool, there are even those whose sang-froid is such that they throw themselves out of the window. No one asks him to go to those lengths. But simply to discover, without further assistance from without, the alleviations of flight from self, that's all, he won't go far, he needn't go far. Simply to find within himself a palliative for what he is, through no fault of his own. Simply to imitate the hussar who gets up on a chair the better to adjust the plume of his busby, it's the least he might do. No one asks him to think, simply to suffer, always in the same way, without hope of diminution, without hope of dissolution, it's no more complicated than that. No need to think in order to despair. Agreed then on monotony, it's more stimulating. But how can it be ensured? No matter, no matter how, they are doing the best they can, with the miserable means at their disposal, a voice, a little light, poor devils, that's what they're paid for, they say, No sign of hardening, no sign of softening, impossible to say, no matter, it's a good average, we have only to continue, one day he'll understand, one day he'll thrill, the little spasm will come, a change in the eye, and cast him up among us. To be on the watch and never sight, to listen for the moan that never comes, that's not a life worth living either. And yet it's theirs. He is there, says the master, somewhere, do as I tell you, bring him before me, he's lacking to my glory. But one last effort, one more, that's the spirit, that's the way, each time as if it were the last, the only way not to lose ground. A great gulp of stinking air and off we go, we'll be back in a second. Forward! That's soon said. But where is forward? And why? The dirty pack of fake maniacs, they know I don't know, they know I forget all they say as fast as they say it. These little pauses are a poor trick too. When they go silent, so do I. A second later, I'm a second behind them, I remember a second, for the space of a second, that is to say long enough to blurt it out, as received, while receiving the next, which is none of my business either. Not an instant I can call my own and they want me to know where next to turn. Ah I know what I'd know, and where I'd turn, if I had a head that worked. Let them tell me again what I'm doing, if they want me to look as if I were doing it. This tone, these words, to make me think they come from me. Always the same old dodges, ever since they took it into their heads that my existence is only a question of time. I think I must have blackouts, whole sentences lost, no, not whole. Perhaps I've missed the keyword to the whole business. I wouldn't have understood it, but I would have said it, that's all that's required, it would have spoken in my favour, next time they judge me, well well, so they judge me from time to time, they neglect nothing. Perhaps one day I'll know, say, what I'm guilty of. How many of us are there altogether, finally? And who is holding forth at the moment? And to whom? And about what? These are futile teasers. Let them put into my mouth at last the words that will save me, damn me, and no more talk about it, no more talk about anything. But this is my punishment, my crime is my punishment, that's what they judge me for, I expiate vilely, like a pig, dumb, uncomprehending, possessed of no utterance but theirs. They'll clap me in a dungeon, I'm in a dungeon, I've always been in a dungeon, I hear everything, every word they say, it's the only sound, as if I were speaking, to myself, out loud, in the end you don't know any more, a voice that never stops, where it's coming from. Perhaps there are others here, with me, it's dark, very properly, it is not necessarily an oubliette for one, or one other, perhaps I have a companion in misfortune, given to talking, or condemned to talk, you know, any old thing, out loud, without ceasing, but I think not, what do I think not, that I have a companion in misfortune, that's it, that would surprise me, they loathe me, but not to that extent, they say that would surprise me. I must doze off from time to time, with open eyes, and yet nothing changes, ever. Gaps, there have always been gaps, it's the voice stopping, it's the voice failing to carry to me, what can it matter, perhaps it's important, the result is the same, one perhaps that doesn't count, exceptionally. They shut me up here, now they're trying to get me out, to shut me up somewhere else, or to let me go, they are capable of putting me out just to see what I'd do. Standing with their backs to the door, their arms folded, their legs crossed, they would observe me. Or all they did was to find me here, on their arrival, or long afterwards. They are not interested in me, only in the place, they want the place for one of their own. What can one do but speculate, speculate, until one hits on the happy speculation? When all goes silent, and comes to

an end, it will be because the words have been said, those it
behoved to say, no need to know which, no means of knowing
which, they'll be there somewhere, in the heap, in the torrent,
not necessarily the last, they have to be ratified by the proper
authority, that takes time, he's far from here, they bring him the
verbatim report of the proceedings, once in a way, he knows the
words that count, it's he who chose them, in the meantime the
voice continues, while the messenger goes towards the master,
and while the master examines the report, and while the messenger
comes back with the verdict, the words continue, the wrong words,
until the order arrives, to stop everything or to continue everything, no, superfluous, everything will continue automatically, until
the order arrives, to stop everything. Perhaps they are somewhere
there, the words that count, in what has just been said, the words
it behoved to say, they need not be more than a few. They say
they, speaking of them, to make me think it is I who am speaking.
Or I say they, speaking of God knows what, to make me think
it is not I who am speaking. Or rather there is silence, from the
moment the messenger departs until he returns with his orders,
namely, Continue. For there are long silences from time to time,
truces, and then I hear them whispering, some perhaps whispering,
It's over, this time we've hit the mark, and others, We'll have to
go through it all again, in other words, or in the same words,
arranged differently. Respite then, once in a way, if one can call
that respite, when one waits to know one's fate, saying, Perhaps
it's not that at all, and saying, Where do these words come from
that pour out of my mouth, and what do they mean, no, saying
nothing, for the words don't carry any more, if one can call that
waiting, when there's no reason for it, and one listens, that stet,
without reason, as one has always listened, because one day listening began, because it cannot stop, that's not a reason, if one can
call that respite. But what's all this about not being able to die,
live, be born, that must have some bearing, all this about staying
where you are, dying, living, being born, unable to go forward
or back, not knowing where you came from, or where you are,
or where you're going, or that it's possible to be elsewhere, to be
otherwise, supposing nothing, asking yourself nothing, you can't,

you're there, you don't know who, you don't know where, the thing stays where it is, nothing changes, within it, outside it, apparently, apparently. And there is nothing for it but to wait for the end, nothing but for the end to come, and at the end all will be the same, at the end at last perhaps all the same as before, as all that livelong time when there was nothing for it but to get to the end, or fly from it, or wait for it, trembling or not, resigned or not, the nuisance of doing over, and of being, same thing, for one who could never do, never be. Ah if only this voice could stop, this meaningless voice which prevents you from being nothing, just barely prevents you from being nothing and nowhere, just enough to keep alight this little yellow flame feebly darting from side to side, panting, as if straining to tear itself from its wick, it should never have been lit, or it should never have been fed, or it should have been put out, put out, it should have been let go out. Regretting, that's what helps you on, that's what gets you on towards the end of the world, regretting what is, regretting what was, it's not the same thing, yes, it's the same, you don't know, what's happening, what's happened, perhaps it's the same, the same regrets, that's what transports you, towards the end of regretting. But a little animation now for pity's sake, it's now or never, a little spirit, it won't produce anything, not a budge, that doesn't matter, we are not tradesmen, and one never knows, does one, no. Perhaps Mahood will emerge from his urn and make his way towards Montmartre, on his belly, singing, I come, I come, my heart's delight. Or Worm, good old Worm, perhaps he won't be able to bear any more, of not being able, of not being able to bear any more, it would be a pity to miss that. If I were they I'd set the rats on him, water-rats, sewer-rats, they're the best, oh not too many, a dozen to a dozen and a half, that might help him make up his mind, to get going, and what an introduction, to his future attributes. No, it would be in vain, a rat wouldn't survive there, not one second. But let's have another squint at his eye, that's the place to look. A little raw perhaps, the white, with all the pissing, there's a gleam at last, one hesitates to say of intelligence. Apart from that the same as ever. A trifle more prominent perhaps, more paraphimotically globose. It seems to listen. It's weak-

ening, that's unavoidable, glazing, it's high time to offer it something to bring it clean out of its socket, in ten years it will be too
late. The mistake they make of course is to speak of him as if
he really existed, in a specific place, whereas the whole thing is
no more than a project for the moment. But let them blunder on to
the end of their folly, then they can go into the question again,
taking care not to compromise themselves by the use of terms,
if not of notions, accessible to the understanding. In the same way
the case of Mahood has been insufficiently studied. One may experience the need of such creatures, assuming they are twain, and
even the presentiment of their possible reality, without all these
blind and surly disquisitions. A little more reflection would have
shown them that the hour to speak, far from having struck, might
never strike. But they are compelled to speak, it is forbidden them
to stop. Why then not speak of something else, something the
existence of which seems in a certain measure already established,
on the subject of which one may chatter away without blushing
purple every thirty or forty thousand words at having to employ
such locutions and which moreover, supreme guarantee, has caused
the glibbest tongues to wag from time immemorial, it would be
preferable. It's the old story, they want to be entertained, while
doing their dirty work, no, not entertained, soothed, no, that's
not it either, solaced, no, even less, no matter, with the result they
achieve nothing, neither what they want, without knowing exactly
what, nor the obscure infamy to which they are committed, the
old story. You wouldn't think it was the same gang as a moment
ago, or would you? What can you expect, they don't know who
they are either, nor where they are, nor what they're doing, nor
why everything is going so badly, so abominably badly, that must
be it. So they build up hypotheses that collapse on top of one
another, it's human, a lobster couldn't do it. Ah a nice mess we're
in, the whole pack of us, is it possible we're all in the same boat,
no, we're in a nice mess each one in his own peculiar way. I myself have been scandalously bungled, they must be beginning to
realise it, I on whom all dangles, better still, about whom, much
better, all turns, dizzily, yes yes, don't protest, all spins, it's a head,
I'm in a head, what an illumination, sssst, pissed on out of hand.

Ah this blind voice. and these moments of held breath when all listen wildly, and the voice that begins to fumble again, without knowing what it's looking for, and again the tiny silence, and the listening again, for what, no one knows, a sign of life perhaps, that must be it, a sign of life escaping someone, and bound to be denied if it came, that's it surely, if only all that could stop, there'd be peace, no, too good to be believed, the listening would go on, for the voice to begin again, for a sign of life, for someone to betray himself, or for something else, anything, what else can there be but signs of life, the fall of a pin, the stirring of a leaf, or the little cry that frogs give when the scythe slices them in half, or when they are spiked, in their pools, with a spear, one could multiply the examples, it would even be an excellent idea, but there it is, one can't. Perhaps it would be better to be blind, the blind hear better, full of general knowledge we are this evening, we have even piano-tuners up our sleeve, they strike A and hear G, two minutes later, there's nothing to be seen in any case, this eye is an oversight. But this isn't Worm speaking. True, so far, who denies it, it would be premature. Nor I, for that matter, and Mahood is notoriously aphonic. But the question is not there, for the moment, no one knows where it is, but it is not there, for the time being. Ah yes, there's great fun to be had from an eye, it weeps for the least little thing, a yes, a no, the yesses make it weep, the noes too, the perhapses particularly, with the result that the grounds for these staggering pronouncements do not always receive the attention they deserve. Mahood too, I mean Worm, no, Mahood, Mahood too is a great weeper, in case it hasn't been mentioned, his beard is soaking with the muck, it's quite ridiculous, especially as it doesn't relieve him in the slightest, what could it possibly relieve him of, the poor brute is as cold as a fish, incapable even of cursing his creator, it's purely mechanical. But it's time Mahood was forgotten, he should never have been mentioned. No doubt. But is it possible to forget him? It is true one forgets everything. And yet it is greatly to be feared that Mahood will never let himself be completely resorbed. Worm yes, Worm will vanish utterly, as if he had never been, which indeed is probably the case, as if one could ever vanish utterly without having been at some previous stage. That's soon said. But Mahood too for that matter. It's not clear, tut tut, it's not clear at all. No matter, Mahood will stay where he was put, stuck up to his skull in his vase, opposite the shambles, beseeching the passers-by, without a word, or a gesture, or any play of his features, they don't play, to perceive him ostensibly, concomitantly with the day's dish, or independently, for reasons unknown, perhaps in the hope of being proven in the swim, that is to say guaranteed to sink, sooner or later, that must be it, such notions may be entertained, without any process of thought. I myself am exceptionally given to the tear, I should have preferred this kept dark, in their position I should have omitted this detail, the truth being I have no vent at my disposal, neither the aforesaid nor those less noble, how can one enjoy good health under such conditions, and what is one to believe, that is not the point, to believe this or that, the point is to guess right, nothing more, they say, If it's not white it's very likely black, it must be admitted the method lacks subtlety, in view of the intermediate shades all equally worthy of a chance. The time they waste repeating the same thing, when they must know pertinently it is not the right one. Recriminations easily rebutted, if they chose to take the trouble, and had the leisure, to reflect on their inanity. But how can you think and speak at the same time, how can you think about what you have said, may say, are saying, and at the same time go on with the last-mentioned, you think about any old thing, you say any old thing, more or less, more or less, in a daze of baseless unanswerable self-reproach, that's why they always repeat the same thing, the same old litany, the one they know by heart, to try and think of something different, of how to say something different from the same old thing, always the same wrong thing said always wrong, they can find nothing, nothing else to say but the thing that prevents them from finding, they'd do better to think of what they're saying, in order at least to vary its presentation, that's what matters, but how can you think and speak at the same time, without a special gift, your thoughts wander, your words too, far apart, no, that's an exaggeration, apart, between them would be the place to be, where you suffer, rejoice, at being bereft of speech, bereft of thought, and feel noth-

ing, hear nothing, know nothing, say nothing, are nothing, that
would be a blessed place to be, where you are. It's a lucky thing
they are there, meaning anywhere, to bear the responsibility of
this state of affairs, with respect to which if one does not know a
great deal one knows at least this, that one would not care to have
it on one's conscience, to have it on one's stomach is enough. Yes,
I'm a lucky man to have them, these voluble shades, I'll be sorry
when they go, for I won't have them always, not at this rate, they'll
make me believe I've piped up before they're done with me. The
master in any case, we don't intend, listen to them hedging, we
don't intend, unless absolutely driven to it, to make the mistake
of inquiring into him, he'd turn out to be a mere high official, we'd
end up by needing God, we have lost all sense of decency admittedly, but there are still certain depths we prefer not to sink to. Let
us keep to the family circle, it's more intimate, we all know one
another now, no surprises to be feared, the will has been opened,
nothing for anybody. This eye, curious how this eye invites inspection, demands sympathy, solicits attention, implores assistance,
to do what, it's not clear, to stop weeping, have a quick look round,
goggle an instant and close forever. It's it you see and it alone, it's
from it you set out to look for a face, to it you return having
found nothing, nothing worth having, nothing but a kind of ashen
smear, perhaps it's long grey hair, hanging in a tangle round the
mouth, greasy with ancient tears, or the fringe of a mantle spread
like a veil, or fingers opening and closing to try and shut out the
world, or all together, fingers, hair and rags, mingled inextricably.
Suppositions all equally vain, it's enough to enounce them to regret
having spoken, familiar torment, a different past, it's often to be
wished, different from yours, when you find out what it was. He is
hairless and naked and his hands, laid flat on his knees once and
for all, are in no danger of ever getting into mischief. And the
face? Balls, all balls, I don't believe in the eye either, there's
nothing here, nothing to see, nothing to see with, merciful coincidence, when you think what it would be, a world without spectator,
and vice versa, brrr! No spectator then, and better still no spectacle, good riddance. If this noise would stop there'd be nothing
more to say. I wonder what the chat is about at the moment. Worm

presumably, Mahood being abandoned. And I await my turn. Yes
indeed, I do not despair, all things considered, of drawing their
attention to my case, some fine day. Not that it offers the least
interest, hey, something wrong there, not that it is particularly interesting, I'll accept that, but it's my turn, I too have the right
to be shown impossible. This will never end, there's no sense in
fooling oneself, yes it will, they'll come round to it, after me it
will be the end, they'll give up, saying, It's all a bubble, we've been
told a lot of lies, he's been told a lot of lies, who he, the master,
by whom, no one knows, the everlasting third party, he's the one
to blame, for this state of affairs, the master's not to blame, neither
are they, neither am I, least of all I, we were foolish to accuse
one another, the master me, them, himself, they me, the master,
themselves, I them, the master, myself, we are all innocent, enough.
Innocent of what, no one knows, of wanting to know, wanting to
be able, of all this noise about nothing, of this long sin against
the silence that enfolds us, we won't ask any more, what it covers,
this innocence we have fallen to, it covers everything, all faults,
all questions, it puts an end to questions. Then it will be over,
thanks to me all will be over, and they'll depart, one by one, or
they'll drop, they'll let themselves drop, where they stand, and
never move again, thanks to me, who could understand nothing,
of all they deemed it their duty to tell me, do nothing, of all
they deemed it their duty to tell me to do, and upon us all
the silence will fall again, and settle, like dust of sand, on the
arena, after the massacres. Bewitching prospect if ever there was
one, they are beginning to come round to my opinion, after all
it's possible I have one, they make me say, If only this, if only
that, but the idea is theirs, no, the idea is not theirs either. As far
as I personally am concerned there is every likelihood of my being
incapable of ever desiring or deploring anything whatsoever. For
it would seem difficult for someone, if I may so describe myself, to
aspire towards a situation of which, notwithstanding the enthusias-
tic descriptions lavished on him, he has not the remotest idea, or
to desire with a straight face the cessation of that other, equally
unintelligible, assigned to him in the beginning and never modified.
This silence they are always talking about, from which supposedly

he came, to which he will return when his act is over, he doesn't
know what it is, nor what he is meant to do, in order to deserve
it. That's the bright boy of the class speaking now, he's the one
always called to the rescue when things go badly, he talks all the
time of merit and situations, he has saved more than one, of suffering too, he knows how to stimulate the flagging spirit, stop the
rot, with the simple use of this mighty word alone, even if he has
to add, a moment later. But what suffering, since he has always
suffered, which rather damps the rejoicings. But he soon makes up
for it, he puts all to rights again, invoking the celebrated notions of
quantity, habit-formation, wear and tear, and others too numerous
for him to mention, and which he is thus in a position, in the next
belch, to declare inapplicable to the case before him, for there is
no end to his wits. But, see above, have they not already bent over
me till black and blue in the face, nay, have they ever done anything else, during the past—no, no dates for pity's sake, and another
question, what am I doing in Mahood's story, and in Worm's, or
rather what are they doing in mine, there are some irons in the
fire to be going on with, let them melt. Oh I know, I know, attention please, this may mean something, I know, there's nothing
new there, it's all part of the same old irresistible baloney, namely,
But my dear man, come, be reasonable, look, this is you, look
at this photograph, and here's your file, no convictions, I assure
you, come now, make an effort, at your age, to have no identity,
it's a scandal, I assure you, look at this photograph, what, you
see nothing, true for you, no matter, here, look at this death's-
head, you'll see, you'll be all right, it won't last long, here, look,
here's the record, insults to policemen, indecent exposure, sins
against holy ghost, contempt of court, impertinence to superiors,
impudence to inferiors, deviations from reason, without battery,
look, no battery, it's nothing, you'll be all right, you'll see, I beg
your pardon, does he work, good God no, out of the question,
look, here's the medical report, spasmodic tabes, painless ulcers, I
repeat, painless, all is painless, multiple softenings, manifold hard-
enings, insensitive to blows, sight failing, chronic gripes, light diet,
shit well tolerated, hearing failing, heart irregular, sweet-tempered,
smell failing, heavy sleeper, no erections, would you like some

more, commission in the territorials, inoperable, untransportable, look, here's the face, no no, the other end, I assure you, it's a bargain, I beg your pardon, does he drink, good God yes, passionately, I beg your pardon, father and mother, both dead, at seven months interval, he at the conception, she at the nativity, I assure you, you won't do better, at your age, no human shape, the pity of it, look, here's the photograph, you'll see, you'll be all right, what does it amount too, after all, a painful moment, on the surface, then peace, underneath, it's the only way, believe me, the only way out, I beg your pardon, have I nothing else, why certainly, certainly, just a second, curious you should mention it, I was wondering myself, just a second, if you were not rather, just a second, here we are, this one here, but I wanted to be sure, what, you don't understand, neither do I, no matter, it's no time for levity, yes, I was right, no doubt about it this time, it's you all over, look, here's the photograph, take a look at that, dying on his feet, you'd better hurry, it's a bargain, I assure you, and so on, till I'm tempted, no, all lies, they know it well, I never understood, I haven't stirred, all I've said, said I've done, said I've been, it's they who said it, I've said nothing, I haven't stirred, they don't understand, I can't stir, they think I don't want to, that their conditions don't suit me, that they'll hit on others, in the end, to my liking, then I'll stir, I'll be in the bag, that's how I see it, I see nothing, they don't understand, I can't go to them, they'll have to come and get me, if they want me, Mahood won't get me out, nor Worm either, they set great store on Worm, to coax me out, he was something new, different from all the others, meant to be, perhaps he was, to me they're all the same, they don't understand, I can't stir, I'm all right here, I'd be all right here, if they'd leave me, let them come and get me, if they want me, they'll find nothing, then they can depart, with an easy mind. And if there is only one, like me, he can depart without fear of remorse, having done all he could, and even more, to achieve the impossible and so lost his life, or stay with me here, he might do that, and be a like for me, that would be lovely, my first like, that would be epoch-making, to know I had a like, a congener, he wouldn't have to be like me, he couldn't but be like me, he need only relax, he might believe what he pleased, at the outset, that he was in hell, or that the place was charming, he might even exclaim, I'll never stir again, being used to announcing his decisions, at the top of his voice, so as to get to know them better, he might even add, to cover all risks, For the moment, it would be his last howler, he need only relax, he'd disappear, he'd know nothing either, there we'd be the two of us, unbeknown to ourselves, unbeknown to each other, that's a darling dream I've been having, a broth of a dream. And it's not over. For here comes another, to see what has happened to his pal, and get him out, and back to his right mind, and back to his kin, with a flow of threats and promises, and tales like this of wombs and cribs, diapers bepissed and the first long trousers, love's young dream and life's old lech, blood and tears and skin and bones and the tossing in the grave, and so coax him out, as he me, that's right, pidgin bullskrit, and in the end, having lived his life, no, before, but you've got my meaning, and there we are the three of us, it's cosier, perpetual dream, you have merely to sleep, not even that, it's like the old jingle. A dog crawled into the kitchen and stole a crust of bread, then cook up with I've forgotten what and walloped him till he was dead, second verse, Then all the dogs came crawling and dug the dog a tomb and wrote upon the tombstone for dogs and bitches to come, third verse, as the first, fourth, as the second, fifth, as the third, give us time, give us time and we'll be a multitude, a thousand, ten thousand, there's no lack of room, adeste, adeste, all ye living bastards, you'll be all right, you'll see, you'll never be born again, what am I saying, you'll never have been born, and bring your brats, our hell will be heaven to them, after what you've done to them. But come to think of it are we not already a goodly company, what right have I to flatter myself I'm the first, first in time I mean of course, there we have a few more questions, please God they don't take the fancy to answer them. What can they be hatching anyhow, at this eleventh hour? Can it be they are resolved at last to seize me by the horns? Looks like it. In that case tableau any minute. Oyez, oyez, I was like them, before being like me, oh the swine, that's one I won't get over in a hurry, no matter, no matter, the charge is sounded, present arms, corpse, to your guns, spermatozoon. I too, weary of pleading an incomprehensible cause, at six and eight the thousand flowers of rhetoric, let myself drop among the contumacious, nice image that, telescoping space, it must be the Pulitzer Prize, they want to bore me to sleep, at long range for fear I might defend myself, they want to catch me alive, so as to be able to kill me, thus I shall have lived, they think I'm alive, what a business, were there but a cadaver it would smack of body-snatching, not in a womb either, the slut has yet to menstruate capable of whelping me, that should singularly narrow the field of research, a sperm dying, of cold, in the sheets, feebly wagging its little tail, perhaps I'm a drying sperm, in the sheets of an innocent boy, even that takes time, no stone must be left unturned, one mustn't be afraid of making a howler, how can one know it is one before it's made, and one it most certainly is, now that it's irrevocable, for the good reason, here's another, here comes another, unless it escapes them in time, what a hope, the bright boy is there, for the excellent reason that counts as living too, counts as murder, it's notorious, ah you can't deny it, some people are lucky, born of a wet dream and dead before morning, I must say I'm tempted, no, the testis has yet to descend that would want any truck with me, it's mutual, another gleam down the drain. And now one last look at Mahood, at Worm, we'll never have another chance, ah will they never learn sense, there's nothing to be got, there was never anything to be got from those stories, I have mine, somewhere, let them tell it to me, they'll see there's nothing to be got from it either, nothing to be got from me, it will be the end, of this hell of stories, you'd think I was cursing them, always the same old trick, you'd be sorry for them, perhaps I'll curse them yet, they'll know what it is to be a subject of conversation, I'll impute words to them you wouldn't throw to a dog, an ear, a mouth and in the middle a few rags of mind, I'll get my own back, a few flitters of mind, they'll see what it's like, I'll clap an eye at random in the thick of the mess, on the off chance something might stray in front of it, then I'll let down my trousers and shit stories on them, stories, photographs, records, sites, lights, gods and fellow-creatures, the daily round and common task, observing the while, Be born, dear friends, be born, enter my arse, you'll just love my

colic pains, it won't take long, I've the bloody flux. They'll see
what it's like, that it's not so easy as it looks, that you must have
a taste for it, that you must be born alive, that it's not something
you can acquire, that will teach them perhaps, to keep their nose
out of my business. Yes, if I could, but I can't, whatever it is, I
can't any more, there was perhaps a time I could, in the days
when I was bursting my guts, as per instructions, to bring back to
the fold the dear lost lamb, I'd been told he was dear, that he was
dear to me, that I was dear to him, that we were dear to each
other, all my life I've pelted him with twaddle, the dear departed,
wondering what he could possibly be like, wondering where we
could possibly have met, all my life, well, almost, damn the almost,
all my life, until I joined him, and now it's I am dear to them, now
it's they are dear to me, glad to hear it, they'll join us, one by one,
what a pity they are numberless, so are we, dear charnel-house
of renegades, this evening decidedly everything is dear, no matter,
the ancients hear nothing, and my old quarry, there beside me, for
him it's all over, beside me how are you, underneath me, we're
piled up in heaps, no, that won't work either, no matter, it's a
detail, for him it's all over, him the second-last, and for me too,
me the last, it will soon be all over, I'll hear nothing more, I've
nothing to do, simply wait, it's a slow business, he'll come and lie
on top of me, lie beside me, my dear tormentor, his turn to suffer
what he made me suffer, mine to be at peace. How all comes right
in the end to be sure, it's thanks to patience, thanks to time, it's
thanks to the earth that revolves that the earth revolves no more,
that time ends its meal and pain comes to an end, you have only to
wait, without doing anything, it's no good doing anything, and
without understanding, there's no help in understanding, and all
comes right, nothing comes right, nothing, nothing, this will never
end, this voice will never stop, I'm alone here, the first and the last,
I never made anyone suffer, I never stopped anyone's sufferings,
no one will ever stop mine, they'll never depart, I'll never stir, I'll
never know peace, neither will they, but with this difference, that
they don't want it, they say they don't want it, they say I don't want
it, don't want peace, after all perhaps they're right, how could I want
it, what is it, they say I suffer, perhaps they're right, and that I'd feel

better if I did this, said that, if my body stirred, if my head understood, if they went silent and departed, perhaps they're right, how would I know about these things, how would I understand what they're talking about. I'll never stir, never speak, they'll never go silent, never depart, they'll never catch me, never stop trying, that's that. I'm listening. Well I prefer that, I must say I prefer that, that what, oh you know, who you, oh I suppose the audience, well well, so there's an audience, it's a public show, you buy your seat and you wait, perhaps it's free, a free show, you take your seat and you wait for it to begin, or perhaps it's compulsory, a compulsory show, you wait for the compulsory show to begin, it takes time, you hear a voice, perhaps it's a recitation, that's the show, someone reciting, selected passages, old favourites, a poetry matinée, or someone improvising, you can barely hear him, that's the show, you can't leave, you're afraid to leave, it might be worse elsewhere, you make the best of it, you try and be reasonable, you came too early, here we'd need Latin, it's only beginning, it hasn't begun, he's only preluding, clearing his throat, alone in his dressing-room, he'll appear any moment, he'll begin any moment, or it's the stage-manager, giving his instructions, his last recommendations, before the curtain rises, that's the show, waiting for the show, to the sound of a murmur, you try and be reasonable, perhaps it's not a voice at all, perhaps it's the air, ascending, descending, flowing, eddying, seeking exit, finding none, and the spectators, where are they, you didn't notice, in the anguish of waiting, never noticed you were waiting alone, that's the show, waiting alone, in the restless air, for it to begin, for something to begin, for there to be something else but you, for the power to rise, the courage to leave, you try and be reasonable, perhaps you are blind, probably deaf, the show is over, all is over, but where then is the hand, the helping hand, or merely charitable, or the hired hand, it's a long time coming, to take yours and draw you away, that's the show, free, gratis and for nothing, waiting alone, blind, deaf, you don't know where, you don't know for what, for a hand to come and draw you away, somewhere else, where perhaps it's worse. And now for the it, I prefer that, I must say I prefer that, what a memory, real fly-paper, I don't know, I don't prefer it any more, that's all

I know, so why bother about it, a thing you don't prefer, just
think of that, bothering about that, perish the thought, one must
wait, discover a preference, within one's bosom, then it will be
time enough to institute an inquiry. Moreover, that's right, link,
link, you never know, moreover their attitude towards me has not
changed, I am deceived, they are deceived, they have tried to
deceive me, saying their attitude towards me had changed, but
they haven't deceived me, I didn't understand what they were
trying to do to me, I say what I'm told to say, that's all there is
to it, and yet I wonder, I don't know, I don't feel a mouth on me,
I don't feel the jostle of words in my mouth, and when you say a
poem you like, if you happen to like poetry, in the underground,
or in bed, for yourself, the words are there, somewhere, without
the least sound, I don't feel that either, words falling, you don't
know where, you don't know whence, drops of silence through the
silence, I don't feel it, I don't feel a mouth on me, nor a head, do
I feel an ear, frankly now, do I feel an ear, well frankly now I
don't, so much the worse, I don't feel an ear either, this is awful,
make an effort, I must feel something, yes, I feel something, they
say I feel something, I don't know what it is, I don't know what
I feel, tell me what I feel and I'll tell you who I am, they'll tell
me who I am, I won't understand, but the thing will be said, they'll
have said who I am, and I'll have heard, without an ear I'll have
heard, and I'll have said it, without a mouth I'll have said it, I'll
have said it inside me, then in the same breath outside me, perhaps
that's what I feel, an outside and an inside and me in the middle,
perhaps that's what I am, the thing that divides the world in two,
on the one side the outside, on the other the inside, that can be as
thin as foil, I'm neither one side nor the other, I'm in the middle,
I'm the partition, I've two surfaces and no thickness, perhaps that's
what I feel, myself vibrating, I'm the tympanum, on the one hand
the mind, on the other the world, I don't belong to either, it's not
to me they're talking, it's not of me they're talking, no, that's not
it, I feel nothing of all that, try something else, herd of shites,
say something else, for me to hear, I don't know how, for me to
say, I don't know how, what clowns they are, to keep on saying
the same thing when they know it's not the right one, no,

they know nothing either, they forget, they think they change
and they never change, they'll be there saying the same
thing till they die, then perhaps a little silence, till the next gang
arrives on the site, I alone am immortal, what can you expect, I
can't get born, perhaps that's their big idea, to keep on saying
the same old thing, generation after generation, till I go mad and
begin to scream, then they'll say, He's mewled, he'll rattle, it's
mathematical, let's get out to hell out of here, no point in waiting
for that, others need us, for him it's over, his troubles will be
over, he's saved, we've saved him, they're all the same, they all
let themselves be saved, they all let themselves be born, he was a
tough nut, he'll have a good time, a brilliant career, in fury and
remorse, he'll never forgive himself, and so depart, thus com-
muning, in Indian file, or two by two, along the seashore, now it's
the seashore, on the shingle, along the sands, in the evening air,
it's evening, that's all I know, evening, shadows, somewhere, anywhere, on the earth. Go mad, yes, but there it is, what would I
go mad with, and evening isn't sure either, it needn't be evening,
dawn too bestows long shadows, on all that is still standing, that's
all that matters, only the shadows matter, with no life of their
own, no shape and no respite, perhaps it's dawn, evening of night,
it doesn't matter, and so depart, towards my brethren, no, none
of that, no brethren, that's right, take it back, they don't know,
they depart, not knowing whither, towards their master, it's possible, make a note of that, it's just possible, to sue for their freedom,
for them it's the end, for me the beginning, my end begins, they
stop to listen to my screams, they'll never stop again, yes, they'll
stop, my screams will stop, from time to time, I'll stop
screaming, to listen and hear if anyone is answering, to look
and see if anyone is coming, then go, close my eyes and go, screaming, to scream elsewhere. Yes, my mouth, but there it is, I won't
open it, I have no mouth, and what about it, I'll grow one, a little
hole at first, then wider and wider, deeper and deeper, the air will
gush into me, and out a second later, howling. But is it not rather
too much to ask, to ask so much, of so little, is it really politic?
And would it not suffice, without any change in the structure of
the thing as it now stands, as it always stood, without a mouth

being opened at the place which even pain could never line, would it not suffice to, to what, the thread is lost, no matter, here's another, would not a little stir suffice, some tiny subsidence or upheaval, that would start things off, the whole fabric would be infected, the ball would start a-rolling, the disturbance would spread to every part, locomotion itself would soon appear, trips properly so called, business trips, pleasure trips, research expeditions, sabbatical leaves, jaunts and rambles, honeymoons at home and abroad and long sad solitary tramps in the rain, I indicate the main trends, athletics, tossing in bed, physical jerks, locomotor ataxy, death throes, rigor and rigor mortis, emergal of the bony structure, that should suffice. Unfortunately it's a question of words, of voices, one must not forget that, one must try and not forget that completely, of a statement to be made, by them, by me, some slight obscurity here, it might sometimes almost be wondered if all their ballocks about life and death is not as foreign to their nature as it is to mine. The fact is they no longer know where they've got to in their affair, where they've got me to, I never knew, I'm where I always was, wherever that is, and their affair, I don't know what is meant by that, some process no doubt, that I've got stuck in, or haven't yet come to, I've got nowhere, in their affair, that's what galls them, they want me there somewhere, anywhere, if only they'd stop committing reason, on them, on me, on the purpose to be achieved, and simply go on, with no illusion about having begun one day or ever being able to conclude, but it's too difficult, too difficult, for one bereft of purpose, not to look forward to his end, and bereft of all reason to exist, back to a time he did not. Difficult too not to forget, in your thirst for something to do, in order to be done with it, and have that much less to do, that there is nothing to be done, nothing special to be done, nothing doable to be done. No point either, in your thirst, your hunger, no, no need of hunger, thirst is enough, no point in telling yourself stories, to pass the time, stories don't pass the time, nothing passes the time, that doesn't matter, that's how it is, you tell yourself stories, then any old thing, saying, No more stories from this day forth, and the stories go on, it's stories still, or it was never stories, always any old thing, for as long as you can remember, no, longer than that, any old thing, the same old thing, to pass the time, then, as time didn't pass, for no reason at all, in your thirst, trying to cease and never ceasing, seeking the cause, the cause of talking and never ceasing, finding the cause, losing it again, finding it again, not finding it again, seeking no longer, seeking again, finding again, losing again, finding nothing, finding at last, losing again, talking without ceasing, thirstier than ever, seeking as usual, losing as usual, blathering away, wondering what it's all about, seeking what it can be you are seeking, exclaiming, Ah yes, sighing, No no, crying, Enough, ejaculating, Not yet, talking incessantly, any old thing, seeking once more, any old thing, thirsting away, you don't know what for, ah yes, something to do, no no, nothing to be done, and now enough of that, unless perhaps, that's an idea, let's seek over there, one last little effort, seek what, pertinent objection, let us try and determine, before we seek, what it can be, before we seek over there, over where, talking unceasingly, seeking incessantly, in yourself, outside yourself, cursing man, cursing God, stopping cursing, past bearing it, going on bearing it, seeking indefatigably, in the world of nature, the world of man, where is nature, where is man, where are you, what are you seeking, who is seeking, seeking who you are, supreme aberration, where you are, what you're doing, what you've done to them, what they've done to you, prattling along, where are the others, who is talking, not I, where am I, where is the place where I've always been, where are the others, it's they are talking, talking to me, talking of me, I hear them, I'm mute, what do they want, what have I done to them, what have I done to God, what have they done to God, what has God done to us, nothing, and we've done nothing to him, you can't do anything to him, he can't do anything to us, we're innocent, he's innocent, it's nobody's fault, what's nobody's fault, this state of affairs, what state of affairs, so it is, so be it, don't fret, so it will be, how so, rattling on, dying of thirst, seeking determinedly, what they want, they want me to be, this, that, to howl, stir, crawl out of here, be born, die, listen, I'm listening, it's not enough, I must understand, I'm doing my best, I can't understand, I stop doing my best, I can't do my best, I can't go on, poor devil, neither can they, let them say what

they want, give me something to do, something doable to do, poor
devils, they can't, they don't know, they're like me, more and more,
no more need of them, no more need of anyone, no one can do
anything, it's I am talking, thirsting, starving, let it stand, in the
ice and in the furnace, you feel nothing, strange, you don't feel a
mouth on you, you don't feel your mouth any more, no need of
a mouth, the words are everywhere, inside me, outside me, well well,
a minute ago I had no thickness, I hear them, no need to hear
them, no need of a head, impossible to stop them, impossible to
stop, I'm in words, made of words, others' words, what others,
the place too, the air, the walls, the floor, the ceiling, all words,
the whole world is here with me, I'm the air, the walls, the walled-
in one, everything yields, opens, ebbs, flows, like flakes, I'm all
these flakes, meeting, mingling, falling asunder, wherever I go I
find me, leave me, go towards me, come from me, nothing ever but
me, a particle of me, retrieved, lost, gone astray, I'm all these words,
all these strangers, this dust of words, with no ground for their
settling, no sky for their dispersing, coming together to say, fleeing
one another to say, that I am they, all of them, those that merge,
those that part, those that never meet, and nothing else, yes, something else, that I'm something quite different, a quite different
thing, a wordless thing in an empty place, a hard shut dry cold
black place, where nothing stirs, nothing speaks, and that I listen,
and that I seek, like a caged beast born of caged beasts born of
caged beasts born of caged beasts born in a cage and dead in a
cage, born and then dead, born in a cage and then dead in a cage,
in a word like a beast, in one of their words, like such a beast,
and that I seek, like such a beast, with my little strength, such a
beast, with nothing of its species left but fear and fury, no, the
fury is past, nothing but fear, nothing of all its due but fear cen-
tupled, fear of its shadow, no, blind from birth, of sound then, if
you like, we'll have that, one must have something, it's a pity, but
there it is, fear of sound, fear of sounds, the sounds of beasts,
the sounds of men, sounds in the daytime and sounds at night,
that's enough, fear of sounds, all sounds, more or less, more or
less fear, all sounds, there's only one, continuous, day and night,
what is it, it's steps coming and going, it's voices speaking for a

moment, it's bodies groping their way, it's the air, it's things, it's
the air among the things, that's enough, that I seek, like it, no, not
like it, like me, in my own way, what am I saying, after my fashion,
that I seek, what do I seek now, what it is, it must be that, it can
only be that, what it is, what it can be, what what can be, what I
seek, no, what I hear, now it comes back to me, all back to me, they
say I seek what it is I hear, I hear them, now it comes back to me,
what it can possibly be, and where it can possibly come from,
since all is silent here, and the walls thick, and how I manage,
without feeling an ear on me, or a head, or a body, or a soul, how
I manage, to do what, how I manage, it's not clear, dear dear,
you say it's not clear, something is wanting to make it clear,
I'll seek, what is wanting, to make everything clear, I'm always seeking something, it's tiring in the end, and it's only the
beginning, how I manage, under such conditions, to do what I'm
doing, what am I doing, I must find out what I'm doing, tell me
what you're doing and I'll ask you how it's possible, I hear, you
say I hear, and that I seek, it's a lie, I seek nothing, nothing any
more, no matter, let's leave it, no harking, and that I seek, listen
to them now, jogging my memory, seek what, firstly what it is,
secondly where it comes from, thirdly how I manage, that's it,
now we've got it, thirdly how I manage, to do it, seeing that this,
considering that that, inasmuch as God knows what, that's clear
now, how I manage to hear, and how I manage to understand,
it's a lie, what would I understand with, that's what I'm asking,
how I manage to understand, oh not the half, nor the hundredth,
nor the five thousandth, let us go on dividing by fifty, nor the quarter
millionth, that's enough, but a little nevertheless, it's essential, it's
preferable, it's a pity, but there it is, just a little all the same, the
least possible, it's appreciable, it's enough, the rough meaning of
one expression in a thousand, in ten thousand, let us go on multiplying by ten, nothing more restful than arithmetic, in a hundred
thousand, in a million, it's too much, too little, we've gone wrong
somewhere, no matter, there is no great difference here between one
expression and the next, when you've grasped one you've grasped
them all, I am not in that fortunate position, all, how you exaggerate, always out for the whole hog, the all of all and the all of

nothing, never in the happy golden, never, always, it's too much,
too little, often, seldom, let me now sum up, after this digression,
there is I, yes, I feel it, I confess, I give in, there is I,
it's essential, it's preferable, I wouldn't have said so, I won't
always say so, so let me hasten to take advantage of being now
obliged to say, in a manner of speaking, that there is I, on the one
hand, and this noise on the other, that I never doubted, no, let
us be logical, there was never any doubt about that, this noise, on
the other, if it is the other, that will very likely be the theme of
our next deliberation, I sum up, now that I'm there it's I will do
the summing up, it's I will say what is to be said and then say
what it was, that will be jolly, I sum up, I and this noise, I see
nothing else for the moment, but I have only just taken over my
functions, I and this noise, and what about it, don't interrupt me,
I'm doing my best, I repeat, I and this noise, on the subject of
which, inverting the natural order, we would seem to know for
certain, among other things, what follows, namely, on the one
hand, with regard to the noise, that it has not been possible up
to date to determine with certainty, or even approximately, what
it is, in the way of noise, or how it comes to me, or by what organ
it is emitted, or by what perceived, or by what intelligence appre-
hended, in its main drift, and on the other, that is to say with
regard to me, this is going to take a little longer, with regard to
me, nice time we're going to have now, with regard to me, that
it has not yet been our good fortune to establish with any degree
of accuracy what I am, where I am, whether I am words among
words, or silence in the midst of silence, to recall only two of the
hypotheses launched in this connection, though silence to tell the
truth does not appear to have been very conspicuous up to now,
but appearances may sometimes be deceptive, I resume, not yet
our good fortune to establish, among other things, what I am, no,
sorry, already mentioned, what I'm doing, how I manage, to hear,
if I hear, if it's I who hear, and who can doubt it, I don't know,
doubt is present, in this connection, somewhere or other, I resume,
how I manage to hear, if it's I who hear, and how to
understand, ellipse when possible, it saves time, how to understand, same observation, and how it happens, if it's I who

speak, and it may be assumed it is, as it may be suspected
it is not, how it happens, if it's I who speak, that I speak
without ceasing, that I long to cease, that I can't cease, I indicate
the principal divisions, it's more synoptic, I resume, not the good
fortune to establish, with regard to me, if it's I who seek, what
exactly it is I seek, find, lose, find again, throw away, seek again,
find again, throw away again, no, I never threw anything away,
never threw anything away of all the things I found, never found
anything that I didn't lose, never lost anything that I mightn't as
well have thrown away, if it's I who seek, find, lose, find again,
lose again, seek in vain, seek no more, if it's I what it is, and if
it's not I who it is, and what it is, I see nothing else for the
moment, yes I do, I conclude, not the good fortune to establish,
considering the futility of my telling myself even any old thing, to pass
the time, why I do it, if it's I who do it, as if reasons were required
for doing any old thing to pass the time, no matter, the question
may be asked, off the record, why time doesn't pass, doesn't pass,
from you, why it piles up all about you, instant on instant, on all
sides, deeper and deeper, thicker and thicker, your time, other's
time, the time of the ancient dead and the dead yet unborn, why
it buries you grain by grain neither dead nor alive, with no memory
of anything, no hope of anything, no knowledge of anything, no
history and no prospects, buried under the seconds, saying any old
thing, your mouth full of sand, oh I know it's immaterial, time is
one thing, I another, but the question may be asked, why time
doesn't pass, just like that, off the record, en passant, to pass the
time, I think that's all, for the moment, I see nothing else, I see
nothing whatever, for the time being. But I really mustn't ask myself any more questions, if it's I, I really must not. More resolutions,
while we're at it, that's right, resolutely, more resolutions. Make
abundant use of the principle of parsimony, as if it were familiar
to me, it is not too late. Assume notably henceforward that the
thing said and the thing heard have a common source, resisting for
this purpose the temptation to call in question the possibility of
assuming anything whatever. Situate this source in me, without
specifying where exactly, no finicking, anything is preferable to the
consciousness of third parties and, more generally speaking, of an

outer world. Carry if necessary this process of compression to the point of abandoning all other postulates than that of a deaf half-wit, hearing nothing of what he says and understanding even less. Evoke at painful junctures, when discouragement threatens to raise its head, the image of a vast cretinous mouth, red, blubber and slobbering, in solitary confinement, extruding indefatigably, with a noise of wet kisses and washing in a tub, the words that obstruct it. Set aside once and for all, at the same time as the analogy with orthodox damnation, all idea of beginning and end. Overcome, that goes without saying, the fatal leaning towards expressiveness. Equate me, without pity or scruple, with him who exists, some-how, no matter how, no finicking, with him whose story this story had the brief ambition to be. Better, ascribe to me a body. Better still, arrogate to me a mind. Speak of a world of my own, sometimes referred to as the inner, without choking. Doubt no more. Seek no more. Take advantage of the brand-new soul and substantiality to abandon, with the only possible abandon, deep down within. And finally, these and other decisions having been taken, carry on cheerfully as before. Something has changed nevertheless. Not a word about Mahood, or Worm, for the past—ah yes, I nearly forgot, speak of time, without flinching, and what is more, it just occurs to me, by a natural association of ideas, treat of space with the same easy grace, as if it were not bunged up on all sides, a few inches away, after all that's something, a few inches, to be thankful for, it gives one air, room for the tongue to loll, to have lolled, to loll on. When I think, that is to say, no, let it stand, when I think of the time I've wasted with these bran-dips, beginning with Murphy, who wasn't even the first, when I had me, on the prem-ises, within easy reach, tottering under my own skin and bones, real ones, rotting with solitude and neglect, till I doubted my own existence, and even still, today, I have no faith in it, none, so that I have to say, when I speak, Who speaks, and seek, and so on and similarly for all the other things that happen to me and for which someone must be found, for things that happen must have some-one to happen to, someone must stop them. But Murphy and the others, and last but not least the two old buffers here present, could not stop them, the things that happened to me, nothing could

happen to them, of the things that happened to me, and nothing else
either, there is nothing else, let us be lucid for once, nothing else
but what happens to me, such as speaking, and such as seeking,
and which cannot happen to me, which prowl round me, like
bodies in torment, the torment of no abode, no repose, no, like
hyenas, screeching and laughing, no, no better, no matter, I've
shut my doors against them, I'm not at home to anything, my
doors are shut against them, perhaps that's how I'll find silence,
and peace at last, by opening my doors and letting myself be
devoured, they'll stop howling, they'll start eating, the maws now
howling. Open up, open up, you'll be all right, you'll see. What a
joy it is, to turn and look astern, between two visits to the depths,
scan in vain the horizon for a sail, it's a real pleasure, upon my
word it is, to be unable to drown, under such conditions. Yes, but
there it is, I am far from my doors, far from my walls, someone
would have to wake the turnkey, there must be one somewhere,
far from my subject too, let us get back to it, it's gone, no longer
there where I thought I last saw it, strange this mixture of solid and
liquid, where was I, ah yes, my subject, no longer there, or no
longer the same, or I mistake the place, no, yes, it's the same, still
there, in the same place, it's a pity, I would have liked to lose it,
I would have liked to lose me, lose me the way I could long ago,
when I still had some imagination, close my eyes and be in a wood,
or on the seashore, or in a town where I don't know anyone, it's
night, everyone has gone home, I walk the streets, I lash into them
one after the other, it's the town of my youth, I'm looking for my
mother to kill her, I should have thought of that a bit earlier,
before being born, it's raining, I'm all right, I stride along on the
crown of the street with great yaws to left and right, now that's
all over, with closed eyes I see the same as with them open, namely,
wait, I'll say it, I'll try and say it, I'm curious to know what it can
possibly be that I see, with closed eyes, with open eyes, nothing,
I see nothing, well that is a disappointment, I was hoping for something better than that, is that what it is to be unable to lose yourself, I'm asking myself a question, is that what it is, to see nothing,
no matter where I look, nor, eyeless, the little creature in his different guises coming and going, now in shadow, now in light, doing

his best, seeking the means of staying among the living, of getting
off with his life, or shut up looking out of the window at the ever-
changing sky, is that it, to be unable to lose myself, I don't know, what
did I see in the old days, when I ventured a quick look, I don't know,
I don't remember. There I am in any case equipped with eyes, which
I open and shut, two, perhaps blue, knowing it avails nothing, for
I have a head now too, where all manner of things are known, can
it be of me I'm speaking, is it possible, of course not, that's another
thing I know, I'll speak of me when I speak no more. In any case
it's not a question of speaking of me, but of speaking, of speaking
no more, this slight confusion augurs well, now I'll have to find a
name for this latest surrogate, his head splitting with vile certainties
and his doll's eyes, later on, later on, first I must describe him in
greater detail, see what he's capable of, whence he comes and
whither he returns, in his head of course, we don't intend to relapse into picaresque, with the stink of Mahood and Worm still
in our nostrils. Now it's I the orator, the beleaguerers have departed, I am master on board, after the rats, I no longer crawl between
the thwarts, under the moon, in the shadow of the lash, strange
this mixture of solid and liquid, a little air now is all we need to
complete the elements, no, I'm forgetting fire, unusual hell when
you come to think of it, perhaps it's paradise, perhaps it's the earth,
perhaps it's the shores of a lake beneath the earth, you scarcely
breathe, but you breathe, it's not certain, you see nothing, hear
nothing, you hear the long kiss of dead water and mud, aloft at
less than a score of fathoms men come and go, you dream of them,
in your long dream there's a place for the waking, you wonder
how you know all you know, you even see grass, grass at dawn,
glaucous with dew, not so blind as all that my eyes, they're not
mine, mine are done, they don't even weep any more, they open
and shut by the force of habit, fifteen minutes exposure, fifteen
minutes shutter, like the owl cooped in the grotto in Battersea
Park, ah misery, will I never stop wanting a life for myself? No
no, no head either, anything you like, but not a head, in his head
he doesn't go anywhere either, I've tried, lashed to the stake,
blindfold, gagged to the gullet, you take the air, under the elms
in se, murmuring Shelley, impervious to the shafts. Yes, a head,

but solid, solid bone, and you imbedded in it, like a fossil in the rock. Perhaps there go I after all. I can't go on in any case. But I must go on. So I'll go on. Air, air, I'll seek air, air in time, the air of time, and in space, in my head, that's how I'll go on. All very fine, but the voice is failing, it's the first time, no, I've been through that, it has even stopped, many a time, that's how it will end again, I'll go silent, for want of air, then the voice will come back and I'll begin again. My voice. The voice. I hardly hear it any more. I'm going silent. Hearing this voice no more, that's what I call going silent. That is to say I'll hear it still, if I listen hard. I'll listen hard. Listening hard, that's what I call going silent. I'll hear it still, broken, faint, unintelligible, if I listen hard. Hearing it still, without hearing what it says, that's what I call going silent. Then it will flare up, like a kindling fire, a dying fire, Mahood explained that to me, and I'll emerge from silence. Hearing too little to be able to speak, that's my silence. That is to say I never stop speaking, but sometimes too low, too far away, too far within, to hear, no, I hear, to understand, not that I ever understand. It fades, it goes in, behind the door, I'm going silent, there's going to be silence, I'll listen, it's worse than speaking, no, no worse, no better. Unless this time it's the true silence, the one I'll never have to break any more, when I won't have to listen any more, when I can dribble in my corner, my head gone, my tongue dead, the one I have tried to earn, that I thought I could earn. I'm going to stop, that is to say I'm going to look as if I had, it will be like everything else. As if anyone were looking at me! As if it were I! It will be the same silence, the same as ever, murmurous with muted lamentation, panting and exhaling of impossible sorrow, like distant laughter, and brief spells of hush, as of one buried before his time. Long or short, the same silence. Then I resurrect and begin again. That's what I'll have got for all my pains. Unless this time it's the real silence at last. Perhaps I've said the thing that had to be said, that gives me the right to be done with speech, done with listening, done with hearing, without my knowing it. I'm listening already, I'm going silent. The next time I won't go to such pains, I'll tell one of Mahood's old tales, no matter which, they are all alike, they won't tire me, I won't bother any more about me, I'll know that no matter what I say the result is the same, that I'll never be silent, never at peace. Unless I try once more, just once more, one last time, to say what has to be said, about me, I feel it's about me, perhaps that's the mistake I make, perhaps that's my sin, so as to have nothing more to say, nothing more to hear, till I die. It's coming back. I'm glad. I'll try again, quick before it goes again. Try what? I don't know. To continue. Now there is no one left. That's a good continuation. No one left, it's embarrassing, if I had a memory it might tell me that this is the sign of the end, this having no one left, no one to talk to, no one to talk to you, so that you have to say, It's I who am doing this to me, I who am talking to me about me. Then the breath fails, the end begins, you go silent, it's the end, short-lived, you begin again, you had forgotten, there's someone there, someone talking to you, about you, about him, then a second, then a third, then the second again, then all three together, these figures just to give you an idea, talking to you, about you, about them, all I have to do is listen, then they depart, one by one, and the voice goes on, it's not theirs, they were never there, there was never anyone but you, talking to you about you, the breath fails, it's nearly the end, the breath stops, it's the end, short-lived, I hear someone calling me, it begins again, that must be how it goes, if I had a memory. Even if there were things, a thing somewhere, a scrap of nature, to talk about, you might be reconciled to having no one left, to being yourself the talker, if only there were a thing somewhere, to talk about, even though you couldn't see it, or know what it was, simply feel it there, with you, you might have the courage not to go silent, no, it's to go silent that you need courage, for you'll be punished, punished for having gone silent, and yet you can't do otherwise than go silent, than be punished for having gone silent, than be punished for having been punished, since you begin again, the breath fails, if only there were a thing, but there it is, there is not, they took away things when they departed, they took away nature, there was never anyone, anyone but me, anything but me, talking to me of me, impossible to stop, impossible to go on, but I must go on, I'll go on, without anyone, without anything, but me, but my voice, that is to say I'll stop, I'll end, it's the end already, short-lived, what is it, a little hole, you go down into it, into the silence, it's worse than the noise, you listen, it's worse than talking, no, not worse, no worse, you wait, in anguish, have they forgotten me, no, yes, no, someone calls me, I crawl out again, what is it, a little hole, in the wilderness. It's the end that is the worst, no, it's the beginning that is the worst, then the middle, then the end, in the end it's the end that is the worst, this voice that, I don't know, it's every second that is the worst, it's a chronicle, the seconds pass, one after another, jerkily, no flow, they don't pass, they arrive, bang, bang, they bang into you, bounce off, fall and never move again, when you have nothing left to say you talk of time, seconds of time, there are some people add them together to make a life, I can't, each one is the first, no, the second, or the third, I'm three seconds old, oh not every day of the week. I've been away, done something, been in a hole, I've just crawled out, perhaps I went silent, no, I say that in order to say something, in order to go on a little more, you must go on a little more, you must go on a long time more, you must go on evermore, if I could remember what I have said I could repeat it, if I could learn something by heart I'd be saved, I have to keep on saying the same thing and each time it's an effort, the seconds must be alike and each one is infernal, what am I saying now, I'm saying I wish I knew. And yet I have memories, I remember Worm, that is to say I have retained the name, and the other, what is his name, what was his name, in his jar, I can see him still, better than I can see me, I know how he lived, now I remember, I alone saw him, but no one sees me, nor him, I don't see him any more, Mahood, he was called Mahood, I don't see him any more, I don't know how he lived any more, he isn't there any more, he was never there, in his jar, I never saw him, and yet I remember, I remember having talked about him, I must have talked about him, the same words recur and they are your memories. It is I invented him, him and so many others, and the places where they passed, the places where they stayed, in order to speak, since I had to speak, without speaking of me, I couldn't speak of me, I was never told I had to speak of me, I invented my memories, not knowing what I was doing, not one is of me. It is they asked me to speak of them, they wanted to know what they were, how they lived, that suited me, I thought

that would suit me, since I had nothing to say and had to say
something, I thought I was free to say any old thing, so long as
I didn't go silent. Then I said to myself that after all perhaps it
wasn't any old thing, the thing I was saying, that it might well be
the thing demanded of me, assuming something was being demanded of me. No, I didn't think anything and I didn't say anything
to myself, I did what I could, a thing beyond my strength, and often
for exhaustion I gave up doing it, and yet it went on being done, the
voice being heard, the voice which could not be mine, since I had
none left, and yet which could only be mine, since I could not go
silent, and since I was alone, in a place where no voice could reach
me. Yes, in my life, since we must call it so, there were three things,
the inability to speak, the inability to be silent, and solitude, that's
what I've had to make the best of. Yes, now I can speak of my life,
I'm too tired for niceties, but I don't know if I ever lived, I have
really no opinion on the subject. However that may be I think I'll
soon go silent for good, in spite of its being prohibited. Then, yes,
phut, just like that, just like one of the living, then I'll be dead, I
think I'll soon be dead, I hope I find it a change. I should have liked
to go silent first, there were moments I thought that would be my reward for having spoken so long and so valiantly, to enter living into
silence, so as to be able to enjoy it, no, I don't know why, so as to
feel myself silent, one with all this quiet air shattered unceasingly
by my voice alone, no, it's not real air, I can't say it, I can't say why
I should have liked to be silent a little before being dead, so as in
the end to be a little as I always was and never could be, without
fear of worse to come peacefully in the place where I always was
and could never rest in peace, no, I don't know, it's simpler than
that, I wanted myself, in my own land for a brief space, I didn't
want to die a stranger in the midst of strangers, a stranger in my
own midst, surrounded by invaders, no, I don't know what I wanted,
I don't know what I thought, I must have wanted so many things,
imagined so many things, while I was talking, without knowing
exactly what, enough to go blind, with longings and visions, mingling and merging in one another, I'd have been better employed
minding what I was saying But it didn't happen like that, it happened like this, the way it's happening now, that is to say, I don't

know, you mustn't believe what I'm saying, I don't know what I'm saying, I'm doing as I always did, I'm going on as best I can. As to believing I shall go silent for good and all, I don't believe it particularly, I always believed it, as I always believed I would never go silent, you can't call that believing, it's my walls. But has nothing really changed, all this time? If instead of having something to say I had something to do, with my hands or feet, some little job, sorting things for example, or simply arranging things, suppose for the sake of argument I had the job of moving things from one place to another, then I'd know where I was, and how far I had got, no, not necessarily, I can see it from here, they would contrive things in such a way that I couldn't suspect the two vessels, the one to be emptied and the one to be filled, of being in reality one and the same, it would be water, water, with my thimble I'd go and draw it from one container and then I'd go and pour it into another, or there would be four, or a hundred, half of them to be filled, the other half to be emptied, numbered, the even to be emptied, the uneven to be filled, no, it would be more complicated, less symmetrical, no matter, to be emptied, and filled, in a certain way, a certain order, in accordance with certain homologies, the word is not too strong, so that I'd have to think, tanks, communicating, communicating, connected by pipes under the floor, I can see it from here, always showing the same level, no, that wouldn't work, too hopeless, they'd arrange for me to have little attacks of hope from time to time, yes, pipes and taps, I can see it from here, so that I might fool myself from time to time, if I had that to do, instead of this, some little job with fluids, filling and emptying, always the same vessel, I'd be good at that, it would be a better life than this, no, I mustn't start complaining, I'd have a body, I wouldn't have to speak, I'd hear my steps, almost without ceasing, and the noise of the water, and the crying of the air trapped in the pipes, I don't understand, I'd have bouts of zeal, I'd say to myself, The quicker I do it the quicker it will be done, the things one has to listen to, that's where hope would come in, it wouldn't be dark, impossible to do such work in the dark, that depends, yes, I must say I see no window, from here, whereas here that has no importance, that I see no window, here I needn't come and go,

fortunately, I couldn't, nor be dextrous, for naturally the water
would have great value and the least drop spilt on the way, or in the
act of drawing, or in the act of pouring, would cost me dear, and
how could you tell, in the dark, if a drop, what's this story, it's a
story, now I've told another little story, about me, about the life
that might have been mine for all the difference it would have
made, which was perhaps mine, perhaps I went through that before
being deemed worthy of going through this, who knows towards
what high destiny I am heading, unless I am coming from it. But
once again the fable must be of another, I see him so well, coming
and going among his casks, trying to stop his hand from trembling,
dropping his thimble, listening to it bouncing and rolling on the
floor, scraping round for it with his foot, going down on his knees,
going down on his belly, crawling, it stops there, it must have been
I, but I never saw myself, so it can't have been I, I don't know,
how can I recognise myself who never made my acquaintance, it
stops there, that's all I know, I don't see him any more, I'll never
see him again, yes I will, now he's there with the others, I won't
name them again, you say that for something to say, you say anything for something to say, some do this, others that, he does as
I said, I don't remember, he'll come back, to keep me company, only
the wicked are solitary, I'll see him again, it's his fault, his fault for
wanting to know what he was like, and how he lived, or he'll never
come back, it's one or the other, they don't all come back, I mean
there must be some I have only seen once, up to now, very true, it's
only beginning, I feel the end at hand and the beginning likewise,
to every man his orbit, that's obvious. But, and here I return to
the charge, but has nothing really changed, all this mortal time,
I'm speaking now of me, yes, henceforward I shall speak of none
but me, that's decided, even though I should not succeed, there's
no reason why I should succeed, so I need have no qualms. Nothing
changed? I must be ageing all the same, bah, I was always aged,
always ageing, and ageing makes no difference, not to mention that
all this is not about me, hell, I've contradicted myself, no matter
So long as one does not know what one is saying and can't stop
to inquire, in tranquillity, fortunately, fortunately, one would like
to stop, but unconditionally, I resume, so long as, so long as, let

me see, so long as one, so long as he, ah fuck all that, so long
as this, then that, agreed, that's good enough, I nearly got stuck.
Help, help, if I could only describe this place, I who am so good
at describing places, walls, ceiling, floors, they are my speciality,
doors, windows, what haven't I imagined in the way of windows
in the course of my career, some opened on the sea, all you could
see was sea and sky, if I could put myself in a room, that would
be the end of the wordy-gurdy, even doorless, even windowless,
nothing but the four surfaces, the six surfaces, if I could shut
myself up, it would be a mine, it could be black dark, I could
be motionless and fixed, I'd find a way to explore it, I'd listen to
the echo, I'd get to know it, I'd get to remember it, I'd be home,
I'd say what it's like, in my home, instead of any old thing, this
place, if I could describe this place, portray it, I've tried, I feel
no place, no place round me, there's no end to me, I don't know
what it is, it isn't flesh, it doesn't end, it's like air, now I have it,
you say that, to say something, you won't say it long, like gas,
balls, balls, the place, then we'll see, first the place, then I'll find
me in it, I'll put me in it, a solid lump, in the middle, or in a
corner, well propped up on three sides, the place, if only I could
feel a place for me, I've tried, I'll try again, none was ever mine,
that sea under my window, higher than the window, and the row-
boat, do you remember, and the river, and the bay, I knew I had
memories, pity they are not of me, and the stars, and the beacons,
and the lights of the buoys, and the mountain burning, it was the
time nothing was too good for me, the others benefited by it, they
died like flies, or the forest, a roof is not indispensable, an interior,
if I could be in a forest, caught in a thicket, or wandering round
in circles, it would be the end of this blither, I'd describe the leaves,
one by one, at the moment of their growing, at the moment of their
giving shade, at the moment of their falling, those are good
moments, for one who has not to say, But it's not I, it's not I,
where am I, what am I doing, all this time, as if that mattered,
but there it is, that takes the heart out of you, your heart isn't
in it any more, your heart that was, among the brambles, cradled
by the shadows, you try the sea, you try the town, you look for
yourself in the mountains and the plains, it's only natural, you

want yourself, you want yourself in your own little corner, it's
not love, not curiosity, it's because you're tired, you want to stop,
travel no more, seek no more, lie no more, speak no more, close
your eyes, but your own, in a word lay your hands on yourself,
after that you'll make short work of it. I notice one thing, the
others have vanished, completely, I don't like it. Notice, I notice
nothing, I go on as best I can, if it begins to mean something I
can't help it, I have passed by here, this has passed by me, thousands of times, its turn has come again, it will pass on and something else will be there, another instant of my old instant, there
it is, the old meaning that I'll give myself, that I won't be able to
give myself, there's a god for the damned, as on the first day, today
is the first day, it begins, I know it well, I'll remember it as I go
along, all adown it I'll be born and born, births for nothing, and
come to night without having been. Look at this Tunis pink, it's
dawn. If I could only shut myself up, quick, I'll shut myself up,
it won't be I, quick, I'll make a place, it won't be mine, it doesn't
matter, I don't feel any place for me, perhaps that will come, I'll
make it mine, I'll put myself in it, I'll put someone in it, I'll find
someone in it, I'll put myself in him, I'll say he's I, perhaps he'll
keep me, perhaps the place will keep us, me inside the other, the
place all round us, it will be over, all over, I won't have to try and
move any more, I'll close my eyes, all I'll have to do is talk, that
will be easy, I'll have things to say, about me, about my life, I'll
make it a good one, I'll know who's talking, and about what, I'll
know where I am, perhaps I'll be able to go silent, perhaps that's all
they're waiting for, there they are again, to pardon me, waiting for
me to reach home, to pardon me, it's the lie they refuse to stop,
I'll close my eyes, be happy at last, that's the way it is this morning. Morning, I call that morning, that's right, shilly-shally a little
longer, I call that morning, I haven't many words, I haven't much
choice, I don't choose, the word came, I should have avoided this
bright stain, it's the dayspring, but it doesn't last, I know it, I call
that the dayspring, if you could only see it. I'm off, you wouldn't
think so, perhaps it's my last gallop, I smell the stable, I always
smelt the stable, it's I smell of the stable, there's no stable but me,
for me. No, I won't do it, what won't I do, as if that depended

on me, I won't seek my home any more, I don't know what I'll
do, it would be occupied already, there would be someone there
already, someone far gone, he wouldn't want me, I can understand
him, I'd disturb him, what am I going to say now, I'm going to
ask myself, I'm going to ask questions, that's a good stop-gap, not
that I'm in any danger of stopping, then why all this fuss, that's
right, questions, I know millions, I must know millions, and then
there are plans, when questions fail there are always plans, you
say what you'll say and what you won't say, that doesn't commit
you to anything and the evil moment passes, it drops stone dead,
suddenly you hear yourself talking about God knows what as if
you had done nothing else all your life, and neither have you, you
come back from a far place, back to life, that's where you should
be, where you are, far from here, far from everything, if only I
could go there, if only I could describe it, I who am so good at
topography, that's right, aspirations, when plans fail there are
always aspirations, it's a knack, you must say it slowly, If only
this, if only that, that gives you time, time for a cud of longing
to rise up in the back of your gullet, nothing remains but to look
as if you enjoyed chewing it, there's no knowing where that may
lead you, on tracks as beaten as the day is long, often you pass
yourself by, someone passes himself by, if only you knew, that's
right, aspirations, you turn and look behind you, so does the other,
you weep for him, he weeps for you, it's screamingly sad, anything
rather than laughter. What else, opinions, comparisons, anything
rather than laughter, all helps, can't help helping, to get you over
the pretty pass, the things you have to listen to, what pretty pass,
it's not I speaking, it's not I hearing, let us not go into that, let us
go on as if I were the only one in the world, whereas I'm the only
one absent from it, or with others, what difference does it make,
others present, others absent, they are not obliged to make themselves manifest, all that is needed is to wander and let wander,
be this slow boundless whirlwind and every particle of its dust,
it's impossible. Someone speaks, someone hears, no need to go
any further, it is not he, it's I, or another, or others, what does it
matter, the case is clear, it is not he, he who I know I am, that's
all I know, who I cannot say I am, I can't say anything, I've tried,

I'm trying, he knows nothing, knows of nothing, neither what it
is to speak, nor what it is to hear, to know nothing, to be capable
of nothing, and to have to try, you don't try any more, no need
to try, it goes on by itself, it drags on by itself, from word to word,
a labouring whirl, you are in it somewhere, everywhere, not he, if
only I could forget him, have one second of this noise that carries
me away, without having to say, I don't, I haven't time, It's not
I, I am he, after all, why not, why not say it, I must have said it,
as well that as anything else, it's not I, not I, I can't say it, it came
like that, it comes like that, it's not I, if only it could be about him,
if only it could come about him, I'd deny him, with pleasure, if
that could help, it's I, here it's I, speak to me of him, let me speak
of him, that's all I ask, I never asked for anything, make me speak
of him, what a mess, now there is no one left, long may it last.
In the end it comes to that, to the survival of that alone, then the
words come back, someone says I, unbelieving. If only I could
make an effort, an effort of attention, to try and discover what's
happening, what's happening to me, what then, I don't know, I've
forgotten my apodosis, but I can't, I don't hear any more, I'm
sleeping, they call that sleeping, there they are again, we'll have
to start killing them again, I hear this horrible noise, coming back
takes time, I don't know where from, I was nearly there, I was
nearly sleeping, I call that sleeping, there is no one but me, there
was never anyone but me, here I mean, elsewhere is another matter,
I was never elsewhere, here is my only elsewhere, it's I who do
this thing and I who suffer it, it's not possible otherwise, it's not
possible so, it's not my fault, all I can say is that it's not my fault,
it's not anyone's fault, since there isn't anyone it can't be anyone's
fault, since there isn't anyone but me it can't be mine, sometimes
you'd think I was reasoning, I've no objection, they must have
taught me reasoning too, they must have begun teaching me, before
they deserted me, I don't remember that period, but it must have
marked me, I don't remember having been deserted, perhaps I
received a shock. Strange, these phrases that die for no reason,
strange, what's strange about it, here all is strange, all is strange
when you come to think of it, no, it's coming to think of it that
is strange, am I to suppose I am inhabited, I can't suppose any-

thing, I have to go on, that's what I'm doing, let others suppose,, there must be others in other elsewheres, each one in his little elsewhere, this word that keeps coming back, each one saying to himself, when the moment comes, the moment to say it, Let others suppose, and so on, so on, let others do this, others do that, if there are any, that helps you on, that helps you forward, I believe in progress, I know how to believe too, they must have taught me believing too, no, no one ever taught me anything, I never learnt anything, I've always been here, here there was never anyone but me, never, always, me, no one, old slush to be churned everlastingly, now it's slush, a minute ago it was dust, it must have rained. He must have travelled, he whose voice it is, he must have seen, with his eyes, a man or two, a thing or two, been aloft, in the light, or else heard tales, travellers found him and told him tales, that proves my innocence, who says, That proves my innocence, he says it, or they say it, yes, they who reason, they who believe, no, in the singular, he who lived, or saw some who had, he speaks of me, as if I were he, as if I were not he, both, and as if I were others, one after another, he is the afflicted, I am far, do you hear him, he says I'm far, as if I were he, no, as if I were not he, for he is not far, he is here, it's he who speaks, he says it's I, then he says it's not, I am far, do you hear him, he seeks me I don't know why, he doesn't know why, he calls me, he wants me to come out, he thinks I can come out, he wants me to be he, or another, let us be fair, he wants me to rise up, up into him, or up into another, let us be impartial, he thinks he's caught me, he feels me in him, then he says I, as if I were he, or in another, let us be just, then he says Murphy, or Molloy, I forget, as if I were Malone, but their day is done, he wants none but himself, for me, he thinks it's his last chance, he thinks that, they taught him thinking, it's always he who speaks, Mercier never spoke, Moran never spoke, I never spoke, I seem to speak, that's because he says I as if he were I, I nearly believed him, do you hear him, as if he were I, I who am far, who can't move, can't be found, but neither can he, he can only talk, if that much, perhaps it's not he, perhaps it's a multitude, one after another, what confusion, someone mentions confusion, is it a sin, all here is sin, you don't know why, you don't know whose, you don't know

against whom, someone says you, it's the fault of the pronouns,
there is no name for me, no pronoun for me, all the trouble comes
from that, that, it's a kind of pronoun too, it isn't that either, I'm
not that either, let us leave all that, forget about all that, it's not
difficult, our concern is with someone, or our concern is with something, now we're getting it, someone or something that is not there,
or that is not anywhere, or that is there, here, why not, after all,
and our concern is with speaking of that, now we've got it, you
don't know why, why you must speak of that, but there it is, you
can't speak of that, no one can speak of that, you speak of yourself,
someone speaks of himself, that's it, in the singular, a single one,
the man on duty, he, I, no matter, the man on duty speaks of
himself, it's not that, of others, it's not that either, he doesn't
know, how could he know, whether he has spoken of that or not,
when speaking of himself, when speaking of others, when speaking
of things, how can I know, I can't know, if I've spoken of him, I
can only speak of me, no, I can't speak of anything, and yet I
speak, perhaps it's of him, I'll never know, how could I know, who
could know, who knowing could tell me, I don't know who it's all
about, that's all I know, no, I must know something else, they must
have taught me something, it's about him who knows nothing,
wants nothing, can do nothing, if it's possible you can do nothing
when you want nothing, who cannot hear, cannot speak, who is
I, who cannot be I, of whom I can't speak, of whom I must speak,
that's all hypotheses, I said nothing, someone said nothing, it's
not a question of hypotheses, it's a question of going on, it goes
on, hypotheses are like everything else, they help you on, as if there
were need of help, that's right, impersonal, as if there were any
need of help to go on with a thing that can't stop, and yet it will,
it will stop, do you hear, the voice says it will stop, some day, it
says it will stop and it says it will never stop, fortunately I have
no opinion, what would I have an opinion with, with my mouth
perhaps, if it's mine, I don't feel a mouth on me, that means
nothing, if only I could feel a mouth on me, if only I could feel
something on me, I'll try, if I can, I know it's not I, that's all I
know, I say I, knowing it's not I, I am far, far, what does that mean,
far, no need to be far, perhaps he's here, in my arms, I don't feel

any arms on me, if only I could feel something on me, it would be
a starting-point, a starting-point, ah if I could laugh, I know what
it is, they must have told me what it is, but I can't do it, they can't
have shown me how to do it, perhaps it's one of those gifts that
can't be acquired. The silence, a word on the silence, in the silence,
that's the worst, to speak of silence, then lock me up, lock someone
up, that is to say, what is that to say, calm, calm, I'm calm, I'm
locked up, I'm in something, it's not I, that's all I know, no more
about that, that is to say, make a place, a little world, it will be
round, this time it will be round, it's not certain, low of ceiling,
thick of wall, why low, why thick, I don't know, it isn't certain,
it remains to be seen, all remains to be seen, a little world, try
and find out what it's like, try and guess, put someone in it, seek
someone in it, and what he's like, and how he manages, it won't
be I, no matter, perhaps it will, perhaps it will be my world,
possible coincidence, there won't be windows, we're done
with windows, the sea refused me, the sky didn't see me,
I wasn't there, and the summer evening air weighing on my
eyelids, we must have eyelids, we must have eyeballs, it's preferable,
they must have explained to me, someone must have explained
to me, what it's like, an eye, at the window, before the sea, before
the earth, before the sky, at the window, against the air, opening,
shutting, grey, black, grey, black, I must have understood, I must
have wanted it, wanted the eye, for my own, I must have tried,
all the things they've told me, all the things I've tried, they come in
useful still, when I think of them, that too, you must go on thinking too, the old thoughts, they call that thinking, it's visions, shreds
of old visions, that's all you can see, a few old pictures, a window,
what need had they to show me a window, saying, no, I forget, it
doesn't come back to me, a window, saying, There are others,
even more beautiful, and the rest, walls, sky, man, like Mahood,
a little nature, too long to go over, too forgotten, too little forgotten,
was it necessary, but was that how it happened, who can have come
here, the devil perhaps, I can think of no one else, it's he showed
me everything, here, in the dark, and how to speak, and what to
say, and a little nature, and a few names, and the outside of men,
those in my image, whom I might resemble, and their way of liv-

ing, in rooms, in sheds, in caverns, in woods, or coming and going,
I forget, and who went away and left me, knowing I was tempted,
knowing I was lost, whether I succumbed or not, have I succumbed
or not, I don't know, it's not I, that's all I know, since that day
it's not I any more, since that day there is no one any more, I must
have succumbed. That's all hypotheses, that helps you forward, I
believe in progress, I believe in silence, ah yes, a few words on
the silence, then the little world, that will be enough, for the rest
of eternity, you'd think it was I, I speaking, I hearing, I making
plans, for the passing hour, for the rest of eternity, whereas I'm
far, or in my arms somewhere, or stowed away somewhere, behind
walls, a few words on the silence, then just one thing more, just
one space and someone within, perhaps, until the end, I believe it,
it's evening already, I call that evening, I wish you could see it,
I believe it this evening, it's announced and I believe it, you announce, then you renounce, so it is, that helps you on, that helps
the end to come, evenings when there is an end, I speak of evening,
someone speaks of evening, perhaps it's still morning, perhaps it's
still night, personally I have no opinion. They love each other,
marry, in order to love each other better, more conveniently, he
goes to the wars, he dies at the wars, she weeps, with emotion, at
having loved him, at having lost him, yep, marries again, in order
to love again, more conveniently again, they love each other, you
love as many times as necessary, as necessary in order to be
happy, he comes back, the other comes back, from the wars, he
didn't die at the wars after all, she goes to the station, to meet him,
he dies in the train, of emotion, at the thought of seeing her again,
having her again, she weeps, weeps again, with emotion again, at
having lost him again, yep, goes back to the house, he's dead, the
other is dead, the mother-in-law takes him down, he hanged himself, with emotion, at the thought of losing her, she weeps, weeps
louder, at having loved him, at having lost him, there's a story
for you, that was to teach me the nature of emotion, that's called
emotion, what emotion can do, given favourable conditions, what
love can do, well well, so that's emotion, that's love, and trains,
the nature of trains, and the meaning of your back to the engine,
and guards, stations, platforms, wars, love, heart-rending cries,

that must be the mother-in-law, her cries rend the heart as she takes down her son, or her son-in-law, I don't know, it must be her son, since she cries, and the door, the house-door is bolted, when she got back from the station she found the house-door bolted, who bolted it, he the better to hang himself, or the mother-in-law the better to take him down, or to prevent her daughter-in-law from re-entering the premises, there's a story for you, it must be the daughter-in-law, it isn't the son-in-law and the daughter, it's the daughter-in-law and the son, how I reason to be sure this evening, it was to teach me how to reason, it was to tempt me to go, to the place where you can come to an end, I must have been a good pupil up to a point, I couldn't get beyond a certain point, I can understand their annoyance, this evening I begin to understand, oh there's no danger, it's not I, it wasn't I, the door, it's the door interests me, a wooden door, who bolted the door, and for what purpose, I'll never know, there's a story for you, I thought they were over, perhaps it's a new one, lepping fresh, is it the return to the world of fable, no, just a reminder, to make me regret what I have lost, long to be again in the place I was banished from, unfortunately it doesn't remind me of anything. The silence, speak of the silence before going into it, was I there already, I don't know, at every instant I'm there, listen to me speaking of it, I knew it would come, I emerge from it to speak of it, I stay in it to speak of it, if it's I who speak, and it's not, I act as if it were, sometimes I act as if it were, but at length, was I ever there at length, a long stay, I understand nothing about duration, I can't speak of it, oh I know I speak of it, I say never and ever, I speak of the four seasons and the different parts of the day and night, the night has no parts, that's because you are asleep, the seasons must be very similar, perhaps it's springtime now, that's all words they taught me, without making their meaning clear to me, that's how I learnt to reason, I use them all, all the words they showed me, there were columns of them, oh the strange glow all of a sudden, they were on lists, with images opposite, I must have forgotten them, I must have mixed them up, these nameless images I have, these imageless names, these windows I should perhaps rather call doors, at least by some other name, and this word man

which is perhaps not the right one for the thing I see when I hear
it, but an instant, an hour, and so on, how can they be represented,
a life, how could that be made clear to me, here, in the dark, I
call that the dark, perhaps it's azure, blank words, but I use them,
they keep coming back, all those they showed me, all those I remember, I need them all, to be able to go on, it's a lie, a score
would be plenty, tried and trusty, unforgettable, nicely varied, that
would be palette enough. I'd mix them, I'd vary them, that would
be gamut enough, all the things I'd do if I could, if I wished, if
I could wish, no need to wish, that's how it will end, in heart-
rending cries, inarticulate murmurs, to be invented, as I go along,
improvised, as I groan along, I'll laugh, that's how it will end, in
a chuckle, chuck chuck, ow, ha, pa, I'll practise, nyum, hoo, plop,
psss, nothing but emotion, bing bang, that's blows, ugh, pooh, what
else, oooh, aaah, that's love, enough, it's tiring, hee hee, that's
the Abderite, no, the other, in the end, it's the end, the ending
end, it's the silence, a few gurgles on the silence, the real silence,
not the one where I macerate up to the mouth, up to the ear, that
covers me, uncovers me, breathes with me, like a cat with a mouse,
that of the drowned, I've drowned, more than once, it wasn't I,
suffocated, set fire to me, thumped on my head with wood and iron,
it wasn't I, there was no head, no wood, no iron, I didn't do anything to me, I didn't do anything to anyone, no one did anything
to me, there is no one, I've looked, no one but me, no, not me
either, I've looked everywhere, there must be someone, the voice
must belong to someone, I've no objection, what it wants I want,
I am it, I've said so, it says so, from time to time it says so, then
it says not, I've no objection, I want it to go silent, it wants to go
silent, it can't, it does for a second, then it starts again, that's not
the real silence, it says that's not the real silence, what can be said
of the real silence, I don't know, that I don't know what
it is, that there is no such thing, that perhaps there is such a
thing, yes, that perhaps there is, somewhere, I'll never know. But
when it falters and when it stops, but it falters every instant, it
stops every instant, yes, but when it stops for a good few moments,
a good few moments, what are a good few moments, what then,
murmurs, then it must be murmurs, and listening, someone listen-

ing, no need of an ear, no need of a mouth, the voice listens,
as when it speaks, listens to its silence, that makes a murmur, that
makes a voice, a small voice, the same voice only small, it sticks
in the throat, there's the throat again, there's the mouth again, it
fills the ear, there's the ear again, then I vomit, someone vomits,
someone starts vomiting again, that must be how it happens, I
have no explanations to offer, none to demand, the comma will
come where I'll drown for good, then the silence, I believe it this
evening, still this evening, how it drags on, I've no objection,
perhaps it's springtime, violets, no, that's autumn, there's a time
for everything, for the things that pass, the things that end, they
could never get me to understand that, the things that stir, depart,
return, a light changing, they could never get me to see that, and
death into the bargain, a voice dying, that's a good one, silence
at last, not a murmur, no air, no one listening, not for the likes of
me, amen, on we go. Enormous prison, like a hundred thousand
cathedrals, never anything else any more, from this time forth,
and in it, somewhere, perhaps, riveted, tiny, the prisoner, how can
he be found, how false this space is, what falseness instantly, to
want to draw that round you, to want to put a being there, a cell
would be plenty, if I gave up, if only I could give up, before beginning, before beginning again, what breathlessness, that's right,
ejaculations, that helps you on, that puts off the fatal hour, no,
the reverse, I don't know, start again, in this immensity, this obscurity, go through the motions of starting again, you who can't
stir, you who never started, you the who, go through the motions,
what motions, you can't stir, you launch your voice, it dies away
in the vault, it calls that a vault, perhaps it's the abyss, those are
words, it speaks of a prison, I've no objection, vast enough for a
whole people, for me alone, or waiting for me, I'll go there now,
I'll try and go there now, I can't stir, I'm there already, I must be
there already, perhaps I'm not alone, perhaps a whole people is
here, and the voice its voice, coming to me fitfully, we would have
lived, been free a moment, now we talk about it, each one to himself, each one out loud for himself, and we listen, a whole people,
talking and listening, all together, that would ex, no, I'm alone,
perhaps the first, or perhaps the last, talking alone, listening alone,

alone alone, the others are gone, they have been stilled, their voices stilled, their listening stilled, one by one, at each new-coming, another will come, I won't be the last, I'll be with the others, I'll be as gone, in the silence, it won't be I, it's not I, I'm not there yet, I'll go there now, I'll try and go there now, no use trying, I wait for my turn, my turn to go there, my turn to talk there, my turn to listen there, my turn to wait there for my turn to go, to be as gone, it's unending, it will be unending, gone where, where do you go from there, you must go somewhere else, wait somewhere else, for your turn to go again, and so on, a whole people, or I alone, and come back, and begin again, no, go on, go on again, it's a circuit, a long circuit, I know it well, I must know it well, it's a lie, I can't stir, I haven't stirred, I launch the voice, I hear a voice, there is nowhere but here, there are not two places, there are not two prisons, it's my parlour, it's a parlour, where I wait for nothing, I don't know where it is, I don't know what it's like, that's no business of mine, I don't know if it's big, or if it's small, or if it's closed, if it's open, that's right, reiterate, that helps you on, open on what, there is nothing else, only it, open on the void, open on the nothing, I've no objection, those are words, open on the silence, looking out on the silence, straight out, why not, all this time on the brink of silence, I knew it, on a rock, lashed to a rock, in the midst of silence, its great swell rears towards me, I'm streaming with it, it's an image, those are words, it's a body, it's not I, I knew it wouldn't be I, I'm not outside, I'm inside, I'm in something, I'm shut up, the silence is outside, outside, inside, there is nothing but here, and the silence outside, nothing but this voice and the silence all round, no need of walls, yes, we must have walls, I need walls, good and thick, I need a prison, I was right, for me alone, I'll go there now, I'll put me in it, I'm there already, I'll start looking for me now, I'm there somewhere, it won't be I, no matter, I'll say it's I, perhaps it will be I, perhaps that's all they're waiting for, there they are again, to give me quittance, waiting for me to say I'm someone, to say I'm somewhere, to put me out, into the silence, I see nothing, it's because there is nothing, or it's because I have no eyes, or both, that makes three possibilities, to choose from, but do I really see nothing, it's not the moment to tell a lie, but how can you not tell a lie, what an idea, a voice like this, who can check it, it tries everything, it's blind, it seeks me blindly, in the dark, it seeks a mouth, to enter into, who can query it, there is no other, you'd need a head, you'd need things, I don't know, I look too often as if I knew, it's the voice does that, it goes all knowing, to make me think I know, to make me think it's mine, it has no interest in eyes, it says I have none, or that they are no use to me, then it speaks of tears, then it speaks of gleams, it is truly at a loss, gleams, yes, far, or near, distances, you know, measurements, enough said, gleams, as at dawn, then dying, as at evening, or flaring up, they do that too, blaze up more dazzling than snow, for a second, that's short, then fizzle out, that's true enough, if you like, one forgets, I forget, I say I see nothing, or I say it's all in my head, as if I felt a head on me, that's all hypotheses, lies, these gleams too, they were to save me, they were to devour me, that came to nothing, I see nothing, either because of this or else on account of that, and these images at which they watered me, like a camel, before the desert, I don't know, more lies, just for the fun of it, fun, what fun we've had, what fun of it, all lies, that's soon said, you must say soon, it's the regulations. The place, I'll make it all the same, I'll make it in my head, I'll draw it out of my memory, I'll gather it all about me, I'll make myself a head, I'll make myself a memory, I have only to listen, the voice will tell me everything, tell it to me again, everything I need, in dribs and drabs, breathless, it's like a confession, a last confession, you think it's finished, then it starts off again, there were so many sins, the memory is so bad, the words don't come, the words fail, the breath fails, no, it's something else, it's an indictment, a dying voice accusing, accusing me, you must accuse someone, a culprit is indispensable, it speaks of my sins, it speaks of my head, it says it's mine, it says that I repent, that I want to be punished, better than I am, that I want to go, give myself up, a victim is essential, I have only to listen, it will show me my hiding-place, what it's like, where the door is, if there's a door, and whereabouts I am in it, and what lies between us, how the land lies, what kind of country, whether it's sea, or whether it's mountain, and the way to take, so that I may

go, make my escape, give myself up, come to the place where the
axe falls, without further ceremony, on all who come from here,
I'm not the first, I won't be the first, it will best me in the end,
it has bested better than me, it will tell me what to do, in order
to rise, move, act like a body endowed with despair, that's how I
reason, that's how I hear myself reasoning, all lies, it's not me
they're calling, not me they're talking about, it's not yet my turn,
it's someone else's turn, that's why I can't stir, that's why I don't
feel a body on me, I'm not suffering enough yet, it's not yet my
turn, not suffering enough to be able to stir, to have a body, complete with head, to be able to understand, to have eyes to light
the way, I merely hear, without understanding, without being able
to profit by it, by what I hear, to do what, to rise and go and be
done with hearing, I don't hear everything, that must be it, the
important things escape me, it's not my turn, the topographical
and anatomical information in particular is lost on me, no, I hear
everything, what difference does it make, the moment it's not my
turn, my turn to understand, my turn to live, my turn of the life-
screw, it calls that living, the space of the way from here to the
door, it's all there, in what I hear, somewhere, if all has been said,
all this long time, all must have been said, but it's not my turn to
know what, to know what I am, where I am, and what I should
do to stop being it, to stop being there, that's coherent, so as to
be another, no, the same, I don't know, depart into life, travel
the road, find the door, find the axe, perhaps it's a cord, for the
neck, for the throat, for the cords, or fingers, I'll have eyes,
I'll see fingers, it will be the silence, perhaps it's a drop, find the
door, open the door, drop, into the silence, it won't be I, I'll stay
here, or there, more likely there, it will never be I, that's all I know,
it's all been done already, said and said again, the departure, the
body that rises, the way, in colour, the arrival, the door that opens,
closes again, it was never I, I've never stirred, I've listened, I
must have spoken, why deny it, why not admit it, after all, I deny
nothing, I admit nothing, I say what I hear, I hear what I say, I
don't know, one or the other, or both, that makes three possibilities,
pick your fancy, all these stories about travellers, these stories about
paralytics, all are mine, I must be extremely old, or it's memory

playing tricks, if only I knew if I've lived, if I live, if I'll live, that
would simplify everything, impossible to find out, that's where
you're buggered, I haven't stirred, that's all I know, no, I know
something else, it's not I, I always forget that, I resume, you must
resume, never stirred from here, never stopped telling stories, to
myself, hardly hearing them, hearing something else, listening for
something else, wondering now and then where I got them from,
was I in the land of the living, were they in mine, and where,
where do I store them, in my head, I don't feel a head on me, and
what do I tell them with, with my mouth, same remark, and what
do I hear them with, and so on, the old rigmarole, it can't be I,
or it's because I pay no heed, it's such an old habit, I do it without
heeding, or as if I were somewhere else, there I am far again, there
I am the absentee again, it's his turn again now, he who neither
speaks nor listens, who has neither body nor soul, it's something
else he has, he must have something, he must be somewhere, he is
made of silence, there's a pretty analysis, he's in the silence, he's
the one to be sought, the one to be, the one to be spoken of, the
one to speak, but he can't speak, then I could stop, I'd be he, I'd
be the silence, I'd be back in the silence, we'd be reunited, his
story the story to be told, but he has no story, he hasn't been in
story, it's not certain, he's in his own story, unimaginable, unspeakable, that doesn't matter, the attempt must be made, in the old
stories incomprehensibly mine, to find his, it must be there somewhere, it must have been mine, before being his, I'll recognise it,
in the end I'll recognise it, the story of the silence that he never
left, that I should never have left, that I may never find again, that
I may find again, then it will be he, it will be I, it will be the place,
the silence, the end, the beginning, the beginning again, how can I
say it, that's all words, they're all I have, and not many of them,
the words fail, the voice fails, so be it, I know that well, it will be
the silence, full of murmurs, distant cries, the usual silence, spent
listening, spent waiting, waiting for the voice, the cries abate, like
all cries, that is to say they stop, the murmurs cease, they give up,
the voice begins again, it begins trying again, quick now before
there is none left, no voice left, nothing left but the core of murmurs, distant cries, quick now and try again, with the words that

remain, try what, I don't know, I've forgotten, it doesn't matter, I never knew, to have them carry me into my story, the words that remain, my old story, which I've forgotten, far from here, through the noise, through the door, into the silence, that must be it, it's too late, perhaps it's too late, perhaps they have, how would I know, in the silence you don't know, perhaps it's the door, perhaps I'm at the door, that would surprise me, perhaps it's I, perhaps somewhere or other it was I, I can depart, all this time I've journeyed without knowing it, it's I now at the door, what door, what's a door doing here, it's the last words, the true last, or it's the murmurs, the murmurs are coming, I know that well, no, not even that, you talk of murmurs, distant cries, as long as you can talk, you talk of them before and you talk of them after, more lies, it will be the silence, the one that doesn't last, spent listening, spent waiting, for it to be broken, for the voice to break it, perhaps there's no other, I don't know, it's not worth having, that's all I know, it's not I, that's all I know, it's not mine, it's the only one I ever had, that's a lie, I must have had the other, the one that lasts, but it didn't last, I don't understand, that is to say it did, it still lasts, I'm still in it, I left myself behind in it, I'm waiting for me there, no, there you don't wait, you don't listen, I don't know, perhaps it's a dream, all a dream, that would surprise me, I'll wake, in the silence, and never sleep again, it will be I, or dream, dream again, dream of a silence, a dream silence, full of murmurs, I don't know, that's all words, never wake, all words, there's nothing else, you must go on, that's all I know, they're going to stop, I know that well, I can feel it, they're going to abandon me, it will be the silence, for a moment, a good few moments, or it will be mine, the lasting one, that didn't last, that still lasts, it will be I, you must go on, I can't go on, you must go on, I'll go on, you must say words, as long as there are any, until they find me, until they say me, strange pain, strange sin, you must go on, perhaps it's done already, perhaps they have said me already, perhaps they have carried me to the threshold of my story, before the door that opens on my story, that would surprise me, if it opens, it will be I, it will be the silence, where I am, I don't know, I'll never know, in the silence you don't know, you must go on, I can't go on, I'll go on.